NIGHTBLADE'S VENGEANCE

BLADES OF THE FALLEN

RYAN KIRK

This is a work of fiction. Names, characters, organizations, places, events, and incidents are either products of the author's imagination or are used fictitiously. Any resemblance to actual persons, living or dead, or actual events is purely coincidental.

Published by 47North, Seattle

www.apub.com

ISBN-13: 9781542047326
ISBN-10: 1542047323

Cover design by Katie Anderson

Printed in the United States of America

NIGHTBLADE'S VENGEANCE

ALSO BY RYAN KIRK

The Nightblade Series

Nightblade
World's Edge
The Wind and the Void

The Primal Series

Primal Dawn
Primal Darkness
Primal Destiny

To Katie,
The most wonderful wife and mother

Prologue

Osamu sensed the prince before he heard him. Yoshi, the future monarch of the Kingdom, had a distinctive presence, strong and vibrant even in a crowd. Osamu poured a second cup of sake and set it down. Yoshi picked it up in one smooth motion as he sat down next to the nightblade.

"I don't know why I think I'll ever be able to sneak up on you. I keep thinking that someday your guard will be down, and I'll be there, right behind you."

Osamu raised his cup in Yoshi's direction. "May we both live long enough to see the day."

Yoshi mirrored Osamu's gesture, and they sipped at the sake silently.

After a while, Yoshi made a show of inspecting the cup. "It tastes better than it did yesterday."

"Your senses are heightened. Even *my* cooking would taste good tonight."

Yoshi laughed, a soft sound on a quiet night. The mood over the camp was somber, given that all gathered knew the work they would be undertaking the next morning.

Curiosity lighting up his face in the firelight, the prince looked at Osamu. "Is it the same for you? Is your sense heightened when danger is near?"

Osamu didn't speak. He just nodded slowly.

Osamu had a question for the prince, but despite the cycles of their friendship, he hesitated to ask. A sip of sake gave him the courage.

"Are you going to be able to live with what we do tomorrow?"

Yoshi leaned closer to the fire, holding his hands near the small blaze for warmth. "Are you afraid we're going to lose?"

Osamu shook his head, a gesture he was certain was barely visible under the hood that he wore. Even here, with only his friend, he hid his face. Who knew who was out there watching, hiding in the camp disguised as a blade? The best defense against an assassin was secrecy.

"No, we will win. It will be dangerous, but we have one of the largest assemblies of nightblades in history for this mission. Some of us will fall, but we will win. No, I'm more worried about the heart of the Kingdom if we do this thing."

Yoshi didn't react to his statements, but Osamu could see that his friend was thinking the same thing. After another moment of silence, Yoshi responded.

"It is not a good decision, but it is the best. If word gets out about what happens here tomorrow, it will be hard for us. But if word gets out about the village, the Kingdom would collapse immediately. In this, I agree with my father."

"Is it worth the cost?"

Yoshi shrugged. "I do not know. I believe so. The Kingdom protects tens of thousands of citizens. It is not a good thing we do, but if the Kingdom requires the sacrifice of a hundred, I will make that sacrifice."

Osamu refilled their cups, and the pair sat together in silence. Osamu's thoughts wandered aimlessly as he tried not to think about tomorrow. He had made tremendous sacrifices for the Kingdom, but nothing quite like this. Yoshi was correct, of course. The Kingdom was worth any cost, but rarely was the cost so high. Normally unshakable, Osamu was filled with dread over tomorrow's task.

"Yoshi?"

"Yes?"

"Do you ever wonder if you will have the strength to be as good a king as your father?"

Yoshi smiled and stood up. "Not often. Only with every breath I take from the moment I wake until the moment I fall back asleep."

Osamu grinned, knowing Yoshi would never see his reaction.

Yoshi handed Osamu his cup back. "Get some rest, friend. Tomorrow is going to be a hard day."

—

Osamu sat with his commanders around a morning fire. The sun had just begun to peek above the horizon, and the day had dawned clear and cold. A part of Osamu had wished for rain to better suit the mood, but it wasn't to be.

They had considered a night raid. If their target had been a more traditional one, such a strategy would have been a wise decision. But the warriors were attacking a village where many nightblades lived, and their life force would be sensed from a distance no matter what time they attacked. At least daylight meant a better chance of avoiding mistakes.

All the commanders and Osamu turned to Yoshi as he entered the circle. Yoshi bowed and waved away the attention. "I know my father appointed this command to me, but we all know Osamu is leading us."

The commanders grinned at Yoshi's easy honesty, and Osamu thought they would be lucky someday when Yoshi became king.

"The plan is simple in its design, but difficult in execution," Osamu said. "Two Falls has its back to a cliff wall, and it's not particularly easy to reach. The nightblades inside have begun very simple fortifications, but that shouldn't prove to be a problem. The latest report from our shadow inside tells us that the walls are just beginning to go up and are easily crossed. Commanders, you know where you're supposed to be attacking from. I want our first wave to wash over them in a heartbeat, fast and hard. I want the second wave ready to catch any stragglers. No one gets out of this village alive."

The commanders nodded, a grim look on their faces. Yoshi spoke up. "I know we are asking you to do a hard thing. The blades have never had to attack their own like this before, and I hope they never have to again. You all agreed to come, and you know nothing less than the future of the Kingdom is at stake here. First, from the depths of my heart, I thank you. Second, no one can escape. The village has women and children inside, many of whom aren't gifted, but no one can survive today. If you can't live with that, I understand, but I need to know now so that you don't put our Kingdom at risk."

Silence hung around the circle like a noose. The men and women knew what they had agreed to. They were blades, and killing warriors on the field of battle was what they had been raised from childhood to do. Now they were asked to end an entire village, to slay everyone, even those who could not fight. The Kingdom may have been at stake, but it was still challenging to find volunteers willing to stain their honor for such a mission.

Osamu gave the final few orders. The commanders stood and bowed and went to prepare their fellow blades for battle.

Osamu stood as well and laid a hand on Yoshi's shoulder. Yoshi turned to look at him.

"I want you to stay with the second wave, Yoshi."

The prince shook his head. "You know I can't do that."

"Yoshi, I know you accept the risk to yourself, but I cannot. The Kingdom needs you. You're a fine swordsman, but you're hopelessly outclassed here. Even an unblooded nightblade would kill you. There's no reason for you to ride in the front."

Yoshi bowed deeply to Osamu, and Osamu knew he had lost the argument.

"I know the danger, friend. But today, of all days, I can't be in the rear. I can't order you all to do this while I sit back and watch."

Osamu understood. He didn't like the prince's response, but he understood. "I thought you might say as much. I've asked a dayblade from Takashi's unit to be at your side for the entire battle. I also ask that you stay near me. I will do my best to protect you."

Yoshi bowed, and they went to find their horses.

Osamu barely used his sight as they rode up toward the village of Two Falls. If he had, he might have been distracted by the natural beauty of the area. Two Falls was well off the beaten path, found near the top of a small valley in between rugged peaks. To each side of the valley, water cascaded down from the mountains, giving the village its name. If the village had more time to build its walls, the site would be a fortress to rival Stonekeep, House Kita's family castle north of the blades' current location.

The location was picturesque, but it wasn't on the way to anywhere. Under other circumstances Osamu might have enjoyed visiting the village—a collection of a few dozen huts, with a single three-story pagoda built to honor the Great Cycle.

Even without using his sight, Osamu could discern much that was happening before him. He could sense all life in the village, could already feel the commotion he and his command were causing. Soon his sense was confirmed as they heard the peal of bells from the pagoda echoing down the valley. The blades wouldn't be surprising the villagers, but they weren't expecting to.

He wished he knew more. The shadow, the nightblade spy the approaching blades had sent into Two Falls, had been there for some time, risking his life to get more information on the village. What they learned was stunning. Not only did the nightblades want to overthrow the government of the Kingdom, but everyone in the village was involved. The shadow reported that everyone, including women and children, was being trained in swordsmanship.

Osamu had lived long enough to know that there was little in the world more dangerous than belief. This village was consumed by it.

The blades didn't use their horses to charge. The valley was long, and there wasn't any way to sneak up on Two Falls. The location was well chosen. No matter how fast the oncoming warriors moved, the villagers would be ready by the time they arrived. Better to save energy for the combat to come.

Osamu remained close to Yoshi near the head of the party. Next to them was Sachio, one of the few dayblades in the party. He would also remain near Yoshi in case the worst should come to pass.

Osamu halted the horses just outside of arrow range. The blades dismounted and handed their horses to their peers, who would remain behind to make sure no stragglers escaped the village. Osamu took one last glance around, ensuring everyone was in place. Satisfied, he started forward, leading the calm walk toward the village.

Arrows came arching down, but small shields protected the warriors well. The nightblades generally eschewed the use of shields, but Osamu had mandated their use for this attack. They had too much open field to cover, and he wouldn't lose his men for honor's sake. A few nightblades fell, but those who did were quickly healed by accompanying dayblades. Sachio tried to go help a fallen blade, but Osamu gently restrained him. The dayblade needed to stay close to the prince, even if such an act meant sacrificing other lives. Sachio glared at him but didn't disobey.

Before long they were at the walls that the village had just begun to erect. The nightblades leapt over the waist-high obstacles with ease, and the battle was joined in earnest.

Osamu focused on the enemies directly in front of him. His sense told him that most were typical civilians, but there was one nightblade within sight of him. Osamu drew his sword as the blade came at him.

Dueling another nightblade was always a challenge. The sense allowed a nightblade to know the moves of an opponent moments before they happened, and thus the victor of such a duel was the warrior whose sense was more refined and whose speed was greater.

Fortunately, Osamu was both fast and skilled. The attacking nightblade made a solid cut that Osamu sidestepped. He responded with a cut of his own that the enemy nightblade sensed coming and stepped away from. The two passed again, neither making contact. On the third pass, steel met steel, and the enemy nightblade tried to overpower Osamu, aiming to force his blade to the side.

Osamu gave up the centerline, and he saw the flicker of satisfaction pass over his enemy's face. But like too many nightblades, his enemy forgot that combat involved more than a sword. Osamu stepped in before the nightblade could seize his advantage, driving his elbow into the man's throat.

The nightblade lost his focus as he struggled to breathe, and Osamu brought his sword around for a fatal cut. He didn't pause to enjoy his victory, not for a moment. He immediately turned his attention to Yoshi, who was fending off three villagers in a vicious battle. Osamu stepped in, and a few moments later, the three villagers were on the ground, bleeding out. Yoshi, normally glib, bowed his appreciation to his friend.

For the next few moments, they had cleared themselves a space. Osamu threw out his sense to feel how the battle was progressing. The fight was not easy, but he could tell the battle was moving deeper into the village, which meant his warriors were winning. But he also sensed the wave of villagers approaching the battle line.

Osamu opened his eyes. He was skilled in the sense, far more than most, but even he had trouble keeping track of everything in a battle involving this many people, especially when he was in the center of the conflict. His heart sank when he saw that the incoming wave was made up of women and children.

To the credit of the nightblades Osamu commanded, they didn't falter, no matter how distasteful they found the task. The sound of steel against steel echoed against the stone walls of the valley.

Another nightblade from the village found Osamu, but their duel was short. The nightblade was older and slower, and she was no match for Osamu's speed.

They were advancing a step at a time, but they were advancing. Osamu kept his sense open, trying to make sure his troops weren't ambushed. Most people in the village were involved in combat. If Osamu's warriors could make it through the next part of the battle, it would soon become a matter of simply cleaning up.

Yoshi stepped into a hut, seeing something. Osamu didn't question; he just followed. A family crouched inside, the mother a nightblade. She cut at Yoshi, but Osamu sensed the movement and was there before she could strike.

The woman was fast, but Osamu was faster. He slipped inside her guard and cut through her with one smooth motion. Behind him, Yoshi killed the husband, a civilian according to Osamu's sense.

When the worst came to pass, Osamu wasn't prepared. He had taken a breath and extended his sense. The sounds of battle outside were fading, and Osamu knew they were near the end.

Osamu sensed the girl attack, but he wasn't concerned. Yoshi was already responding, and the prince was between Osamu and the girl. There wasn't much Osamu could do.

Then he heard a soft grunt, and Osamu's well-ordered world fell apart. He sensed what had happened, but he didn't believe his own gift. It couldn't be right. His path unraveled in front of him, possibilities cut from the fabric of the future one heartbeat at a time. Yoshi hadn't finished his cut.

Yoshi turned around, a short sword embedded in his chest, a look of surprise and mirth on his face. Osamu's mind slowed to a crawl. The stab was fatal. It had penetrated Yoshi's heart.

The girl came at Osamu unarmed, and some deep part of him, honed by cycles and cycles of training, numbed by shock, cut at her with one powerful blow, his mind not registering what he had done.

A second thought pierced through his mental haze. Dayblades were nearby. If one got to Yoshi soon enough, they could still save his life. Sachio—he was supposed to be here. Osamu looked around, but he couldn't see Sachio. He tried to use his sense, but he couldn't summon the necessary focus.

Osamu opened his mouth to scream, but Yoshi's lips were moving, and Osamu wanted to hear his friend.

"Never thought it would be a little girl that killed me. Always thought it would be politics."

Osamu, despite himself, laughed, but it was hollow and couldn't last. His friend's lifeblood was slipping through his fingers.

He remembered there was still a chance. Osamu yelled for help, his voice echoing in the small hut.

"Osamu?" asked Yoshi.

"Yes?"

"Will you show me your face?"

Osamu didn't hesitate. For the first time in cycles, in front of another, he drew back the hood that was a permanent fixture over his head. Yoshi looked for the first time upon the face of the man he had called a friend.

Yoshi forced a grin. "Uglier than I thought you'd be." The mirth was evident in his eyes.

Osamu shook his head. "I don't know if this is a good time for jokes."

Yoshi laughed, blood coming up through his mouth. The wound must have cut through his lungs. "Life is funny."

With that, the light faded from Yoshi's eyes, and Osamu felt the prince's energy return to the Great Cycle.

—

Osamu wasn't sure how long he knelt there, staring at his friend. He was no stranger to death and he had lost those he was close to before, but somehow, this was different.

Yoshi and Osamu were beyond friends. They were brothers, even if they didn't share the same bloodline. And Yoshi was heir to the Kingdom. The only heir. His death didn't just affect Osamu; it affected every person in the land.

Part of Osamu knew the battle was concluding outside the hut, but he couldn't bring his mind to focus on anything other than the body in front of him.

He heard movement behind him. He put his hood back up, turned his face to the door, and saw Sachio standing there, shock on his face. Beyond the dayblade, he saw a handful of villagers being rounded up, Osamu's nightblades collecting them in the center of the village.

Osamu's mind felt as though it kept missing a beat, like a drummer who just couldn't keep up. There was no reason to round up the villagers. He had made it clear before: their orders were to kill everyone. This wasn't a battlefield, ruled by the dictates of honor and convention. This was, and always had been, the eradication of the village.

A thought settled in Osamu's mind. Sachio was supposed to have been next to them. He should have saved Yoshi. Blind rage fought against Osamu's iron control.

He stood up. There was still a mission to complete. This wouldn't end in total failure. He walked toward the door, prepared to order the nightblades to finish the work they had started. The villagers who had been rounded up were largely women and children, but as horrible as the work was, it was necessary to the survival of the Kingdom.

Sachio, understanding his commander's intent, put up his hand to stop Osamu. He grabbed Osamu's shoulder, trying to stop him from leaving the hut. It was his last mistake. Osamu, his rage overwhelming his control, drew his blade in one smooth motion, slicing right through Sachio's neck. Osamu didn't even stop to see the look of surprise on the dayblade's face. He charged right to the center of the village, where the other blades stared at him, dumbstruck at what he had just done.

"Kill them all. Burn the village. I want us to move on before the middle of the day." His tone allowed for no argument, and given what had just happened, no one dared disagree.

The nightblades went to their terrible work, and Osamu stumbled outside the village.

He looked out on the scenery, the beautiful, lush valley below him. It was hard to reconcile the natural beauty in front of him with the horrors lurking behind. His mind refused to do anything but run in circles, replaying Yoshi's death and Sachio's murder. Yoshi's death brought tears to his eyes, but Sachio's murder tore his heart.

Osamu fell to his knees, his entire body shuddering in doubt.

—

Hundreds of leagues away and many days later, a young girl was weeding in her family's fields. It was hard work, but the girl's mind kept wandering, mostly to her stomach. Mother had told her there wouldn't be any breakfast today. She had spoken with a smile, but the girl thought her mother looked like she was about to cry. She often looked like she was about to cry.

The girl was used to going hungry. Hunger was normal. If you didn't think about your stomach for long enough, sometimes you could make the hunger go away. The girl tried to focus on getting the weeds out of the field, but today was going to be one of those days where the hunger wouldn't leave. The girl listened for the sounds of her mother's voice, calling her and her brother in for lunch. But when she looked up, the sun wasn't anywhere near the middle of the sky. Her hunger would have to wait.

A shadow crossed over her, and she looked up to see her brother standing there. As always, her face immediately lit up with a smile.

Her brother was a hero. He was big and strong and nice. Someday she wanted to work in the fields as fast as he did. He could do much more than she could.

Her brother returned her smile. He had been bigger last winter, when their father was still around. Now he was skinny, like her, but still, he was very strong.

"I thought maybe I would scare you. You were being very still," he said.

The girl shook her head. She was ashamed because he was right. She hadn't been working very hard. But she was also ashamed because she had a secret. She knew where her brother was all the time. The girl didn't know how she knew, but she did. That was why she was never surprised by him.

"Don't worry. You keep picking as many weeds as you can. Maybe we can finish this part of the field by the end of the day if we work together."

The girl nodded enthusiastically. If that was what her brother wanted, that was what she would do.

Her brother smiled, but then just as suddenly, his smile turned to a frown. The girl followed his gaze and saw a man in black robes approaching their house. Instinctively the girl knew who it was.

"A nightblade," her brother confirmed.

Her brother started running toward the house, but when the girl tried to follow, he told her to stay in the fields.

The girl waited for her brother to stop paying attention, then followed anyway. She wasn't going to miss a visitor.

By the time she was able to sneak down close enough to the house, she could hear her mother weeping. It was a hard sound for the girl to hear, but she knew why her mother was crying. There could be only one reason. Their dad wasn't coming home.

The man in black stepped out of the house, and the girl scrambled backward. Something was inherently menacing about the man and the steel tied to his waist.

He gave her a curious look.

"You can sense me, can't you?"

Her confusion must have been evident from the look on her face. He tried again.

"You can feel me, can't you? I feel different from the other people, correct?"

The girl nodded, and the man smiled, a smile that still seemed dangerous. The man knelt down, bringing himself to her level. He looked her squarely in the eyes. "Your father is dead, girl. A blade should hear it from another blade."

Somehow the girl had already known this, but her mind was filled with questions, and one came out of her mouth before she could decide whether to stop it or not.

"How did he die? He was a dayblade, sworn to heal, not to kill."

The nightblade didn't hesitate. "Your father was killed by his own commander, the man who was supposed to protect him."

The girl didn't understand, but she nodded anyway. The man studied her, as if he could see right through her. He stood back up.

"Good luck, girl."

Chapter 1

The night was cool and fresh with the scents of spring. A full moon had just risen over the horizon, its brightness drowning out the light from stars unfortunate enough to be too close. The wind blew softly over the plains, picking up bite as it brushed over the small deposits of snow still dotting the landscape.

Asa didn't mind the breeze. She had trained herself to ignore both heat and cold. The feat was a matter of discipline, a trait she had more than enough of. Her attention was focused on the village in front of her, pulsing with the life of innocents and criminals alike.

To the untrained eye, the village might have seemed much like any other—decently sized, with dozens of huts and shops and a handful of larger buildings. A casual glance wouldn't catch anything more interesting.

An astute observer would notice items that seemed out of place. Two swordsmiths worked in the small village, a fact even more out of place when one considered how far from the mountains they were. The ore had to be hauled a long way to get here. Yet even at this late hour, Asa could sometimes hear the clang of metalwork carried on the breeze. By itself, the presence of two smiths would be odd, but Asa felt what others couldn't see.

She sensed the guards walking the perimeter at regular intervals, armed as heavily as a lord's soldiers even though there was no military. Not out here, far from Haven and the king's court.

The locals were behaving strangely as well. In a normal village, at this time of night, the movement of people would be random. Asa would expect to sense a few villagers out eating at food stands, a few drinking, a few gambling, but most at home, with their families. But even at this distance, she could feel how most of the people out at night had only one destination in mind, a larger building near the center of the village.

Asa closed her eyes and her sense expanded, reaching out toward the life energy of the village. She could feel a few people in their beds, sleeping soundly, mostly women and children. With her eyes closed, she could easily discern the pattern of the patrols that surrounded the village, more than she had expected. A problem, but not insurmountable.

Her focus was drawn to the building near the center of village, where a crowd was congregating. It felt packed, but not uncomfortably so. Clusters of people were gathered around, but on one side of the building, there was a warrior, alone except for two bodyguards. Asa took a deep breath and focused on the lone man. As she did, she could feel his own sense, subdued among such a large crowd. The two bodyguards had also developed the sense, but it was weak.

Asa came back to herself, opening her eyes and scanning her surroundings. Her sense told her she was alone, but it never hurt to be more certain. The fields around her were empty.

She took another deep breath. The patrols were regular, and if her timing was perfect, she'd be able to slip through them without a problem. Once inside the village, she only had to worry about the chaos she would cause in the hall. The fact that the bodyguards were sense-trained was disturbing. Stealth would be much harder.

Asa ran the challenges through her mind, but there was never any hesitation. The night was hers.

As a final check, Asa ran her fingers over all the different blades concealed on her person. The casual observer wouldn't notice weaponry, and even trained guards weren't likely to be suspicious. But she was a woman who liked to be prepared. A short sword was strapped to her right thigh, accessible through a wide slit in her traveling clothes. A long knife was strapped to her left thigh, also easy to reach. And a very thin blade was strapped to the inside of her left thigh in case of emergency. A dagger rode on her left arm, and several throwing blades accented her right forearm. Everything was in place.

Asa strode down toward the village, moving from cover to cover, staying out of sight of the patrols.

Getting past the patrols was no more than a test of patience. Asa hid behind a pile of brush thirty paces from the edge of the village, relying on her sense to track the movements of the guards. The patrols circled in groups of two, moving slowly, trying and failing at acting natural. Each pair was always in sight of another pair, in theory leaving no gaps to sneak through. But people weren't perfect. The shadows' report on the group had been scant. The village was too small and tight-knit, hard to penetrate, but the Council of the Blades believed it was mostly angry ex-soldiers and disgruntled civilians. They had some training and were getting better, but they weren't an army, not yet.

The lack of training showed in their movements. Asa could sense this as one group would fall behind and then rush to catch up to the pair in front of them, causing other pairs to speed up behind them. Their pacing was uneven, and soon Asa's chosen route into the village would be hidden from view. Until then, she bided her time, letting the cold breeze blow through her robes as though they were open windows. Spring was coming, but the weather seemed to have forgotten.

The gap appeared, one pair pausing just out of sight. Asa sprang into action, sprinting silently behind another pair, trusting her dark clothing to hide her from a wayward glance. The pair she passed behind was oblivious to what was happening behind them. And why not? Their backs were supposed to be guarded by the following pair.

In just a moment, Asa was among the huts on the outskirts of the village. From there, she could easily approach the large hall she had pinpointed earlier as the group's meeting place. She used her sense to avoid anyone wandering the paths between the huts. There were plenty of dark corners, and she was never in danger of being discovered.

The smell of sizzling beef from a nearby food stand was almost too tempting to pass up. She had subsisted on trail rations for most of the past moon, and this part of the Kingdom was known for the quality of their cattle. She could imagine the fat melting off the meat and catching fire on the charcoal underneath. The aroma tested her will to continue without stopping.

Her next challenge was getting into the hall. She could sense the people inside and the pair of guards at what she assumed was the front of the building. A few moments later she came in sight of the hall, and her suspicion was confirmed. Two guards stood at attention at the door, and their easy and alert stance let Asa know right away these two were far more experienced than the patrols she'd gotten past.

She discarded options almost as fast as they came to her. She could try to get onto the roof and hear what was happening, but with her target and the two bodyguards being sense-trained, they'd likely notice her. There were windows in the hall, but if she loitered outside them, she would also be sensed. Killing the two guards outside was an option, but a huge risk. The village, although quiet, still had a number of people moving around, and the bodies would likely be discovered before the meeting was over.

Deception was her only chance. Her intended ploy brought risks as well, but was most likely to succeed. If it failed, she could chance killing the guards.

Asa took a single breath. She threw up her hood so her face was in shadow and walked into the lights.

The guards noticed her immediately. She could sense it in the way their stances shifted. They were wary, but not worried. Asa wasn't surprised. She wasn't a tall woman, and her stature would appear slight, even under the generous folds of her traveling cloak.

Asa approached them slowly, trying to seem as though she posed no threat to them. She added just the slightest sway to her hips, accenting her femininity. The elders claimed they were trying to discover ways to use the sense to manipulate minds, but Asa would believe such a possibility when she experienced it herself. Until then, there were other ways to manipulate people. Especially men.

She stopped a short pace away from the sentries. She wanted to be close to them, both for them to get a good look at her, but also to be within easy reach of their long swords. If the worst came to pass, she would be inside their guards even if they had the reflexes to draw their blades. Her short weapons would be a definite advantage.

"Halt right there," one of the guards said, realizing too late she had already stopped. He covered up his mistake quickly. "What is your business here?"

"I am one of his shadows. I came here to speak to him."

The other guard, the one Asa labeled the smart one, frowned. "He's holding a meeting right now. What is so important it can't wait?"

Asa shook her head. "I can't say, but I can wait until he finishes."

The second guard was still suspicious. Asa decided to take a risk based on a whisper she had heard from a shadow. Her target liked women, perhaps more than was good for him. "My news is important, but I want to catch him before he goes back to his house." She lowered her voice. "I want him to myself tonight."

Slowly, the second guard raised his hand and drew back her hood. The first guard whistled when he saw her face. Asa was beautiful, and she knew it. The first guard couldn't help himself, and Asa was grateful he was unintentionally supporting her story.

"I can see what he sees in you."

She turned to him and gave him a look full of promise. "Thank you."

The second guard was the one she had to convince. "I need to search you for weapons," he said.

Asa needed to bluff the guards or she'd have to kill them. "You're welcome to, if that's what you want. But I can assure you, my weapons aren't steel." Her voice held a hint of warning.

The second guard was willing to call her bluff, but the first one stopped him. "Wait. If she's with him, do you think it's a good idea to proceed? You know how jealous he gets."

The smart guard hesitated, and Asa stayed there, her posture open and relaxed.

The silence lasted only for a moment before the second guard made his decision. "You're right." He turned to Asa. "I'll escort you in. If you try anything, you won't live long enough to regret it."

"Thank you." Internally, she felt a rush of relief. She was certain killing the guards would make the rest of the evening far more challenging.

She stopped using her sense, cutting herself off from her gift. Without it, she felt naked and exposed, surrounded by darkness. But if she used her sense in the hall, the man she had come for would certainly order her death.

The second guard opened the door and let her in. She took a single step inside and waited for the guard to close the door behind them. She wouldn't give him any chance to doubt her.

Fortunately, all the attention in the room was on the speaker—a good thing, as she was the only woman in a room of about thirty men. No surprise. The chance of any women being included in such a gathering was almost zero.

Asa could understand why attention was drawn to the front, where Takashi stood on a simple, small, raised platform. It was the first time she had seen Takashi, and she was surprised by him. All the reports talked about him being larger than life, but in stature he was perfectly normal and unassuming. She could see by the way he held himself that he was a dangerous man, fully in control of his body, but if you passed him on the street, you wouldn't think twice about the encounter.

But his stature was far overshadowed by his presence, which elicited an almost physical sensation. Asa felt it the moment she stepped into the room. Takashi didn't shout or even speak loudly, but his voice carried throughout the hall, and he had the full attention of every person there. She had arrived well into his speech, but it wasn't hard to catch up.

"Friends, we've talked and talked about this. The desire for action burns in each of you. I know. I feel it, too. It feels as though all we do is talk. Our blood is hot and screams for death. I can assure you, the time will come, but it will not be today, and if we are fortunate, it will not be for many cycles."

Asa was immediately taken by Takashi's words. He paused between sentences, allowing each one to sink in, confident he wouldn't be interrupted. He knew he was worth listening to. His words were also interesting and not what she had expected to hear. She could see from a glance around the room that some men didn't like what he was uttering, but they held their tongues, respecting Takashi's space.

"I don't need to repeat my story to anyone here. You each know me personally, and some of you have fought beside me. We will see the Kingdom fall, but it won't be through the violence you propose. Not yet. Look around you. Think about how many people were beside you at this time last cycle. You are surrounded by soldiers, scholars, wise men in many disciplines. And all of us have found a place to call our home, a place ruled by the consent of the people. Every day we grow stronger, and every day our ability to win our freedom grows one step closer.

"Here we have food and space. It is not convenient, but we are not bothered. We have no fear of the military, and even the blades themselves can't harm us here."

Asa smiled slightly.

"But we are not invincible. Not at all. If we draw attention to ourselves, we will fall. There are those among you who think that as soon as word of us gets out, everyone will flock to our cause. How I wish I shared your belief. But I cannot share such naive optimism. Yes, the Kingdom is the weakest it's ever been. An old man without a successor holds the throne; and petty lords, focused only on their own power, bicker over his remains like feral dogs over scraps of food. It is not enough. Discontent is rife, but still the land is at peace. So long as people are fed and feel safe, they aren't likely to disobey under the threat of death."

Takashi looked around the room, judging the mood of the men gathered.

"I know some of you aren't convinced. But look around this room again, closely. Think of every person here. We grow every day, but every person who joins us has a story, an event, something that pushed them one step over the edge. Mere discontent wasn't enough, not even for us."

Asa could feel the shift of attitude in the room. Some had disagreed with Takashi, but his final argument had hit them hard. She realized how close this group was and understood why no outsiders had managed to get in and stay safe.

"For now, we stay our course. Word of us is spreading, and every day more settlers come here. Let us grow slowly, learning more as we grow. When we have grown large enough, we will not be overlooked. But by that time we will be strong enough to stand against the might of the Kingdom, and we will know our system of government works. We will know that a government chosen and led by the people can thrive, no matter how large it gets."

Asa turned Takashi's words over in her mind. Takashi was proposing a radical system of running the Kingdom, an idea he had supposedly developed while serving in the military as a blade. He believed people could govern themselves, and this village was the heart of his grand experiment. Conveniently, he had been chosen by the people as their leader.

Asa found his argument . . . interesting, she supposed. The whole idea seemed foolish. Peasants running the land? The concept was laughable. They didn't have the education, experience, or resources. And they were peasants. But looking around the room, she could see many thought his ideas had merit.

Yet Takashi's philosophy had an inherent hypocrisy, evident in a single glance around the room. Sharing power, to him, meant sharing it with other men, not everyone. No one here would recognize that simple fact. They were embedded in Takashi's new system of power and wouldn't take kindly to anyone questioning their authority. Asa fought the urge to shake her head.

She hadn't gotten where she was without a sharp and objective mind, and she could see the appeal of Takashi's idea, especially to the lower classes. He was promising power, power to those who didn't have it. And people loved having power. The only problem, as Asa saw it, was that very few people could handle such responsibility. Takashi's dream would collapse on itself eventually, a victim of its own hubris. A part of her wished that he would be able to see it. That his rebellion could last long enough for him to see it collapse, for him to understand how foolish all his planning had been.

She alone in the room was aware that he would never have the chance.

Because she was here to kill him.

Asa waited patiently as the meeting concluded. Even though her mission was clear, she couldn't help but be interested in this sect of people. As misguided as they were, they believed, and Asa respected them for that. Takashi was right about one thing: the houses that ran the Kingdom were corrupt and increasingly chained to sycophants and power-hungry lords. Asa had spent a little time at court as part of her training, and the number of honest people she had met was less than the number of weapons she carried.

But Asa couldn't see how Takashi's idea could work. The government didn't need to be run by peasants. In her opinion, it needed a strong king, one stronger than the last two, who had reigned for forty cycles. The Kingdom could be strong and unified and serve the people, but only if an appropriate leader rose from the bickering houses.

The moon was high in the sky when the meeting disbanded. Asa could feel the tension growing within her as the time for action came near. Takashi had dismissed the group, and in ones and twos, the people trickled out, leaving only a diminishing number of small conversations in scattered groups throughout the hall. As the people left, some noticed Asa, but they couldn't see her face under the shadow of her hood. Whatever curiosity they had was sated by the presence of the guard.

Not long after the meeting's end, Takashi noticed her. He had been going from group to group, presumably winning favors and being the corrupt politician Asa assumed he was.

Asa kept her mind empty. He would be able to sense her intent, and surprise was essential. After Takashi finished his conversation with a pair of men, he made his way toward her. She kept her face hidden, her eyes only able to see his feet. To attack first was her best chance.

He only took seven steps to reach her, but she felt as if those steps took forever. She hated the idea of tracking down another blade, but Takashi had gone too far a long time ago. Again, she felt naked without her sense. She imagined he was studying her, trying to decide who she was and if she was dangerous. His own sense would be playing over her.

Finally, she saw his feet stop in front of her, the feet of his guards a step behind him and to the side. He had stopped outside of her arm's reach, and Asa had to give the man credit. He knew she didn't carry a long sword, so he stood back just far enough that she would have to step toward him to attack. That told her a lot about him. She was dealing with someone both smart and cautious.

"Who is this?"

The guard responded. "My lord, she claims to be one of your shadows. She says she comes with important information."

Everything happened in an instant. Takashi took a step back and motioned for his guards. He didn't panic, just gave an order. "Kill her."

There was no hesitation in his voice, and Asa knew she wouldn't have a chance to convince him with words. She reconnected with her sense, gladly drinking in the new information it provided. She could sense the guards drawing their weapons and the complicated intertwining of four people all using the sense in a small place. Self-preservation demanded she run, but her combat instincts were honed sharper than the edges of her blades. She darted forward, her hand finding the slit in her traveling cloak and drawing her short sword.

Takashi was the one she needed to worry about. He was trained as she was, and he would not fall easily. But she didn't want to kill him, at least, not yet. For her own reasons, she wanted him alive long enough for her to have a conversation with him.

Takashi was faster than his guards, his sword clearing its scabbard first, slicing out at her before she could launch her first attack. But Asa was fast. Her short blade was lighter and quicker than Takashi's longer curved blade, and she deflected his cut with ease, directing it over her head toward the ceiling. Asa was underneath his blade and inside his guard, and Takashi realized his mistake. He had underestimated her.

Asa spun, driving her small, sharp elbow into Takashi's center. She felt all the breath leave his body, and he involuntarily started to fold in half. Asa completed her spin by stepping forward and bringing up her knee, catching Takashi's falling chin. She felt the crunch of his jaw and wondered how many teeth she'd broken. Takashi fell backward, unconscious, and Asa could safely ignore him. Her vicious attack had the added benefit of sending the guard who had escorted her in running for the door, frightened as a hare.

His two guards were right behind Takashi, their swords trying to catch her. They were strong young men with rudimentary abilities with the sense. They had probably been trained by Takashi himself after leaving the military. But they were too young to know the information she was seeking.

Asa's sense let her know where the blades were going to be, and she slid around them, giving herself the slimmest of margins. Then she was behind the warriors, and she took another few steps to put space between them. She turned and faced her assailants, drawing a throwing blade in her left hand to complement the short sword in her right.

"Run now or lose your lives."

Asa knew there was little chance they would listen. They were on fire, the scream of battle in their blood, and they were too inexperienced to know how to control such passion. But she didn't want to kill innocent men.

Her prediction was accurate. Though the rest of the hall had emptied in panic as soon as swords were drawn, the two bodyguards were too focused on Asa to join their companions. They came at her together, a perfect example of how the military academies trained soldiers to attack in pairs. Asa had the fleeting thought that these two must have been great students.

But she wasn't a traditionalist. Asa moved to her right and crouched low. As a smaller woman, crouching brought her below the heights men usually trained at. The guard on her right tried to bring his sword down on top of her, but she had her short sword angled above her head, allowing the cut to slide down the steel and past her shoulder. She sliced the guard's leg as she swept by, carefully avoiding the major blood vessel. Her cut peeled apart his muscle, and he collapsed onto the ground.

Asa returned to standing as the second guard came at her. Her left hand came up, whipping the throwing knife at him point-blank. The blade caught him in the meaty part of his upper right arm. The guard didn't seem to realize what had happened. Instinctively, his right arm loosened as it was hit, and the blade spun out of his hands as he tried to raise it to attack her. She sidestepped his charge.

When she turned around, she saw the fight had gone out of the guards, but they were still torn. They were sworn to Takashi, and she saw the battle of honor and self-preservation play across each of their faces.

"Leave now. There is nothing you can do. Save your own lives and fight another day. It is what he would want you to do."

She watched the duo closely, waiting to see if her words would have the effect she desired. She had no idea what Takashi would order them to do were he awake, but it was a kind lie.

The guard with the throwing knife in his arm shifted his stance, and Asa's sense gave her a picture of exactly what he was intending. In one smooth motion, she grabbed another throwing knife and sped it toward him. Even if he could have sensed the blade coming, there was too little time to react. He started shifting his weight to avoid the attack, but the knife caught him in the left arm, an almost perfect mirror image of his other arm. Asa's point was made.

"You know I can kill you. I've let you both live with only minor wounds. If you try anything, you're throwing your lives away meaninglessly."

The two suddenly saw the truth of her statement. Together, one guard hobbling, they made their way toward the exit. Asa shouted after them.

"If anyone tries to come back in, I will kill them. I can use the sense much better than you can, and if anyone comes within fifty paces of this hall, I will kill them. And him."

The guards nodded, and Asa surveyed her work. She wasn't certain her threat would be enough to keep the villagers away, but she hoped so. It was time to have a conversation.

—

Asa slapped Takashi across the face to awaken him. She had tied him up in a corner of the hall with cloth torn from his clothing, trying to find a spot where an archer wouldn't be able to hit them from outside the windows. The hall wasn't the safest place to have a conversation, but she had waited too long for an opportunity like this.

Takashi came to quickly, and Asa felt him immediately take in his surroundings with his sense. She could feel his tendrils go throughout the village, and she saw his shoulders relax as he discovered his people were fine. He saw that she noticed.

"I thought you were an advance for a raiding party."

Asa shook her head. No point in lying to a dead man.

"My bodyguards?"

"Wounded, but neither fatally. They were hard to convince."

Takashi bowed his head to her just slightly. "Thank you."

Asa ignored the gratitude.

"Did the council send you?"

Asa nodded.

Takashi sighed. "As much as I respect some of them, they are part of the problem as well. They need to open their eyes."

"I'm not here to discuss your politics."

"Then why are you here? If the council sent you, you only have one purpose, and it isn't to talk to me."

"I want to know about Two Falls."

Takashi laughed, blood spewing from his mouth. "That's over twenty cycles ago. Everyone knows about the massacre at Two Falls."

Asa drove her fist into Takashi's stomach, doubling him over again. She snatched his hair and pulled his head back up.

"You and I both know that's not true. I want the real story. I want to know what happened that day. Every detail you remember."

Takashi's eyes met hers, the mirth having left. Asa could see the pain in his face, the sorrow over a memory he'd never quite been able to erase.

"You should know, that day started me on the path that led me here. When the sun rose on that day, I was like you. Obedient and blind."

Asa didn't respond, and Takashi studied her. She felt as though he was searching for something, a truth just a little too elusive for him to hold onto. He spoke carefully. "No, I wasn't quite like you. You're not really obedient, are you? You're more like me. Searching for truth. Only your path is different than mine."

Asa didn't know how to respond. It was as though he knew. Either that or he was very intuitive. Or very lucky.

"I'll tell you what happened that day."

Asa knelt down next to Takashi, and he began to recite his story. As she had asked, he left out no details, no matter how insignificant. As he continued, she realized he had lived with the consequences of that day for over twenty cycles. Every step he had taken that day was ingrained in his memory, and he shared all with her. She listened closely, having to remind herself to pay attention to the outside world. The village was still on edge from her attack, but they didn't attempt to retaliate. They must have believed her threats.

When Takashi finished, the sun was just beginning to rise. The story was everything Asa had managed to piece together on her own, and more. She was surprised to find tears running down her face. She wiped them away, ashamed of the bond she had developed with Takashi as he told his story.

"Thank you."

Takashi nodded. "I don't know if I've ever told the full story to anyone before. It was good to tell. That day should never be forgotten."

"And the commander who was responsible?"

"Osamu? He disappeared soon after. Everyone assumed he went off into the woods to kill himself, but no one could be sure. He was never seen by anyone again." He studied her once more. "If you are hoping to find him, you should not hold out hope. Personally, I believe he killed himself. But even if he hadn't, he would be an old man by now, over sixty cycles of age. I'm certain he's dead. Revenge isn't worth it."

He spoke as though he understood.

Asa held his gaze. "You know who I am?"

Takashi nodded. "I wasn't sure at first, but now I am. He was in my unit, but I suppose that's why you've tracked me down. He and I were close, you know."

Asa shook her head. "I didn't."

Takashi looked up at the ceiling of the hall, apparently trying to hold back tears. "I suppose you wouldn't. You must have only been, what, five or six when it happened?"

"Six."

"I'm sorry. I can't even imagine."

Asa didn't know what to say, so she didn't speak. The past was vivid in her mind.

"He spoke about you all the time."

Asa smiled at the thought.

"He would have been proud of your becoming a nightblade. He was proud of being a dayblade. He thought it was the best way to help others, but until that day, he always saw the need for the nightblades, too."

Takashi met her eyes again. "You know, that day, when everything descended into chaos, he was one of the few people who kept his head. He tried to save lives. He was the only one who did the right thing that day. When I do what I do, a lot of it is because of him."

"Thank you." Asa's gratitude was genuine. She had been so young and known so little.

Takashi straightened himself. "You're welcome. But enough. Let's finish what you came here to do."

Asa didn't want to, but she knew she would anyway.

"Will you grant me a request?"

"If I can."

"Will you allow me to take my own life? I do not want the council to have the pleasure. I would ask that you make the final cut. It is the greatest honor I can give him."

Asa didn't bother to hide the tears. She wasn't an emotional woman, but Takashi had worked his way deep into her heart, taking the only path that still existed. She nodded.

With caution, she undid his bonds, never taking her attention off her fellow blade. She wanted to trust him, but she wasn't so foolish as to believe he wouldn't try to fight back if given the chance. She granted him his short sword and took his long blade in her hands. It was a well-made sword.

Takashi knelt and said a short prayer. He took several deep breaths, and Asa watched as he settled into his final action. She took a cutting stance, ready at a moment's need. Takashi looked up at her. "I wish you the very best."

With a single motion, Takashi drove his short blade into his stomach. Asa forced herself to watch. He deserved that, if nothing else. Every moment seemed an eternity, and Asa forgot to breathe. Takashi's face was made of stone, not showing the slightest bit of emotion. Blood poured from the wound in his stomach, but he didn't move a single muscle. Asa wanted him to show something, some sign she could end his suffering, but he remained still, defiant, just as he had in life.

Finally, he bent his head forward. As he did, the expression on his face changed, and he started to smile.

Asa's cut was clean, and she felt the energy that had been Takashi empty from his body and join the Great Cycle.

Chapter 2

Minori looked over the board, only half paying attention. Hajimi wasn't a bad player, but Minori was much, much stronger. They had played together dozens of times, and Hajimi had never won, yet he kept coming back, always ready for another chance. Minori didn't take any particular joy in playing him, but he respected the older man's determination. Minori was only a few moves away from finishing the game, but he didn't think Hajimi recognized this.

Across from him, Hajimi focused, his stare boring holes in the wooden board. When Hajimi smiled, Minori knew the game was over for good. Just as Minori had expected, Hajimi moved one of his peasants, setting up a trap one move later. From a certain perspective, the stratagem would have been a good one, but Hajimi lacked the foresight to see the result of his move. Blinded by the prospect of short-term gain, he missed the threat looming on the horizon.

Minori pretended to think over his move while his opponent spoke. Hajimi never talked while he was debating his next move, making any conversation a ponderous affair.

"This has been a good game, Minori. There are days when I wish we had fewer responsibilities and could play all day."

Minori looked up and smiled. He couldn't think of anything more boring. "It would be a relaxing way to spend our time, but the Kingdom must come first."

Minori sacrificed his lord, one of his strongest pieces, to set up the endgame he wanted. Hajimi took the bait without question, and a few moves later, the game was over.

Hajimi had the grace to laugh about his loss. "Minori, you are the best player I have ever come across! How do you do it?"

Minori was pleased at the compliment. "Everyone has different weaknesses. It's simply a matter of being able to find and exploit them."

Hajimi's sharp eyes pierced into Minori's. "And tell me, what's my weakness?"

Minori paused, as though considering. Hajimi would never realize Minori had hoped for just that question. "You're a strong player, but you have a tendency to focus too much on the center of the board."

Hajimi frowned. "But the player who controls the center of the board controls the game. Basic strategy."

"Yes, but the mistake is to think the center of the board is controlled by the pieces at the center. You're so focused on the pieces there that you miss the threats coming from the edges of the board. When I play you, I control the center by controlling the edges and working my way in."

Hajimi nodded in understanding. "This is why you suggested we send an assassin to kill Takashi? Because the actions near the edges of the Kingdom affect the center?"

"I fear the key events of our generation have happened on the edges of the board. Takashi is dead, but his ideas still spread from peasant to peasant. Two Falls was on the very edge of the Kingdom, but that day reverberates through history. If we wish to control Haven, we must be able to control the boundaries of our land."

They stood up and walked in silence for a while, enjoying the sights and sounds of the garden where they had been playing. As they walked, Minori gave a small bow to the master gardener, carefully raking the pattern into a small stone garden. Minori appreciated the man's efforts, and he wielded a rake with the same care Minori wielded his sword.

His thoughts were interrupted by Hajimi. "Minori, one reason I so enjoy our matches is because of the way you approach the game. You are thoughtful and always looking at the larger picture. It's for these very reasons that I have a new assignment for you."

Hajimi stopped, and Minori paused beside him. "I hate to ask this of you, because you already do so much for the council, but many of us are convinced there is no better person for the task."

Minori only had a moment to wonder what the mysterious task could be. Knowing Hajimi, it could be almost anything.

"We'd like you to travel down to Haven and act as a liaison to the king."

Minori, through cycles of practice, controlled his reaction. Instead of the joy he felt, he affected a concerned expression. "Has something happened to Kiyoshi?"

Hajimi shook his head. "No, but the council believes the current situation requires a stronger presence at court. Kiyoshi will continue in his duties, but I'd like for the two of you to work together. Kiyoshi's wisdom can be your guide, but your intelligence and perspective could be very valuable."

Minori bowed to Hajimi. "I'm honored to serve."

Hajimi waved away Minori's bow. "Come, now. We've known each other for many cycles. I knew you'd accept, even though it means you'll have to leave these gardens you love so well."

"A worthy sacrifice."

"I do not think you'll be saying as much a few moons from now."

"How may I best serve the council at the capital?"

Hajimi looked around, almost as if worried about shadows. Minori smiled at the thought. If there was any spy bold enough to sneak into the Hall of the Blades, where everyone could sense your presence, they deserved the secrets held within. But still, Hajimi hesitated, and Minori had to encourage him to speak openly.

"The council believes we need to have a stronger voice at the king's side. Kiyoshi's strength is in his ability to work with people, but time and time again, he has been willing to make concessions that we believe weaken the Kingdom."

Minori knew what Hajimi was referring to. The blades' power had been strongly curtailed in the past few cycles, while the three great houses' power continued to grow. The only balancing force against the lords was the blades, loyal only to the Kingdom, and by extension, the king. The great houses might bicker and skirmish among themselves, but no one would dare to endanger the Kingdom with the blades around to maintain order. Though they were far fewer in number than the armies the lords wielded, their strength as warriors would decimate any opponent on the field.

So the houses resorted to politics, playing on the latent fear that existed in the populace. The blades were almost mythic in their status and, for better or worse, feared as much as they were respected. The houses had been spreading stories of abuses. Some were mundane, such as blades demanding payment for services or deciding who to help based on their wealth. But those mundane stories allowed for even more dangerous rumors to spread. Rumors of murders, rapes, and robberies. True or not, rumor by rumor, the people began to fear the blades.

The houses seized on that fear and, with Kiyoshi at the capital, had managed to push through a number of laws that limited the ability of the blades to act. It had started with a census and a registry, so that every blade in the Kingdom was known. Then, step by step, the houses insisted that the Council of the Blades seek approval for almost any action within their families' lands. The council could now do little without first seeking approval from at least one house, putting the council in a dangerous position. The blades were and had always been the glue that kept the Kingdom together.

Hajimi continued. "The council has debated long and hard, and we have decided it is time for us to make more dramatic moves. Strength must rule this land. None of the lords have the will. We are the only ones fit to rule."

Minori agreed. Blades would make the best rulers, not driven by fear in the way of lords and citizens. Being gifted with the sense, they could see further and understand more than any normal person could hope to. But long ago their ancestors had decreed that no blade would take the throne. They had decided it was too much power in one place.

Minori respected his ancestors, but disagreed with them. Power should be concentrated. Any swordsman knew focus was essential in both battle and life. Power was no different. Concentrated, power could effect change as decisively as a killing cut with a blade. Spread out, power was weakened. He would fight until the day he died to see a blade on the throne.

He looked at his superior. "If I can see or create opportunities to acquire more authority for the blades, should I pursue it?"

Hajimi nodded. "The houses are too strong, and if the pattern continues, it can only result in open conflict. More than anything, we would prefer to see a future without violence. You will be instrumental in bringing that about."

The two men walked in silence for some time, Minori soaking in the peace of the gardens. He cultivated an image of a man who loved the gardens, only half a lie. He did enjoy the peace they provided, but he would never hesitate to give the green up if he could serve the blades.

Minori hid his smile, as he was delighted at this turn of events. He had been prodding the council in just this direction for quite some time. He had thought he wouldn't have a chance until Kiyoshi died. Rumors circulated of the old man's illnesses, but he seemed to stubbornly hold on to life. Some days Minori worried that he might pass away to the Great Cycle before Kiyoshi.

One pressing question still remained unanswered.

"Forgive me for the bluntness of this query, but I must ask, to fully understand the council's will. How far am I permitted to go to gain the advantages we seek?"

Hajimi fixed his subordinate with a cold stare, but Minori didn't back down. Minori might be advanced in age, but he had made his name with legendary assassinations, and his skills had not dulled with age. If anything, the cunning developed with age gave him a tremendous advantage.

Hajimi's answer was as direct as any he was likely to give: "You may go as far as is necessary."

Chapter 3

Kiyoshi inspected the message in his hand. It bore the king's seal, which seemed unnecessary to Kiyoshi, but he believed that was true of most of the trappings of office. The writing was in Masaki's hand, but Kiyoshi could see the note had been scribed in a hurry. Given the nature of the message, that wasn't surprising. He suppressed a sigh. Another day, another scheme brewing. Crisis was almost becoming monotonous.

Despite the urgency of the king's hand, Kiyoshi didn't hurry. Haste led to mistakes, and those he couldn't afford to make. He browsed through his outfits, settling on a plain white set of robes, the daily wear of a dayblade. Then he took both his long and short swords and tied them to his hip.

It was unusual for a dayblade to walk around with swords. A healer had little need for them. But these blades were gifts from Masaki. They would also remind the lords that Kiyoshi, unlike any of them, was allowed to wear his steel in the presence of the king. A petty display of status, but it was all the lords responded to. As much as he desired to draw the swords, he wouldn't. Such gestures would do the Kingdom no good.

After he finished preparing, he walked deliberately toward the receiving hall. His footsteps caused the nightingale floor to sing underneath, and he knew his arrival would be noticed. The lords would also notice he didn't hurry. Let them know he had no fear of their power.

He entered the hall and took in the scene. His eyes narrowed at the sight of all three lords sitting around the table with King Masaki. Whatever move they were going to make, it was going to be serious today; he could see that plainly from the looks on their faces. Kiyoshi let his sense wander over the room. The energy coming from the lords was palpable. None were blades, but all were powerful leaders. They weren't to be underestimated. In contrast to the young and healthy lords, Masaki was sick, as he would be until the day he died.

Kiyoshi knelt and bowed his head to the floor, suppressing his pride. Yes, they were lords, but he was a blade, and he had no desire to bow to anyone but the king. His knees didn't bend like they had forty cycles ago, but his movements were still strong.

Kiyoshi took his place next to Masaki, whose face was grave.

"I apologize for my delay, lords. I had just finished a healing and was not prepared for this meeting."

Lord Isamu, head of House Fujita, who controlled the lands in the south third of the Kingdom, was the first to speak. "Your apology is accepted. We understand how important the work you do is. Thank you for your haste."

Kiyoshi bowed in gratitude. The lord's words were empty, but he was a polite man. Isamu was a large man, born into riches and opulence. Even if Isamu would rather see Kiyoshi with a sword through his chest, he would never say an impolite word, especially not in the King's Council.

"Thank you, Lord Isamu. My summons from the king did not speak as to the cause for this meeting. What has happened?"

Kiyoshi didn't like Isamu, either—a visceral reaction. He detested the lord's rich dress and condescension. His hands were soft, never having held a blade or done hard work. But though Isamu was clever in his own way, he wasn't the one Kiyoshi worried most about. That honor was held by the lord who spoke next.

Lord Shin, the head of House Amari, answered, "I am sorry to be the bearer of bad news, Kiyoshi."

Kiyoshi knew that to be a lie. A tension, tighter than any bowstring, could be felt between the two men, but Shin was exceedingly clever. He was the lord of the lands to the north and west of the Kingdom, and he had the ability to manipulate people to his own ends. Like Isamu, he was not a warrior. His hands had never held a sword, but they were bloody all the same. He was tall and thin, and more than once, Kiyoshi had wanted to cut him down. Whenever Shin smiled, Kiyoshi got the impression he was witnessing a man who could see the strings, the motivations of everyone, and pull as he needed. In Kiyoshi's opinion, Shin was the most dangerous man in the Kingdom.

Shin continued, "It deals with another offense by a nightblade."

Kiyoshi fought against his own reaction. Their scheme was always the same. For just a moment, he wished his enemies would have more imagination, just so he could have a new problem to deal with.

Again he placed his forehead to the floor. "I apologize for my people. What has happened?"

Masaki asked Kiyoshi to sit up straight. "I appreciate your sorrow at this turn of events, but you do not bear the responsibility for every blade in the Kingdom. I don't scrape my forehead against the floor for every crime committed by one of my citizens. Let us work together to solve this problem."

Kiyoshi appreciated Masaki's kindness, but he worried the king would look weak in front of the lords.

"Please, my lords, let me know what has happened."

This time Lord Juro spoke. Juro was the head of House Kita, which managed the mountainous lands to the north and east of the Kingdom. Of all the lords, he was the one Kiyoshi most respected. He had been raised as a warrior, and he was an honorable man. His hands were well calloused, and he moved with a grace that told of his cycles of training with a sword. Unfortunately, he wasn't wise enough to understand the plots of a man like Shin. "There was an incident in my lands. Some of my smaller villages near the mountains were being harassed by a well-organized group of bandits. Some of my militia units attempted to discover their lair, but were unsuccessful. The bandits must have found some hiding place deep in the mountains.

"Because of the militia's failure, a nightblade was summoned to help discover the bandits' lair. At first, everything went well. The nightblade intercepted several raids before they reached villages, and the villagers were pleased with his service. From what we can tell, the bandits gathered everyone for one all-out assault. They wanted to overpower the nightblade with sheer numbers."

Kiyoshi nodded. There were no guarantees when fighting a nightblade, but the best hope for someone without the gift of the sense was to try to outnumber the nightblade as much as possible. A common strategy. Not efficient, but sometimes effective.

"The battle ended with the nightblade victorious. The villagers rejoiced until the nightblade began demanding remuneration for his services. At first the villagers were happy to contribute, but his requests became more and more extravagant, and now the villagers are more in fear of the nightblade than they ever were of the bandits. It is said the nightblade even killed a farmer who refused his request for rice."

Kiyoshi's eyes narrowed. This news was almost impossible to believe. But who knew what the truth was? The story was already likely being circulated throughout the Kingdom.

Kiyoshi searched for more information. "What actions have you taken?"

Isamu answered, his loud voice carrying over Juro's calm tone.

"What do you mean what actions have been taken? We can't take any action against a nightblade! Indeed, Lord Juro could send dozens of his men to die, but that's not how the rule of law works. Nightblades are supposed to keep the peace. Their gifts make them perfect for such endeavors, but they need to be controlled. It is up to your people to keep yourselves in line. If not, we'll have to remove the blades from service to the Kingdom."

Kiyoshi struggled to control his expression, only succeeding because of his cycles of practice. He had listened closely, not just to Isamu's words, but to his tone. Near the end, it had shifted from practiced indignation to something more terrible—truth. Lord Isamu wanted to remove the nightblades entirely from the Kingdom. Kiyoshi focused on the other two lords. Juro seemed oblivious to the impact of the statement, but Shin was watching Kiyoshi with the same intensity that Kiyoshi used studying them. Shin also recognized the statement of truth, and waited for the dayblade's reaction. Kiyoshi had to step carefully, more so than ever before.

"Lord Juro, I am deeply sorry for the actions of my brethren. Give me the nightblade's name, and I will ensure the affair is taken care of."

Lord Shin interrupted. "You must forgive me, Kiyoshi. I know you are a man of honor, but we need to know more. Incidents like this one are happening more and more frequently. People have always had a combination of fear and respect of the blades, but the scale is shifting too far toward fear. Lord Isamu spoke well. For hundreds of cycles we have entrusted the peace of the Kingdom to your people, but how can we continue to trust the blades when these acts of violence toward the citizens of the Kingdom continue?"

Kiyoshi paused. His answers were important here. "You ask hard questions, but I would also ask that we look to the wisdom of the king. As he has stated, it is difficult to assume responsibility for every single blade. Despite appearances, we are human as well, and flawed. There will always be those who don't represent the greater part of us."

Shin pressed the issue. "So, answer my question. How will you censure the nightblade who has visited such terror on an innocent village?"

Kiyoshi didn't allow himself to hesitate. He needed to project confidence more than ever before. "If possible, we will take the nightblade into custody. He will stand trial, and if found guilty by the council, he will suffer whatever consequences are deemed appropriate."

Shin's voice rose. "I'm sorry, Kiyoshi, but that is not enough. The nightblade has killed an innocent farmer. The only punishment suitable to one in his position is death."

Kiyoshi took a deep breath to calm himself. The lords were pressing more than they ever had before. He didn't dare glance to Masaki for help. If the king stepped in, he would declare himself for a side, and that was the worst action he could take. The king knew this as well. Masaki remained silent, waiting patiently for Kiyoshi's response.

"My lord, I can pass your words on to the council, but I do not have the authority to proclaim the death of a nightblade."

Shin eyed Kiyoshi, judging his next step. "See that you do. Make it clear to the council that if the nightblade is not put to death, our faith in your order will be lost."

The rest of the meeting passed quickly. Kiyoshi was given the information on the nightblade allegedly responsible for the atrocities described. He didn't recognize the name, but that didn't surprise him. The lords disbanded, certainly off to plan their next steps. A glance from the king told Kiyoshi that Masaki wanted to talk with him alone.

As Kiyoshi watched the three lords exit the chamber, he wondered how the blades would react to being told to kill their own.

King Masaki and Kiyoshi sat across from each other, each sipping some of the finest tea in the Kingdom. Kiyoshi was a man of few desires, but one advantage of his position that he very much enjoyed was access to the best tea. He would miss the experience when he passed into the Great Cycle.

The two sat in silence, each finding peace in the company of the other. Kiyoshi took a moment to use his sense on the king. He could feel the energy moving through the older man's body, but more and more, all he could sense was the disruption in his stomach.

Kiyoshi didn't know how to describe the ailment, but something amiss was growing in the king's stomach. Daily, Kiyoshi used his powers to heal the king, nonetheless fighting a losing battle. He kept the king alive, but soon his administrations would fail. Masaki knew this, but he didn't let the knowledge keep him from his duties. He would discharge the office of the king until his last breath passed.

Masaki met Kiyoshi's eye. "Tell me, old friend, what is happening."

"The lords grow bolder every day. Particularly Lord Shin. Cycles ago, I thought he could be calmed, but I was wrong. He never wanted to reach an agreement. He wanted to keep pushing until he reached his goal."

"And what is his goal?"

"I believe Shin and Isamu, at least, seek to remove the blades from the Kingdom."

Masaki scoffed, but then saw Kiyoshi was being serious.

"You think so? I've always thought they sought to bring more power to their houses."

Kiyoshi nodded. "They do. There's no doubt of that. But the best way to do that is to eliminate the threat of the blades. As it stands, the blades won't take a side, preventing any house from gaining dominance over the others. If we're gone, they'll have unprecedented opportunities."

Masaki considered his friend's words. "What would the blades do if I die without an heir?"

Kiyoshi almost argued, but a look from the king silenced him. They both knew Masaki was sterile, something to do with the growth in his stomach. It was a secret only the two of them shared. Masaki had lost his only son, Yoshi, over twenty cycles ago and had never raised another heir.

Kiyoshi shook his head. "I don't know. I would hope we would remain neutral, but this council is one of the most political I've ever seen. I'm not sure how they will react to your passing."

A fire lit in Masaki's eyes. "We need to ensure the continuation of the Kingdom. Peace needs to be maintained."

"You need an heir."

The fire in Masaki's eyes flared. "We've had this discussion a hundred times. There is no one worthy that the lords would accept."

Kiyoshi sighed over the debate they had far too often. After Yoshi had died, Masaki had named various successors, but each had been blocked by the King's Council. They would only accept another lord, one of their own, but Masaki didn't think any were suitable. The stalemate had lasted for cycles. Foolish as the conflict was, neither side would budge.

"Is there any way we could prepare Lord Juro for the throne?" Kiyoshi asked.

Masaki shook his head. "I wish there were. You and I both know he'd be eaten alive by Shin. If it was somehow possible to combine Juro's training and honor with Shin's intelligence and skill with people, we would have a king for the ages."

They needed to make a decision quickly. If Masaki died without an heir, power passed to the King's Council, an unstable situation. Splitting power three ways would never work over the long term. The only way to ensure the continued peace of the Kingdom was to name an heir the council would accept before the king died.

Kiyoshi gestured to the floor with his hand. "Lie down. I will attempt to ease your pain."

"Is it obvious?"

"Not to one without the gift. Your control of your expressions is better than almost anyone I've ever met. But my sense tells me your energy is blocked, and you must be in a great deal of pain. Let me help."

The king didn't argue, turning over and lying down on the floor. Kiyoshi reached out a hand and laid it on his king's stomach. He extended his sense into Masaki's body, resting his mind and allowing it to trace the movement of energy within. The mass in his stomach continued to grow. Kiyoshi glanced briefly at the king, who was resting with his eyes closed. The pain had to be incredible.

The dayblade went to work. Using his sense, he pressed his fingers on particular parts of the king's body, redirecting the energy as best he could. When he had done all he could using physical methods, he took a breath and focused his own power.

The blades were unique because they controlled a power called the sense, allowing them to observe the flow of surrounding energy. Nightblades specialized in being able to sense events at a distance, making them warriors without equal. They could predict the movements of an opponent and thus never be ambushed by conventional means. In combat, blades could feel an opponent's moves moments before the cuts were made, making them nearly impossible for a normal soldier to defeat.

Dayblades focused on understanding the proper flow of energy internally. Much of the dayblades' work involved redirecting the energy within the body, sensing particular pathways and altering them as necessary. Bones could heal in moments instead of moons. Sicknesses could be removed and injuries soothed away. It was the most potent medicine that had ever been known.

Yet there were far fewer dayblades than nightblades. Everyone had their own theory as to why that might be, but Kiyoshi wasn't interested in the why. It simply was, a fact to be dealt with. If he had been forced to answer, he would have responded that the skills required to be a dayblade were harder to acquire than those of a nightblade. One's ability with the sense had to be much more refined as a dayblade. The flows of energy around a sword strike or punch were far more obvious than the subtle change in a person whose heart wasn't beating correctly.

Kiyoshi focused on the king's energy. He tried to cut off the flow to the mass in Masaki's stomach. A stronger dayblade might have been completely successful, but Kiyoshi could only cut off most of the energy. He was trying to starve the mass, giving the king's body the chance to fight the tumor on more equal terms. He held the altered flow as long as possible, but eventually had to break away.

Kiyoshi took his hand off his friend's stomach. As he wiped sweat from his brow, he used his sense again. The mass was smaller, but by a meaningful amount? Kiyoshi wasn't sure. "How do you feel?" he asked.

"Better."

It wasn't much, but it was something. "We need to know who will replace you."

The king laughed, a grim sound. "How long do I have?"

Kiyoshi shook his head. "There's no telling. I can continue to do all I can, but I'm fighting a losing battle. If you allowed me to call a stronger dayblade, perhaps we could eliminate the growth completely."

Masaki stood up. He was moving better than he had been after the King's Council. That was something, at least. "No. You do more than enough for me, and I can tell my time here is almost at an end. All we need to do is finish my work."

"A successor?"

This time it was Masaki's turn to shake his head. "No. The great houses will only accept one of their own, but choosing among those three is no choice at all. They are all strong leaders, but they are all self-serving. None of them would put the Kingdom first."

The two had traveled this road before, but Kiyoshi was drawn into the same arguments. "The Kingdom has had bad kings before."

Usually Masaki argued about his general unease about the state of affairs, but today he took a different approach. "And we've always had the blades to help us hold the course. But you and I have had to make concession after concession to the houses, and even if the blades aren't driven from the Kingdom, your authority has been substantially curtailed. I'm not sure the blades can help balance the Kingdom much longer."

Kiyoshi wasn't sure how to respond. He wanted to tell the king he was wrong. That there was still a way forward. But Masaki spoke the truth. In their efforts to maintain the peace, they had backed themselves into a corner, and Kiyoshi wasn't sure the blades could effect change moving forward.

Kiyoshi followed Masaki to his private quarters, a comfortable silence between them. When they arrived, the king waved Kiyoshi away.

"I'm sick, not useless."

Kiyoshi stepped back. He admired his old friend's resilience.

"Kiyoshi, thank you, both for trying to heal me and for all you do for the Kingdom. I am aware it hasn't been easy, and I know you've made a lot of sacrifices. I wanted to say it doesn't go unappreciated."

Kiyoshi bowed deeply to his king. "You are welcome, Masaki. Please rest."

He ensured the king was sleeping comfortably, then turned around and walked back to his quarters, his mind racing, trying to find some answer to the problems that plagued them.

When Kiyoshi returned to his quarters, he saw that another message had been delivered to his door. He let out a long sigh, knowing no one was nearby to hear him. He had hoped for peace and quiet of his own before having to deal with more politics.

The decision to become the king's adviser had been an easy one. Kiyoshi had seen how the Kingdom was drifting apart. The houses continued to get stronger and stronger, and after the king's only heir had died, an opportunity for power reared its head, causing political dissensions stronger than anything Kiyoshi had ever seen or heard.

Kiyoshi believed that although the blades weren't perfect, they were the only ones capable of keeping the Kingdom moving forward on a peaceful path. But for that to be true, the blades had to be politically neutral. They had to have the interests of the Kingdom at heart, not their own self-interest. Kiyoshi had struggled for cycles to bring that truth to reality.

He knew the Council of the Blades felt that they should have more power. He didn't know the depth of their desires, but he feared their conviction. Kiyoshi had seen what happened to blades when they were presented with the opportunity for control. He would spend the rest of his life fighting against seeing that happen again.

The path hadn't been easy. Kiyoshi remembered his first few days with Masaki. The blade hadn't been sent by the council as advisers typically were. His situation had been unique, and one day he had ended up at the king's feet, being ordered to serve by Masaki himself. Since that day he and Masaki had grown steadfastly closer. Kiyoshi had come to know him not just as the ruler of the Kingdom, but as a person.

Kiyoshi saw from the seal that the letter was from Hajimi. Given how rarely the head of the blades wrote to him of late, the news could only be bad. He considered, just for a moment, throwing the letter into a fire and ignoring it, but he sighed again and broke the seal.

His eyes wandered over the short missive quickly. Kiyoshi and Hajimi hadn't seen eye to eye in many cycles, and Hajimi had long ago abandoned the pretense of courtesy. The letter was short and to the point, and it caused Kiyoshi to raise his eyebrows in surprise.

Minori would soon be arriving. The letter, undoubtedly on purpose, had been timed to give Kiyoshi minimal warning. Minori might already be in Haven. Kiyoshi fed his early desire by taking the letter and throwing it in the fire. It was the closest he would come to violence.

Everyone was self-focused. Cycle after cycle, the Council of the Blades had let him know how displeased they were with his work. Until now, Kiyoshi had long been the only royal adviser from the blades. The others had been dismissed from service.

Hajimi's letter had been clear that the council would not take it lightly if Minori was not allowed to serve the king. The letter didn't go so far as to say that Kiyoshi was dismissed, but the act was implied.

Kiyoshi forced himself to take a deep breath and focus on the consequences of the council's newest action. Everything could be reduced to actions and consequences. A wise man never lost sight of that.

First, his position of trust with the king was safe. Barring some dramatic event he couldn't imagine, Masaki would never exclude Kiyoshi from his confidence. The other lords might have different reactions. If they felt there was a schism within the blades, they would exploit the division. And Kiyoshi couldn't ensure they wouldn't succeed.

But the actions of the lords were generally shortsighted. Kiyoshi was less worried about them than he was about Minori himself. He had met the nightblade a handful of times. There was much to recommend. He was brilliant, probably one of the best strategists the blades had seen for two or three generations. He was slow to speak, meaning none of the lords would be able to trap him in their petty verbal squabbles.

But at the same time, Minori was cold, aloof. Kiyoshi knew Minori believed that the blades should have a more prominent role in current affairs, but he didn't know the man's motivation, and that concerned him. He seemed as inflexible as a piece of steel and just as sharp. If Minori was on your side, he could be a formidable ally. But if he was your opponent, one had best beware.

Kiyoshi closed his eyes, thinking that no matter what he did, disaster was coming.

Chapter 4

Asa sipped quietly at her bowl of noodles, her second of the meal. The restaurant she sat in was small, suitable for the tiny village she was passing through. But the venue's size was no indication of the quality of its food.

She was considering ordering a third bowl. She had been on the road, traveling leagues on foot every day. Asa had enough coin to afford a horse, but the walk gave her time to reflect on what she had learned and to decide what to do next. But walking led to ravenous hunger. And hunger, as she had often been told by the masters who'd trained her, was the best seasoning. Asa thought she was eating the best noodles she had ever tasted.

Word of Takashi's death spread faster than she walked. He had been well known and well loved in the area, and Asa was on edge. She worried there would be a call for her execution, but the lack of pursuit was almost more worrisome than a posse on her tail. She didn't wear her black robes, the ones given to her on the day she passed the trials that confirmed her as a nightblade, in public. Not now. She preferred to remain anonymous.

Leaving Takashi's village had been a nerve-racking affair. The whole town had surrounded the hall, and Asa had worried the locals would retaliate. Fortunately, they feared her too much to attack, and she had left as quickly as she could. She went into the wild, always using her sense to see if anyone followed. But no one did.

Since then, Asa had stayed off the roads as much as possible. These parts weren't very populated, and all strangers passing through tended to draw attention. The fewer people Asa came across, the happier she would be. But the aromas drifting from the restaurant as she passed outside the village had been too tempting to ignore.

The restaurant, like the village, was quiet and sleepy. Asa was one of three customers, and the only one present who was actually eating the food. The other two were local boys who were more interested in the pretty server—the old shop owner's granddaughter, no doubt—than the food. Asa didn't mind. A part of her mind tracked the boys' feeble attempts to romance the server. She had at least four cycles on them, in Asa's estimation, and there was no likelihood they would succeed. But Asa enjoyed watching them try.

For a moment, everything seemed right with the world. Her legs were tired but ready for another half day of walking. Her stomach was almost full, and the warmth of the broth drove away the chill of the spring air. For a moment, she was a little girl again, in a village not too different from this one. Her village, the one closest to her childhood farm, had also contained a small noodle shop, with another old man who spent his entire life pursuing the perfection of noodle making. One of her last memories of her father was from that shop, enjoying a meal with him. He had taken her there alone, a special treat for just the two of them.

Thoughts of her father pushed her attention back to the present. Asa's mind ran over everything she had learned from Takashi. Again and again she saw Takashi's face. He had met his death calmly, and that had shaken her. She had taken life before, but the deaths had always been violent. Asa had never seen a man let himself go calmly into the Great Cycle. She had heard stories of such suicides, but Takashi's dignity in his final moments indicated a peace with himself that Asa envied.

Takashi had told her more than she had expected. He had told her everything. The problem was, most of his account only confirmed what she had already guessed. Asa had spent almost fifteen cycles getting her hands on every piece of information about the massacre at Two Falls, and although the real story had never been made public, she had searched resolutely for the truth.

She thought she had put the story all together, but it was all circumstantial. All she had was logical deductions and her intuition. Until she met Takashi, there hadn't been any evidence for any of her suspicions.

Takashi had confirmed everything she'd suspected. He had added a few details she hadn't been aware of and had shown her she was wrong in a few places, but mostly, he confirmed she had been right, that her journey thus far hadn't been wasted. There had been a conspiracy, but Takashi hadn't known enough for Asa's liking.

However, he had given her a name: Commander Osamu. The name was unfamiliar to her. Takashi had been convinced Osamu had died after the massacre. She worried she had come all this way only to be thwarted by the past.

Asa tried to control her frustration. She had hoped that taking the assignment to kill Takashi would bring her closer to closure.

She remembered the initial rush of excitement when her master had shown her the letter from the council ordering Takashi's death. Asa didn't believe in fate, but passing that outpost only days after the letter arrived was luck almost too good to be true. After considerable persuasion, Asa had convinced her master to accept the order and give it to her. She thought that after all those cycles of waiting, her family could rest in peace, the man responsible for her father's death a part of the Great Cycle.

Instead of closure, all she found was another clue, another journey to go on. The commander the blade had referred to, all those cycles ago, hadn't been Takashi, but Osamu. The realization made her consider giving up, but then the memories would return. She had to keep going, no matter how long it took.

Asa finished her second bowl of noodles and sat back against the wall of the restaurant, her eyes wandering up to the ceiling as she thought. There was only one possibility—the archives at Starfall, the seat of the Council of the Blades. Asa had long avoided Starfall, even though she had always suspected it would be necessary to return there.

Asa valued her independence. She had become a nightblade because she had the gift of the sense. Even now she could feel a pair of villagers walking down the street outside the restaurant. But her purpose had never aligned with that of the council. Asa often turned down requests to patrol areas of the countryside, and she absolutely refused to guard any lords or nobles.

In Asa's mind, her purpose was clear: she lived so that her family would be revenged. Fortunately, her master was lazy and preferred to spend most days with a bottle instead of a sword. Most days she was allowed to do as she pleased, and he would make no fuss. So long as she didn't bring attention to either of them and shared credit on completed assignments, he would remain silent.

Thus, she focused on missions that were short and exposed her to new places and people. Although young, she had already traveled over much of the Kingdom, raiding archives and questioning scribes and historians whenever she could get a chance. Over time she picked away layer after layer of lies, finally getting to the truth of what had happened at Two Falls.

Going to the seat of the council meant risking her freedom. She didn't have the authority or permission to investigate the massacre, but because she kept her true purpose secret, no one had stopped her from digging up the truth of Two Falls. The council, if her presence became known to them, wouldn't be so friendly toward her actions, and her arrangement with her master would be jeopardized.

But Starfall was the only place she could go where there might be answers. She had looked at every possible document she could get her hands on related to the massacre, and she had never found mention of a Commander Osamu. That meant whoever had cleaned up the incident had erased the name from most of the records. If there was a record that existed on the man, who had to be a nightblade, the only place it could be was with the council. As much as she hated the idea, Starfall was the only place for her to go.

Asa paid her bill and gave the two boys a sly wink. Both noticed her for the first time, and for a few precious moments, the poor serving girl got a break from their unwanted attention as the boys turned to Asa and made suggestions about nicer places they could go to eat. Asa just smiled and bowed as she left the restaurant.

—

Asa walked along the path leading from the village. After a few more leagues, she would reach a small town where she would rest for the night. Her feet were sore from a day on the road, and she looked forward to resting at a nice inn and having a wonderful bath.

The two boys had followed her out of the restaurant, but when it was clear their antics would not be successful, they went back to tormenting the serving girl. At times, Asa missed parts of having a normal life. She missed having boys and men flirt with her, and when she was traveling through villages like the one she had just visited, she missed the scenes of day-to-day life she encountered: women going about performing their daily chores, men out at work in the fields, and the noise and bustle of local markets.

Asa loved being a nightblade. She loved the power it gave her, and she loved that she had the strength to make a difference. But the cost was high.

Blades were a part of the world, and yet separate. Civilians held them in awe and a little bit of fear. Wherever blades went, they were the center of attention. Asa often tried to travel incognito, but being a woman alone on the roads often gave her away.

There were days, like today, when she wasn't certain about how to move forward, where she yearned for the simplicity of village life. When she had been younger, she sometimes dreamed of settling down with a husband and starting a family.

Those moments still hit her with the force of a punch to the stomach, but they were rarer now. She was old enough to recognize that she loved her freedom, and while the idea of domestic life wasn't without its appeal, Asa knew she would never submit to another.

Asa stopped walking and looked around. Her thoughts and footsteps had carried her far from the village. She was in the plains, which made up the vast majority of the northwest lands of the Kingdom. The land rolled for as far as the eye could see. People who hadn't traveled here or lived here always thought plains meant flatland. Sometimes that was true, but here the grass rose and fell in hills, like a gently rolling sea.

Asa turned around and took in her surroundings. The path she was on was empty, and as far as she could see, she was alone. She smiled. Perhaps the thought of being alone scared some, but it was a feeling she craved. She had been born on a farm, and the emptiness of fields was as close as she ever got to a feeling of home.

When she was young and the sense had first developed in her, cities had been terrifying places. Cities already contained enough new sights and sounds to scare a young child, but add to that an awareness of everything happening around you, an awareness no one else can explain, and the visits had been a trying, if not traumatic, experience. No matter how much older she grew, she always hated cities and loved the countryside.

Out here, Asa could let her sense run free. It was possible to control how strongly the sense acted. Like plugging your ears with your fingers, you could slow the information down to a trickle and quiet the noise of the outside world. Or you could focus on your sense and allow it to sharpen every experience. You could pick out the organized dance of the ants below your feet or feel the vast, quiet presence of old woods. With enough training, you could shut the sense down completely. But most of the time, your awareness sat somewhere in the middle. In many places, at least some small part of your consciousness had to be expended to ensure the gift didn't extend too far.

But out here in the prairie, with no one to bother her, here she could let her abilities go. And she did. She focused on her sense, closing her eyes and calming her breathing. She could feel the tendrils of her sense spread far and wide across the prairie. Many people thought the prairies were lifeless, but Asa knew differently. She could sense the bugs moving in the dirt, the hundreds of ants making their home where humans would never bother them. She jumped as a group of small songbirds flew overhead. There was plenty of life here; one just had to pay attention.

When Asa felt the tendrils of another person with the sense, her eyes opened with a snap, and she lost all focus. The world returned to normal, or as close to normal as it could be for one gifted with the sense. Asa's first instinct was to spin around again, to search for the person the sense was emanating from. Only blades were able to use the sense, and there was no reason for another one to be nearby. A warning in her mind told her not to move suddenly.

Asa listened to her gut. If someone else was out here, someone else who could use the sense, something was wrong. There was no reason for another blade to be here. Trying to learn a little more, Asa took a deep breath and turned around slowly, acting as though she were trying to take in all the scenery. She spun in a lazy circle. As she turned, she focused her gaze in the direction the sense had come from, but she couldn't see anyone.

Someone was hiding, and if someone were hiding and using the sense, it meant she was being tracked. But on the other hand, no one else was around. Asa figured if the blade meant her any harm, there would be no reason to hide. This place was as good as any to attack. If the blade were hiding, she wasn't in any immediate danger.

Perhaps that was why no posse was in pursuit. Perhaps the town had sent one assassin after her instead of a group. But still, if there were a time to attack, it was now. So she was safe, at least for a while.

Asa turned around again. She closed her eyes and focused on her breath. This time, she channeled her sense, pushing it farther in the direction from where she had felt the other sense. She felt her tendrils stretch out ever farther, and she was worried because for a few moments, she couldn't feel the other sense. Had she imagined the entire experience?

She patiently kept her sense crawling in the direction she wanted. As far as people knew, there was no limit to the distance the sense could travel; the only limit was how much information one person's mind could handle. The farther the sense traveled, the more information it brought in. If the sense traveled too far, your mind couldn't understand. Legends said that if you pushed too far, you risked snapping your mind.

She felt the tendrils again, the sure signs of another person using the sense. But they were farther away, or the tendrils lacked some of their previous strength. Someone was trying to hide from her. She pushed her sense out even farther, nearing the edge of her ability. For just a moment, she thought she found where the tendrils were emanating from, but she couldn't sense anyone there.

The effort of keeping her sense extended so far exhausted Asa, and the fact that she couldn't feel the person at the center was too much for her mind to endure. She broke her connection, bringing her sense back into line with its normal work. She knelt down in the grass, considering what she had felt.

Asa had a hard time figuring out what was happening. Whoever was following her was far away, and his or her ability with the sense was probably more developed.

There was no way to hide from the sense, so she must have not been able to reach the person's hiding place. If the blade were following her, which seemed increasingly certain, the tracker could sense Asa far beyond where she could funnel her sense.

Asa fingered her short blades. The most obvious solution was to try to kill whoever was following her. Under most circumstances that would be her decision. But today the idea made her uncomfortable. Whoever was out there had skills beyond Asa's, and she had to assume someone had assigned that person to track her. If that was true, she was probably outclassed. Asa was a strong warrior, but she was far from the strongest nightblade. She could name at least a dozen off the top of her head who were better, and those were only the ones she knew.

The other action was to pretend as though she hadn't noticed. The other person would have felt her sense, but if the nightblade was confident in his or her ability to hide, Asa's stalker might feel safe. Asa had never turned around suddenly or given any definitive indication she was certain she was being followed. The person following her would be suspicious, but if Asa could sell her ignorance, perhaps the other person would get overconfident.

Asa grabbed some dried fruit from her bag and stood back up, chewing slowly. If the blade could see her, the gesture would reveal a reason for having knelt down. Taking a deep breath, Asa started walking forward, wondering if the person following her was a shadow or an assassin.

Chapter 5

Minori looked down at himself, making sure he appeared presentable. He wasn't comfortable admitting how much time he had spent deciding what to wear for this meeting, but it was crucial that he make the right impression. He and Kiyoshi had met several times in the past, but the introductions had always been brief. The two of them knew each other primarily through reputation alone.

Despite their political disagreements, Minori had a great deal of respect for Kiyoshi. The older man was a fool when it came to the way the world worked, but a noble fool at least. Like Minori, Kiyoshi believed. He believed the actions he was taking were in the best interest of the blades. Minori disagreed. If Kiyoshi's philosophies continued to become policy, Minori was certain the blades wouldn't have any voice in the direction of the Kingdom. But if he had any chance at all of working with Kiyoshi, it all would start with this meeting.

To that end, he had dressed and re-dressed himself, considering the statement each outfit made. He knew Kiyoshi was a simple, straightforward man. But though the dayblade was simple, he was not unintelligent. The man was brilliant and knew whom he'd be dealing with. Minori couldn't help whatever impression Kiyoshi already had of him, but he could determine how that impression would change.

Minori had settled on simple black robes, the traditional garb of the nightblades. The fabric was of quality, but wasn't so fine as to be only for decoration. The garment had seen wear and tear. After much debate, Minori wore his sword. Kiyoshi didn't always, but the man was also a dayblade and had little need. Minori wondered if the sword would be considered too martial, but decided to stick with his values. He was a nightblade, and he would wear a sword wherever he went.

Satisfied with his appearance, he knocked lightly on the door. The two had agreed to meet at a teahouse Kiyoshi favored. While Minori waited for Kiyoshi to welcome him in, he studied the teahouse. Though placed in the heart of the city, the venue was surrounded by a small bamboo grove and thick walls, serving as one of the most peaceful locations in the city. Minori approved. Whoever managed the grove was diligent about their work.

The details always mattered. A small rock garden sat next to the path to the teahouse; no stone was out of place. Minori could hear the soft trickle of the stream that ran through the property, and the plants were trimmed with a thoughtfulness that spoke volumes about the caretaker of the teahouse.

He didn't hear movement, but he could sense Kiyoshi moving through the house. Minori frowned. Despite his advanced age, Kiyoshi moved with surprising strength and grace. He was a man who clearly took care of himself. Minori reminded himself again not to underestimate his fellow blade.

Kiyoshi opened the door and bowed deeply, a deeper bow than Minori warranted. Minori returned the gesture, bowing equally low. The move made him uncomfortable, but he wouldn't be rude to his host. He hadn't bowed so low in some time.

"Come in, please. I am grateful for the opportunity for us to have a conversation."

Minori noted the older man's choice of words. There was no possibility Kiyoshi was grateful to have Minori here, at least not yet, but he hadn't alluded to that. He was trying to be both honest and polite, confirming everything Minori suspected about the man.

"Likewise, I am grateful that we can get to know each other after all this time."

Minori saw the fire of intelligence in Kiyoshi's eyes. There was a mirth there, a hint of a man who saw humor in the day-to-day situations he found himself in. Reflexively, Minori decided he liked Kiyoshi. He wondered, if they played chess together, who would win.

Kiyoshi gave him a brief tour of the teahouse, but there wasn't much to see there. Minori paid attention to the space, certainly arranged by Kiyoshi prior to Minori's arrival. But there was little to learn. Kiyoshi didn't weave any subtle messages into the arrangement of the house. Everything was organized for an ideal tea-drinking experience.

The two sat down, and Kiyoshi served tea. Minori sipped at the brew gently, pleased with its quality. Kiyoshi might be simple, but he was a man of refined tastes. The leaves imparted a rich flavor that finished with just a hint of sweetness. The tea was excellent. Kiyoshi's preparation was flawless. Minori would have led with the polite exchange of remarks mandatory to such settings, but he decided to break the rules of etiquette and see how his host dealt with the pressure.

"Kiyoshi, we have much to discuss. I'm sure you have several questions about why I've been sent."

Kiyoshi's smile was gentle, as though he were talking to a child. His eyes were still lit with laughter, and Minori saw the old man didn't mind the breach of etiquette at all. Despite himself, Minori drew parallels between himself and the king's adviser. Perhaps they were more similar than he thought.

"I don't think there's any question as to why you're here. The council is displeased with the way I've handled affairs. They hope by sending you, they can pursue a more ambitious strategy that gives the blades more political power."

Minori found himself on the defensive. His first impulse was to lie, but he could see deception would do him no good. For now. Kiyoshi knew exactly why Minori was here, and if Minori wanted the older man to be his ally at all, he would have to become far more comfortable telling the truth.

"You are correct, of course. The council believes you are too amenable to constraints being placed on the blades."

Kiyoshi's smile grew. "I have heard much about you, but your honesty is a refreshing change from the politics of the castle."

Minori held his own grin in check. He could already feel Kiyoshi warming up to him. If he played this right, the old dayblade would be helping him in no time at all. He replied, "I can imagine. I've seen the politics that dominate the Council of the Blades, and I suspect it is even worse here."

A small silence blossomed as they both sipped their tea at the same time. Minori saw Kiyoshi was perfectly at home in the silence. It would be his responsibility to move the conversation forward.

"I believe you mean well by your work. You are doing what you think is necessary. If I were to guess, I would say you believe the way to quench the dissension among the lords is to make the sacrifices they request. You believe that by doing so, you'll keep the Kingdom functioning smoothly."

Kiyoshi's grin remained on his face, but he nodded. Emboldened, Minori continued.

"I understand your beliefs. But you're wrong. What happens when you've sacrificed so much authority the blades aren't able to effect change any longer?"

"It's the same question that keeps me up almost every night."

"So explain yourself. Why is giving up our legal powers a better plan than maintaining them, or even strengthening them?"

Kiyoshi sipped his tea, clearly thinking through Minori's question. When he did answer, his response surprised the nightblade.

"I'm not sure it is the best plan. But I can predict your thoughts as well. You'd like to see the blades become stronger. You see the pettiness that drives the lords, and you believe the blades must be strong to protect the Kingdom. You even believe the blades should influence or direct the policy of the Kingdom."

Minori was delighted. He hadn't been sure what he would encounter when visiting Kiyoshi, but he certainly hadn't expected an honest debate. He couldn't imagine this conversation happening anywhere else, at least not between two people whose opinions and actions could actually shape the future of the Kingdom.

"You are right, of course," Minori replied.

Kiyoshi spoke carefully. "So, as you can see, we already agree on quite a bit. The world is changing, and the role of the blades has to change with it. You worry I will make us too weak, and I worry you will make us too strong. The fact is, if I had to choose between the two extremes, I much prefer my own, even if it leads to the decline of the blades many cycles from now."

Minori had to take a sip of his tea to hide his surprise. At the Council of the Blades, Kiyoshi's argument would be considered treasonous. He'd be thrown out of the council, maybe even executed.

Minori's mind raced, trying to understand Kiyoshi's reasoning. "You don't believe we can handle the extra responsibility, do you?"

Kiyoshi shook his head. "I wish that I did. If we could be both strong warriors and strong leaders, we would begin a Kingdom the like of which the world has never seen. But we're human. We're not any wiser than any other civilian. Combine that with our power, and you've got a plan for disaster. Ideally, I'd like for the world to continue as it has. Now we have the strength to influence decisions, but we don't make them. And that's a good thing. But like you, I've seen the future. The current state of affairs will not hold for much longer, and as a people, we must decide how we move forward."

Minori thought about what Kiyoshi said. What surprised him most was that he understood Kiyoshi. He disagreed with the dayblade, but he saw how Kiyoshi's beliefs might have come about. There was only one idea Minori didn't agree with. The blades weren't just normal humans.

A normal human lived in fear of death. It drove every action, from work to sex. It colored every decision they made. But not a blade. A blade grew up befriending death. With the sense, you could feel the energy that made a person unique. When a person died, you could feel that energy become one with all life. Blades didn't have to question death. They knew.

Their abilities gave them a perspective no regular human could ever have. Blades would make better leaders. Of that, Minori had no doubt.

"Is there anything that would change your mind?" Minori asked.

Kiyoshi thought about the question. "I don't think so. Even if you could present me an ideal leader, I'm not sure I trust us any more than I'd trust a regular human to lead this Kingdom."

Minori nodded his head. The old man had given him much to think about. They wouldn't reach an agreement. Not today. The conversation was coming to an end. He finished his tea and bowed low, this time doing so sincerely.

"Thank you for your hospitality. I look forward to many more conversations in the future."

Kiyoshi's words echoed in Minori's head. While he hadn't been sure what to expect, he hadn't planned on having a civil disagreement with the single most influential blade in the Kingdom. He had known they would disagree. But he hadn't expected his respect for Kiyoshi to grow significantly.

Minori was a man who respected strength. He despised politicians who bent with the slightest changes in the breeze. There was a strength in standing for principles, and there was a definite strength in choosing decay over dominance. Minori knew Kiyoshi was wrong, but he respected the man for standing his ground. He still might have to kill the old dayblade, but such an act wouldn't be his first choice.

His next errand was also important. Others might have waited, but Minori thought procrastination was another form of weakness. Far better to fill your days with meaningful activities.

He made his way to the king's guards' outpost. The king had armies scattered throughout the land, but the best warriors made their way to the king's guard. Haven, although it resided in the lands of Lord Isamu's house, was considered separate from the rest of the Kingdom. The king's guard were all experts not just in the sword, but also in the spear, one of the few weapons that gave a soldier any chance to harm a nightblade. As an army, they were small, only a few hundred strong, but Minori wouldn't bet against them in a battle with any lord's army.

The guard was responsible for the protection of the capital, and their fort was a sight to behold. The walls were three times the height of a man, made of solid stone that had never been breached. But the fort barely registered in Minori's mind as he approached. His black robes were more than enough to get him through the front gates, and a set of papers marked with the sign of the Council of the Blades gave him entrance to the cells inside the fort.

In a matter of moments, he was sitting across from another nightblade, Koji. Recently, Koji had been in the realm of House Kita, Lord Juro's land, saving a town from bandits. When he had returned to civilization, he had been detained based on an order from Kiyoshi. Although the young nightblade was unaware of his fate, Minori had learned that he would be sentenced to death in the next few days. Another sacrifice Kiyoshi was willing to make to keep the peace.

Koji bowed to his guest, and Minori returned the bow, although less deep. His eyes ran over the captured nightblade. Koji looked as though he was being cared for. His eyes were bright, and there were no signs of abuse. Minori wasn't surprised. The guards would fear even a chained nightblade, and from the way this one held himself, Minori agreed with their assessment. The boy was stronger than Minori had been led to believe. He could sense the energy radiating from the captive.

"You don't know me, but my name is Minori. I'm a representative of the Council of the Blades."

"It is good to see you. Are you here to straighten out what has happened?"

Minori nodded. "There are many stories being circulated about what occurred in the mountains, but I have difficulty believing them. We hold ourselves to a higher standard, and just observing that you allowed yourself to be chained and imprisoned indicates you aren't the sort of man the stories claim you are."

The look of relief in Koji's eyes was palpable. Minori kept his eyes on the young nightblade. The truth was he had no idea what had happened up in the mountains. The stories didn't seem true, but Minori didn't care. Koji had become a pawn, and Minori wanted to take control.

Koji spoke. "I'm very grateful. I've been trying to tell the truth to anyone who will listen, but no one seems to care what I have to say. The truth differs greatly from what others would have you believe."

Minori leaned back, preparing for a long story. "Please, tell me what happened, briefly if you can."

"As you know, I was sent to the mountains to root out a group of bandits. Some of the local army units had tried to find the thieves, but based on the difficult geography, they were unsuccessful. The bandits were well hidden. It was thought that a nightblade, with the ability to sense the rogues, would be able to track and follow them.

"Everything began well. I was able to wander the mountains, and with my sense, I intercepted a few small raids before they began. One time I followed a survivor of a raid quite deep into the mountains before I lost him."

Minori stopped Koji. "How did you lose a bandit?"

Koji's face reflected his failure. "Even though I could sense him at quite a distance, he knew he was being followed, and his skills on a horse were far superior to my own in the mountains. He took paths I was not able to follow mounted, and on foot I was not fast enough to catch him."

Minori was frustrated. Such weakness shouldn't be tolerated. But to Koji he said, "Do not worry. I'm sure you tried everything you could. Please continue."

"Even though I wasn't able to track the bandit back to his lair, I had a much better idea of where he and his cohorts were located. I returned to the nearest village and began preparations for a small expedition. My plan was to go deep into the mountains and attack the bandits wherever they were hiding. I stocked up on supplies and left.

"What I didn't know was that the bandits were already planning their own counterattack. I had made enough of an impact that they wanted to kill me. I ended up meeting them deep in the mountains. They had meant to set up an ambush, which wasn't successful, but I was still outnumbered. The fight was intense, and someday I hope to share more of that. But, in short, I won, even though I lost my horse and supplies in the battle.

"Losing the horse was the worst event that could have happened. I was days away from the village, and game was scarce in the mountains. I won't waste your time with the details of my journey back, but by the time I made it back to the village, I was near death. Most of the villagers were very kind. I asked for food and aid, and most were more than willing to provide assistance. But as I recovered, I felt like something was wrong.

"There was a farmer in the village, a farmer who had never been friendly toward me. I assumed he just had a general dislike of blades, but as I thought more about it, I realized this man's farm had never been attacked. I became suspicious. His wasn't the only farm unharmed, but I followed my instinct. Something felt wrong. After I recovered, I approached the farmer. I suspected he had ties to the bandits. When I questioned him, he attacked me with a knife. I reacted instinctively, killing him with a single blow.

"I left the village that day. My work was done. But I hadn't shared my suspicions with anyone else, and I suspect the farmer's wife spread lies after I left, perhaps telling people I demanded extravagant amounts of rice and then murdered her husband when he refused. When I returned to well-traveled roads, I was soon spotted and arrested. I made no fuss because I figured the matter could be straightened out once I was brought here. So I'm grateful you've arrived to end this."

Minori considered the nightblade's story. It had the ring of truth, and he didn't get any impression the boy was lying. "I am here to help, but I have bad news for you. The lords have seized upon the widow's story, and it has become widely accepted as the truth. The people are clamoring for your head."

Koji paled but maintained his composure. "What will happen?"

"You know Kiyoshi?"

Koji nodded.

"I believe he plans to sacrifice you. There is a great deal of political pressure on him, and he believes your life will maintain the peace."

Minori studied Koji's reaction carefully, all hinging on this point. He saw the rage cross Koji's face, but the young nightblade controlled it well. Koji's countenance was stony and silent. Good. The boy was angry.

Minori commented, "I am here because I believe every blade is valuable. Too valuable to be sacrificed on the altar of petty political struggles."

He could see the relief in Koji's shoulders. This was almost too easy.

"What would you have me do?"

Minori smiled. "First, don't worry. I will not let you die for performing your services admirably. I will help you escape, but you'll need to leave the city immediately. The council will find you a new line of work, but you won't be acting in public as a nightblade, not anymore. Is that an acceptable compromise?"

Koji didn't hesitate. "I will do whatever you ask."

"In the next night or two, I will come for you. Until then, be a model prisoner. Give them no reason to suspect anything. Be ready to move when I arrive."

Koji bowed deeply. "Thank you."

Minori stood. "Think nothing of it. I will return soon."

Two days later, the night was dark, and the cloudy skies portended rain. Minori couldn't have asked for a better night to mask his plans. From underneath his black robes, he pulled out more black fabric, wrapping the cloth over his face, rendering him almost invisible against the darkness of the skies.

His heart beat faster, but his breath was calm and consistent. It had been far too long since he had done anything truly useful. His recent work was largely of the mind, shaping the path of the Kingdom, but words could never match the thrill of physical accomplishment. Minori was no longer young, but he kept his body in peak physical condition and knew he would be successful tonight.

As he picked his way toward the fort, the skies opened, pouring water upon the inhabitants of Haven. Where others hid from the rain, Minori embraced the deluge. It was only water, and it gave Minori an edge as he approached the fort. No guard, no matter how disciplined, liked standing in the rain. They would find shelter, and as they did, they would leave gaps in their defenses.

Minori reached the walls of the fort without being seen. Families were inside enjoying the warmth of their fires, and businesses were closed. He studied his first obstacle. The wall was daunting but wouldn't be difficult to scale. There were plenty of holds, and he was an excellent climber. He hoped Koji would be just as good on the way out.

Using his sense, Minori determined where the sentries were on the walls. As he had suspected, the guards had taken cover from the rain. He just needed to find a climbing route that the guards couldn't observe. He spotted one potential route, but the guards would spot him if he took it. He wasn't dismayed.

Minori crept around the fort, finding another route farther along the wall. He studied the path and decided it would suit his needs. Again, he extended his sense and searched for guards. They were nearby, but no one was paying attention to the section of wall upon which he gazed. The path was open, so he ran forward. His first step upon the barrier was about waist height, with upward momentum. His hand grasped a crack, and his grip was solid. He hung by his hand for just a moment. He needed to be careful.

Finding handholds and footholds, Minori moved up the wall, not hurrying, not hesitating. Within a few breaths, he was near the top, the rain beating down against his head. He extended his sense, double-checking that his route was still unobserved. No guard was looking his way, so he clambered onto the top of the wall. He paused for a moment, studying the courtyard below. There was no reason for any guards to be in the courtyard. No alarm had been sounded, and the rain was still pouring. The guards' limited attention would be focused on what lurked outside the walls, not inside their home. Minori dropped down and walked across the courtyard without interruption.

His next challenge would be the first guard in the cells. When he had visited Koji two days ago, he had noted the guards, one at the door and another patrolling the halls at random. Wariness was required, but he didn't expect a problem.

Minori reached the door to the cells and gently pushed it. As it had been when he had visited, the door was unlocked. The guards had no reason to expect anyone sneaking in. After all, they were behind well-protected walls. The unlocked door was a lapse in security they wouldn't repeat after tonight. Minori opened the door just a crack, exposing the guard standing close by. Minori drew a small tube from the fold of his robes and brought it to his lips. He blew, and a dart embedded itself in the guard's neck. The poison wasn't fatal, but it would render the guard unconscious for most of the evening.

Minori wasn't sure what repercussions his actions would have, but he had played through a few different scenarios. Through all of them, one necessity was that he not kill anyone; otherwise, the outcry against his actions would be far too strong to mitigate. So the guards couldn't know he was there, and they couldn't be killed.

Minori opened the door and slipped the rest of the way in. He knelt in a corner and reloaded his tube. Like his previous visit, there would be another guard nearby. He stopped for a moment to pull his first dart out of the guard's neck. He wasn't planning on leaving any evidence behind.

With his sense extended, Minori had no trouble finding the second guard, wandering the halls around a corner. Minori stood up and walked toward the corner, his footsteps silent compared to the rain pounding on the roof. When he was certain the guard's back was to him, Minori stepped around the corner, as silent as the grave, put the tube to his lips, and blew again. His aim was true, and the guard collapsed into a heap. Minori came up to him and pulled out the second dart. This guard also had a set of keys, to which Minori helped himself.

Koji was awake. No words passed between the two nightblades. Minori let the younger blade out using the keys, locking the door again once Koji was out. He didn't think his deception would actually confuse anyone, but there wasn't any harm in trying. Walking back through the hallways, Minori replaced the keys on the guard's belt.

At the door Koji found his sword and personal effects, meager as they were. He was about to leave, but Minori stopped him.

"Follow me, and whatever happens, kill no one. We're not here to cause any harm."

Koji nodded his understanding. Minori took a deep breath and extended his sense out the way he had come. Luck was on their side. As far as he could tell, the path was open. He opened the door, and the two went back toward the wall. Minori led the way, climbing on top of the wall in one smooth motion. Koji followed, and together they looked down. Koji whispered to his fellow blade, "You know, you're very capable for your age."

The respect was evident in his voice, and Minori took the words as the compliment they were intended to be. "Follow me closely. The wall is slippery."

Minori kicked his legs over the wall and let himself down, his feet finding the same holds they had previously used. Moving carefully, ensuring each hold was solid before adding his full weight, Minori picked his way down the wall. Koji took a different route. With a leap, he plummeted from the top, rolling smoothly when he landed. Minori shook his head. The feat was stupid, but he could understand the boy's desire to move after being locked away for several days. In his younger days, Minori might have attempted the same stunt, but he knew if he was to try such a feat now, he would break a bone.

He smiled for a moment at the thought of Kiyoshi being summoned to heal him, and the thought led to another. A new plan formed in his mind, and by the time he reached the ground, he was certain of his way forward. He grinned and met Koji down at the bottom. The younger nightblade was covered in mud slowly being washed away by the rain. He was smiling from ear to ear, with a look of loyalty in his eyes that Minori would never have been able to buy.

They walked away from the castle, and Minori removed his mask. The rain was becoming torrential, and between the weather and their sense, no one would spot them leaving the fort.

Koji looked over at him. "What do I do next?"

Minori decided to try out his new plan. "I've spoken with the council, and they have given me permission to make you my direct aide. The type of work I do is special and very secret. Do you think you are up for it?"

There wasn't even a hint of hesitation in Koji's voice. "I owe you my life."

"Good. Let's go home. Your new life starts now."

Chapter 6

Kiyoshi ambled through the streets of Haven, his mind wandering to a thousand different places as he approached his destination. Shin had demanded haste, but Kiyoshi had no desire to follow the lord's orders. He felt as though the world he had worked so hard to build was unraveling, one strand at a time, and he was left clutching at the various strings that had once been the fabric of his life.

As usual, he was wearing the plain white robes of the dayblades, and his presence attracted attention on the streets. Blades were hardly rare, but because of their gifts, they tended to avoid public places, and thus people didn't get to see them often. Kiyoshi noted the different reactions his presence created. Small children were fascinated. One young boy wanted to run up and talk to him, but his mother caught the child and held on to him tightly.

Some stared openly, but most tracked him with their eyes while trying to pretend they weren't. Kiyoshi sighed. He had lived with the gift of the sense for more than sixty cycles now, and it was an old friend. There was still much he didn't understand, but he had learned more about his powers than many ever did. There was nothing mysterious about the sense, but it was impossible to say as much to those who didn't possess the gift. They would always view it as something too powerful to understand.

Kiyoshi stopped by the stand of a local fisherman he knew. The old vendor was an expert at finding fish in the river a day's journey away from Haven, and his fish were often wonderfully fatty, with a buttery flavor when eaten raw. Kiyoshi spoke briefly with the man and selected a fish to be delivered to the palace. If nothing else, he would eat well tonight, and that would give today's outing more value.

Kiyoshi focused his thoughts as he approached the fort. The meeting was a trap, and the worst trap was the one you knew about but had to walk into anyway. At times, Kiyoshi wished he cared less about the Kingdom, but that wasn't who he was, and Lord Shin knew that.

He was stopped at the front gate. Kiyoshi had visited the fort before and his robes had always been enough to gain him entrance, but the soldiers now fixed him with a stare that made it clear his robes weren't enough anymore. Reasonable, although disturbing. If this were the way the soldiers felt, soon the populace would follow suit. Kiyoshi felt like he was dancing on the edge of a knife.

A messenger was sent, and a short time later, Lord Shin's chief aide came to escort Kiyoshi into the fort. The blade felt dozens of eyes on him as he walked into the center courtyard, but he did his best to ignore the attention. He had answers to find while he was here, too. He scanned the walls, considering different entrance and egress routes. It had been a long time since he had studied a fort with such intent, a skill he had once developed well.

It had been raining last night, which meant most guards would have sought shelter. Most forts had shelters built at intervals along the walls, and the guards would have retreated into them with the storm, leaving potential gaps in their vision. Kiyoshi spotted at least three locations where someone could have conceivably entered, if the intruder had known which slots the guards would be looking through. Not a surprise, but unsettling. The discovery meant he was probably right about what had happened last night. Only one type of person would have been able to enter the fort unseen.

Shin's chief aide escorted him into the cells where Koji had been imprisoned. Kiyoshi analyzed the layout quickly and decided a skilled individual would have had no problem breaking Koji out.

His thoughts were interrupted by a livid Lord Shin. "Kiyoshi! Tell me, what is the meaning of all this?"

Kiyoshi had rehearsed his response. "Lord Shin, I know no more than you do. I was hoping we could find answers together."

Lord Shin drew himself up to his full height as he stepped toward Kiyoshi. Had the moment been less serious, Kiyoshi might have found humor in the situation. Shin had never been a warrior, and even Kiyoshi, a dayblade, had nothing to fear personally from the lord. "That is a blatant lie, and we both know it! You had Koji broken out of the prison last night—admit it!"

Kiyoshi shook his head. "I'm sorry, Lord Shin, but that isn't true, and I am offended you would implicate me in this. As you well know, it was I who signed the warrant for Koji's arrest. It would hardly be reasonable for me to then break him out. I want to know what happened here just as much as you do."

Kiyoshi's calm demeanor seemed to pierce Shin's anger, but the blade suspected it had been a facade to begin with. Lord Shin was creating a show for the soldiers. He was not to be underestimated. Kiyoshi wondered, just for a moment, if Lord Shin had orchestrated the escape to create this very situation. An entertaining thought, but Kiyoshi dismissed it quickly. Lord Shin would have had to cooperate with a blade, and Kiyoshi didn't see that happening. Shin was clever, but his dislike of the blades was too strong.

"Very well, Kiyoshi. What do you think happened?"

"I don't know. I just arrived and know nothing besides the fact that Koji is no longer in his cell. What have you found so far?"

Lord Shin looked pained to have to explain last night's events, but Kiyoshi didn't mind. "Last night, Koji escaped from his cell."

Kiyoshi frowned. "Your message said as much, but my question was much more specific. What do we actually know happened?"

Lord Shin's frustration was obvious. "Much less than I'd like. The guards claim everything was normal. They don't remember, but the two guards inside the cell block apparently passed out. They realized there was a problem when they woke up and found Koji gone. No one saw anything, and there's no evidence of any combat. The keys were still on one guard's belt."

Kiyoshi put the pieces together quickly, but he wondered what Lord Shin was thinking. "What's the best theory for what happened?"

"I think it's obvious. Koji found out he would be executed, and he decided to leave."

"How did he escape?"

"I don't know! Who knows what powers the nightblades have? Somehow he must have put the guards to sleep and opened the door to his cell."

Kiyoshi didn't even try to dignify that comment with a response. Unless Koji had somehow developed skills far beyond current understanding, he didn't possess those sorts of abilities. People without the gift erroneously believed those with it were capable of anything.

Lord Shin continued. "Otherwise, one of your people came in and helped him escape. Either way, you are responsible."

Shin's second theory was much more reasonable, but Kiyoshi couldn't have the blame for the prison break placed on the blades. "Until we know what happened, it is far too soon to be making baseless accusations, Lord Shin. I have ordered a manhunt for Koji. We will find him and bring him to justice."

Shin sneered. "I don't think your manhunt will do very well when your blades are the ones who broke him out in the first place. No, I have called a manhunt of my own. I have summoned a number of my honor guard into the city, and they will conduct an intensive search. There won't be anyplace for him to hide."

It took everything Kiyoshi had not to let his anger show. "I am thankful you will help us in this search. It was very wise of you. If there is nothing else, I must go now. I have my own hunt to complete."

Lord Shin waved his hand. "You are dismissed."

Turning on his heels was one of the most satisfying actions Kiyoshi had taken in a long time. Before he left, he stopped and spoke to a guard at the door of the prison. The soldier seemed uncomfortable talking to the blade but answered his questions.

"Has anything been different around here lately? Did Koji have any visitors?"

The guard thought for a moment. "He had only one visitor. Another nightblade. An older man. I don't remember his name."

Kiyoshi didn't need it. He knew where his next stop would be.

—

Kiyoshi knew where Minori had set up his household. Kiyoshi prided himself on being aware of as many of the happenings in the Kingdom as possible, and in Haven his attention was even more focused. He headed directly to the nightblade's home, his mind racing faster than he could walk.

There was only one reasonable explanation for what had happened in the prison, even though Kiyoshi had a hard time believing Minori would go so far. Kiyoshi had been impressed in their first meeting. Minori had been honest and direct, qualities that surprised Kiyoshi. Minori had seemed reasonable, and he had to know what effect his actions would have.

Kiyoshi worried about Lord Shin bringing more troops into the city. The Kingdom continued to survive because of a balance of power. Certain cycles were generally peaceful, allowing more room for mistakes, but this cycle was as tense as any Kiyoshi had lived through.

Shin was grabbing an opportunity right now. Under the pretense of a manhunt, he was moving more troops into the capital. The other lords would complain in the council, but they wouldn't take action, and the king could hardly push back. If he did, he would appear to be on the side of a murderous nightblade. With the extra manpower, if anything happened to the king, Shin would be in the best position to take control of the capital, and most likely the Kingdom.

All because of Minori's shortsightedness. That was what surprised Kiyoshi more than anything. They might disagree, but Minori had a reputation as a man who knew what he was doing. A man who made change happen. Well, he was certainly causing change now, but he was playing right into Shin's hands.

By the time Kiyoshi got to Minori's house, he was almost running, driven as he was by rage. He had worked too hard for too long to let something like this happen. He pounded on the door, and a young man came and answered. Kiyoshi demanded to see Minori, and the young man bowed and escorted him into the house.

Minori was kneeling at his desk, writing a letter that Kiyoshi imagined was going back to the Council of the Blades. It caused a thought to run through Kiyoshi's head that he hadn't yet considered: What if Minori was working on the direct orders of the council? Would they be so bold as to undermine Kiyoshi so thoroughly? It seemed unlikely, but he had been out of touch for some time. He reminded himself to stay calm and not make hasty mistakes.

Minori smiled, and Kiyoshi knew he would play this game to the end.

"Kiyoshi, it's wonderful to see you again so soon. What brings you here today?"

Kiyoshi noted that the young man took up station by the door. His presence caused Kiyoshi to pause. There wouldn't be any reason for an aide to remain here for this conversation, not unless Minori had something else planned. Was he in danger? The thought seemed almost ridiculous, but perhaps he needed to stop making assumptions when dealing with Minori. He immediately became more alert.

"Let's get right to the point. Where were you last night?"

Minori's smile never left his face. "And what do you want me to say?"

"The truth."

Minori seemed to juggle a few options in his mind, but then he shrugged. "Very well. I was helping Koji escape from jail."

Even though Kiyoshi had been certain Minori had been responsible, it still defied belief that the blade would sit here and acknowledge the truth so openly. Minori had to be crazy or stupid, or both. Kiyoshi could feel his emotions getting the better of him, but he couldn't stop the fury that erupted.

"Do you have any idea what effect your actions had?"

Minori's smile faded as he answered. "I assume one of a few possibilities. The most likely was that the king would be forced to declare a large, public manhunt for a nightblade. There was also a chance that one of the lords, most likely Shin, would bring in more soldiers under the pretense of hunting for Koji."

Kiyoshi knew his mouth was hanging open. He couldn't believe what he was hearing.

"What were you thinking?"

"Two things. First, it was criminal what happened to Koji. I assume you already know I went to the prison to talk with him. He told me the truth of what happened, and not only is he innocent, but he upheld his duties with an honor and wisdom far beyond his age. He's an honorable man, and I won't allow you to sacrifice him just because you think it serves the greater good. Once you do, who knows how much farther you'll go to protect the peace?

"Second, it is time that the Kingdom makes a decision. For too long the blades have held a precarious position in our society. The Kingdom relies on our strength to keep the peace, but no one respects us. They fear us. They fear what they don't understand, and this can't continue. Either we need to be accepted, or the Kingdom needs to find another way to protect itself."

Kiyoshi was stunned. Yet part of him understood what Minori was saying. Maybe, just maybe, that same part of him even respected how Minori stood for his beliefs. But the greater part of him knew that the nightblade's actions were wrong. Perhaps Minori could justify his deeds, but if he was trying to push the Kingdom toward some sort of conflict or decision, then a time of chaos was on the horizon. People would suffer, and Kiyoshi didn't want any more blood on his hands.

"Minori, perhaps Koji was innocent. But what you did could lead to conflict. People could die as a repercussion of your action."

"Perhaps. But we know Koji certainly would have died, and forgive me for saying so, but I value the life of a fellow blade more than any citizen of Haven."

Kiyoshi stumbled backward. Minori's philosophy and his self-belief were unshakable, and Kiyoshi didn't know how to attack. All he knew was that this was far too dangerous a path to take.

"I'm sorry, Minori, but I need to launch a manhunt for Koji. I understand your intent, but if his life will save the lives of others, it's a price I remain willing to pay."

Kiyoshi turned to leave, but Minori seemed set on having the last word.

"Your manhunt will never find him."

Kiyoshi turned back to Minori. "What do you mean?"

Minori grinned viciously, a laugh threatening to break out on his face. "Kiyoshi, meet Koji, my new personal chief aide."

Kiyoshi spun around so fast he thought he might wear a hole in his sock. Koji was bowing to him. Kiyoshi extended his sense and discovered the young man was gifted. Koji hadn't been using his sense at the door.

Kiyoshi knew suddenly he'd been played, and he'd put his own life in danger.

Minori was deadly serious. "Kiyoshi, I do not want to cause the loss of life, but I do plan on reasserting the authority of the blades in the Kingdom. These lords are focused on petty plays for power, but the blades already possess all the power this land needs. Our advice and guidance should lead this Kingdom, and I will do everything I believe is necessary to bring that day closer. You can either join me or oppose me, but if you oppose me, you will lose."

Mind racing, Kiyoshi moved to slap Minori. The nightblade sensed the movement coming and easily caught Kiyoshi's hand. He looked at Kiyoshi condescendingly. "I expected better from you."

Anger burned in Kiyoshi's gut. He wasn't sure if he was in danger, but he needed to escape Minori. Twisting his wrist, he broke Minori's grip and grabbed the blade's arm tightly. Kiyoshi sensed Koji stepping toward them, but it would take the dayblade only a moment to teach Minori a lesson. He focused his sense and pushed into Minori's body, sending his energy into every nerve ending the warrior had. Minori's eyes went wide and his body collapsed, a moan escaping his lips.

Koji was close but hadn't drawn his sword. Kiyoshi grabbed a short blade strapped to one of his forearms, hidden by his robes. He drew the blade and pressed the back side of it against Koji's neck. The young nightblade, taken by surprise at the collapse of his master, didn't know how to react. Kiyoshi had been very fortunate. If they had been prepared for a fight, he likely would have died.

"I won't kill you, because I can't undo what Minori did. But realize this: you were born to serve, not yourself, but others. If you turn yourself in, you can save lives. I know you're an honorable man who is scared. Make your choice."

With that, Kiyoshi withdrew his blade and walked out of Minori's house, thankful to still be taking breath.

Chapter 7

Asa was up with the morning sun, not typically her way. But she had struggled to sleep last night, and when the sun rose, she gave up all hope of a decent night's rest.

She had arrived in Starfall two nights ago. The journey from Takashi's village had been long, and more than once Asa was convinced she was being followed. But no matter what steps she took to find her stalker, she found nothing but empty space. She was certain her sense hadn't misled her, but she still didn't have any explanation for what she was experiencing. Because of her uncertainty, she had struggled to sleep on the road. She had hoped that being at the seat of the Council of the Blades would ease her fears, but her concerns had only been replaced by a fear for her future.

There was only one way forward she could see. She needed to access the archives in Starfall. More specifically, she needed to access the archives in Starfall that were off-limits to all but a few.

Being allowed into the general archives wasn't a problem. Any blade was given access without having to explain themselves. Asa had spent the better part of the last two days, searching. But all she had earned for her effort was a pounding headache, unrelenting in intensity. If she never saw another word on a page, she'd be plenty happy.

Still, there was one part of the archives she was restricted from accessing, which stood behind a thick door with a sign proclaiming no admittance. The door that blocked her wasn't even locked. Locked doors were for civilians, not blades. The problem was that the archives had blades constantly wandering through them. The moment she stepped through the door, everyone nearby would know.

Asa's plan wasn't complicated. If it had been, it would have had even less chance of succeeding. She would go into the archives very early in the morning, when the fewest people were around. By now, the blades who maintained the archives had gotten used to her presence. She needed to wait for an opportunity to access the forbidden section when no one was nearby. The building was far from populated; she just needed to wait for the right moment.

Asa gathered her notes and materials and left the common bunk she had been assigned when she entered town. Like many blades, she didn't have a permanent home. Starfall, considered the home of the blades, housed only a few permanent residents. The other blades were scattered throughout the Kingdom.

When a blade came to Starfall, she or he received a place to stay. Someone like Asa, who planned on remaining for only a few days, slept in a common bunkhouse. If she had had plans to stay longer, she would have received a more permanent residence. The gifted who were a part of the council lived in houses that, although nothing special by Kingdom standards, were opulent by blade standards.

Asa made her way through the streets, taking in the relative peace of morning. Starfall wasn't a huge city. At times the population could swell to almost five thousand if there was a festival or gathering of blades, but on most days, far less than a thousand blades were present. Still, this was the largest gathering of people Asa had been around for quite some time, and it took practice to be able to use the sense in more densely inhabited locales.

The limits of a blade's sense were all about the ability to process information. In a city, crowded with life, most blades could only extend their sense maybe a dozen paces. Asa was no different, but upon her return to civilization, she wasn't able to sense even four paces away. She needed time to build the ability back up, stretching her mind like a muscle that hadn't been used for moons.

The calm of the morning was a good time for her to be about. Far fewer people were making their way through the city, and she could extend her sense farther than she could have otherwise. The city itself was situated by a lake, and Asa could smell the fresh air carried over the water by the soft breeze. The sun still hadn't warmed up the spring air, and she pulled her robes closer as the breeze turned into an unexpected gust.

Suddenly she became uneasy. She stopped and tried to focus on the sensation, to figure out what warning her body and senses were interpreting.

Asa stopped in the middle of a small square. Due to the hour, only a handful of people strolled in what would otherwise have been a crowded intersection. But what was wrong?

Her instincts guided her to a man walking parallel to her. She guessed he had seen maybe thirty cycles, and he moved with a grace she associated with nightblades and their training. At first, nothing seemed suspicious about him, until she realized she couldn't sense him. He was right there in front of her, but when she tried to focus her sense, she felt nothing.

Asa's world twisted. She didn't believe in ghosts or the supernatural. She had felt men and women die, and she knew how their spirits rejoined the Great Cycle, which governed all things. But her senses warred with one another. Her sight told her a man was nearby, but her sense, her ability to detect all living things, told her the space he occupied was empty.

His eyes came up and met hers, and just for a moment they seemed to twinkle. Then he smiled and was gone.

Asa blinked. She couldn't say for certain what had just happened. Had the man disappeared like smoke from a fire? Or had he just turned a corner and left her line of sight? Try as she might, she couldn't focus her memories, and she felt the image of him, once so vivid, slip from her mind.

Asa frowned and kept walking toward the archives. She shivered and pulled her robes tighter, even though there was no breeze.

—

Asa tried but failed to shake her encounter with the man she couldn't sense. She tried telling herself there was plenty about the world she didn't understand, but the rationalizing didn't ease her nerves.

Asa continued toward the archives, but then a sudden memory stopped her, almost in midstride. She remembered the plains outside Takashi's village and the blade she couldn't sense. Was this the same person? For a moment, her heart raced as she considered for the first time that she had been followed for hundreds of leagues.

Her rational mind soon took over. She was getting inside her own head and making connections that didn't exist. No one would go to such lengths to pursue her, and she was certain no one knew what drove her. She had never told another living soul.

Asa continued walking toward the archives, pausing often to turn around and make sure she wasn't being followed. Although she was certain the man was always right behind her, she never saw him again.

Her nerves were too jittery. Some part of her life had changed when she killed Takashi.

When she had stepped into that room with Takashi, she had thought that her journey was over. She had approached him filled with thoughts of revenge, and even as he confessed himself to her, her rage cooled but never died.

Asa flashed back to the scene, Takashi in front of her, right before she took his head. The emotions the memory evoked were every bit as powerful as those she felt in the moment. Frustration that all she had been given was another clue. Sorrow, for Takashi had proven himself an honorable man at the end.

But more than that, as she brought the sword down to end his life, she had understood a truth: she wanted to kill him. Before Takashi, killing had been an action, devoid of emotion. But as her sword sliced through the skin of his neck, finding the space between the bones of his spine, she discovered that she desired his death.

Takashi may not have been the one who killed her father, but he hadn't saved him. For that, she had wanted him to die, and a part of her worried that her desire didn't bother her at all.

Asa forced her thoughts to the present as she got to the archives. Whatever thinking she had to do could wait until she found the information she needed. Until then, she had to pay attention to the present moment. She would need her wits about her to have any chance of succeeding.

The archives were always open but staffed only during the day. At this early hour, the library was almost abandoned. If she were an optimist, she could embrace the fact there were thus fewer blades around to detect her presence. The pessimist in her countered that with fewer people, her own presence would shine more brightly, like the only candle in a dark room. But Asa was a realist, and she wouldn't know unless she tried.

Asa entered the archives through the front door, relieved that the dayblade who usually sat nearby wasn't yet present.

She wandered the halls, walking into a few random rooms to check her surroundings more closely. If she was certain she was alone, she would pause for a moment to extend her sense. After a few attempts, she was sure she was in the archives alone. There would never be a better time to try for the forbidden section.

Asa went to the room nearest her goal and stopped to check her surroundings one last time. She hesitated. Up until this point, everything she had done had been in accordance with the wishes of the council.

If she proceeded, that would no longer be true. She had no idea what type of punishments awaited her if she was caught, but this intrusion was the first real risk she'd ever taken on her personal quest.

The moment passed, and Asa walked toward the forbidden section. She opened the door and closed it silently, turning around to see what awaited her.

Her first reaction was one of disappointment. For all her planning and second-guessing, the forbidden section of the archives looked much the same as any other section. Stacks of scrolls and books lined the walls, with a set of nearby documents detailing what was where. She started looking for information about the massacre at Two Falls.

The first level of information, stored in books of records, was easy to find, but was barely more interesting than everything she had already pieced together. She read through it, taking notes as necessary. She found a list of every blade involved with the massacre and copied it quickly. When she came across her father's name, she paused and took a deep breath. The discovery hit her harder than she'd expected, but she felt relief that somewhere, her father would be remembered for what he had done.

Once the first layer of information was processed, Asa worked her way through her notes, looking at names and other facts. A part of her had hoped that the hidden archives would have a complete, written record of Two Falls, but the hope was in vain. She would dig deeper.

As Asa worked, she remembered to take temporary breaks to extend her sense and check the area around her. Although she dared not extend her sense too far and give away her own presence, she examined the immediate vicinity to ensure she wouldn't be discovered. She presumed she was alone, but she knew she wouldn't have much more time.

After more digging, Asa eventually found new information. When no complete record of Two Falls was found, she focused on the name Takashi had given her: Osamu. Records seemed to be scarce, but she discovered a few mentions of a nightblade by that name who seemed to fit the profile she had made of him. She started reading, and as she did, the rest of the world slipped away. The more she read, the less real he seemed to be. His life seemed to be the type of story young boys dreamed of when they talked about becoming blades. He was a serial womanizer, Yoshi's right-hand man, and a shadow for the king himself. Although the reports he wrote were dry, they had to have been full of tremendous adventure. How was it that Asa had never heard of him? If half the information she was reading was true, he would be a nightblade legend.

Asa was so absorbed by what she was reading, she didn't notice when the doors to the forbidden section of the archive opened to reveal two nightblades. She *did* hear them enter the room. She glanced quickly around, already aware there weren't any other exits. The only way out was through the two nightblades, and she didn't think her skills were sufficiently developed to attack. Even if they were, it would do her little good to fight. Her name was on the records for the archives, and it wouldn't take a genius to figure out who had been there. Better to surrender peacefully and hope for a lenient punishment.

The nightblades who entered didn't take kindly to her presence. Even though she didn't put up any fight, they apprehended her in moments, pinning her to the ground and roughly tying her hands behind her back. Asa didn't struggle, but as she was pulled to her feet, she saw the same man from the square framed in the doorway. He looked at her for a moment, face expressionless, before disappearing again.

The first stop Asa and her captors made was to a block of cells she had never known existed within Starfall. She didn't resist, and as the night-blades who guarded Asa began to understand she would not put up a fight, they stopped trying to control her and simply remained in a state of relaxed awareness.

In the cells she was treated well. The guards brought her food and drink, and at her request, they even brought her sleeping pad from the bunk she'd been staying in. A guard was posted at all times, and Asa could feel his sense constantly wandering the grounds.

She made good use of her time. Asa stretched and ran through some of her practice routines, her moves filling the small space of the cell with energy. When the sun fell below the horizon, she went to bed, her mind wandering over the facts of the day.

In the archives she had found some interesting information, but nothing that changed her outlook. Her beliefs about what had happened at the massacre at Two Falls were confirmed. Osamu was interesting, but there was no doubt his name had been scrubbed from the records. She imagined a vow of silence had been ordered regarding him, and it would be hard, if not impossible, to find an old blade willing to bend the wishes of the council. If her investigation ever continued, she would need to find another way to get information on Osamu.

Asa's more immediate concern was the man she couldn't sense. She refused to believe in ghosts, but he was haunting her. With nothing but time on her hands, she worked through the problem. If the man wasn't an apparition, then there was a type of blade who could hide his presence from other blades. She had never heard of the skill before, but the explanation seemed to be the most rational.

A blade who couldn't be sensed would explain the sensation she had experienced after leaving Takashi's village, and if she was dealing with the same man, it meant he had been following her for quite some time. With that level of skill and her inability to sense him, he would be a very dangerous opponent. But he didn't seem interested in killing her. That meant he was a spy, a shadow sent by someone to watch her moves.

She was making a lot of assumptions, but the idea felt right to her. Someone with wealth and influence had hired a shadow to spy on her. The skills of a man like that wouldn't come cheaply, and most nightblades shunned material wealth. But what had she done to attract this type of attention? The only thing that made Asa stand out was her quest to find out what happened at the massacre at Two Falls. If all her assumptions were right, it meant she had to be getting close to the truth.

If only she knew the truth. Asa had turned over a lot of stones, but all she seemed to find was more dirt underneath. The information she had was dangerous, she supposed, but she didn't have any plans to share it. That had never been her purpose.

Having decided she wasn't in any immediate danger, Asa slept well, waking up to a new guard bringing her breakfast. She tested her surroundings with her sense again, but this new guard was just as cautious as the overnight sentry. The guard was a young nightblade, a woman only a few cycles younger than Asa. This would be an important assignment for her, and she wouldn't drop her awareness enough for Asa to escape. With no other options, Asa ate eagerly, surprised at how hungry she was. When the guard came back, she was working through her morning exercises.

The guard waited until she finished. "You have been summoned by the council."

Asa wasn't surprised. She took a deep breath and steeled herself. "Thank you. I'm ready."

"Do we need to bind you?"

Asa shook her head. "I will cause you no trouble. May I have my blades to present myself to the council?"

The guard paused, considering for a moment. It was potentially dangerous to give Asa the swords, but for her to show herself to the council without them would be almost as shameful as asking her to appear naked. "Very well."

Asa and the guard were soon walking together toward the hall of the council. The sentry stopped at the door, knowing she wasn't invited in. Asa turned and bowed deeply to her. "Thank you for your kindness."

The guard returned the bow, less deeply than Asa had. Asa turned to the hall of the council and walked in.

She was surprised to find the space almost empty. Only one blade sat in the hall, and Asa recognized him immediately: Hajimi, the head of the Council of the Blades. As soon as he noticed her, Asa bowed deeply. Hajimi returned the bow with a curt nod of his head. In front of him was a stack of papers and scrolls he had evidently been reading.

"Come in, Asa. You have made my past two days much more interesting."

Asa stepped forward, her mind tripping over the different possibilities. If there was going to be a trial, she would have expected more than one council member. She supposed Hajimi had all the authority needed to hold court, but his behavior toward her didn't seem to indicate she was on trial. She considered apologizing, but didn't. Her words would have been a lie, and the head of the blades deserved more respect than that. She maintained her silence.

Hajimi was more than happy to fill in the silence. "First, I learn that someone tried sneaking into the forbidden section of the archive. This is surprising enough, and I assumed one of the lords was up to his foolish games again. No blade would be so stupid as to try. But then I find out I'm wrong. So all the information we have on you is given to me, as well as the information you were found with.

"I know from your records you are not foolish. Your master spoke highly of you, but you seem determined to disappoint him. No matter. So you knew the information in the archives would likely get you caught, which meant it was valuable to you.

"Finally, when I dig further into your past, curious about what was happening, I find a wall. Not a physical wall, mind you, but a wall nonetheless. There's nothing about your past anywhere in our archives. The first information we have of your existence is when your master started training you at an advanced age. There's no record of you in the first census, which you are more than old enough to have been a part of. So we have mysteries wrapped in mysteries, and I'm hoping you can explain them."

Hajimi seemed to be done, but Asa was unsure what to tell him. So many unanswered questions lingered in his comments. "Where would you like me to begin?"

"All stories have a beginning. Let's start with yours. Who are you, Asa?"

"I was born to a small farming household in the lands of House Fujita. The only point of my upbringing worth mentioning is that my father possessed the gift of the sense. He elected not to be trained as a blade, content with his lot in life as a farmer. It was only shortly after I was born that he changed his mind. I was too young to know what was happening, but according to my mother, there were a series of bad harvests. My father struggled to make ends meet, and in an act of desperation, studied and passed the trials and became a dayblade. The stipend provided fed our family. Of his service there is little of note. His most notable achievement was dying at the massacre at Two Falls."

Hajimi's eyebrows raised. She could see he was putting the pieces together.

"I don't want to assume anything. Please continue."

Asa debated how much to tell Hajimi. Ultimately, her mother had raised her to be honest, and old habits died hard. She could tell most of the truth. "His death destroyed my life. The blades only pay a stipend for active service, and without it, our family had no means to support itself. I had an older brother who tried to keep the farm going, and for almost eight cycles he succeeded. They were hard times, but pleasant memories. My brother died after a cut became infected. My mother didn't have any more options. By the time we had sold everything and spent the money, I had already demonstrated an aptitude with the sense. When the census began, my mother hid me. She didn't want me to follow in the footsteps of my father. But when there was no choice, my mother forced me to enter training, even though I was already far older than most of my peers. I do not know what happened to my mother."

Asa let the truth be unspoken. There was only one profession for widows, and it didn't bear mentioning.

"So, you've been driven to figure out what happened at the massacre since you started training?" Hajimi's voice was encouraging.

"Yes. The story always felt wrong to me, and my father was a dayblade. There was no way he should have died at that battle." Asa still didn't want to bring up that she had been told her father had been killed by his own commander.

Hajimi paused and sipped at a cup of tea sitting next to him. "That was why you requested Takashi's assignment."

Asa nodded.

"How much do you know?"

Again Asa wondered if it was wise to speak the truth, but she saw no other path forward. "Everything, and yet nothing. I know the massacre wasn't a battle between the blades and a well-organized group of bandits. It was a civil war between blades. I know that Osamu, the commander of the mission, ordered the entire village burned. I know my father died trying to protect the villagers."

Hajimi shook his head. "It sounds more like you know everything than nothing."

"I disagree. I want the person responsible. I had thought perhaps Takashi was culpable. He was my father's direct commander at the time. But we spoke before I let him kill himself. It's Osamu I want."

Hajimi finished the thought. "That's why you were in the archives. You were trying to figure out if Osamu still lived, and if so, you were going to kill him."

Asa nodded. "I accept whatever punishment you see fit."

Hajimi took another sip of tea and allowed the silence to fill the room. Asa was calm. She had never told her story to someone, and now felt a weight lifted off her shoulders. Perhaps this was the end of her journey, but if so, she had tried everything she could. She could die content.

Hajimi's voice brought her back to the present. "I don't think you will be reprimanded."

Asa thought her surprise must have been evident.

"Osamu is one of the great mysteries of our age. I don't know how much you picked up from the files, but I'm old enough to have lived through many cycles of his adventures. What the records might not show was that he was a very private man. Few people saw his face. Most of us thought he was ridiculous, but it seems to have served him well."

Asa wondered where Hajimi was going.

"You are searching for Osamu, and the truth is, you aren't the only one. Two Falls led to the calls for the census, and the decline of the blades since then can be directly linked to that day. His actions put us all in danger. Together, the king and the Council of the Blades agreed on the lie that most people today accept as the truth about Two Falls. That lie has been responsible for the decline in our strength, but if the truth ever got out, we would see an uprising against the blades the likes of which we have never seen. Combined with the king's poor health, the conflict would tear the Kingdom apart.

"No one knows what happened to Osamu. Most of us on the council hope he is dead, that he committed suicide after word of the massacre got out. But we don't know. We searched for him for several cycles, but no one knew what he looked like, so we never found him. Perhaps your passion will lead you where we never could go."

Hajimi paused for a moment.

"Asa, I'm going to give you a new mission. An official one, on behalf of the council. I grant you full access to everything you need. You will also be given the title of Master. You may act on your own officially now. I don't need to tell you what will happen if the truth becomes public, but you must find out what happened to Osamu. If he's still alive, your orders are to kill him. Regardless, keep the council updated on your progress. Understood?"

Asa bowed deeply. This was the mission she had always wanted, and she was eager to continue the hunt.

Chapter 8

Minori kept running through the scene in his mind, already having done so hundreds of times. The event was burned in his memory, more potent and surprising even than the first time he had been with a woman.

It was difficult for him to comprehend what had happened. The old dayblade had moved with a speed and ruthlessness Minori never expected. If he hadn't known better, he would've thought Kiyoshi was a nightblade. But Kiyoshi's credentials were well established. He healed the king himself.

What obsessed Minori was the initial slap. The more he thought on that moment, the more certain he was the move had been premeditated by Kiyoshi. At the distance they had been standing, Kiyoshi had no ability to hurt Minori. With Minori's ability to sense intent before action, Kiyoshi would have been unable to lay hands on him. But by slapping at the nightblade, he lured Minori in to grab his wrist. Then Kiyoshi was close enough to send that shock, or whatever it was, through Minori's body.

If Minori had had more time, he would have further explored Kiyoshi's unique talents. He had never heard of dayblades using their powers to harm as well as heal.

At first, the incident had enraged Minori. He had been so pleased with himself and his small coup over Kiyoshi that he had let down his guard. He hadn't expected a direct confrontation, and he certainly hadn't expected to lose. In retrospect, he should have known better, having heard of Kiyoshi's passion.

Fortunately, Minori thought, he was a rational and analytical man, and he forced himself to take a wider perspective. The rescue of the young nightblade had been a lark, an opportunity to create waves. Besides Lord Shin moving more of his household guard into the city, there had been no other fallout. Minori had been surprised at first, but perhaps the lords were not as bold as he had originally thought.

He couldn't get firsthand experience, though. Since their little scene, Kiyoshi had effectively blocked him from any formal proceedings. Minori had done his best to stay abreast of council meetings, but they were often held with short notice, and Kiyoshi's messenger always seemed to have difficulty finding Minori's household. Minori wasn't even sure if the king knew he was in Haven.

It was a setback, but Minori didn't despair. Politics never had a single solution.

But time was a precious commodity. He'd been able to glance at the king only once, but he was surprised by what he saw. Everyone knew the king was ill, but the council had hidden the true extent of his sickness. Using his sense, Minori had just barely been able to feel the king's presence. He suspected that if not for Kiyoshi's intervention, Masaki would already be dead.

Minori idly played with the letter from the Council of the Blades he had received that morning, another piece of a puzzle he didn't yet understand. Most of the information was meaningless, Hajimi relating information Minori had no need or desire to know. But one piece of news was buried in the letter that had his head spinning. A young nightblade named Asa was researching the events at Two Falls. She was searching for Osamu.

The name echoed in Minori's thoughts, causing him to lose focus and forcing his mind to wander. He hadn't thought of that name, or the images of the massacre it brought to mind, in a long time. It had been, what, more than twenty cycles since those events had happened? Still, the echoes of the actions taken that day haunted the present. He wondered just how persistent Asa was and what her persistence might mean for him.

Minori's thoughts were interrupted by a messenger at his door. With so few friends in the city, he wondered who it could be. His curiosity was sated when the messenger announced himself as a vassal of Lord Shin.

The blade's interest was immediately piqued. His presence had not gone unnoticed. The messenger bowed deeply, as befitted Minori's station.

"Sir, my lord requests your company as soon as you are able to visit."

Minori was curious. "Did your lord happen to mention what he wanted to see me about?"

Minori saw the hint of fear in the man's eyes. After more than fifty cycles of life, he had become all too familiar with the look. No matter how common the blades were in the Kingdom, they would always be feared by those who didn't understand their power. This poor messenger was terrified, and he was only delivering an invitation.

The messenger shook his head. "I'm afraid, sir, he did not. However, he did mention he was happy to make himself available at all times for you. It is not a statement he often makes."

Minori closed his eyes and thought for a moment. Sometimes in chess, it was important to be in control of the board, to know there was only one move your opponent could make. But there were other times when the board was in complete chaos, and you had to be comfortable making the best moves amidst uncertainty. This was one of those times.

"Please let your lord know I will be there at my earliest possible convenience."

With a relieved look on his face, the messenger turned and almost ran out of Minori's receiving room. Minori stifled a chuckle and wondered what one of the three lords of the Kingdom had to say.

Shin's messenger had come in the morning. Minori's instinct had been to leave almost immediately for the lord's household, but reason gave him pause. It was important he create the impression he wasn't at the lord's beck and call. Despite his overwhelming curiosity, Minori forced himself to wait until late afternoon.

As Minori walked through Haven, he paid attention to the talk of the commoners and the merchants. One of the blind spots of all the blades was their pride. On an individual level, their power was so much greater than any other member of the Kingdom, they had a tendency to forget about the importance of everybody else. Minori believed that was a mistake. Despite the strength of the blades, they were vastly outnumbered by regular citizens. Few agreed with him, but Minori believed that if the commoners ever revolted against the blades, there was little the blades would be able to do. So he did his best to pay attention to what was being said on the street and in the teahouses.

Most people seemed to be going about their daily business. Minori heard a few mentions of Lord Shin's soldiers, but the troops had been well behaved and brought good money into the city. Because of the lack of any incidents, the people viewed them favorably.

Minori was surprised, as he always was, by how little the citizens seemed concerned about the king's health. The king could die at any time, and without an heir named, the king's death would bring confusion at the best and civil war at the worst. Minori thought the subject should be foremost on everyone's minds, but perhaps he was one of the few who cared. He had to remind himself that most people were concerned with the little problems in life and often ignored the bigger, more dangerous issues.

Minori found Lord Shin's household with little difficulty. The abode was one of the biggest complexes in the city, rivaling even the king's castle. Thick and tall white walls cut the grounds off from the rest of the city. The center structure, Shin's palace, was massive—two stories tall, with a sloped tile roof that added half that height again. A nearby pagoda towered over the massive stone walls. Minori wondered how Shin, who wasn't even the lord of this land, could have built such an enormous complex in the capital. The payments to Masaki must be significant, to say the least.

Minori wore his robes, and after a short introduction, was ushered directly to Shin's office, a nightingale floor singing under his feet as he walked. He kept his face neutral, but he was surprised by this prompt attention. Whatever the lord was up to, it was clear he placed a great deal of importance on this visit.

Minori was shown into the office, and he recognized the lord immediately. He gave Shin a small bow, and Shin barely bowed his head in return. The rudeness angered Minori. Shin was a lord because of birth. He had never had to earn his position. Minori was a blade, sharpened and hardened through cycles of training and experience. But Minori stifled his reflex and kept his face as featureless as a stone.

As host, Shin had the responsibility to speak first. When he spoke, Minori noticed that his voice was strong and firm, the voice of a man used to giving commands.

"Thank you for seeing me on such short notice. I realize my summons came as a surprise, and I am grateful you could come as soon as you did."

"The honor is all mine. It is the first time since my arrival in the city I've had the chance to meet with any of the lords."

Minori had little doubt that Shin already knew he hadn't seen any lords, but his remarks turned the conversation in the direction the blade wanted to go.

"I am very sorry to hear that, but I'm glad the mistake is rectified today."

For a moment, Minori worried they were going to have to go through all the formalities of a polite conversation. In other circumstances, he wouldn't have minded, but today he was grateful when Shin got to the point.

"I asked you here today because I believe our interests might align."

Minori hoped his face gave nothing away. An alliance with Shin might be very powerful, but he had to walk carefully. As a general matter of principle, the blades did not align with any of the great houses, electing instead to serve only the Kingdom.

"Thank you, Lord Shin, for your careful consideration. It would be an honor to assist you in any way." Working with Shin could be lucrative, but some things could be said, and others could not.

Minori looked around the lord's office. The room was barren, except for one carefully groomed tree and a set of swords on the wall. That, combined with Lord Shin's presence, led Minori to believe this was a man he could work with. Shin's reputation was one of a bold and clever leader, and if Minori played the game well, he could use the lord to help bring the blades to power in the Kingdom.

Shin's posture changed, and Minori paid more attention. "Let us not play any more games that society would expect of us. I've seen you looking around my room, and I know you are judging me. Likewise, I've studied every move you've made since you came in this room, and I believe your reputation is well earned. Can we do business together?"

Minori met Shin's gaze calmly. "I believe we can, although much depends on the nature of your offer."

Shin stood up. "I am grateful for your honest response, and it confirms what I've already suspected. You know as well as I do that, despite the calm of its citizens, the Kingdom is in crisis. The king will rejoin the Great Cycle soon, and despite the pressure of all the lords, he will not name an heir. This can no longer stand, and I hope to resolve the situation."

The lord didn't need to say anything else to Minori. He had already moved his troops into the city, and according to the reports Kiyoshi was feeding to the Council of the Blades, the other lords were not half as bold as Shin. He had put himself in the ideal position to become king should the old man die without naming a successor. Minori also knew there was only one faction that stood in his way: the blades.

Shin saw that Minori understood and was pleased. "My request is simple. I request the support of the blades in the event I take action."

Minori blinked in surprise. Talking so openly was close to treason. Shin was taking a calculated risk. The blade responded, "And in return?"

"Name your price. I know many of the recent reforms pushed by the lords have met with significant resistance within the ranks of the blades. It would be my pleasure to look at those reforms again to see if they serve the needs of the Kingdom."

Minori didn't buy Shin's offer outright. "That is a dramatic reversal from a man who has proposed many of the very reforms we're discussing."

Shin nodded, and Minori got the impression the lord had hoped he would ask just that question. "That is true, but the recent events surrounding the young nightblade, I believe he was named Koji, have led me to contemplation. He was broken out of the middle of the king's guards' fort with apparently no difficulty at all. That feat has reminded me of the power of the blades."

Minori studied Shin silently, wondering where this was going.

"Let me ask you a question. If you were to encounter a dragon of myth and legend, what would you do?"

Minori had no adequate response, so he fell to humor. "Regret whatever decisions had led to me being in front of one."

Shin smiled politely at the joke. "For the past cycles, we have tried to put a wall around the dragon. But a dragon will never be caged. It is too strong, and a smart builder knows this. Far better to harness that power and make one's self stronger as a result."

Minori stood in silence, considering the ramifications of what Shin was offering. If real, such an agreement could return a great deal of authority to the blades, and could be enough to allow Minori to consider his mission to Haven as a success. He still didn't trust Shin, but the lord's reasoning seemed rational enough.

Shin filled in the silence with another line of reasoning. "You and I both want what is best for the Kingdom. I fear that if steps are not taken, the Kingdom will descend into chaos. This is a way for us to move forward in peace."

Minori mentally chastised himself. He hadn't even thought of the health of the Kingdom, but what Shin said was true.

In an instant, Minori decided. It was the best play he had. "I will see what I may do. In return, I ask you make me one of your advisers and invite me to all future meetings of the King's Council."

Shin nodded, and the deal was done. Minori left soon after, wondering how to play this new situation to its greatest advantage.

Chapter 9

The candles flickered in Kiyoshi's room, but he paid them no mind. His eyesight was slowly failing anyway, another symptom of old age he didn't want to admit to. The decline wasn't great, but Kiyoshi knew his vision was only going to get worse. It would be a sad day when he could no longer read, a habit he had developed later in life. As part of his training as a blade, he had learned to read and write, but that had always seemed superfluous and secondary to his real training. Later on, he realized the magic of words.

It was good that he enjoyed reading, he thought as he looked over the stack of papers scattered across his desk. As chief adviser to the king, there was more than enough correspondence to go around. Everyone wanted something from Masaki, and one of Kiyoshi's main tasks every day was to act as a barrier between the monarch and the multitude of people who would seek his time.

Unfortunately, Kiyoshi was having trouble focusing. One letter among many had news he would rather not hear. Asa, the young nightblade who had taken the assignment to kill Takashi, was pursuing leads related to the massacre at Two Falls. Kiyoshi rubbed his temples to try to ease his frustration. The massacre had been more than twenty cycles ago, but they were still dealing with its aftermath. Masaki had lost his son, Yoshi, the prince, on that day. His wife had already passed away, and the king had never recovered. When he lost his son and heir, he was unable to return to his duties with the same vigor.

Kiyoshi remembered what Masaki had been like as a younger king—dynamic, but more than anything, he had smiled. When Kiyoshi first met Masaki, he thought for the first time he was experiencing a man who truly enjoyed his life. Masaki was always at hand with a joke, and even when times were difficult, he negotiated challenges with a calm acceptance.

But the deaths of his wife and son couldn't be overcome. Some days Kiyoshi saw hints of the old Masaki, a genuine gladness at a wedding or a birth, but those moments were now few and far between. Instead, he saw a man weighed down by the burdens of his responsibilities, one of which he seemed determined not to fulfill. After the prince died at the massacre, the entire Kingdom was abuzz about Masaki's marriage choices. Would he select someone from one of the great houses, to strengthen the alliance, or would he find a commoner to build a closer bond with the people? Every woman who had come within fifteen paces of the king had been endlessly speculated about.

But Masaki had never remarried. At first, he made the excuse he was still dealing with grief, but as time went on, those who knew him best saw it wasn't a temporary decision. Masaki couldn't bring himself to remarry. They never spoke directly of such intimacies, but Kiyoshi suspected Masaki didn't want to open himself up to the possibility of loss again. Even the bonds of duty couldn't compel him.

Masaki and his grief had created a dire predicament for the Kingdom. The great houses were at odds about who would be king next, and if Masaki didn't name an heir soon, Kiyoshi couldn't imagine a situation in which the houses wouldn't enter into war. Kiyoshi's shadows reported that all the great lords were planning intense military drills this summer, a field of dry grass just waiting for fire.

And into it all walked Asa, stirring up the past. Kiyoshi knew, better than anyone, what had happened at the massacre of Two Falls, and if the knowledge ever became public, there would be an immediate outcry. The public would revolt, possibly led by one of the great houses.

Unable to focus, Kiyoshi stood and started his forms. The movements had been drilled into him long ago, and although he was old, he still practiced them every day, the strength of his youth replaced by the precision and grace of his age. He moved slowly, aware of each muscle in his body, cognizant of every action.

His breath slowed and deepened. There was something about movement that his mind craved. No matter how busy his daily life was, when he was going through his routines and forms, time stopped. Only the body and breath mattered.

Kiyoshi was interrupted by a loud knock. He opened his eyes, and the temporary peace he had felt was gone faster than a hawk released from its cage. The knock was repeated, and his name was called loudly through the door. It was late at night. Kiyoshi's heart sank. Had it finally happened?

He answered, almost getting struck as the red-faced messenger was about to rap the door again.

"Sorry, sir, but you need to come with me. The king is dying."

Kiyoshi ran through the halls of the castle, each passageway a familiar nightmare. He always thought he had more time, but if this was it, he wasn't ready. The Kingdom wasn't ready. Masaki had to live.

The messenger didn't take Kiyoshi to the king's quarters, which surprised him. At this time of the night, what had Masaki been up to? The question ran through Kiyoshi's mind again and again. They eventually skidded to a stop outside of the king's practice chambers. Despite the terror running through his heart, Kiyoshi managed the slightest smile. This was just like the Masaki he once knew, practicing his martial skills this late into the evening.

Kiyoshi's heart sank even farther when he saw the king lying on the ground, his body tense. Masaki's doctor was present, but the look he gave Kiyoshi wasn't reassuring.

Kiyoshi sprinted in and knelt down next to his friend. "What happened?"

The doctor spoke. "He was in here practicing with the sword. According to his guards, everything seemed fine until he suddenly collapsed. My guess is he overexerted himself and his body couldn't take the strain."

Kiyoshi studied the king's body as he listened to the doctor's report. "What have you tried?"

The doctor shook his head. "Nothing, yet. Were it up to me, I would give him a sedative and try to help him rest, but I'm not sure there's anything my medicines can do. You and I both know how far the illness has come."

Kiyoshi hated that the doctor was right.

"Prepare a sedative. If I heal him, he's going to need to rest to recover. Otherwise, keep this room silent. I must focus."

Kiyoshi put his hands on the king, one on Masaki's forehead and one on his chest. He closed his eyes and opened up his sense.

The transition, made hundreds of times by Kiyoshi, was effortless. He was no longer just one person, but two people at once. He used his sense to explore the king's body. The first abnormality he noticed was in the king's head. The flow of energy was disrupted, blocked. This was what had caused Masaki to collapse and still threatened his life. Kiyoshi didn't bother scanning the rest of the body. He knew the king better than the king knew himself, and he realized immediately he had found the cause. He focused his energy on Masaki's head, giving some of his own energy to tear the blockage apart.

Kiyoshi knew he was witnessing a blood clot in the brain, and as his healing broke the clot apart, he kept his focus on the smaller pieces, ensuring they disappeared completely. If a remaining bit lodged in the king's brain, he was certain it would be the end. Once the detritus was dissolved, he honed in on where the clot had formed, focusing his energy on healing the area. The work was delicate and painstaking, but Kiyoshi was in his element, and he refused to give up.

When he was satisfied he had tended to the king's brain as much as he could, Kiyoshi scanned the rest of Masaki's body. Everything else felt normal, or at least as normal as it typically was. Kiyoshi spent some of his time fighting the growth in the king's stomach, but he could tell he was losing his focus. He elected instead to give as much of his energy to Masaki as he could.

More than anything, this lack of energy kept the king spiraling downward. His will to live had diminished day by day, and with very little now left, only his responsibility to the Kingdom kept him tethered to life, and that was a thin strand. Kiyoshi gave Masaki what energy he could, which felt meager. Kiyoshi wasn't young anymore, and only had but so much of his own strength to give.

When he was done, he opened his eyes. Masaki looked healthier and more relaxed, but Kiyoshi knew they were fighting a losing battle.

"Give him the sedative and get him to his bed. He shouldn't be disturbed for at least a day, but he should live."

The doctor's relief was palpable, but Kiyoshi didn't stay to hear his gratitude. Every part of his body ached, and he knew he didn't have many healings of that magnitude left in his body. He stumbled back to his room, his body held up by the messenger who had come to get him in the first place. He soon let go of the aide and collapsed onto his bed, and the world immediately went black.

Chapter 10

Asa rubbed her forehead, trying to ease the strain she felt there. She had learned to read as part of her nightblade training, but she hadn't ever had to put the skill to such intense use. Papers surrounded her as she sat in the same archives she had broken into. She shifted her weight, and her body reminded her she had been sitting in one place for too long. She stood up to take a short walk around the archives.

When she left the room, she was surprised to find night had fallen. An old dayblade, one of the keepers of the archives, gave her a friendly smile. "Are you done for today?"

"I didn't realize it had gotten so late."

The dayblade laughed. "It's not time to be buried in books. A sensible young person should either be drunk or asleep."

Although the comment was meant in jest, Asa felt a truth to what the keeper said. A break sounded like a good idea. "From now on, you should come get me when it gets dark out."

The old man laughed again. "I did come to get you. I even came in the room and called your name. But you were so engrossed in your work, you didn't even notice me. I figured I'd let you keep working."

Asa was touched by the old man's kindness, but also concerned by what his words really meant. She was a nightblade who hadn't sensed someone in the same room. She had gotten so wrapped up in her study, she had opened herself up to danger. Mentally chastising herself, she replied, "Thank you. I will pack things up for today and return tomorrow."

Soon Asa was outside the archives, breathing in the fresh air of early summer. Even though the moon was already high in the sky, the evening was still warm.

She walked to her quarters slowly, her mind wandering over all the information she'd learned. Osamu had to be one of the most interesting people who had ever lived, but information on him was in short supply. He had been obsessed with anonymity when he had been active, and it seemed as though he had been through the archives himself, destroying major records of his life before he disappeared. All Asa could do was piece together parts of his history from secondhand accounts and educated guesswork.

Osamu had been a nightblade of extraordinary skill. Everyone who encountered him agreed on that point. Not only was he an expert in swordsmanship; he seemed to have an innate grasp of battlefield command. His units were never ambushed and always had the upper hand. Even reading some of the secondhand accounts, Asa was impressed by what Osamu was capable of. He was physically skilled, but from what she understood, his ability with the sense also exceeded anyone else's she had ever known.

In one account, a fellow nightblade spoke with unabashed admiration as she described Osamu commanding a small group of soldiers in a larger battle. In the midst of combat, he had sensed a flanking maneuver, thus enabling his warriors to turn the tide of the battle.

Asa couldn't even imagine this level of control over the sense. In her combat experience her sense was limited to ten to fifteen paces. Osamu had demonstrated an ability to take in far more information than Asa had ever dreamed of trying to consume at once. She realized that even if she met the blade, she wasn't sure she'd be able to defeat him.

After the massacre there had been a few sightings of Osamu, including his appearances in Starfall. Asa assumed he was trying to erase any record of his presence. And then, after just a few moons, he was gone. No one saw him again, even though the blades had launched the biggest manhunt in their history.

The common assumption was that Osamu had committed suicide, a tempting theory that Asa couldn't accept. This was a man who had been on top of the world. From what she understood, he had been supremely patriotic, willing to make any sacrifice for the Kingdom. That, along with his skill, was the primary reason he had been selected to attack Two Falls and end the blade rebellion. He wouldn't kill himself.

Asa assumed Osamu was still alive. If that were true, she had to put herself in his place and try to figure out what he would do. But she didn't understand him well enough. Although Osamu had been famous once, he had also been a private person, and when she had asked Hajimi if she could speak to blades who knew him, he said there wasn't anyone he could recommend. Plenty had come across Osamu, but no one had called him friend.

There was only one lead left, found in a genealogical chart buried deep in the archives, but Asa wasn't hopeful. Osamu had a brother, a man who lived in Haven, where they had grown up together before Osamu was identified as gifted and placed in a nightblade training camp. Although the blades didn't keep detailed records of civilians, he might still be alive. Additionally, Osamu had spent a fair amount of time in Haven. The city was big enough to hide in. Perhaps that was where he had returned. Her lead was thin, but it was the best she could do, and the archives no longer held any secrets.

By the time she returned to her bunk, Asa had made up her mind. In the morning she would go to Hajimi and report her findings. After that, her next step was on to the road once again. She would go to Haven and try to find Osamu's brother, or anyone else who knew the legendary blade. If she could understand him, perhaps she could hunt him.

Once Asa decided to travel to Haven, she had little to do but prepare and leave. Asa couldn't remember the last time she had slept in a place she considered home. Her journey had taken her across the Kingdom several times, and she never stayed long in one place. She required little time to gather her few belongings and find transportation to Haven.

Before she left, she spoke with Hajimi to keep him updated on her progress and plan. It was a formality she preferred not to bother with, but he had helped her with her mission, and she felt like she owed him the courtesy.

Asa bartered for transportation with a moderately sized caravan heading for Haven. The services of a nightblade were always in demand, and while Hajimi had provided her with enough money to purchase transportation, she was naturally frugal and preferred to save what currency she had for more urgent situations. She was an old hand at exchanging her services for transport and bartered for a seat in a wagon as well as meals provided in promise of her protection on the journey.

As soon as the caravan left, Asa tried to reconstruct everything she knew in her mind. After all this time, the cycles spent searching, she had a feeling she was finally getting close. Osamu would pay for his actions.

Asa's mind wandered, and she paid only a little attention to her surroundings. The roads were muddy from recent rainstorms, and the wagons gouged deep tracks in the road. Besides small villages and farmland, there was little to see. She had promised protection, and there was a chance she would be needed, but the odds were small. Asa wasn't sure how many nightblades were active in the Kingdom, but at least hundreds wandered to and fro throughout the land, keeping roads and paths safe for travelers. Besides that, the Kingdom was largely prosperous, with little need for people to resort to thievery. Most bandits had been pushed to the edges of the Kingdom.

The caravan had been on the road for several days before Asa realized that something wasn't right. She noticed it first as a feeling, a tension in the faces of the people the travelers passed. When the caravan passed through villages, instead of being greeted by a boisterous crowd, they were met only by merchants who had need of their wares. Asa wondered how many villages they had passed where she hadn't even noticed this dynamic, too distracted by her own thoughts.

After Asa observed the third quiet village in a row, curiosity got the better of her. She made her way to the front of the caravan and spoke with the owner, the merchant she had bartered with originally.

"Greetings, nightblade," the merchant said. Asa, now that she was paying attention, noticed that even the merchant seemed on edge.

"The mood of the villages we pass is tense, but I have heard no news," Asa said.

The merchant looked somewhat taken aback. At night, when they made camp, Asa sat far away from the others, far away from the fire. It was too hard for her to use her sense when she was near people, and at night, the sense was a far better method than sight for noticing danger. But the merchant hadn't gathered that because of this, Asa wouldn't know what was happening in the world.

"The news isn't good. The king has taken ill. They say he lives, but he does not wake up, and there is no telling how much longer he will draw breath."

"Has a successor been named?"

The merchant shook his head. "The Kingdom is stuck between a dying king and three lords. There are many rumors, but I'm not sure what is true. The best I can tell is that no decision has been made. The lords are all in Haven at the moment, probably arguing with one another over who will become the next ruler, but none has been named that I know. If the king doesn't wake up, I fear what will happen next. The Kingdom hasn't been through anything like this in many lifetimes."

Asa remembered her history well. The last time a monarch had died without an heir, he had been a young king, not even alive long enough to marry. Asa had been taught that the nightblades were the only reason the various lords hadn't descended to war. The blades kept the peace, forcing the lords to negotiate and decide who would be next in line.

But the blades didn't have the same authority they once had. Much of the problem could be traced back, again, to the massacre at Two Falls. The public outcry had been tremendous. Nightblades had decimated an entire village and razed it to the ground, and the prince had died. Never before in memory had such a deed happened, and with that event, the public attitude toward the blades changed.

Once, blades had been heroes to the people, almost godlike, treated with respect and awe. But after Two Falls, the public realized that the power that kept common folk safe for so long might one day be turned against them. As a result, the lords passed laws limiting the power of the blades. For the first time in Kingdom history, the blades became subject to the same laws as ordinary citizens.

It began with the census, undertaken when Asa was young. Her mother had hid her far away from civilization for a time, so she hadn't been counted. But the census was an act by King Masaki to ease the fears of the people. The move made him look as if he were acting to check the power of the blades, and as the cycles wore on, the constraints against the gifted became more and more strict.

Asa often wondered why the blades didn't just revolt. Asa had known her fair share of blades over the course of her short life, and in her experience, they were mostly decent men and women. If they took over the Kingdom, it would be in everyone's best interest.

But the Council of the Blades was comprised of honorable blades who followed the king's orders, as they always had. They might chafe under certain restrictions, but they would obey. They believed, at least for now, that was how they could best serve the Kingdom. Asa disagreed, but ultimately she didn't care enough to get involved in political matters. All she wanted was to find Osamu.

The caravan was back on the road, and as they got closer to Haven, they were joined by more people wandering in the same direction.

Despite Masaki's illness, or perhaps because of it, trade was brisk. Everyone wanted to get their goods sold in Haven before the king died and uncertainty became the order of the day.

Because of the crowds, Asa had to be more aware. When they were in remote parts of the Kingdom, she could easily use the sense to discover anyone approaching. But in crowds, security became more difficult. All her attention was required to ensure the caravan stayed together and wasn't infiltrated by strangers.

A strange unease settled over Asa. Something tickled at the edges of her awareness, something that wasn't quite as it should be. As the day dragged, Asa became more certain her shadow was following her. She couldn't quite pinpoint him, but with all her recent experiences, she was learning to trust her instincts. She let her sense wander freely, taking in the surrounding life. Then she felt the hole, the place where life should be, but wasn't.

He wasn't trying to use the sense. As close as he was, it would have been a dead giveaway. But all life moved around him, and if the spot had been stationary, Asa might have assumed it was a rock. But the hole moved, and people moved around it. Asa opened her eyes, careful not to give any indication she had felt him.

Asa no longer felt any danger from the tracker. If he wanted her dead, he'd certainly had plenty of opportunities. With his ability to hide from her sense, Asa wasn't even sure there was anything she could do if he wanted to kill her. She was certain he was a shadow, hired by someone to follow her.

Asa turned the problem over in her mind. She wanted to interrogate him, but he held all the advantages. He could sense her, and she could only sense him indirectly. Under most circumstances, she wouldn't have a chance. But there had to be a way. Asa thought through the problem until an idea occurred to her.

—

Deception was the first step. The next time the caravan came to rest, Asa called for a bottle of wine, and although the merchant was wary of providing his protection drink, he brought one over. She assumed the shadow following the caravan was close enough to see her. With so many people on the road, it was the only way to ensure he didn't lose her.

As she drank, she allowed her sense to fade and return, as though she was having trouble maintaining her focus. When her sense was out, she allowed herself to stay relaxed, visually examining the surrounding area. She didn't want the shadow to have any warning, but she needed to keep an eye on the caravan. The merchant deserved that much at least.

The caravan continued on, and the sun was falling when Asa finally found the building she was looking for in an approaching village. It was a two-story inn, typical of the area. The wooden walls stretched upward, topped with a slanted roof that Asa noticed was missing a few plaster tiles. She went up to the merchant to speak and received a lucky break. The merchant was planning on stopping at the inn for the evening meal without any intervention from Asa.

As the caravan came to a stop, Asa helped with the horses. Although she wasn't drunk in the least, she added just a little sway to her gait. She needed the shadow to feel comfortable, to move in a little closer. Although she was tempted, she didn't check her surroundings. She didn't want the shadow to have any clue she was aware of him this time.

After the horses were taken care of, Asa stumbled into the inn. Once she did, she cut herself off from her sense completely, something she always hated doing, like she was taking off a warm and comforting cloak. Her other five senses didn't feel like they gave her any real information at all.

When she wasn't extending her sense, her presence would feel much the same as anyone else's. Asa was betting the shadow didn't know her well enough to sense her presence in a crowd. He would have gotten used to tracking her by sensing her power, not her actual presence.

To make the shadow's work even harder, Asa went from crowd to crowd in the inn. She didn't mingle, but moved in and out of groups, appearing as natural as possible and remaining patient. It didn't seem likely the shadow would come into the inn. Asa knew what he looked like, and he would want to remain hidden. He would stay outside the main entrance, waiting.

Her actions brought back a flash of memory from her days of training. Her masters had ordered her to track a single person while engaging in combat, a drill to test her use of the sense, and she had failed miserably. She had tracked her target well, but once others started attacking with wooden swords, her target slipped away. Even worse, because she was trying to focus on the target, she had taken several painful hits from the swords. She only hoped her own ruse would be as successful.

Eventually Asa worked her way upstairs. She had no way of knowing if the shadow could track her or not anymore, but she had to hope. Once upstairs, she continued her mingling, trying to hide her presence as well as possible. Mostly, she avoided windows, but every once in a while, she would drift close to one just to look outside.

First, the shadow had to believe Asa would let down her guard near the inn. Second, he had to lose her presence in the inn, and finally, he needed to keep most of his attention on the first floor. It had always been Asa's experience that people hesitated to look up. Most people were far too focused on the ground in front of their feet.

On one of her passes near a window, she saw that her plan had worked. Outside the inn, reclining on a hay bale, was her shadow, focused on the exit of the inn. Asa grinned. She needed answers, and she believed her shadow was somehow linked to Osamu. Did the old blade know she was getting closer? If so, she would question the shadow and be one step further.

Asa sprinted toward the window and jumped out.

She had always loved jumping off things. Growing up, sometimes in the rare moments her brother wasn't focused on keeping the farm going, they would climb trees together and leap. As she got older, she was able to jump from higher places. She learned how to land and roll, avoiding injury. Today, that training paid off.

Asa landed on her feet, rolled over her shoulder, and came back to her feet at a full sprint. The shadow was on his feet in an instant. He turned to run down a narrow passage between two buildings, but he had made it only a few steps before Asa caught him. She tackled the shadow, and they went down together in a pile of arms and legs.

Asa was initially on top, but the shadow drove an elbow into her face, knocking her to the side. In the narrow passage, there was no space for her to roll, and she crashed into the side of the building. The shadow struggled to rise, but Asa regained her wits and wrapped her arms around his ankles, causing him to crash down again.

The shadow tried to kick at her, but Asa's grip was too tight. Her mind raced. She needed to find a way to overpower the shadow for interrogation.

In a desperate heave, Asa pulled herself up the shadow's body, reaching for any handhold. She managed to wrap her hand in his clothing and pull herself up farther. He tried to elbow her in the head, but with her newly freed arm, she was able to deflect the attack.

After a moment of struggling, Asa was again on top of the shadow, letting her weight settle over his hips, trying to pin him down. For a moment she was balanced and drove an elbow into his face, feeling a satisfying crunch as her blow landed.

The shadow managed to plant his feet on the ground and thrust his hips into the air. Asa, unprepared for the sudden shift in weight, was thrown forward, losing all grip on her opponent. She rolled forward and back to her feet, turning around just as the shadow got to his own feet, his back to her. He was about to run again.

Asa grabbed his left shoulder, and in response, his left arm came snapping back in an effort to knock her down. Asa saw the blow coming and stopped it with her own left arm. She slid her right hand, which had been on the shadow's shoulder, down to his elbow. She shoved with all her body weight, locking his joint and throwing him into the building.

At least that had been her plan. The shadow rotated, turning his torso toward her. Instead of slamming face-first into the building, his back crashed into the wall. They stood there, facing each other. Asa was angry, furious at being followed for so long, but the shadow seemed to be enjoying himself.

Asa's mind raced. If it came down to a matter of strength, she was going to lose.

The shadow planted one of his feet against the building and, with a strong shove, reversed their positions. Now Asa was pinned to the opposite wall, with the shadow's body stretched across the narrow opening, his feet on the wall he had once been pinned against.

Despite her situation, Asa was amazed at the shadow's skill. She had never seen anyone use their environment so well.

In her moment of distraction, the shadow's grip on Asa's hands changed, and he had one hand on her wrist and another on her elbow. The shadow twisted, his body parallel to the ground, forcing Asa's elbow up and her wrist down. A classic throw, but Asa had never even considered the move as a possibility in such narrow circumstances. If she didn't want to break her arm, she had only one choice—to be thrown. She launched herself into the throw, trying to roll out smoothly.

Unfortunately, the shadow's grip on her wrist was strong. His move caused him to crash down as well, but he still controlled her wrist and, with a firm grip, kept her on the ground for a moment while he regained his balance. Asa saw his face, just for a heartbeat, and the man looked almost sad to see the fight had come to an end.

The shadow drove his fist into Asa's stomach, and all the breath was driven from her. He immediately let go, and Asa doubled over as she sucked and sucked, trying to get air back into her body. As soon as she did, a wave of coughing ran through her form, and the agony of the shadow's punch took a few moments to subside.

Asa struggled to her feet and looked around. Her shadow was gone.

Chapter 11

Minori meandered the dark streets of Haven, lost in thought although there was plenty to observe. Shin's troops seemed to be everywhere, many more than the small personal guard the lord had claimed to summon. But Shin was a concern for another day.

Minori was thinking about the blades. He had served as a blade for more than forty cycles, and in that time he had seen both the best and the worst of his peers. When he was feeling charitable, he could see Kiyoshi's perspective. The blades, for all their strength, made mistakes.

Despite that, blades were still better leaders, and that was where he and Kiyoshi separated. They had been forged in a kind of training civilians would never understand. Minori would choose a foolish blade over a wise merchant any day.

It was his purpose to bring order and direction to his community of warriors and healers. The main problem blades faced, Minori believed, was that they had an amazing amount of power but no way of focusing it. Since they were distributed throughout the Kingdom, their influence didn't present a threat to any of the lords or the Kingdom itself. But because the blades were so widely spread, they couldn't bring about change, either.

Minori didn't like to admit it, but he was an optimist. He believed the blades, given the proper leeway, could change the Kingdom. They could bring a lasting order, making war and conflict a distant memory.

But the blades needed unity, and for them to achieve that, Minori knew they would have to walk through flames.

Minori traced over his train of thought, as he often did, just to ensure there were no mistakes in his logic. The first premise he held to was that the power of the blades gave them an independent attitude—only natural. Even the dayblades had the power of life and death, as Kiyoshi had so kindly reminded him earlier. Therefore, the traditional means of exerting power, such as overwhelming force, weren't applicable to the blades. They needed to be ruled by consent.

The second premise followed from the first. To gain the consent of the blades, Minori needed an issue to rally the blades around, an issue to convince them that the current system was broken and they needed another. Fortunately, Kiyoshi had dropped just such an issue in his lap with the order to kill Koji.

This was related to Minori's third premise. The blades were honorable people, much to the benefit of the Kingdom. But they were also proud, and there was a limit to which their pride could be swallowed. Being counted was one thing; being asked to kill your peer was another entirely. The blades were already upset about Koji's sentence, but with a little prodding, he could push them further. He needed to play to their honor and their pride. If he did, he would have their consent. With their consent he could guide them and focus their strength, and the gifted would take the place of authority so long denied to them.

Tonight was an experiment to test Minori's ideas. Koji, faithful as he was, had already laid the groundwork. Despite the reward on his head, he had traveled through Haven, letting other blades know what Minori had done for him. A risky move, but Minori needed Koji's help. Simply bragging about his work wouldn't get him anywhere. But Koji was living proof, a blade with a bounty on his head.

Koji's information had brought Minori to a darker section of Haven, a section rarely frequented by the well-to-do. Here the streets weren't well lit, and the buildings cast deep shadows to hide any number of illicit activities. Minori walked calmly through the middle of the road, his sense alert. He was wearing the robes of a nightblade, and it would be a very courageous—or very drunk—criminal who would dare attempt anything against his person.

Minori remembered a time when blades had interacted with the people on a daily basis, a time when a blade could enter an inn and attract little more notice than a well-known local musician. But after the massacre, those times had ended. Awe and respect had turned to fear, and although a blade was never refused at an inn, they certainly weren't welcome.

Because of this, special places had been created, places where blades could congregate without disturbing the people. Unfortunately, those places were often located in neighborhoods like this. Minori was furious that the blades would allow themselves to be treated thus.

The building he was looking for didn't have any external markings, and a casual glance wouldn't have revealed anything remarkable. It was a place that served blades, and the venue didn't feel any need to advertise its presence. Minori's sense came alive as he felt so many others like him, those with power and strength.

Minori paused for a moment before entering. Part of him wondered if this was the most reasonable course of action. His hand came to the door, but he didn't open it. Anyone watching would have wondered what was going through his mind. Then Minori opened the door.

At first, no one paid any attention to him. Everyone in the room had felt his presence outside, so no one was the least bit surprised to see the door open and a blade step through. Minori's eyes scanned the room. A small fire was in the back corner, lighting the space and the almost dozen bodies inside. Most of the patrons were nightblades, but a few dayblades were scattered among the tables. Other than its clientele, the bar could have been any bar in the Kingdom. Cups in various stages of emptiness sat around the tables, and assorted games of chance were being played.

A nightblade near the back of the room glanced at Minori, and he saw a flicker of recognition pass across the woman's face. Minori didn't recognize her, though. The nightblade stood, an action that focused the attention of everyone in the room. The quiet din became silent as the two blades took each other's measure. Minori recognized the dynamic. Whoever the nightblade was, she was a respected member, a leader of this community.

Slowly the blade reached down, and for a moment, Minori wondered if she was going to draw her sword. But the nightblade grabbed her cup and raised it to the ceiling. One by one, the other blades in the room raised their cups. Some apparently recognized Minori, while others seemed more likely to have just been following suit.

The nightblade spoke, her voice clear throughout the small room. "To the man who saved Koji's life."

At that, everyone's attitude seemed to change, transforming from neutral to friendly in just a moment. "To our brother."

Everyone drank, and the nightblade who had led the toast made her way between the tightly crowded tables to greet their champion. Minori bowed to her. Perhaps this would be easier than he thought.

He spoke, his voice casual. "Friend, I'm afraid you have me at a loss."

The nightblade answered, "My name is Akane. It is a pleasure to meet you in person."

Minori considered his options. He had come to the bar hoping to find a friendly ear. He hadn't expected such a warm welcome. Koji had laid the groundwork of his plan better than Minori had dared to hope. He rolled the dice.

"Koji told me this was a good place to find a drink. A place with strong blades. But I didn't expect such a welcome."

The nightblade led Minori to a table and ordered two drinks. "There are many who feel these are dark times. Your actions are a light to us."

"There are those who don't feel that way."

Akane looked as though she were ready to spit on the ground. "Kiyoshi is a fool. He hopes to placate the lords, but they will never be satisfied. They will take and take from us until we have nothing left to give."

Minori nodded. "I agree. Kiyoshi is a good man, but misguided."

"You are far more charitable than I. He was willing to let one of us die for the whim of a lord. There is no strength, no honor, in that behavior. But you, you are a different story."

Minori didn't respond, wondering what the nightblade was getting at.

"Koji told us what you did. He told us how you snuck into the prison and helped him escape. That, friend, was an act of courage, strength, and honor. All of us were taught not to leave our brothers and sisters behind on the battlefield, and you didn't. That's a true leader, one we would look up to."

Minori bowed. "Your words flatter me and are kinder than I perhaps deserve. It is no more than I'd do for any blade."

Akane was far bolder than Minori expected, and Minori wondered how deep the nightblade was into her cups. "Koji also tells us that you were sent here by the council to replace Kiyoshi."

Minori let a frown develop on his face. "Koji is a little off. I have the backing of the council and I was sent to advise the king, but I was never supposed to replace Kiyoshi. More like balance him out."

This time, Akane did spit on the ground. "If you ask me, you should replace him. Someone needs to remind the lords and the king that we are here as the protectors of the Kingdom, not their enemies."

Minori knew he would never have a better chance. He leaned forward, and Akane mirrored his action instinctively. "Sister, I am glad you think so. I fear the time is coming when the blades will have to choose sides. When that day comes, will you be there for me?"

Akane didn't hesitate. "My blade is yours, yours and the council's. As it always has been."

"Thank you. Will you find others, others who will stand up for the blades?"

Akane agreed, and Minori was done at the bar. However, because he wanted to maintain good form, he stayed for a while longer, drinking and allowing himself to be introduced to other blades. He memorized everything, knowing the warriors and healers in the bar were some of the first he'd be able to rely on.

Conflict was coming, and he wanted to have the strongest allies at his side.

Minori wasn't sure what to make of his first impression of Asa. Hajimi had sent the young nightblade to him hoping he would lend her a hand on her personal quest. Hajimi, foolish as he was, apparently somehow thought that tracking down Osamu was worth someone's time. Minori hadn't heard that name in cycles and would have been perfectly content to never hear it again. The mere mention of Osamu brought a wave of bile to his throat. But Asa had made her way to Haven, and now she was another problem he had to deal with.

He studied her again, wondering what he had missed. On the surface, she seemed almost entirely unremarkable. She was short, but not substantially below the average height of women in the Kingdom. Although her robes draped over her body, Minori could tell she was strong. Even in his old age, though, he suspected he would be able to overpower her. Battles with a sword rarely came down to strength, but if they did, she would be at a disadvantage.

If she had anything to recommend her, it was her appearance. Asa was one of the most attractive nightblades Minori could remember meeting. There was a stereotype, and Minori accepted it, that most nightblade women tended to pay little attention to their looks. As a nightblade, one's identity was formed around swordsmanship. Most women—and men—focused on that to the exclusion of everything else. Asa was different. Although she didn't strike Minori as vain, she clearly spent some energy every day combing her hair. A clue, but of what, Minori couldn't guess. Perhaps it was just an indicator of her past. Minori knew she had joined the blades far later than most. Maybe she had developed habits living among civilians that had carried over to her life as a blade.

Regardless, Minori was sure he was missing something. If someone was tracking Osamu over twenty cycles after he had disappeared from the face of the earth, that implied a certain dedication, a focus that he didn't yet see in the young lady who stood before him. Her eyes darted about frequently, but not because she was checking her surroundings. She seemed impatient and uncaring.

Koji had let her into Minori's study, and still he stood behind her, his stance relaxed and ready. Minori took a deep breath. Koji was one of the greatest assets he could have asked for, but the boy had literally pledged his life to Minori. Unless he was explicitly dismissed, he stayed for every audience, guarding his savior.

Minori shook his head. He had to stop his mind from wandering. The silence had settled over the room for long enough and didn't seem to be having any effect on Asa.

"Asa, it is a pleasure to meet you. Hajimi told me I could expect you."

Asa's gaze fixed on him, and for a single moment, Minori thought he saw a spark in her eyes. There was a fire there, but well hidden.

Who was this woman?

"Did you know Osamu?" she asked.

The question caught Minori off guard, with both its bluntness and its directness. In polite company, the question would have been considered unforgivably rude. Surprised, Minori listened to himself answer honestly.

"I did. Well, at least as well as anyone knew Osamu."

Asa's entire expression seemed to change, and Minori saw for the first time the focus that drove this woman. She formed a query with her gaze, piercing Minori and making him uncomfortable. He wondered at the change in her, but he had already started down this path and would have to continue. Minori's mind wandered back through his long, long history as a nightblade, and he debated what he should tell her. The fact was, Minori didn't want her to find Osamu. But he needed to give her enough information to leave him alone. Far more important matters were at stake.

"You've probably already figured much of this out, but Osamu was the legend of our time. It is only because of Two Falls that his name will be struck from the record of history. If not for that decision, every young nightblade would want to be him, and even civilians would dream of his exploits."

Minori's answer didn't seem to satisfy Asa at all, but he hadn't thought it would. "What was he like?" she asked.

Minori wondered about the easiest way to answer that question. Osamu had been a lot of things. "If there was one quality that made him stand out, it was his focus. Osamu was a patriot, the type you never see anymore. He was fiercely loyal, both to the king and to the Kingdom. He and the prince were close friends, and had Yoshi lived, Osamu undoubtedly would have been his top adviser.

"But Osamu was single-minded. There are all sorts of theories for why he always hid his face, you know. Some people said he was disfigured. Others claimed he was so attractive no one took him seriously. But those are silly. The reason he hid his face was because it wasn't about him. He didn't want the attention he received, even before Two Falls. For him, his life was all about the Kingdom. He would have done anything for the Kingdom. And he did."

Minori was lost in thought, memories coming and going through his mind. The girl was sending him on a trip he'd rather not take.

"I take it Hajimi allowed you into the archives? You know everything Osamu did?"

Asa nodded.

"If there was ever a man who would do everything that was necessary, it was Osamu. Not only was he strong, but he believed. That, more than anything, was why he was chosen to lead the Two Falls expedition."

Another silence fell over the room. Minori hadn't meant to say so much about Osamu, but even the mention of the name evoked strong feelings. It had been a long time, but apparently not long enough.

Asa broke the silence. "What do you think happened to him?"

Minori laughed. "Oh, if only you knew how many times I've been asked that question. The truth is, I really don't know. Osamu was a singular man, and many enemies rejoined the Great Cycle because they thought they could predict him."

"Do you think he killed himself?"

Minori wasn't thinking, lost in memories and emotions. "I know he didn't."

Asa's attention was piqued, and the elder blade immediately realized his mistake.

"How do you know?"

Minori studied the young girl. She had already gotten far more out of him than he should have said. Her eyes were focused on him, and he knew that if he lied or misled her, she would keep hounding him until she was satisfied. Minori cursed himself. He had dug himself into a hole. The only way to be left alone was to tell her enough of the truth to get her to leave.

"Because he believed he was right in what he did at Two Falls. I can guarantee that if you find him, he'll tell you as much. He may regret having to do what he did, but if you ask him, he'll tell you he'd do it again. He would never take his own life because he doesn't believe his honor was tarnished by his actions. The only way he would have killed himself was if the king asked him to, but the king never did. Thus, he didn't."

Asa's next question was also unspoken, but her gaze said more than enough: How could Minori know this?

He sighed. He hated giving out more information, but there was only one way forward.

"I was there, at Two Falls. Osamu was unrepentant about the massacre."

Asa's eyes narrowed, and Minori would have given anything to know what was going through her mind at that moment. Something he had said was wrong, and he wondered what she knew that he didn't.

Minori felt a sudden and strong urge to end this audience. From the beginning, it hadn't gone as he wanted.

Fortunately, Asa seemed to have come to the same conclusion. She had learned something, and Minori suspected her discovery was because he had said too much. The new information was enough for her to continue on, so perhaps that was a small benefit.

They exchanged the necessary pleasantries, and Koji escorted Asa out. Minori noticed how his young aide couldn't take his eyes off her. He fought the urge to roll his eyes. If he was right about Asa, she wasn't the sort of woman who accepted many, if any, advances.

After she left, the room was empty, and Minori ran his hands through his beard, wondering what had just transpired. Was Asa a threat? If she was stirring up the past, she might raise a hornet's nest. Minori exhaled, undecided as to what to do next.

As Minori turned the corner on the way to Shin's castle, he couldn't help but think about how different Lord Shin's estate was from the bars where he had been meeting with nightblades. The taverns were dark, unmarked, small. Even if the blades weren't criminals, it felt that way walking into one of their establishments. Shin's palace in Haven, on the other hand, was as ostentatious as a building could be.

Minori was admitted to the grounds without problem. There was plenty to dislike about Shin, but he ran a well-organized household and lands. Minori believed you could tell how people would handle great responsibility by how they handled small ones. Based on what he observed around the household, Minori had little doubt Shin would be a strong leader. Since their unofficial alliance two moons ago, Minori had come to genuinely believe Shin was the best choice to be the next king.

One of the household guards informed Minori that Shin was taking his daily walk through his gardens. The guard gave Minori directions, which he followed, finding the lord without difficulty. On the way, he passed what had to be dozens of guards. Minori noted it. He suspected Shin had more troops in Haven than he was claiming, but this was the first direct evidence he had gathered.

Minori bowed deeply to the lord, who returned the bow. He gestured for Minori to join him.

He remembered when Hajimi had first sent him to Haven, apologizing for sending Minori away from his gardens. Minori hadn't minded that much, but there had been a grain of truth in Hajimi's statement. Minori did love gardens. He loved the peace a well-maintained garden radiated, which let his troubled heart beat easily. He well understood why Shin would take a daily walk.

For a few moments, Minori allowed himself to forget the concerns of the day. Shin wouldn't discuss matters of importance on his walk, and Minori was comfortable in the silence. They strolled the gardens, taking time to pause at various points. Minori looked down and saw the path they walked was well worn.

The garden was exquisite. One section was a small bamboo grove, which swallowed the sun and sound. The two men stood silently, and Minori studied the placement of the bamboo. At times, he imagined there was a larger pattern, but recognizing the pattern remained elusively out of his grasp. As they continued, they came upon a small rock garden, formed around three larger stones. The sight captured Minori's attention. The three stones could only represent the three lords or the three great houses. He looked for a message, some symbolism that would help him understand Shin better, but again understanding eluded him. Regardless, when they finished their walk, Minori felt a sense of peace he hadn't felt since leaving Starfall. He thanked Shin.

The two men sat down in a teahouse adjoining the garden. Shin poured the tea and made an observation.

"Minori, although we haven't known each other long, I don't think I have ever seen such pleasure on your face."

Minori acknowledged the statement. "One of the most significant sacrifices I made in coming to Haven was abandoning my garden in Starfall. It pales in comparison to what you've shown me today, but still, it provided a measure of peace."

"You are welcome to come and walk my gardens at any time. If another can gain the same peace from the gardens as I do, I happily offer them to you."

It was a kind offer, which Minori accepted. He sipped at his tea, recognizing it would be rude to discuss business so soon.

After enough pleasantries were exchanged, Minori updated Shin on his progress. Minori's nights had been as full as his days, and he had started to gain a more complete picture of where the blades stood on the events of the day.

Shin's primary question was very direct. "Should the worst come to pass and force become necessary, how will the blades respond?"

Minori handled the question gently. "The blades do not act as a unified whole, one of our greatest weaknesses. A great deal will depend on Kiyoshi. There are many blades who despise the actions he has taken but would still hesitate to go against him directly. Although he is losing support among both nightblades and dayblades, he does have a small, loyal following that could interfere with a smooth transfer of power. That being said, I now believe most blades will support whomever I back."

"Even if it comes to force?"

"Yes. There is a great deal of discontent with the current state of affairs. Word has spread that you will treat the blades differently, and many will fight for that opportunity."

Shin nodded.

"There is one other challenge I would like to discuss with you."

Shin's face was a mask as Minori continued.

"A while ago a new nightblade came into town. She has the backing of the council, and I'm afraid that if her mission succeeds, I will become a liability to our plans."

Shin frowned. He clearly wanted more of an explanation, but Minori was loath to give him one. When it was clear Minori wasn't going to say more without prompting, Shin replied, "Why can't you take care of this?"

"I've built my goodwill on standing up for the rights of blades. Even my closest advisers would abandon me if I sent someone after one of our own."

Shin gazed out into his gardens, contemplating the consequences of his actions.

"Very well. I have a unit that has been specially training for such a purpose. She's alone?"

Minori nodded, relief flooding through his body. A part of him felt sorry for Asa, but she was swimming in waters far deeper than she understood, and Minori had no choice. Thankfully, she would soon cease to be a thorn in his side.

Chapter 12

Kiyoshi was deep inside a world that few people understood. His mind and energy traveled pathways closed to all but those whom fate selected. He could sense the king's energy and feel the blockage in his mind and stomach. Healing the mind was delicate work, work that few of his peers would have even considered doing. If the consequences weren't so dangerous, even Kiyoshi would have held back. But he had no choice.

First among Kiyoshi's thoughts was that even the power of the dayblades had limits, limits that were far too apparent to him today. While the dayblades could extend life, they couldn't defeat death. Sooner or later, the body gave out, and a person rejoined the Great Cycle.

Gently, as though he were trying to open a door without the owner knowing he was there, Kiyoshi focused his attention on Masaki's mind. He knew if Masaki had been able to speak to him, the king would have ordered Kiyoshi to let him die. Kiyoshi knew he went against the king's wishes, but they needed him alive, at least for a while longer. As soon as he publicly proclaimed an heir, he could pass on to the Great Cycle in peace.

Kiyoshi studied the flow of energies in the king's head. Even a healthy mind was like looking at a knot of tangled strings, but Masaki's was even more jumbled. With a careful touch, Kiyoshi went in and tried to subtly alter the flows of energy, like poking at a giant knot with a finger, hoping it would magically unravel. Sweat beaded down his brow, and with a firm but focused touch, Kiyoshi felt a piece of the knot fall away. He retreated. It was more success than he saw some days. The temptation was always to do more, but one of the fundamental truths of being a dayblade was that one wanted to do as little as necessary. Nowhere was that truer than working inside someone's mind.

The mind was amazingly intricate and sensitive. In ages long ago, when the power of the dayblades was still being refined, there were stories of healers going into the minds of patients and causing horrors as a result. A gentle nudge the wrong way could destroy a person's memories or power of speech. Most dayblades avoided the mind, but Kiyoshi took a certain pleasure in pushing himself further. His actions were born out of necessity, but he still felt pride at his abilities.

Done for the day, Kiyoshi allowed most of his own energy to flow into the king, to give him strength for the next day. Kiyoshi gave probably more than he should, but the king's life was far more important than his own.

Kiyoshi gently broke contact with the king. Time had no meaning when a dayblade was healing, and he was surprised to see the morning sun rising through the king's windows. Kiyoshi looked down at Masaki, one of the few men he considered a friend in this world. The king was still alive, and for the moment, he looked well, but Kiyoshi wrestled with his own private doubts. The only reason Masaki lived was Kiyoshi's daily healings. And living was a strong word for what the king was doing. More accurately, the king was breathing on his own. Kiyoshi wasn't sure he'd ever get the king to wake up again.

Kiyoshi went to stand up, but his leg buckled underneath him, and he fell back onto the cushions he had been using for support during the healing. He cursed himself and old age. He had no fear of death. Some days he thought the idea sounded rather appealing. But he had work to do, and he would leave the Kingdom better than when he found it. Then he could pass to the Great Cycle peacefully.

He knew he couldn't keep up these daily healings for much longer. Even if he had been young and vigorous, it would be difficult for his body to recover.

Eventually Kiyoshi was able to stand up. After several deep breaths to keep his balance, he stumbled forward toward his own room, just down the hall. By the time he got to his bed, he felt as though he had run from Haven to Starfall. Twice. Carrying an obese lord.

Kiyoshi saw a note in his room before he lay down. Fighting apathy, the blade opened the note and scanned the letter. Another cursed King's Council. Kiyoshi called for a guard and asked to be awakened at the appointed time. Then he lay down on his bed and allowed the blackness of rest to take him.

—

Kiyoshi was startled awake by persistent shaking from the guard. His eyes opened, and for a moment, he feared he was being attacked. He rose and tensed his body for combat. He reached for one of the short blades hidden on his body, but his mind reasserted itself.

Kiyoshi relaxed back onto his bed and nodded his thanks to the guard. With any luck, he would look like any other old man startled awake. The guard, surprised by Kiyoshi's reaction, bowed and left the room.

The old dayblade sighed and rubbed his eyes, his body demanding more rest. He knew he had been pushing his limits, but even he didn't realize how far he had gone. His sense should have warned him someone was nearby, waking him before they approached.

Lying in bed, almost unable to move, Kiyoshi questioned himself. He knew he would do anything for Masaki, including give up his own life. There was no question of that. But was he walking the right path? His hopes hinged on Masaki gaining consciousness again and declaring an heir. He had to acknowledge, however, that such an act now seemed far-fetched. The two had always thought they had more time, until they didn't.

Any other decision seemed worse. The king's line had always been separate from that of any of the three lords. Legend had it that the first king gave up his land as a sacrifice to the Kingdom. It had always been understood that one couldn't be a just king when predisposed to a certain house. If any of the lords became monarch, they had to cut their line off from their clan's for all time, and Kiyoshi had a hard time believing most would give up their family's rights to the land. Juro, very likely, would, but the others—never.

Kiyoshi wanted Masaki to declare for Juro. The choice and transference of power would be far from ideal, but they were backed into a corner, and Kiyoshi saw the warrior lord as their only chance.

It took Kiyoshi a while to realize that a substantial amount of time had passed. He cursed himself. He had been so tired that he had thought nothing about lying in bed even though he had a council meeting to attend. In this time of chaos, his calming presence was needed more than ever.

He groaned as he rose. He would have gone through his morning forms, but since he had been spending so much time with the king, every routine he once had was a distant memory. Moving stiffly, Kiyoshi shuffled through the halls toward the council chamber.

When he arrived, he could see that the meeting had already started. The initial pleasantries were done, and if Kiyoshi's sense of time was any sign, they hadn't lasted long.

He stopped in his tracks when he took in the room. Shin was standing, while the other two lords were sitting. What really drew Kiyoshi's attention, though, was Minori, sitting calmly at the table like he had been a part of the council his entire life.

Kiyoshi's tired mind tried to figure out what was happening. Even though he was a dayblade, he could tell he was walking into a trap. He wasn't worried about physical violence. Minori wouldn't dare try, not here. But how had he figured out the timing of a council meeting? The schedules were always secret, and Kiyoshi had conveniently had trouble delivering timely messages to Minori.

There was only one logical explanation: Minori was connected to one of the lords. If that was true and Minori was half as intelligent as Kiyoshi assumed he was, then the nightblade had sided with Lord Shin. Kiyoshi wasn't even able to track the potential consequences of that relationship. His exhausted mind simply wasn't able to continue. He stepped forward, wondering how the trap would snap shut on him.

Lord Shin stopped whatever he had been saying when he saw Kiyoshi move into his peripheral vision. "Kiyoshi, it is good to see you. We all know how you have driven yourself to the brink of collapse to keep Masaki alive, and all of us here are grateful. I've heard you already know Minori, sent here as a representative of the Council of Blades."

Shin's words were kind, but his voice was anything but, leaving nothing to the imagination. Kiyoshi was taken aback. The situation was worse than he thought if Shin was being so bold. But he wouldn't sink to the lord's level. This was the King's Council, a place of respect. He bowed deeply to Shin, as befitted the lord's station.

"Thank you for your kind words, Lord Shin."

It was no surprise Minori had shown Shin and the other lords his letter from Hajimi, but it complicated Kiyoshi's situation. From an official standpoint, there was no need for two blades on the King's Council, and there would be plenty of people who would see having two blades as a bid for more power. Minori could argue his more recent appointment overrode Kiyoshi's older one, and if he did, there was little Kiyoshi could do. He suspected if he appealed to the Council of Blades, Hajimi would default to Minori. Kiyoshi would have to tread lightly.

Kiyoshi sat at his typical place at the table, and Shin continued his previous line of questioning.

"What do we know about this wave of crime in Haven?"

Kiyoshi was surprised again. He had heard nothing of this, but from the looks of the lords, Shin's words weren't news to any of them. He realized his efforts to save the king were isolating him from events in the Kingdom.

Lord Isamu spoke first, his voice angry. "The streets of Haven have become almost impassable. Even trying to get here today, I didn't feel comfortable with less than a hundred guards. The populace is furious."

Juro turned to Isamu. "I struggle to believe you can't control your people."

Kiyoshi interjected, using his own ignorance in the hope it might calm the situation.

"Forgive me, lords, but with my time spent at the king's side, I'm afraid I'm not aware of what's happening in Haven. Would someone be so kind as to update me?"

Minori replied, highlighting the difference between the two blades. "As of late, the city and, indeed, the entire Kingdom have become unsettled. Word of the king's illness has spread, and the people fear what will happen if our majesty rejoins the Great Cycle without naming an heir. There have been calls for the council to take action, but due to our respect for the king, none has been taken. The lack of action is causing greater unrest."

"And how has this unrest manifested?"

Minori answered again. "Here in Haven, the streets are not as safe as they once were. There are many more reports of petty crime, but more concerning to the lords are the gatherings that are gaining momentum. I'm sure every lord here has their supporters calling for their elevation to the post of king, but there are other fringe gatherings promoting treasonous ideas. On my morning walk, I heard one group calling for an end to lords and kings. One young man was arguing that all taxes should be abolished forever and people should be free to live as they please. Reports show the gatherings are getting larger, indicating a greater level of discontent with the situation."

Kiyoshi was surprised.

"What actions have the king's guards taken?"

Isamu answered this time. "They are doing all they can, but they aren't prepared for this type of work. They need more men, and money to pay them."

In a flash of insight, Kiyoshi saw what was happening. Even though Haven was controlled by the king, it resided on Isamu's family lands. Chaos here would reflect poorly on Isamu. The other two lords could argue that a man who couldn't control his own city was in no position to control the Kingdom. He wondered how much of the unrest was natural and how much was being encouraged by the other lords.

Shin spoke, the voice of reason at the table. "Lords, this is no time for these petty squabbles. May I propose a solution? My honor guard is scheduled to change the day after next. If you are willing, I would allow my present honor guard to remain in the city to assist the king's guard. I would be happy to pay their wages, so no new money would need to be raised, and the king's guard could be put in command. An extra hundred men would surely be useful, would they not?"

Isamu fixed Shin with an icy glare. "You'll have to forgive me, Lord Shin, but I hesitate to allow an extra hundred of your men into the city."

Minori spoke up. "My lord, I'm new to the council, so you must forgive me, but may I provide a piece of support?"

Isamu gestured at the nightblade to continue.

"My lord, I'd also be willing to request the presence of more warriors from the Council of Blades. Even a dozen nightblades walking around the city would quickly help restore order. It would take at least a half moon for the blades to arrive. I would suggest you take Lord Shin up on his offer for now. If you are concerned about the balance of power, rest assured it would be for only a little while. Once the blades arrive, I'm certain Shin would be willing to remove his extra guards."

Shin nodded his agreement. "I would be more than happy to do so."

Minori continued. "In fact, I may even be able to summon a few blades from the surrounding area who could be here in a few days."

Kiyoshi watched as Isamu struggled with his decision. Minori had sweetened the deal considerably. Kiyoshi was worried. If Minori and Shin were working together, as he expected, this entire scene might have been coordinated. It meant the blades were taking a side, and nothing scared Kiyoshi more.

Isamu reached his decision. "Very well. Lord Shin, your offer is accepted. Thank you for your willingness to help."

The rest of the council passed quickly, and Kiyoshi wondered what he had just seen. The blades were aligning with Shin, and Kiyoshi could see only one way this path ended. Perhaps he was overly pessimistic, but Kiyoshi, better than anyone else, understood what happened when the blades chose a side. He feared that blood was going to be spilled. Far too much blood.

Chapter 13

If Asa never stared at another piece of parchment again, it would be too soon. Outside of the bit of excitement at the inn, Asa felt like she hadn't moved at all in ages. She put away all the papers she had been going through, wondering why anyone would ever choose to be a scribe. When she was a blade in training, she had befriended a scribe in training, and he had spoken about the excitement of words, the magic of transmitting an idea through both distance and time. Asa supposed language was powerful, but it certainly was boring. Give her a sword and an opponent any day.

Asa returned the papers to the young scribe who managed the archives at Haven. As was becoming a pattern in her research, she was hitting dead end after dead end. She had also been trying to track down Osamu's brother, but she had had no luck on that end, either.

Asa wondered if she should just follow her gut. For the past few days she had been trying to control her excitement. After cycles of searching, could her quest almost be over? She was pretty certain she had discovered not just where Osamu was, but who he was—Minori.

She didn't have any direct proof, but the circumstantial evidence was strong. He claimed he had been at Two Falls, and he was a nightblade around the correct age. He had also clearly been hiding secrets. He was by far the most likely candidate she had come across yet.

The best piece of evidence she had was his claim he had been at Two Falls. Afterward, she went over all the records and notes she had taken. She had been right. The name of every blade who had been at Two Falls had been recorded, and Minori's name wasn't on the list. But he didn't know she had access to that information. She didn't think he had intended to reveal his participation in the massacre, but he'd also been too smart to try to lie to her.

Thus, if Minori had been at the scene and his name wasn't on the list, the explanation that was most reasonable was that Minori was Osamu. To confirm her theory, she could try to go through Osamu's brother, or she could return to Starfall. Hopefully Osamu's brother would recognize Minori, but Asa still had to find him, and there was no guarantee he was still alive.

But going back to Starfall didn't seem to be any better a decision. Minori was chosen by the council and likely a friend of Hajimi's. Either Hajimi already knew his identity or he didn't want to know the truth. Going back to Starfall would only cause Asa more headaches.

More importantly, Asa didn't want to be too far away from Minori, especially the way events in the Kingdom were unfolding.

Asa walked out of the archives, her mind lost in thought. She wasn't interested in politics, but she had never seen a city where the tension was so high. People stayed home, and when they came out, they were angry and scared. It was unsettling to wander the streets. She could feel the people all around her, but she could not see them, hidden behind the walls of their homes.

Even though she hated to draw attention to herself, Asa had started to wear the robes of a nightblade wherever she walked. She couldn't blend in, but robberies were becoming more and more common, and it was far easier to wear the robes than deal with random attacks.

Though she cared little about politics, she was concerned. If Haven exploded into violence, it would be much harder for her to complete her mission.

Asa was a nightblade, and a patient one. She had waited for cycles, and she had never been closer to her prey. She was a hunter, and Minori couldn't escape.

Asa sat in a public teahouse, gazing out at the city, considering her next steps. She had been going to the archives for days now, but she wasn't going to learn anything new there she didn't already know. She had been going because it gave her something to do, and it provided her with the feeling she was moving forward and accomplishing something.

It wasn't true, though. Asa was wasting time, lying to herself. Multiple times she fingered her weapons, considering going back to Minori's home and killing him. But she never went beyond brushing her weapons with her fingertips. Instead, she sat at her table, drinking her tea, her frustration rising.

She told herself she didn't act because of the challenges facing the Kingdom; her situation was complicated by political events. Asa had heard the news, as it was on everyone's lips. The king was going to die without an heir, and there was no clear successor. Unless something dramatic unfolded in the next half moon or so, everyone seemed certain the Kingdom was heading for a war of succession. Minori sat on the King's Council and could prevent the war from becoming reality.

That excuse wasn't really why she didn't act, though. Asa tried, but she couldn't bring herself to care about politics and power struggles. All that mattered was avenging her father's death, and she didn't care what ramifications Minori's death would have.

Asa sipped at her tea, savoring the slight sweetness of the liquid. Teahouses were some of her favorite places to visit, places where people gathered to soak in a calm ambience and talk. Asa enjoyed dressing as a civilian and listening to the discussions. She rarely chimed in. She was reminded of when she had been very young, before her father had donned the white, when guests would come by their house and have long and loud discussions.

Nothing of the sort was happening today. There were a few people in the teahouse, but they stared down into their cups, unwilling to meet the eyes of anyone else. Everyone was afraid. When they walked in and saw Asa in her robes, people stayed even farther away.

Asa knew there were places where blades could go and not be the center of attention, but that wasn't what she wanted. She wanted to bask in the pleasure of a conversation that was pleasant but ultimately meaningless.

She wasn't going to find it here, not tonight. She finished her tea and paid her bill, moving slowly so as not to startle any of the other patrons. The owner bowed deeply to her, but Asa could tell the old man was glad she was leaving.

Night had fallen, and before Asa went on her way, she looked up to see the moon high above. She smiled as a random thought crossed her mind. If someone lived there, looking down on all of this, what would he think? Would he think that all the actions of humanity were as foolish as Asa felt they were?

She smiled softly at her own thought and began walking to the nightblades' quarters. Asa didn't like it there, but the space was free and she didn't attract attention, which was enough for her.

Asa quickly realized she was being followed. Her sense was always with her, even if she didn't consciously recognize it. She felt the two men behind her, turning the corners just moments after she did. Asa's heart started pumping more wildly, but she willed her breath to be calm. Nothing good came from rash decision-making. She turned a corner, breaking from her normal route to the bunks. As she did, she glanced toward the men. They were tall and dressed in dark clothes. From their movement, Asa assumed they were wearing a fair amount of armor underneath. They carried spears, in public, without concern.

Everything about them screamed soldier to Asa's mind, and she accepted her instincts. She didn't know why she had attracted their attention, but she suspected there was only one way this ended.

Asa wanted to avoid drawing additional scrutiny and thus didn't want to fight. She could take two soldiers without any problem. Her sense let her know that despite their intimidating presence, they weren't blades and had no chance against her. But if she left a trail of bodies behind, she would receive far more attention than she needed. That would interfere with her hunt, an inexcusable possibility.

She considered running, but the soldiers seemed content to follow. Maybe they were supposed to intimidate her? Foolish. A regular soldier could never intimidate a nightblade.

Asa considered her options. She settled on returning to the bunks where the blades slept. Once there, she wouldn't have to worry about being attacked. In the light of day, perhaps she could find answers about who would send soldiers after her. She altered her course, returning once again to the path to the bunks.

Her sense warned her before she could see them. Down the street, two more soldiers waited, directly in her path. Asa started down a side alley, but paused. Warnings were going off in her mind. This was a trap, and if so, she was being guided in a specific direction. She took a deep breath and closed her eyes, expanding her sense.

At any other time, here in the city, she would have been inundated with information, and her mind would have collapsed under the pressure. But now, due to the mild fear that had gripped the city, no one was on the streets. She could push out her sense without worry. At the other end of the alley were two more soldiers, waiting for her. She swore, fear threatening to take her heart. She kept her focus, pushed a little farther, and felt two more, covering an alley heading in another direction. Asa opened her eyes. She was surrounded.

The soldiers weren't in any rush. They knew she was a nightblade, but she didn't sense any hesitation in their steps or their bearing. They were willing to give her the choice of battleground.

Normally Asa would have chosen the alley. Against a spear, the narrow walls would favor her short swords, but pieces were starting to fall into place for her. She had heard rumors, but they had never been confirmed. If they had, the blades would have acted, Asa was certain. She was surrounded by a unit of eight, purposefully selected and trained to kill nightblades.

If the warriors' training was as good as Asa suspected, going into an alley would be a death sentence. They wouldn't advance one at a time, like enemies did in plays. They'd form two lines, using the greater length of their spears to skewer. The tight space, normally her ally, would doom her.

Asa's odds didn't seem much better in the center of the street, but at least she'd have room to move. Their strategy would be simple but effective. They would try to narrow her space, using the spears to keep her at a distance. If they were in pairs, one would likely be in forward position, threatening her with his spear while his partner stood behind him, protecting him with a second deadly shaft.

All of this occurred to Asa in an instant, as did her strategy in return. If they wanted to reduce her space, she needed to stay mobile. And that she was good at.

Asa scanned the area one last time with her sense. No help was coming. No one else was walking the streets. Asa took a deep breath and steadied herself. She drew her short sword and stood her ground.

The four pairs of soldiers converged on her, leaving at least ten paces between themselves and her. Torches flared up all around her as one of each pair lit the lights. They tossed the torches around them, forming a circle of light. No shadows would hide Asa or her attacks. She swallowed her fear. She couldn't sense any hesitation from anyone.

For a moment, the scene was still. Asa spun slowly around, her sense fully alive, waiting for the first move. More to ease her own fear, she spoke loudly. "What, no threats? I'm disappointed."

Even to Asa's ears, her attempts at bravado sounded empty. She was no hero. Just a nightblade with one man she wanted to kill.

The thought spiked her focus. Only one person could be responsible for this ambush—the man who knew his secret had been exposed: Minori. She would eliminate his minions and go after him this very night.

She chose a pair that seemed slightly off guard and dashed toward them.

Asa prided herself on her speed, but no matter how fast a person was, it took plenty of time to cover ten paces. As soon as she moved, the circle tightened around her. The pair on either side of her tried to keep pace. They were a little slower, but the extra reach of their spears would make enough of a difference. Asa might shift the shape of the circle a little, but she knew she wasn't going to escape.

She shifted tactics. In a single smooth motion, practiced hundreds of times, Asa drew one of her throwing knives and hurled it at one of the pair standing right in front of her. At the same time, she slid to a stop and started dashing the other way, trying to break through the pair of soldiers who had been pursuing her first sprint.

She sensed her knife catch the soldier by surprise. The blade embedded itself in him, but she didn't sense his life force diminish at all. She swore again. She had forgotten the armor they were wearing underneath. Her throwing knives would only be effective as distractions, or she'd have to make really powerful throws.

There wasn't time to worry. She reached the pair that had been behind her. She slapped away the first spear with the flat of her sword and slid under the second one, her body throwing dust into the air as she hit the ground. Asa ignored the pain and allowed her momentum to bring her back up to her feet, her sword leading the way. She was inside the guards of both soldiers, and the point of her sword stabbed deeply into the chest of a warrior, cutting cleanly through his armor. She twisted and pulled the sword out, drawing plenty of blood in the process. The dying soldier's partner swung his spear. She was well inside the range of the shaft's sharp point, and Asa assumed he was trying to strike her upon the head. She sensed the blow coming and got her sword up to block. Her blade cut through wood, slicing the spear in half and sending the point spinning off into the darkness.

Asa had enough time to kick the soldier in the chest, but she couldn't kill him before the other six were on her.

Four of them went straight at her, but a single pair had the presence of mind to circle instead. Asa thought she saw a window to escape, but was blocked by the point of a spear.

Trapped, all Asa had was her speed and her sense. She dodged underneath a cluster of spears, but the pairs were well trained. She could avoid an attack and get inside the guard of the attacker, but the attacker's partner was always there, right behind, protecting his comrade. Asa was staying alive, but she wasn't able to threaten any of her attackers, and soon the battle would be over. Asa raged against her fate. She had always thought that if she was going to die, it was going to be at Osamu's hand, not by pathetic regular soldiers.

The soldier Asa had kicked returned to his feet and grabbed his dead partner's spear. He joined the other six, and a flurry of attacks and counters were exchanged. Fortunately for Asa, only half the soldiers ever attacked at any one time, and four spears were marginally easier to manage than seven. But after the strikes were exchanged, Asa was bleeding from half a dozen shallow cuts. She could feel the blood trickling down her arms. Soon she wouldn't be able to hold on to her sword.

They came in again, and Asa used her sense to predict the strikes. Even so, she could move only so fast, and one of the strikes finally got through her defense. A spear cut through Asa's side, the first time she'd ever been deeply wounded. The agony brought her to her knees. The soldier pulled out the spear as she fell, readying himself for another strike.

Asa's sword dropped from her hand. Rage, sorrow, and regret demanded she get to her feet, but she couldn't summon the energy. There was no chance of winning this fight.

She didn't know why the soldiers didn't attack her right away. The battle was over. Perhaps they weren't certain who should strike the killing blow. Perhaps they were taking a moment to savor their victory over a nightblade. Either way, their short pause saved her life.

Out of the shadows of the alley, a man appeared. It took Asa a moment to realize why the man looked so familiar. It was the same man who had been following her since she had killed Takashi, and possibly even before then. Who knew how long he had been there before she noticed his presence?

Everything clicked into place. He was behind everything. She had been followed by Minori's minion. The shadow had known all along she was after him, and he had decided she had finally gotten too close. She should have been furious, but she couldn't summon up any more emotion.

But the man didn't gloat, and the soldiers didn't notice him behind them. He drew his sword, the first time Asa had seen him do so. With two smooth cuts, he felled two of the soldiers.

Asa struggled to comprehend what was happening. Her thoughts felt as though they were tumbling over one another, but as the soldiers turned to face this new threat, it dawned on her that she was being rescued.

The battle had turned from seven-on-one to five-on-two, appropriate odds by any nightblade's estimation. The mysterious nightblade focused on Asa before the fight resumed. "Get up," he said.

The note of command in the nightblade's voice sparked something in Asa that had died. She grabbed her sword.

The single soldier, the one who had watched his partner die, tried to stab at her. He was the only one who had kept his focus on Asa as the others turned toward the new threat. She sensed the strike coming and slapped it away with her empty palm. Gritting her teeth against the pain, Asa got to her feet and grasped her sword firmly in both hands. The sight and feel of cold steel gave her strength.

She remembered the words drilled into her so long ago. She couldn't even remember who had said them. "Be as strong as steel, and flow over obstacles like water."

Asa sensed the single soldier bringing his spear up for another attack. Although she wasn't as fast as she had been due to her injury, Asa was easily able to get inside his guard and draw her knife across his neck, the lone soldier no match for a nightblade.

Her attention was drawn to the other fight. The four soldiers had tried to surround the nightblade, but they knew they didn't have the numbers they needed. They wanted to fight as pairs, but they couldn't surround a nightblade from only two sides.

Asa was fascinated by the shadow. He was far older than she and not as fast, but he moved with an effortless grace born from cycles and cycles of training. He didn't move much, but every spear strike missed cleanly. The nightblade was also patient, waiting for opportunities as they presented themselves. In this way, he was able to dispatch another soldier in a move Asa never would have imagined succeeding against a spear, a low cut that sliced through the artery in the inner thigh.

The kill snapped Asa out of her reverie. She drew a throwing blade, and without the pressure of being attacked, she took a moment to aim carefully. She threw, striking a soldier in his back, near the base of his skull. He collapsed, spasms racking his body.

After that, the end was only a matter of time. The two soldiers knew they had no chance, but they still fought. Asa engaged one, but it was the older nightblade who killed them both. The battle done, Asa looked around, processing what had just happened.

Her gaze met that of the older nightblade. The pain in her stomach was returning as the energy from the fight drained away, and she wasn't sure how much longer she'd be able to stay on her feet.

"Who are you?"

The nightblade flicked blood off his blade, knelt to the ground, and used a dead soldier's clothes to wipe off the rest. After a careful but quick examination, the nightblade slid his weapon into its sheath with an easy, practiced motion. Asa couldn't sense a thing coming from him, even though he was right in front of her. Eerie.

"My name is meaningless. I'm a shadow, assigned to follow you. The time has come for me to take you to my master. He will be able to heal you, and you'll find some of the answers you're looking for."

Questions swirled in Asa's mind, but she knew, just by looking at the stranger, that he'd never answer them. He'd said as much as he was going to say. She decided to trust him. She also wasn't sure if there were any dayblades back in her quarters. If she didn't receive treatment, she might die. He was her best hope.

She sheathed her bloody sword. "One moment."

Digging through her pockets, she found an unmarked piece of paper she had been using to take notes. She scribbled down a few characters and dropped the paper on one of the bodies. Let it serve as a message.

She fell toward the other nightblade, who caught her with ease. Together they stumbled into the shadows.

Chapter 14

Shin's gardens, which usually gave Minori the moments of peace he craved, were failing to do so today. It was no fault of the gardens themselves. They were as serene and peaceful as always, untouched by the chaos and uncertainty of the world outside. The failing was Minori's. Even though he sat in what might be the calmest spot in Haven, he couldn't get his analytical mind to slow down.

He had gotten Shin's note that morning, informing him of the loss of the assassination squad but little else. The missive requested a meeting, which was why Minori was here.

Minori didn't understand. The girl had been right in front of him, and she hadn't seemed special. The only quality she possessed of any worth, in Minori's estimation, was her drive for revenge. But revenge didn't make you any better with a sword.

Eight dead. Minori was no slouch with a blade, but he was certain he couldn't take on eight soldiers attacking him at once. By his estimation, the girl couldn't be much better than he was. If she was good enough to kill eight highly trained soldiers, word of her skill would have trickled up to him before.

The logical explanation was that she had help. But Minori couldn't imagine who. He'd had her watched, and all she ever did was visit teahouses and search the archives. Blades tended to isolate themselves from civilian society, their powers a wall between them and the rest of the Kingdom, but she was a loner even by that standard.

Minori's thoughts were interrupted by Shin's approach. The blade stood and bowed.

With a gesture from Shin, both men sat down. Minori waited for Shin to start.

"Who is this girl?"

Minori fought the urge to shrug. He had requested more information from Starfall with his last letter to Hajimi, but days would pass before his message was answered. All he knew about her was what Hajimi had written in his introduction, which was little.

"I thought she was working alone. She doesn't have the skill to kill eight soldiers. I apologize for the loss of your men."

Shin waved the apology away. "There are far more where they came from."

Minori's eyes narrowed. Was Shin admitting that he had more nightblade death squads, or just making a general claim about how many men he had?

Shin didn't pause. "Anyhow, their deaths will serve a purpose. They were wearing armor taken from the king's guard. People are already talking about how the guards were killed last night. Their grip on the city loosens by the day."

Minori kept his posture and face still. Shin was the sort of man who always had plans within plans, who couldn't be underestimated.

"There are two problems for you, however."

Minori's eyes came up and met Shin's, the question unspoken.

"First, rumor on the streets say that it was a nightblade who killed the guards. While I suppose it is true, I worry the rumor is going to be damaging to your people. I've asked several of my plants within the city to argue against the rumor, but it is like trying to stop a grass fire with a single cup of water."

That was unfortunate, and Minori wished he'd taken a moment to get the feel of the city this morning. But with eight soldiers dead and no other bodies, of course people would assume a nightblade. This wasn't something he'd considered. Granted, he hadn't thought it was something he'd even have to consider. He wondered just how hard Shin's people were trying to change public opinion. Anger against the nightblades only served the lord in the long run.

"The second problem?"

Shin pulled out a piece of paper and handed it to Minori. There were only a few characters, which Minori read quickly. The message was simple. "M, I'm coming for you."

Shin seemed to find the paper amusing. "It seems the girl knew you were behind the attack. Are you getting sloppy, Minori?"

Minori debated, just for a moment, if there could be anything else to the note. But there wouldn't be. The girl was not one for guile. "No. I believe she thinks I am someone I am not. But the note speaks truly. She will be coming for me."

Shin didn't respond, clearly waiting for Minori to continue speaking. The nightblade knew what the lord was waiting for.

"It doesn't change anything. The blades should be on their way shortly, and they will pledge loyalty to you. Haven will be yours in a little while."

Shin nodded and stood, signaling the end of the meeting. "Good. I look forward to hearing from you soon."

With that he turned and walked away, leaving Minori alone, unable to find peace in the gardens.

Minori left Shin's grounds and let his feet carry him wherever they desired. A walk always helped to clear his head.

He pushed aside all thoughts of the girl and the problems associated with her and focused on his next actions. He didn't trust Shin, but it was only through the lord that he could realize a future in which blades held more sway in the land. To bring Shin into power, several events had to happen. First, the king had to die. Minori wasn't sure how much longer Kiyoshi could keep the old man alive, but it couldn't be for much longer. Minori could always try to kill Kiyoshi. Without the dayblade, the king wouldn't last for more than a day or two.

That left the other two lords. They would never hand power over to Shin, at least not under any terms that Shin would accept. Killing them was an option but provided only a temporary solution. They both came from large families with a clear designated heir. If either died, the entire family's holdings would most likely rise in revolt. Perhaps they could be held hostage long enough for Shin to consolidate power?

Minori's mind wandered over the different options, and eventually he found that he was nearing the grounds of Lord Isamu. He was surprised to have wandered so far. Driven by curiosity and convenience, the blade decided to investigate Isamu's holdings more carefully. Perhaps the information would be useful one day.

When Isamu's holdings came into view, Minori was immediately surprised. The walls were surrounded with guards. On the one hand, it made sense. Haven, although the capital of the Kingdom, was part of Isamu's family lands. As such, he wasn't required to observe the same limit on soldiers the other two lords were. Minori had expected there would be a few more guards, but Isamu's grounds were practically crawling with military. Even at night, there wouldn't be any chance of sneaking into the castle without taking at least a few lives.

Fortunately, as a nightblade, Minori didn't have to get inside to know what was happening. He found a quiet alcove and situated himself so he wouldn't be jostled. He took a deep breath and tried to calm his mind. Driven by an actual purpose, the meditative act was easier than he expected. His sense came alive, and he threw it forward, toward Isamu's castle.

He sensed the massive number of guards surrounding the castle, but he lingered on them only a moment. Most were bored, and there was little he could learn from such bodies. He pushed deeper inside the castle.

What he felt shocked his mind and almost forced him to retreat inside himself. There were even more guards inside. Isamu hadn't advertised anything in council, but he had far, far more men in the city than he was letting on. Minori wanted to look deeper, toward the center of the castle, but the gathering was too much information for his mind to take. He'd have to get closer, and he didn't want to show himself.

The intelligence was good enough for today. Minori returned his sense to his immediate surroundings, an experience made all the more disconcerting when a blade was placed against his throat. He hadn't sensed a thing.

Minori's heart leapt, and if not for the firm pressure of steel, he would have jumped. It was one thing to scare a civilian. It was impossible to sneak up on a nightblade. Or at least, that's what Minori had thought until a breath ago.

Reflexively, he attempted to turn his head, to see who had pulled off such an incredible feat. But as soon as he did, he was shoved forward into the wall of the alcove he'd been standing in. A gravelly voice, clearly someone attempting to disguise himself, spoke. "Try to turn around, and this blade goes a little deeper into your throat. I'm not supposed to kill you, but I won't have a problem if I have to. I'd ask you if you understand, but you're a smart man, so I know you do."

Minori's mind, usually so useful to him, shut down. He was used to being in control, to knowing everything that was happening. But this man, whoever he was, had taken that all away in a moment, and Minori didn't know how to react.

Frozen, Minori listened as the man spoke again. "I'm here to deliver a message. You think you're clever, but you're not. If you go anywhere near one of the lords again, you are giving up your life. We're always right behind you. Always."

The voice stopped, and Minori wondered what was going to happen next.

He didn't have long to worry. The man removed the blade, but before Minori could move, the man drove his fist into Minori's kidney. The blade shuddered in pain, but he felt the warrior's hand against the back of his head before he could react. With a single, sharp, violent move, Minori felt his head being driven toward the wall in front of him, and his world went black.

Chapter 15

A long time had passed since Kiyoshi had to heal injuries sustained on a battlefield. In a way, it was a pleasant relief. While the work required energy and focus, the damage was easier to repair, and the results were much more apparent.

The work had been finished a while ago. Kiyoshi doubted the wisdom of his decision. Because he had healed Asa, it would be more difficult to heal Masaki. But Kiyoshi had the distinct feeling that Asa was important to everything that was happening. Events seemed to swirl around her, and despite his decision regarding Koji, he hated to see a fellow blade die.

He sat by her side. When she was brought to him, she had succumbed to unconsciousness. Her wound, although not immediately fatal, had been serious. It had been an easy decision to heal her. While he waited for her to awake, he caught up on some of his reading. Despite the chaos in the world, there was little for him to actually do. His decisions had been made, and those who listened to him, like the shadow who had been following Asa, already knew what to do. It was hard at times for a leader not to act, but Kiyoshi felt the skill was one far too few had mastered.

Asa soon woke up. He wasn't surprised to see her stir so soon after a healing. Her physical strength wasn't great, but her will was strong.

She started, as they always did. Kiyoshi had been careful not to place himself too close to Asa. When he was younger, he had experienced a few close calls as formerly injured warriors came to. Now he simply smiled at a fellow blade and waited for her to gain her bearings, which didn't take long. Everything he knew about Asa supported the idea that she was intelligent, and she scanned her surroundings and calmed down in just a moment. Kiyoshi was impressed.

Her eyes met his. "Who are you?"

He kept his smile gentle. "My name is Kiyoshi."

"*The* Kiyoshi? The dayblade who serves the king directly?"

Kiyoshi nodded.

"And you're behind the man who's followed me since I killed Takashi?"

"He's been following you since before then."

Her face twisted, and Kiyoshi allowed his grin to grow. He could tell she was trying to figure out what to ask next.

"I'm certain you have many questions. They will all be answered. Perhaps, though, you would like something to eat while you question me?" Kiyoshi gestured toward a plate of food set off to the side of the room, and Asa dug into it without question. People were often starving after being healed, which took energy both from the dayblade and the injured. Kiyoshi had already eaten a healthy meal himself.

As she ate, Kiyoshi studied Asa. She was using the time to organize her thoughts, and she was studying him without hesitation. He liked her.

"Where would you like to begin?"

She didn't hesitate. "Why have you had someone following me?"

"Because you are trying to find Osamu. When word came to me about what you were trying to do, I decided to have you followed. It seemed like of all people, you had the best chance of finding him after all this time."

"How did you know what I was doing? The first person I ever told was Hajimi, and that was less than a moon ago."

Kiyoshi smiled. "I'm smarter than Hajimi, and I think there is nothing more important to a blade than information. In my many cycles, I have developed many friendships, and we are always sharing all sorts of information. I know the man who trained you, so I know your background. It wasn't hard to determine what your real motives were."

Asa's eyes focused on him, and Kiyoshi saw for the first time the drive she possessed. She asked, "What do you want with Osamu?"

"My business with him is personal, and I'd rather not share."

She wasn't happy about that, but it was all she was going to get.

"Will you stop me?"

"From what?"

"Killing him."

Kiyoshi stroked his beard as he considered his answer. "No. If you decide to kill him, I won't stop you."

Asa looked as though she was turning the words over in her head. "Fine. What do you know?"

"Probably nothing more than you."

"Where's Osamu's brother?"

"Dead. He joined the Great Cycle almost fifteen cycles ago."

"Where do you think Osamu is?"

"Somewhere still in the Kingdom. He never would have left."

"I agree."

The younger blade seemed to be considering her next question, so Kiyoshi asked one of his own. "Do you know why you were attacked?"

Asa stared at him, and Kiyoshi could see she did know and was debating whether to tell him. "Because I know who Osamu is."

A simple statement of fact, and it rocked Kiyoshi. After all this time, could she really have figured out the truth? He didn't trust himself to speak. If she was going to share with him, that would have to be her own choice. She hesitated for only a moment.

"It was Minori who sent the men after me. He knows that I know he is Osamu."

Kiyoshi leaned back, his mouth wide open. "How do you know?"

She shook her head. "I don't have any real proof yet, which is why he's still alive. But when I met with him, he told me he had been at Two Falls. What he didn't know was that I'd looked at the lists. I know every blade at that battle, and Minori's name was never on the lists."

Kiyoshi saw the same connection Asa had. "So, he has to be Osamu."

Asa nodded. "He fits the profile. He's a nightblade, and not only is he old enough to have been there, he's admitted it. I think he realized his mistake and tried to have me killed. Thank you, by the way, for saving me."

Kiyoshi brushed the gratitude away. Events were happening too fast for him to follow. For so long, nothing had happened in regard to Osamu's fate; but in just a few days, Asa had changed the entire situation.

"May I ask one final question?" Kiyoshi said.

Asa nodded.

"I know you want to kill Osamu. But what really drives you? Osamu killed plenty of people in his time, and no one has pursued him as relentlessly as you have. Why you?"

Asa frowned. "Why do you want to know?"

"Because I want you to work with me. But before I ask you to, I want to know you. I know you're driven by revenge, but I want to understand your character."

Asa took a few bites of food to give herself time to think. "I won't claim it's because of justice. I'm not that noble. It's revenge, but it's revenge motivated by wanting to do what's right. Osamu did a great wrong at Two Falls, and he should go to his grave knowing it was his actions that came back to haunt him. Not only did he kill my father without cause; he killed my brother and mother as well. By killing my father, he destroyed my family."

"So you want to kill him because it's right. It's what he deserves?"

Asa nodded.

"If your theory about Minori is correct, this is a pointless question, but I need to understand you. What if he spent the last twenty-some cycles doing only good deeds? Would you still insist on killing him?"

To Asa's credit, she considered the question carefully before answering. "Absolutely. No matter how good his intentions were or what he has done since, what he did deserves punishment. Even if he was a great man, I would still seek his death."

Kiyoshi considered her answer, which was what he had expected. Then he sensed someone at his door. He called for the visitor to come in and was greeted by Daisuke, his best shadow, the one he had assigned to Asa and, most recently, Minori.

Daisuke, in many ways, was unremarkable. He was of average height, with a face that wouldn't attract any special attention. Only when he moved did onlookers get any idea of his true nature. His footsteps were smooth and silent, and Kiyoshi knew Daisuke to be one of the physically strongest men around. From his bearing, the dayblade could immediately tell that something had happened. The shadow looked to Kiyoshi for permission to speak freely in front of Asa, and Kiyoshi nodded.

"Minori met with Lord Shin again. I assume they were speaking about the events of last night. Afterward he went to Isamu's castle. He was using his sense to gain a better understanding of the troops inside."

Kiyoshi could tell there was something more. "What did you do?"

"I became concerned he was plotting an assassination attempt. I warned him and knocked him unconscious. When he wakes up, he's going to have quite a headache."

Kiyoshi supposed it was good news. Minori was a bold player, more than willing to take dramatic moves. If he was trying to elevate Shin, he might also consider an assassination attempt.

Asa looked at the elderly blade with unconcealed curiosity. "Who are you, really?"

Kiyoshi gave her a short smile, but his mind was distracted by the information he had to process. "As you've guessed, I'm far more involved in the affairs of the Kingdom than most people assume. That's the way I like it."

He paused, trying to find a metaphor. "There are plenty of people who have plans and plots. Including you. But very few people can understand how all the pieces come together. For example, when many dayblades are training, they become so enamored of their ability to sense the flow of energy within a body, they forget to look for external cues. Is the person sweating and running a fever? Once a dayblade in training missed a bone sticking out of a child's arm. But people are no different. Everyone is focused on their own lives and their own problems. My goal, my real gift, is to see everything and how it all comes together. Then I try to keep the Kingdom intact."

"And how do I fit into all of this?"

A sudden thought occurred to Kiyoshi. "May I give you a demonstration?"

Asa, confused, agreed.

"Good. Find something refined to wear. If you need help, I can have people assist you. Tonight, you'll be my date to a wedding."

—

The look of confusion on Asa's face itself was worth the evening. They met at the house Kiyoshi had told her about, the house of a wealthy merchant who was a close friend of Masaki's. At least, as close a friend as one could be to a king.

From the looks Asa was giving all the participants of the ceremony, it was obvious she was completely out of her element. Kiyoshi wasn't surprised. Like many nightblades, Asa's life focused on the sword, and her life in particular was focused on revenge. She wouldn't have made time for weddings and celebrations. Perhaps that was one of the reasons the blades faced the challenges they did. For all their power, they didn't understand what life was about.

Even though Asa wore civilian clothing, Kiyoshi knew she was carrying at least three weapons.

Kiyoshi offered Asa his arm, which she took after only a moment of hesitation. Together they walked into the receiving hall of the massive house. Kiyoshi watched as Asa took the scene in. He sometimes forgot about the opulence with which the upper class lived. While his own existence was simple, he lived a life surrounded by men of wealth and power, and at times even he took their lifestyle for granted.

The merchant who owned the house saw Kiyoshi and hustled toward him. He bowed deeply. "Kiyoshi, thank you for your presence. We are honored to have you here."

Kiyoshi returned the bow. "It is the least I can do, but I'm afraid I'm a poor substitute for Masaki. I wanted to let you know that if he were awake and well, he wouldn't have missed this day for any business of the Kingdom."

The merchant was visibly moved. "It is very kind of you to say so. He is in our thoughts, and we all wish him a full recovery."

With that, the merchant continued on his way, greeting the guests. Asa turned to Kiyoshi. "Why are we here?"

"We are here because this man is a friend to the king. Not in a political way, although that is also true. They are actual friends, two boys who knew each other growing up. The king was invited, but because he can't make it, I'm here to maintain his relationship."

Asa shook her head. "That's nice, but what I meant is, why am I here?"

Kiyoshi smiled. "I hope this evening shows you something, something very important."

"What is that?"

Kiyoshi's smile turned mischievous. "For that, you must wait awhile. If you don't mind, of course."

For a moment, Kiyoshi thought she might turn and leave to resume her hunt of Minori, but something held her back. "Very well."

They wandered the ceremony without any real purpose. Kiyoshi knew a few of the people present, but not enough to keep them involved in constant conversation. The two sampled all the food that was offered, and Kiyoshi paid attention to the dishes. The food they ate was indicative of the state of trade. Mostly, everything looked to be continuing more or less as normal. He enjoyed watching Asa try dishes far beyond anything she'd ever experienced before. In many ways, it was like taking a child out into the world for the first time. Everything was new, and despite Asa's nature, he could tell she was enjoying the experience.

A young man came up to them, and although Kiyoshi wasn't immediately certain, it was soon clear this was the groom. The young man bowed deeply, far deeper than required by manners.

"My bride pointed you out. You are Kiyoshi, who cares for the king?"

Kiyoshi nodded.

"My bride tells me of how kind the king was to her when she was growing up. When he visited, he always brought gifts, and she remembers him fondly."

"No more than Masaki remembers her. She was always a special girl to him. Were he awake, nothing would stop him from being here."

The young man seemed unsure of exactly what to say next. "I don't have much, at least not compared to the king, but if there is ever anything I can do, know our new family will always be there."

Kiyoshi bowed, more deeply than he had to.

"Thank you. I will make sure Masaki is made aware of your generosity."

The man, satisfied, left, and Asa turned to Kiyoshi.

"Are you here to make political alliances?"

Kiyoshi glanced at her with a hint of anger. It was the only thing so many people could see, only the advantages to themselves. "No. There's no doubt my presence here will strengthen the alliance already in place, but that's not why I'm here." He looked at the young man as he rejoined his bride. "I'm here because Masaki would want to be here. Once, when that little girl was sick, Masaki sent me to heal her. There was no need. She would have recovered with rest. The merchant and the king were already fast friends, so there was no further political gain."

He glanced over at Asa and saw her gaze fixed on him.

"He put my gifts to use because he cared. No other reason. And that's why I'm here today. Because he cares. I do, too."

He could see a new question forming in her mind. Then she asked, "You've given up everything for him, haven't you?"

Kiyoshi hadn't ever really thought about it that way. "Perhaps. But not for him specifically. For the Kingdom."

"What did you do before you came here?"

Kiyoshi laughed. "Nothing worth mentioning."

They circled the room for a while longer, but once all the guests had arrived, the ceremony began.

For a family of such stature, the affair was simple, lacking unusual extravagances. Although the quality of the food and the clothing showed the clan's wealth, in many ways the ceremony did not differ from one held in the smallest village. Kiyoshi wasn't surprised, knowing the family as he did. They were wealthy, but they didn't lord their money over others, as many were likely to do. They lived well but quietly. Kiyoshi imagined this was one reason Masaki had remained close to them even after his ascent to power.

When the groom read his vow of commitment, Kiyoshi beamed. When the bride read hers, Kiyoshi couldn't hold back his tears. It was such a bold decision, the choice to spend the rest of your days with another. Kiyoshi had never had such a relationship, and there was a simple beauty there that left him speechless. He remembered healing the little girl, how she had been so polite even when she was sick. To see her now as a young woman, taking this next step, was moving.

Asa noticed his tears but didn't say anything.

The ceremony was short and soon ended. Afterward came the celebration. Music began, more food appeared as though by magic, and people danced with one another. Kiyoshi, moved by the moment, joined in the dancing. He tried to get Asa to join, but she refused. He felt sorry for the blade, but his joy was such he couldn't worry much about her behavior.

Kiyoshi lost himself in the beat and even danced with the bride for a few moments before other eager guests got their turn. Eventually his body reminded him he had seen more than sixty cycles of life. He found Asa and sat down next to her. Her patience was clearly running thin.

She let him catch his breath, but then fixed him with her stare. "So, what is it I'm supposed to learn?"

Kiyoshi studied her, saddened that on a day like today, she wasn't able to see what was right in front of her face.

"What do you see when you look around you?"

Asa looked quickly. "A wedding?"

Kiyoshi sighed. He had held out hope for the girl, but her single-mindedness closed her off. She could have been an ally, but now he wasn't so sure. "This, right here, this is all that matters. Two lives coming together, to follow the same path for the rest of their lives. All the politics, all the power struggles, your desire to kill Osamu—all of it is meaningless. The only thing that matters is this, that people have the opportunity to live full and happy lives. The Kingdom is only worthwhile so long as it provides these moments. Serving the people is all that matters."

Kiyoshi stopped. He could start a rant, but it would do no good. He could already see the range of emotions running over Asa's face. She didn't like that he had called her life's purpose meaningless, and she couldn't see beyond that.

Asa confirmed his suspicion by standing up and leaving the room. Kiyoshi used his sense and felt her leave the house. Why were they all shortsighted? Asa's happiness had been taken from her by Osamu's actions, but even she didn't recognize how important it was that such events never happen again.

Kiyoshi pushed her out of his mind. He loved weddings, and it would provide him a small glimmer of light in the darkness of daily life. He stood up, ignoring the aches in his body, ready to dance some more.

Chapter 16

Asa left the wedding, her mind more of a mess than it had ever been. Kiyoshi was unlike anyone she had met, and she was struggling to figure out just how he fit into her view of the world. Part of her understood his perspective and even found it appealing. Kiyoshi seemed to have something she didn't, answers that came from cycles of experience. But the part of Asa that had guided her for so long was strong.

She thought of the long days and nights of her training to become a nightblade. The endless afternoons of meditation and combat practice. The brutal tests of endurance and mental fortitude. Becoming a blade had been the hardest thing she had accomplished, but the thought of revenge had pushed her through.

Her memory stretched back further, and she thought of the final moon of her brother's life. How he had worked relentlessly to provide for the family, to do what their father should have done. Even when he knew he was sick, he pushed himself out in the fields every day. Asa had tried to get him to go to the village to find a physician, but he always told her he was fine. She didn't realize until later that they didn't have the money to pay for a doctor.

For Asa, her revenge always came back to first causes. She couldn't blame her father for becoming a dayblade. The role wasn't what he had wanted from life, but if he could make a sacrifice to save his family, he was more than willing. As a dayblade, he had seen little risk in what he was doing. The world had been a relatively peaceful place. She remembered him being eager to heal others.

But he had been at Two Falls, and there was only one person who was responsible—Osamu. The same chain of thoughts had sustained her for countless cycles. As a child she imagined a nameless commander giving the order to kill her father. She had always pictured the commander as a demon from the plays she had seen, with white face and horns. Now, for the first time, she replayed those childhood dreams, this time substituting Minori for the demon. Just like when she was young, the vision fueled her anger and sharpened her focus. It didn't matter what Kiyoshi said or how noble his dreams were. This was the real world, and justice needed to be delivered.

Night was falling, and the streets, although still relatively empty for Haven, were clearing of people. No one wanted to be out after dark, including Asa. She was more than happy to spend the night ensconced in the bunk she had never reached the night before.

She turned a corner and ended up following a mother and child. Asa didn't think anything of it until the little girl, who had not seen any more than four or five cycles, stumbled and fell. The tears gathered in her eyes, and although she looked like she would wail, her mother knelt down and comforted her right away.

Perhaps it was because of her recent conversations with Kiyoshi or the paths of remembrances she had already been following, but Asa was reminded of a memory she had suppressed a long time ago.

She had been with her mother not long before she had been sent away. Asa's recollection was vague, but she remembered being angry, furious that her father wasn't around. She had always been her father's girl. She had raged and cried and screamed. Everyone else had dads who came home when the sun set. She didn't understand why her father never returned.

Asa hadn't been old enough to understand how her mom must have felt. But the memory struck her like a slap across the face. She always remembered the rage, but today she remembered how her mom had embraced her, her arms wrapped around her daughter in an attempt to keep the rest of the world away. Her mother never said anything, never tried to explain the loss away. She just held Asa, and Asa felt for a moment that on the streets of Haven, she could feel her mom's tears on her hair.

Asa wasn't sure she'd remembered the full memory before. Previously, she had always held on to the hate and the rage. But one memory led to another, and the only times she could remember her mom being angry was when Asa misbehaved.

A deep, stabbing guilt struck Asa, deeper even than the spear she'd taken the night before. She pictured herself as a righteous avenger, taking the justice her mother and brother deserved but never received. But they had never raged against their fate. They were sad, but they pulled themselves up and tried to put their lives back together. It wasn't a new insight, but Asa held her past in a new light as she watched the mother and daughter. Her family had sacrificed everything for her. Everything had always been for her.

When her brother died and she had been identified as sense-gifted, there had been only one way forward for her. Had everything been wrong? She always assumed that if her family knew of her actions, they would look down on her with pride. But they had never wanted revenge. All they had desired was happiness.

Her thoughts brought her full circle, back to Kiyoshi and his little speeches at the wedding. All he wanted was to try to guarantee the most happiness for the greatest number of people. Was he right and she wrong?

Her mind raced in circles, and for a moment, she wondered if she would actually cry. It had been so long. Had all her cycles been misspent? What could she have done with a different goal? What if her family was disappointed in her? Why did she insist on avenging them?

The mother successfully calmed her girl down, and with an apologetic glance back toward Asa, she continued on. A simple moment, no different than any of thousands that happened every day, but it hit her hard. She cursed Kiyoshi for bringing such doubt into her life. What was it about him that caused this?

Then she put her finger on it. He radiated a feeling of peace, of satisfaction with his life. His path brought him contentment—hers, only anger.

Asa swore to herself and turned randomly down another street. She needed to think this through. Perhaps she should take his offer of alliance more seriously.

—

Asa was surprised by how angry she was. She supposed she should be grateful to Kiyoshi. Not only had he saved her life; he had been kind. After a moment of reflection, she realized she wasn't angry at him. She was angry at herself. Angry at allowing herself to doubt.

Kiyoshi posed hard questions she had never asked of herself. All she knew, everything she lived for, was based on her desire to see Osamu die for his crimes. She had never questioned, just allowed herself to be driven forward. Kiyoshi didn't know what she had been through, what the death of her father had done to her family. It was easy to judge someone when you were at a wedding, celebrating and enjoying delicious food, but another when you watched your brother slowly work himself to death and not be able to do anything about his fate. On the day he had died, her brother had been out in the fields, toiling.

But a small part of her wondered if Kiyoshi was right. She had never encountered another person with such a clear vision of their purpose. Kiyoshi gave everything for the Kingdom, and he knew why. He made her feel insecure in her own beliefs, and that angered Asa more than she thought possible.

The observation took longer than it should have, but soon she realized she had walked the streets of Haven alone for the second time in two nights. Her heart sped up for a moment before she calmed. She was still a nightblade, and despite her experiences last night, there wouldn't be another group of assassins waiting for her. If nothing else, Minori would need several days to plan another attempt on her life. If what Kiyoshi's shadow said was true, Minori might have other problems on his mind right now.

She sensed him before she saw him. She couldn't feel his presence, but she could feel his sense, and he was focused on her.

Asa's heart stopped. It wasn't impossible for another nightblade to be out on the streets at this time, but given her recent history, she was more cautious than before. She could tell he was waiting for her, and there was no way she could avoid or hide from him, not with the streets so empty.

Asa calmed herself. Perhaps it would come to battle, but perhaps not. She steeled herself and walked forward. As she did, he detached himself from the shadow of the building.

He was a younger man, taller than Asa and built with a wiry strength. It took her a moment to recognize him, but when she did, her heart raced. He was the nightblade who had welcomed her into Minori's residence. She reached down through a slit in her robes and drew her short sword, strapped to the outside of her thigh. Her two throwing knives would be useless against an opponent who could sense her throw. She regretted hiding only one sword on herself for the wedding. She raised the blade, drawing the weapon parallel to the ground, ready to fight.

His confusion was evident. "I'm not here to fight. I wanted to meet you."

Asa's blade wavered for a moment, but she regained her control and held it steady. There wasn't anything to say. Despite what he said, there was only one reason he would be here: to kill her. She wouldn't give him the chance.

Asa sprinted forward, blade in front. She stabbed straight out at the man, right at the center of his torso. The nightblade twisted to the side, but Asa slid to a halt and twisted her wrists, bringing the sword back into line. She snapped her wrists, and the blade was forced to throw himself aside to avoid being cut. Asa followed him as he rolled backward, cutting down sharply with her blade.

The nightblade came to his knees, his own sword drawn. He brought his blade up, deflecting her own overhead strike down and to the side in a classic umbrella block. This put him inside her guard, and Asa backpedaled before he could cut at her. Instead, he took the moment to get back on his feet. A look of confusion bloomed on his face.

Asa was deciding on her next attack when the nightblade leapt at her. With her speed and short sword, she was easily able to deflect the strike, and the battle began in earnest.

She was surprised by his speed. His attacks were strong, but she suspected he could have struck with more strength. Instead, he sacrificed power for quicker cuts. Smart swordplay against Asa's shorter sword, but unusual. Most of the time when she fought men, they instinctively sought to overpower her. Because of this, they often let themselves get off-balance, providing her openings. Not this man. His skill and technique were excellent, and he didn't attempt to win by brute force. In doing so, he prevented any openings.

Asa was used to being the faster fighter in a duel. Ever since she had first started training, she knew she wouldn't win duels based on strength. Speed was her ally. But this nightblade was easily as fast.

After a flurry of attacks, he paused, and Asa leapt into the space. Attacking with a short sword was rarely a good idea against a longer blade, but if he wouldn't make foolish mistakes, she would have to try to force his hand.

The nightblade responded by holding his blade straight out in front of him, parallel to the ground, the point as far away from his torso as he could comfortably hold it. A very defensive stance, and as Asa moved, the nightblade moved with her, always keeping the point directed right at her chest. She was unable to get anywhere near him.

They broke apart again, and Asa studied her opponent. Though the nightblade was younger than she, he was one of the best swords she'd ever fought, if not the best. She wasn't surprised someone like Minori could recruit a man like this, but his access to resources made her angry.

The nightblade seemed to study her as well, an unreadable expression on his face. Somehow, Asa felt as though the blade were trying to figure something out, like she was a puzzle he didn't understand. His face changed, and Asa thought he had come to a decision.

"My turn."

The blade shifted his stance, bringing his sword down low. Before Asa could take any action, she sensed his intent. She took a step back, trying to give herself more room. Knowing where the attacks were coming from didn't make any difference if she wasn't fast enough to block them.

The man sprang forward, his sword coming up in a strike very similar to a sword-drawing technique. Asa knew exactly where the first strike was coming, and she blocked it easily. But within a heartbeat she was surrounded by flashing steel. She did her best to deflect and keep up, but her guard was already uncomfortably close to her body, and she could feel herself falling behind. Even with her short sword, she wasn't fast enough to make a difference.

Finally, he cut with the perfect strike. She was already off-balance trying to deflect his blade, and he struck at her short sword with power she hadn't yet seen. Asa was knocked forward and to the side, and he slid behind her easily, rotating around and bringing his sword to her neck.

As soon as she felt the steel, Asa stopped fighting. Her mind raced, wondering what she could do to turn the situation around. Had a normal soldier gotten the better of her, she would have trusted her own speed, but as a nightblade, the stranger would be able to sense forthcoming movement.

Without options, Asa relaxed. The fight was over. Her journey was over. She was surprised to find that a part of her was relieved. Rest sounded appealing.

The young nightblade held the sword against her neck for a few moments, but then he released it. He brought his weapon down, sheathed it, and pushed her gently forward. "I told you already, I'm not here to kill you."

Asa regained her balance, and despite the warnings screaming in her mind, reciprocated the gesture of the nightblade, sheathing her own sword against her thigh.

The two studied each other again. Asa had to admit he didn't look impressive, but he had beaten her far more easily than any of her teachers had. She was impressed.

The other nightblade still looked confused. "You are the nightblade who killed the eight guards last night, right?"

The question was perhaps the last Asa had expected. If he worked for Minori, she assumed he would be familiar with the events of last night. And if he was working for Minori, why hadn't his master just sent him last night? A far more certain kill would be the result of sending a nightblade after a nightblade.

"I am."

The look of confusion deepened on the other's face. "You're not strong enough to take on eight guards. I saw their bodies after. They weren't typical city guards. If I had to guess, they were specialists. Each of them looked strong and well trained, even in death. You're good, but not that much better than an average nightblade."

She could see him working through the problem. Strong as he was, it didn't seem like he was the smartest man in the world. The answer occurred to him finally. "But a number of them had cuts on their backs! You had help from someone else, didn't you?"

Asa didn't know what to think. Either this young man really didn't understand what was going on, or this was the strangest way of getting around to killing her.

"Why would you care what happened last night?"

The look of innocence on the nightblade's face almost made Asa believe him. She felt as though she was seeing a boy full of power, but lacking wisdom. "I've been walking the streets a lot lately for my master. Everyone is talking about how one nightblade killed eight of the king's guards. I know pretty much every nightblade in the city, and none of them would try something like that, so I figured it must be you. I wanted to come and see how strong you were. I thought maybe you'd be strong enough to be a challenge for me."

The boy didn't seem to realize how many veiled insults were contained in his reasoning. Asa realized she was dealing with someone honest and unguarded.

She looked around. The street was no place to be talking about the previous evening. She stepped closer to him, arms out to her side so as not to present a threat. "I'll tell you what happened last night. But not here. Care to join me for a drink?"

The young man looked like she had just given him the entire treasury of the Kingdom.

The nightblade, whose name was Koji, sat across from Asa as she told her story. He was already deep into his third cup, but he didn't seem to suffer from any ill effects. Asa had no idea how Koji managed that much drink. She was finishing up her first cup, and she could already feel her thoughts and tension loosening.

Asa had just gotten to the point in her story where she had been attacked. Until this point, there hadn't been any danger in telling Koji everything. But now she had to decide. Should she trust the young nightblade? Everything in his attitude and bearing indicated she had nothing to fear, but trust didn't come easily, especially not now.

She looked in his eyes and made a judgment.

"I believe the attackers were sent by Minori."

Koji's entire expression changed. While before, he had been listening with rapt attention, now he looked angry. Asa had assumed Minori was simply Koji's employer, but she realized now that assumption was wrong. There was something more there, a deeper relationship than she had expected. But she had already made her decision, and now she had to ride out the consequences.

"I don't believe you," he said. "Minori saved me from certain death."

There was a tale there, and with a little coaxing, Asa convinced Koji to tell her his own story. Slowly, he told her how he had been sent on one of his first missions as a blade and what had happened. He told about how he had been sentenced to death by Kiyoshi's own hand and how Minori had broken into the prison and released him.

It was Asa's turn to listen with rapt attention. Koji was undoubtedly telling the story as he believed it, but Asa was having a hard time accepting his words as truth. Kiyoshi didn't seem like the type of person who would order another blade's death.

But then she thought more about Kiyoshi. She turned her image of him just a little, and suddenly, the pieces fit. Kiyoshi would sacrifice a nightblade. He wouldn't like it, but if he felt like such an act furthered the Kingdom, he wouldn't hesitate. She thought back to the wedding and realized Kiyoshi wasn't making idle commentary. The happiness of the people of the Kingdom was paramount for him, and if that meant tremendous sacrifice, so be it.

Asa decided to test Koji. She told the rest of her story, including how she had been saved from death by Kiyoshi and how she suspected that Minori was Osamu under a different name.

To Koji's credit, he listened to her story and theory without interrupting. She couldn't tell whether he believed her, but he was at least willing to listen, something more indicative of his character than anything she had seen so far.

When she finished, Koji sat back and ordered another drink. They sat across from each other in silence, and Asa saw that Koji was turning all the facts over in his head. Her first impression of him had been wrong. He wasn't a fool, but a very slow, logical thinker, a refreshing change of pace after Asa's interactions with people adept at politics and quick thinking.

The silence felt long, and Koji had finished his fourth drink by the time he spoke. "I do not know what the truth is. I believe you are telling the truth as you see it, but my story is true as well. At least one of us is misguided. Perhaps both of us. But there is no way of telling who."

Asa wanted to claim it was him, but as she thought more carefully, she realized he was speaking accurately. Her accusations, so far, carried no proof. She acknowledged his point.

Koji continued, "Because of this, I suggest that both of us continue to walk our respective paths. However, I would like to make a pact with you. I believe Minori is a good man, but I have crossed blades with you, and because of this, I know you better than I know him. I know you are a good woman. Let us meet regularly, so we can sort this problem out."

Asa was curious. "To what end?"

Koji looked at her as though she'd asked a dumb question. "Lies got me imprisoned. As I was brought back to Haven, I had much time to reflect, and I realized that nothing is more important than the truth. At least one of us is ensnared in a lie, and we owe it to ourselves to discover the truth."

Asa felt a weight lifted off her chest, a weight she had only recently realized she was carrying. She felt a sudden kinship with this young blade, a companionship she wasn't sure she had experienced before.

"Thank you."

On an impulse, Asa ordered another drink, as did her companion. She was excited to see that for the first time, she was seeing some of the effects of the drink on Koji. Business was forgotten as the two night-blades talked about their lives and their training.

Later that evening, Koji escorted her back to the bunkhouse. Asa wondered if maybe he would come inside with her and was surprised to realize she wouldn't mind at all. However, if the thought crossed Koji's mind, he managed to suppress it completely, even as tipsy as he was. He escorted her all the way to the entrance, and she felt safer than she had in a long time. Once there, he bowed deeply. She returned the gesture, slightly less deep so as not to offend him, and then turned around and walked to her room, feeling a peace she hadn't felt in many cycles.

Chapter 17

Minori's head still hurt whenever he stepped outside. After a restless night of sleep, he had hoped the fresh morning air would ease his pain, but the sunlight had caused his head to explode in agony, and he retreated to the more comfortable shelter of his home.

Minori's head hurt for more reasons than one. His attacker had left a deep bruise across his cheek and forehead, and every time he moved too quickly, his head reminded him just how injured he was.

Beyond that, Minori's head swam with possibilities. He knew the endgame was about to start. All the pieces were slipping into place, and he had only to figure out the final moves.

He sensed Koji return to the house. The boy had been out all night, and even though Minori hadn't given him any instructions or expectations, it was unlike the blade. Most days, it took every persuasive technique Minori knew to get Koji to leave his side. Minori wasn't upset the young nightblade had left for the evening. He was just curious. Had Koji found pleasure in a woman's arms? Minori realized he knew very little about the warrior he had rescued.

Koji made a line straight toward him, and Minori knew something important had happened last night.

He came in and bowed deeply. Minori noted the gesture. It looked as though Koji didn't consider their relationship to be any different. If he had, he would have changed the depth of his bow.

Minori got right to the problem. "I can see that something troubles you."

Koji needed no further encouragement. "Last night I sought out Asa."

Minori's eyes narrowed, and he wondered at Koji. Despite the nightblade's youth, he had an important role to play in Minori's game. In his mind, the pieces on the board continued to move, and he wondered where Koji would end up. Before he could catch himself, he said, "To what end?"

Koji didn't seem to think there was anything wrong with the question. "Yesterday, when I was walking the streets, I heard stories of a nightblade who killed eight city guards. I was curious, so I investigated. I'll admit, when I started, I thought perhaps if there was a nightblade with that strength here in town, they would be a worthy ally, or at least a worthy challenge. It took the entire day, but eventually I found her. We dueled."

Minori's heart skipped a beat. Had Koji unintentionally done exactly what Minori needed? Of all the players on the board, Asa was the one he understood the least, and as such, she was the most dangerous to his plans. If she was removed, Minori's path was much clearer.

"I was disappointed in the result. I was able to beat her easily."

"You killed her?"

Koji shook his head. "No. There was no reason. Instead, she and I spoke at length."

"And what are your impressions of her?"

It wasn't a line of questioning Koji wanted to pursue, and Minori already saw how the conversation would likely go.

Koji spoke with care, choosing his words exactly. "At first, I thought she was strong. Her personality, even when she came here to visit you, was powerful. But I don't think she is strong. She is driven. But if her purpose is taken away or even completed, I don't know what she would do. I suspect she would shatter like poorly made steel. Her purpose lends her power, but it is also her greatest weakness."

Minori was surprised. Koji's analysis was deep, and probably correct. The young blade was far more astute than Minori had believed.

As Minori had expected, Koji wasn't distracted from his true purpose. His eyes met Minori's. Like any nightblade Minori had ever met, he charged straight into battle. "Is it true?"

Minori took a deep breath. He hated to lie, and he couldn't think of a denial that would dissuade Koji. The young man was clearly torn. He didn't want to believe what he had heard, but at the same time, he thought there might be a hint of truth. In his mind's eye, Minori rearranged the board, adapting to new information.

First, he had to deal with Koji. He saw the nightblade had unconsciously taken an offensive posture, ready to attack as needed.

"Tell me, Koji. If you were a commander of men, and one of your soldiers was only a few heartbeats away from giving away your position, dooming hundreds of your men, what would you do? And let's assume you've already tried all other forms of persuasion."

Koji's face changed rapidly as he understood what Minori was saying.

"You're saying that sometimes it is necessary to sacrifice one to save many?"

Minori didn't respond. He could see his answer had gotten under Koji's skin. Sometimes the true mark of wisdom was knowing when not to say anything at all. Minori fingered a poison blade he had started carrying after his little incident with Kiyoshi.

"I think Kiyoshi made a similar argument about the necessity of my death," mused Koji. "You two are more similar than you're willing to admit."

The comment stung, but Minori recognized the truth. He didn't want to be compared to Kiyoshi, but it was deserved. "In our determination perhaps. May I tell you a story? One that very few people have ever heard, and one you may never repeat."

Koji looked at Minori with suspicion in his eyes. "What good will a story do?"

"All the good in the world. When I'm done, I will release you from any obligation you have given. At that time, you have a choice to make, whether to continue serving me or not. Either way, your honor will be intact."

Koji appeared to debate with himself for a moment, but Minori knew his offer would be too tempting to the young nightblade. At his age, honor was an all-important concept, and if he could leave his sworn service for the price of listening to a story, he certainly would.

Minori loosened his grip on the poisoned dart. He motioned for Koji to sit, and he served tea. He had never spoken this story out loud, and he wanted to make sure he got every detail just right.

"Many, many cycles ago, there was a group of blades. Both nightblades and dayblades. It was mostly nightblades, but that won't come as any surprise to you. You know just how outnumbered the dayblades are. It was a pretty large group as far as our people go. Maybe thirty or forty total. I forget the exact number now.

"These blades decided that they weren't happy with the way their lives were going. They had all passed the trials and been wanderers for some time. All had seen much of the world, and in those days, things were different. The blades had far more authority than they do now. A nightblade could cut down the elder of a village in the middle of the day, and no one would question it, at least not out loud."

Minori noticed the surprised look on Koji's face. Such an action would be unheard of today. "Remember, these were very different days. It was assumed that if a blade cut down a civilian, there was good reason. And for the most part, there was. The blades rarely overstepped the bounds of good judgment.

"The group of blades decided they deserved more power in the Kingdom. A famine was beginning, and they saw the suffering that the shortsighted policies of the lords and king had caused. They believed they could do better, and separated from the guidance of the Council of the Blades."

Koji was surprised again. Today such an action meant imprisonment or death.

"Remember, the council existed largely as a figurehead. There was no need to control the blades, and the council was an honorary position. The council didn't have the authority it does today. They didn't need to. There was no census at the time, so no one kept track of the blades, and the splinter group just slipped away and built Two Falls. They took husbands and wives and tried to live normal lives. Most tried to farm the land, as difficult as that was for them.

"But at the same time, they met regularly to discuss the future and began to lay plans for assuming authority in the Kingdom. For a little while, several cycles in fact, everything seemed to go well. The village grew, and the blades lived in peace. Those who lived there felt called to a larger purpose, and everyone, even those who weren't gifted, worked toward the same end. The village wasn't too populated and was far off the typical trading routes, so people only visited if that was where they wanted to be.

"But call it fate or call it horrible luck, the good times came to an end. The cycle of famine hit, and I assume you've studied your history, so there's not too much I have to say about it. The famine struck the village of blades just as hard as it hit anywhere else.

"The famine tested them. Because of their foresight, the village itself didn't suffer from the effects of hunger. But they decided it was time to expand their reach. They knew nearby villages were suffering, and they believed they could ease their pain.

"The conflict began when House Kita sent soldiers to acquire grain from the village. Rumors had spread claiming the village was feasting during the famine, and a troop of soldiers came to redistribute the food. The blades wouldn't allow it, and the conflict became violent. The soldiers didn't know they had walked into a town of blades. Needless to say, the troop disappeared.

"Eventually, word of the attacks made it to the king. It wasn't the first time such reports had reached his ears. In the cycle of famine, more and more people were resorting to violence, and the king always responded the same way. He launched large-scale attacks against the hideouts, the better to send a message to everyone else who was tempted. The king needed to make the cost of hoarding food far greater than the possible reward.

"So another troop marched up to the village of the blades. And now came the second test. The orders of the troop were clear: kill all the men, and kill any women or children who resist. A death sentence for the entire village, even if not all by the sword. Everyone was involved. The blades didn't feel like the time had come to set their plans in motion, but they also felt as though they had no choice but to act. Tell me this, Koji. If you were one of those blades, would you accept death calmly, or would you fight for your family and your land?"

Koji's expression said enough.

"The blades made the same decision. The blades left their homes and met the king's troop on their way to the village. They laid into the troop, leaving no survivors.

"When word reached the king, he was racked with uncertainty. He had sent in the troop assuming he was attacking a small, helpless village. They shouldn't have met any worthwhile resistance. He didn't want to send more troops in until he knew what was going on. So he went to the Council of the Blades and asked them to send a shadow into the village. To make a long, boring part of the story short, the shadow went and discovered Two Falls wasn't your typical village, but one comprised of blades trying to establish a better Kingdom. As the meager harvest concluded, the shadow made his report to the Council of the Blades.

"Now the king faced a challenge. Word of the destruction of his troops was spreading through the ranks. Most people believed that the village was hiding a huge number of bandits, some sort of tremendous hideout. But the king knew better and knew the truth was even worse. The blades, sworn to protect the Kingdom, had turned against it, killing its own soldiers.

"The king was a strong man, and he made a tough choice. He met with the Council of the Blades, and together they summoned an expedition of blades to attack the village. The mission was very difficult and marked the first time that blades had been asked to kill other blades in large numbers. For the best chance of success, they assigned the mission to their most prized leader, a commander everyone looked up to.

"Koji, I was at that battle, and my actions that day continue to haunt me. They were people who were only trying to do their best."

Minori paused and thought about what he wanted to say. There were too many memories from that day.

"It was the first time I ever fought another nightblade to the death, and I'm happy to say it was my last. I remember fighting with one blade in particular, the third one I came across. He'd already been hit with two arrows, and he knew he had only a few breaths left. His impending death gave him energy, but he just couldn't move fast enough. He didn't have a chance, but that didn't stop him from coming at me with everything he had.

"His strikes were strong, and if any of them had come close, I certainly would have died. But I could sense them coming, and he wasn't fast enough to overcome my advantage. For a while I let him strike at me. I think I was hoping he would die from his arrow wounds so I wouldn't have to draw my sword again. But he managed to back me into a corner, and I was forced to respond. He could sense me, but he wasn't fast enough to react. I killed him easily.

"Now, mind you, I wasn't young at this time. I already had a long history as a nightblade and I was no stranger to death, but nothing could prepare me for what that felt like. I couldn't believe what I had done. When I finally looked up, I saw a woman and child huddling inside their house. I believe they were his family. I looked into their eyes, and I saw hatred and sorrow like I've never seen before."

Minori stopped his story again. He could continue his confession, but he saw from the look on Koji's face he knew how the story went. To say more would be wasted breath, and Minori wasn't sure he ever wanted to visit those moments again.

"I need you to understand this: I was ambitious then. You may think I'm still that way, but you'd be wrong. I no longer seek power for my own ends. Today I want to use my power to make a difference. Back then my ambition convinced me to follow orders, and I made decisions for which I'll never forgive myself.

"Afterward, you know what haunted me the most? It wasn't the killing, not exactly. It was the idea that we were punishing other blades for making a rational choice. They had chosen to live a different type of life, and yes, it went against the wishes of the Kingdom, but they had not harmed a single person until they were pushed. For that, we ended their lives.

"I've thought a lot about those days, and I've realized that our freedom to choose is all that matters. It's what separates us from the animals, who only react on instinct. We can choose to create art, remain chaste, dedicate ourselves to a cause, or do horrible things. But it's always *our* choice.

"Perhaps you're right. It angers me to admit such things, but maybe Kiyoshi and I are similar in many ways. Still, there is one aspect of our personalities that divides us, a gap we will never bridge. Kiyoshi accepts the idea of taking away the freedom of nightblades. I understand his philosophy. He believes we are servants to the Kingdom, and I agree. But he believes that as servants, we should give up our ability to choose.

That we should be beholden to the will of the lords. And that, I will never agree with. Servitude without choice, without intent, is slavery, pure and simple. It makes us less than human. Like Kiyoshi, I believe we should serve the Kingdom, but we should choose to do it in our own ways."

Minori looked at Koji, meeting his eyes without hesitation. "The reason I rescued you wasn't because it would give me some political edge over the others. You had done your duty well, and still you had been imprisoned. It reminded me uncomfortably of that battle, and I couldn't sit by and let all your freedoms be taken away for good."

Minori took a breath and leaned backward.

"That's all I have to say. Now you know what motivates me and why I'm willing to go to any length to succeed. The cost is higher than what I'd like to pay, but my heart is already black. I'm willing to make the sacrifice.

"And now, I leave you with a choice. You know me, better than maybe anyone else does. You can choose to follow and help me. The end of our journey is coming close—this I can feel. Know that if you do join me, I may ask you to do tasks you won't find pleasant, but I wouldn't ask for them if I didn't think they were absolutely necessary. You can also choose to leave. As I promised, I release you from your duty to me. You have served me well, and I respect your strength."

Koji stood up from the table. "Would you ask me to kill Asa?"

"Possibly."

"I wouldn't. Not without a good reason."

"I won't take that choice away from you."

Koji paced the room, and Minori studied him in a new light. He had always considered Koji to be a bit of a simpleton, but he realized now he had underestimated the young man. Koji was a strong blade and far more intuitive than Minori had expected. A powerful ally, but a dangerous enemy.

Koji stopped and stared at him. "There's another choice."

Minori raised an eyebrow.

"I could kill you now."

"Certainly. If you do, all I ask is that you do it face-to-face, honorably. I've had enough of being attacked from behind for the foreseeable future."

Koji looked around the room, as though the answer would be written on one of the barren walls.

"I think I'll need more time to make my choice."

"Take it. I don't know how much time you have to decide, but I will give you as much as I am able. Until then, you are still welcome to live here. If you want to continue in your other duties, I would be indebted to you."

Koji nodded and bowed deeply. Minori noted the gesture, and in his mind he thought about how the pieces were moving on the board.

His conversation with Koji had helped clarify Minori's own mind. The elder warrior had been honest with Koji. His entire goal in life was to earn autonomy for the blades. He hated to see what had been happening to them in the past several cycles, and he wouldn't be content until they all had the same rights as normal citizens.

Second to that, he did want to see stability in the Kingdom. In his mind, there was no other option but Shin. The lord would provide the strong leadership the Kingdom would need in a time of transition, and his heavy-handed nature would be ideal to pit the blades against a few cycles from now, when they had the support of the people. But getting Shin into power through nonviolent means just didn't seem likely. Minori had tried to solve the problem over and over during the past moon, but every option he came up with eventually resulted in violence. There just wasn't any reason for any of the other lords to accept Shin. Their claims were equal to his.

Minori realized he had been putting off a major decision, and he now had to take a stand. He had asked Koji to make a choice; now it was time for him to do the same.

To distract his mind, Minori looked over a chessboard. So many options, but the path to victory was always clear.

Minori turned over different ideas in his head. It would be hard to take the Kingdom by force, but it might fall by subterfuge. Unlike so many, Minori had a different concept of honor. Honor wasn't the rules and structures placed by society. Honor was doing the right thing, your actions in line with your conscience. If those actions were distasteful to others, that didn't matter. Minori considered himself an honorable man, but he wouldn't hesitate to take any action he felt was right.

Minori stood up. His decision was made. He would go as far as necessary. He looked down at the board. The key piece was Kiyoshi. If he fell, the king fell. It was time for the Kingdom to have a new king. It was time for Kiyoshi to die.

Chapter 18

As he had been doing every day, Kiyoshi wandered the energy pathways of Masaki's brain. Every day when he came to work with Masaki, the damage was a little worse, a little more widespread.

The dayblade did his duty, realigning the intricate pathways with the gentleness of a mother caring for a newborn child. When he had given all the energy and focus he could, he gently broke contact with Masaki, lying backward and exhaling. He had never felt as old as he did now. He could feel his own end approaching, but he would go to the Great Cycle fighting.

It was a measure of Kiyoshi's focus and subsequent exhaustion that several breaths passed before he noticed he wasn't alone in the room. He frowned. The guards had specific instructions. No one else was to be let in. When he turned around, he was surprised to see Asa.

Kiyoshi tried to summon a smile for her, but there wasn't one left in him.

She came to him and knelt down. "Can I help?"

Kiyoshi noticed the difference in her voice. Before, she had been all determination and hardness. But now there was a hint of kindness in her voice that hadn't been there before. Something was starting to change. After their meeting, Kiyoshi stopped having her followed. He hadn't seen much point.

He nodded, and Asa helped him stand.

They walked together, Kiyoshi putting far more of his weight on Asa than he cared to. They moved in silence down several halls, Kiyoshi wondering exactly what question he wanted to ask.

"What changed for you?"

Asa looked at him, surprised he had seen so deeply into her intentions. She smiled and shook her head. "I was thinking about what you said and thought maybe you were right."

Kiyoshi had to let out a small laugh. Asa's glance indicated her offense.

"I'm sorry; it's just that no one changes their mind based on rational argument. Not anymore. If you did, you truly are a rare and special woman."

Asa wasn't sure how to respond and didn't say anything until they got back to Kiyoshi's room. "I would like to help you, if I can."

Kiyoshi lay down on his bed, not caring at all if it was rude. He was drained. He swiveled his head to face Asa. "Does this mean you've given up on revenge?"

There was hesitation on her face, and Kiyoshi's heart sank. She met his gaze. "No. But I am at an impasse and have decided that perhaps there is room in my life for other pursuits. I want to help the Kingdom. I want to help those who need protecting. It seems, from everything I've seen, that means helping you."

Kiyoshi closed his eyes. He didn't know why, but he felt like so much was pinned on Asa. His heart raced, risk and reward balanced precariously in his mind's eye. He took a deep breath to calm himself.

He opened his eyes. "Your offer is accepted."

She bowed slightly to him.

"Now, for your first task."

Asa leaned forward, curious.

"Leave me alone so that I may sleep. I gave everything I had to the king and need to recover." This time he did manage a grin, to let her know he wasn't being too serious.

Asa nodded her head, and as Kiyoshi closed his eyes, she stood up and left the room.

It seemed like no time at all had passed when Kiyoshi was woken up by a firm, familiar hand on his shoulder. He opened his eyes slowly, awareness reluctant to return to his mind. In his windowless room, he couldn't tell how long he had been out, but it hadn't been long enough.

Daisuke had woken him up. The nightblade who couldn't be sensed was Kiyoshi's closest friend and ally, in addition to his best shadow. There was a look of concern in his eyes that brought Kiyoshi to attention. It almost felt physically painful to focus.

"What's wrong?"

As his mind came to him, Kiyoshi saw that Asa was in the room as well. That surprised him. Daisuke caught his glance. "I ran into her as she was leaving the castle. She told me she had joined your service, and so I brought her with me."

Kiyoshi nodded, which was all he could do in his state.

Daisuke told his story.

"Something is happening. Shin's grounds are emptying in ones and twos. All the guards are leaving. They've been leaving all day, but it took me a while to realize what was happening. If I couldn't send my sense into the grounds themselves, I might never have figured out what they were doing."

Kiyoshi was slow to understand, his mind still struggling against the chains of sleep and exhaustion. "What do you mean?"

"They've been leaving the castle but not the city, and none have been returning to the estate. By the time I figured it out and started making my way here, Shin's castle was almost empty of guards. I think they're preparing to take over the city."

The healer's mind spun in confusion. What was Shin up to? Did he know Isamu had gathered far more troops in his own castle than Shin had? If it came to open combat, Shin's troops would be overwhelmed. Although, he considered, if Shin's troops were able to station themselves in key places throughout the city, they could put up far more of a fight than otherwise possible.

Daisuke looked at his old friend. "What would you like me to do?"

Kiyoshi struggled to a sitting position, his mind racing. What could they do? They didn't have the men necessary to stop combat. The night-blades in the city would be caught by surprise, but unless they received a clear order, they would probably stay out of the fighting. After all, Shin and Isamu had equal claims to the throne.

Unless Minori was prepared to issue an order. Kiyoshi wasn't sure he would be so bold, but he wouldn't put it past the nightblade.

Before Kiyoshi could come up with an answer, there was a knock at his door. All three blades looked over expectantly, Daisuke and Asa both keeping hands on their swords. Kiyoshi invited the guest in. A castle guard appeared with a note for Kiyoshi. The dayblade took the message and tore it open as the guard left, his mission complete.

He looked up at his two allies. "They've called a King's Council, and my presence has been requested."

Kiyoshi tried to stand up, but he fell back down. He had given far too much to Masaki. He needed more rest, more food. Daisuke's look of concern was impossible to miss, and Asa clearly wasn't sure what to think.

He looked at the two. He had made the same mistake people always seem to make. Everyone always thinks they have more time. It's rarely true. Life moves quickly, and action is constantly necessary.

"Daisuke, I need you to take Asa with you."

Daisuke disagreed. "Kiyoshi, if something is happening, you're going to need me here."

"You're probably right, but Minori is clever, and I have no idea what he's got planned. A sword fight between equals goes to the warrior willing to wait for his opponent to reveal his intent first. The same is true here. I need Minori to reveal his hand before we decide what we will do. You know me as well as I know myself. You'll know what to do based on what happens."

Daisuke was ready to argue, but Kiyoshi glared daggers into him. "I know you don't like it, but it gives us the best chance we're going to have. I need you to do this."

There were a few moments of tense silence between the two old friends, and for a while, Kiyoshi wondered if Daisuke would see the wisdom in his approach. Finally, his eyes softened, and Kiyoshi knew his orders would be followed.

Kiyoshi spoke softly. "Thank you."

Daisuke bowed deeply, and Kiyoshi got the impression his old friend thought this would be the last time he saw him. Kiyoshi returned the bow as well as he was able.

—

Kiyoshi summoned a guard to escort him into the meeting hall. As they walked, the healer's eyes and sense took in everything. From what he could see, everything in the palace seemed as normal as it ever was. Had Daisuke overreacted? No, Kiyoshi believed his old friend. Whatever was happening hadn't reached the palace yet.

When he entered the meeting hall, he saw all the lords were present. If he could have, he would have dismissed the guard, but he wasn't certain he would reach his seat without support. Better to appear weak than to be proven weak.

Kiyoshi couldn't see Minori anywhere. He extended his sense, not very far given his current state, and couldn't feel him, either. That fact worried Kiyoshi more than Daisuke's report. If Minori was associated with Shin, he would have known about this meeting, and if he knew about it, he would want to be here. If he wasn't here, more important matters were occurring somewhere else.

After Kiyoshi was settled, Isamu started the discussion. He looked right at Shin. "Lord Shin, why have you called this council?"

Kiyoshi's fears doubled instantly. His note hadn't said anything about Shin calling the meeting. Suddenly he was very glad he had sent Daisuke and Asa away.

Shin looked around and took a deep breath. "Lords, it's time for us to have an honest discussion. We've danced around the topic long enough. What are we going to do when Masaki joins the Great Cycle?"

Lord Juro looked over at Kiyoshi. "We have no idea that will happen. Kiyoshi is giving everything he can to heal the king."

Shin looked as though he was going to laugh, but he didn't. "Everyone can see Kiyoshi is doing all he can. He wasn't even able to enter the room unassisted. And we all hope the king will make a full recovery. But we can't count on such a possibility, and we can't keep acting as though it will happen. We need to prepare for the worst. When Masaki dies, what will we do?"

The other two lords looked at each other, wondering where this was going. To bring the king's demise up so straightforwardly was almost certainly an indicator Shin had a greater plan in mind.

Isamu spoke, his words measured. "It would be the most rational to assume one of us would ascend to the kingship."

Juro nodded, and Shin looked like a predator ready to attack his prey. "I agree. But who is it going to be?" Juro asked.

A heavy silence fell across the table. Kiyoshi watched with wary eyes. Shin was building to something.

Shin only let the silence last a few moments. "Let's speak honestly. All of us have our eyes on the throne, and even though each of us would renounce the claims to our lands, the agreement, as it has been made, is going to be broken. Even if we tell ourselves we will rule with fairness, we're going to give preferential treatment to our own lands, and maybe even think about consolidating all the great houses.

"Furthermore, there's not going to be any good way of deciding who's going to be the next king. We could hold some sort of vote, but I would win, because my lands are the most populous. Likewise, we could go by resources, and then Lord Juro, you would be the clear winner. We could choose any number of factors, but choosing a factor is just a facade for choosing one of ourselves. None of us are willing to do that.

"I don't think I'm surprising any of you when I talk about the buildup of troops at the borders. I've been doing so, as have both of you. None of us want war, but each of us is willing to fight because we believe we're the best choice.

"So, I pose my original question to you all again: What are we going to do when the king dies?"

This time the silence was thick, and Kiyoshi could feel the anger and confusion emanating from the other lords. They hadn't expected this. Kiyoshi didn't blame them. To be having this conversation while Masaki was still alive and unable to contribute was the height of poor manners. But perhaps that was Shin's advantage. He was willing to do what others weren't to see his ends met.

As energy slowly returned to Kiyoshi, he began to notice a change. Off at the edge of his ability to sense, he felt other blades. He closed his eyes—another rude gesture in the council meeting—but he needed to focus his attention.

Blades were entering the palace, perhaps twenty or thirty in number, and all grouped closely together.

His first thought was for Asa and Daisuke. Had they gotten out in time? He pushed his sense out toward his room and followed the path they'd have to take. He wouldn't be able to sense Daisuke, but he could find Asa. Fortunately, she didn't seem to be anywhere to be found.

His second thought was to Shin. He had a few moments. The lords were sitting around the table unaware, each one absorbed in their own ruminations. Minori's plan must hinge on Shin, and if Kiyoshi could kill the treacherous lord, it would all fall apart.

But Kiyoshi couldn't bring himself to action. This wasn't about stopping Minori. This was about saving the Kingdom, and he wondered if Shin wasn't the best choice for king. He was smart and ruthless and possessed the qualities a monarch would need. Kiyoshi might not approve of Shin's methods, but at this point, it didn't seem justifiable to kill him.

Shin's voice intruded on Kiyoshi's thoughts. "Well, if no one else has any ideas, I'd like to present my own proposal. Make me king."

Isamu looked up, anger on his face. Juro rose, his hand going down to his sword. A part of Kiyoshi detached, interested in what was going to happen next. He felt as though he had become a spectator in his own life.

Juro was first to find the words. "You're mad if you believe we're just going to make you king."

Shin smiled, as though he had been waiting for just such a response. "I don't think you understand. I'm not offering you a choice. You will make me king."

Juro drew his sword. "Enough of this. Our families are strong enough without us. Let us settle this in the old ways. The person who leaves this room alive is the next king."

The detached Kiyoshi watched, his eyes widening. He didn't worry about his own life. None of the men in the room posed any personal threat to him, even as tired as he was. But he was reminded, memories flooding his thoughts, of how quickly civilized humans can lose everything that makes them better than animals. In just a few moments, they had come to violence as the only answer.

Kiyoshi sensed the blade coming, so it came as no surprise to him when Minori strode into the room. He looked around, the grin on his face so wide Kiyoshi wondered if he was under the influence of some drug. But the only drug at work here was power.

"My lords, there's no reason for any of this." He turned to Shin and bowed deeply. "My king, the palace is yours."

Both Juro and Isamu stared at Minori, their jaws wide open. They made the connection instantly and turned to Kiyoshi. "Kiyoshi, have the blades aligned with a single lord?"

Kiyoshi looked from face to face, unsure of how to answer. He wasn't certain what powers and permissions Minori had received from Starfall, but he had a hard time believing Minori would act without the council's blessing. "I hope not. But the Council of the Blades gives my advice less and less credence. I know nothing of Minori's actions."

Minori's smile of victory was almost sickening, but in his pride, he backed Kiyoshi up. "Well, that's certainly true. A new age is dawning."

As he finished speaking, a number of Shin's soldiers and nightblades entered the room. Considering all the people in the immediate vicinity, Kiyoshi couldn't sense what was happening in the entire castle, but most of the fighting was apparently over. The takeover, as violent as it had been, was quick. The military aspect of Kiyoshi's mind had to give Minori and Shin respect for their clean invasion of the palace. Not bloodless, but perhaps as bloodless as possible.

Juro and Isamu were speechless. Shin was clearly prepared for this moment. "Guards, take Lords Juro and Isamu from the grounds to their palaces."

Shin turned to the lords.

"We will have plenty of time to speak in a day or two. I will come to you and discuss what has happened here today and what options you have. You can choose to believe me or not, but it is my desire not to harm either of you. I will be king, but I would prefer to do it in as peaceful a manner as possible. You each will have the option of supporting me and maintaining the lives you are used to, or you can elect not to. Choose wisely."

Rage consumed the faces of the other two lords, and Kiyoshi worried they wouldn't be making choices based on wisdom anytime soon.

Yet they both managed to keep their mouths shut, and they were led firmly out of the room by Shin's guards.

That business completed, Shin and Minori turned to Kiyoshi. Minori still had the grin of victory on his face, and Shin spoke first. "Kiyoshi, your service to the Kingdom is well known. As I expect you've guessed already, Minori and I have been planning this moment for some time. Minori is no supporter of yours, but I have nothing but respect for what you've done. I know you are an honest man, so I'll ask you directly. Will you support me as king?"

Kiyoshi's answer was firm, but he spoke softly. "Perhaps if Masaki were dead, I would, but while the true king lives, I cannot."

Shin nodded. "I had expected nothing less from a man of your reputation. I have many things to take care of, and I cannot worry about a devoted dayblade. Minori would have you thrown in prison with a death sentence, but for now, you are confined to the palace. Any attempt to escape will result in violence."

Kiyoshi met Shin's steely gaze with one of his own. "I thank you for your generosity. What about Masaki?"

Shin didn't flinch. "There are messages being spread throughout Haven and the Kingdom. As far as anyone knows, Masaki died tonight."

Kiyoshi didn't respond.

Shin sighed, as though he didn't think he was making the right decision. "Rationally, I should just kill him and put him out of his misery, but I spoke truly to the lords. I'd prefer to shed as little blood as possible. You are closer to him than anyone else. I know you've kept him alive to prevent just this moment, but now that it has happened, you can choose based on your own conscience. If you think he should live, you are welcome to keep trying to heal him. Otherwise, you can let him pass into the Great Cycle like he should have a half moon ago."

Minori looked as though he were about to argue but thought better of it. Kiyoshi had to admit the terms were more than fair from a conqueror.

Minori turned to several of the nightblades who had come into the room after him. "Escort Kiyoshi back to his quarters. If he tries anything, don't hesitate to kill him. I want at least four of you with him at all times, even when he's asleep. He may not look like much, but he's not as helpless as he'd have you believe. Am I clear?"

One of the nightblades bowed slightly to Minori. "Yes. Never less than four."

With that, four nightblades detached from the rest of the group and came over to Kiyoshi. He nodded, and they formed a loose perimeter around him. Kiyoshi walked with his guards, now a prisoner in the palace he had once considered home.

Chapter 19

Asa's world was turned upside down yet again. She was getting to the point where she wished she could have a single day without being in danger. Perhaps saving the Kingdom wasn't for her. She didn't understand why Daisuke was so worried. All in all, a few troops leaving a compound didn't seem like that big a deal, but Daisuke looked as though he was ready for the battle of a lifetime.

After Kiyoshi left, Daisuke went rummaging around Kiyoshi's small room, pulling out various vials and packages. He took each of them and threw them into a small sack.

"What are you doing?"

Daisuke didn't even spare Asa a glance as he continued ransacking Kiyoshi's place. "I don't think we're going to be returning. Many of the items here are valuable and have powerful healing properties. It is best if Kiyoshi has them wherever we go."

Asa couldn't hide her disbelief. "You really think this is that serious?"

Daisuke paused for a moment, turned, and stared at her. "If I'm right, tonight is the night the Kingdom collapses."

Asa's jaw opened in amazement. "What do you mean?"

Daisuke had gone back to rummaging through the small room. "Minori and Shin have been working together. I believe Shin is preparing for an assault on the palace. That's why there is a council meeting tonight. He's going to catch them by surprise, and by tomorrow, he will have declared himself king. But the other lords and their families will not stand for it. We're going to be looking at war in a matter of days."

"You're not very optimistic, are you?"

He laughed. "Just realistic."

"That's what all the pessimists say."

A few moments later he was done packing. He slung the sack over his back and stood up. "It's time to go."

They stepped out into the hallway, and Daisuke looked up and down. "Come on, this way."

Asa frowned. "Isn't the exit that way?"

"We're going to have to take a different route."

Without waiting for her to agree, he took off. Asa frowned, but before she asked any foolish questions, she took a moment and extended her sense. What she felt surprised her. The palace was a hive of activity; there were so many people that she had to back off or risk stunning her mind.

"We're being attacked."

Daisuke didn't bother to respond. He walked, but his steps were fast and determined. Asa realized she'd never really met anyone like him. The fact that she couldn't sense him was still disorienting, although she was getting used to his ability. But the world seemed to be collapsing all around them, and he was walking through the chaos like he knew every step he had to take.

The palace was a maze. Asa knew only the route to Kiyoshi's chambers and was quickly lost. Daisuke turned and turned again, and if he hadn't looked so calm and focused, Asa would have guessed he was choosing hallways at random. But at times she would extend her sense, and she could tell he was avoiding different groups of warriors.

Finally he came to a stop. He looked at Asa and seemed to ask himself a question. She had no idea what it was, but he seemed to answer decisively. "There's no way we're getting out of here without fighting.

However, I think I can find us a path that won't have any more than one or two nightblades. Don't kill anyone."

His statements were simple, but they raised dozens of questions in Asa's distracted mind. There were nightblades fighting in the palace? What was actually going on? And why was he prohibiting her from killing people? If they were enemies, shouldn't they die?

Daisuke didn't give her any time to ask the questions. Instead, he turned around and continued the pace he had set before. Asa took a deep breath. She was a nightblade, and here she was acting as though she was useless. Daisuke clearly didn't think so. His comments indicated he expected her to fight, so conflict seemed likely.

She centered herself and extended her sense out past her immediate vicinity. She couldn't extend her sense very far, but it was enough to give her ample warning. She drew one of her swords and took off after Daisuke.

Asa caught up with him after a few running steps, but as she did, with her newfound awareness, she started noticing other things. For one, Daisuke was focusing his sense ahead of him. She understood, her training inserting itself into her memory once again. They were moving like a small convoy, and he expected her to cover the path behind them, allowing each to focus a little farther out.

Asa couldn't remember the last time she had worked so closely with someone else. Her dedication to finding and killing Osamu had made her a loner, but with Daisuke's calm competence, she slipped into the pairing without difficulty. They moved forward, finally starting to turn toward the palace door.

Asa sensed two soldiers behind them, but they weren't in line of sight and neither was sense-gifted. In general, the commotion seemed to be moving toward the center of the palace, which was understandable if the Kingdom really was being taken over.

Ahead, two soldiers turned and headed straight for the blades, but they weren't sense-gifted either and didn't have a chance. Daisuke slowed just slightly, timing his gait so that he would run into them right at the intersection of the hallway.

The pair of guards was taken by surprise. Daisuke turned the corner and struck the first guard with the hilt of his sword, knocking the breath out of him and bringing him to the ground. The second guard was just beginning to react when Daisuke chopped at his throat with his hand. The man also went down, clutching at his throat, trying desperately to bring air into his straining lungs.

Asa helped. The first guard was trying to get his feet underneath him, but she stepped forward and snapped a kick into his midsection. He collapsed again and decided to stay down. Daisuke gave her a small nod of acknowledgment, and they continued on.

Asa used her sense to make sure their little fight hadn't been noticed. After they had taken a few more turns, she could feel they had a reprieve from being attacked.

She was so focused on what was happening behind them, she almost didn't notice that Daisuke had stopped. Her sense warned her right before impact, and she halted just in time. Daisuke looked at her and whispered, "There is a nightblade around that corner. She's waiting for you."

Asa shifted her sense forward and felt exactly what Daisuke was talking about. If she stalled much longer, the nightblade would get curious and come around the corner for her. She guessed what Daisuke's plan was. The intersection ahead was T-shaped.

Asa took the lead, crossing through the intersection of the hallways without paying any particular attention to the nightblade. As Asa had hoped, the woman called after her.

Asa turned around and hid a smile as the nightblade stepped into the intersection, her back to Daisuke.

The blade looked at Asa, a question on her face. "Who are you?"

Asa gave her name as she studied the other nightblade. She recognized her from the quarters she stayed in. The only odd fact about her appearance was that she had a red piece of fabric tied around her upper left arm. Asa assumed the fabric identified her as a blade who supported Minori.

She was so interested she almost missed the blade's next statement. "I'm sorry, but you're going to have to come with me. Minori is looking for you."

Asa didn't have to come up with an explanation. Daisuke slid behind the nightblade, as silent as the grave and invisible to the warrior's sense, and with one strong blow, knocked her unconscious to the floor.

Daisuke took a short moment, and Asa assumed he was trying to sense their path ahead. "I think we should be safe now. We'll need to move quickly."

Asa didn't need to be told twice. Before she left, she reached down and untied the ribbon from around the nightblade's arm and tied it around her own. Daisuke gave her a short look. "It might work," she responded.

Without another word they took off, Daisuke setting his confident pace once again. Just before they got to the front gate, Daisuke veered away. Asa knew better than to question him by this point. The front gate would be guarded, and Daisuke seemed to have another plan for getting out of the palace.

They paused at the entrance to a garden as a set of four guards walked past. Only moments after their footsteps faded, Daisuke crept into the garden, Asa right behind him. He pulled on a rope attached to the palace wall, and a ladder unfurled from the top. Asa was surprised but followed Daisuke up to the top of the wall.

Asa wasn't sure what she'd find when she reached the top, but she wasn't expecting what she saw. From the wall she was able to see much of Haven, and the night was quiet. The city wasn't burning, and there weren't any sounds of combat. The peace was disconcerting after the tension of their escape.

The duo waited for another set of guards to pass below them, and then Daisuke looked back at Asa.

"From firsthand experience I know you're fine jumping from heights. Follow me."

He leapt, and rolled as he landed in the street that surrounded the palace walls, and Asa followed suit. She came to her feet, and for the first time that night, Daisuke broke into a run. Asa ran, too, but their sprint was short-lived. As soon as they reached the line of buildings across from the palace, they stopped, and Daisuke took a moment to use his sense to scan the surroundings. A few moments later, Asa saw why they had fled. Another set of guards passed by the spot they had just occupied.

Daisuke gave his head a little jerk, indicating they should be off. Asa, following without hesitation, stepped into the shadows.

The two walked through the night, following alleys and backways. If Asa hadn't been following Daisuke, she would have been lost almost instantly. It was obvious Daisuke had a deep understanding of all of Haven, and he never paused as he turned from back alley to back alley.

Asa couldn't get over just how quiet the city was. Her heartbeat was returning to normal after their escape from the palace. Even though they hadn't run except for at the very end of their escape, Asa felt as though she had just finished a long race. The tension of uncertainty had sapped her strength.

Outside of the palace, it could have been any other night. The streets were quiet. People could feel the potency of the situation, and they stayed in their houses, safe. But all the same, Asa could hear a few drunks wandering down roads, and she could sense the life in many of the houses. Her world might be upside down, but for tonight at least, she had little company.

Her thoughts turned from the city and its inhabitants to Daisuke. Even though she had spent a fair amount of time with him, his special ability was still disconcerting. Asa had sensed all the life around her for almost as long as she could remember, but here in front of her, the man might as well have not even existed.

His skill, as unusual as it was, wasn't what captured her attention, though. What she was really surprised by was his competence. She was certain that even with her skills, she wouldn't have had a chance of getting out of the castle as smoothly as they just had.

Daisuke was striding in his typical confident manner, and it seemed like he had a particular destination in mind. She considered asking about where they were headed, but decided not to. She trusted him.

They eventually stopped in front of a nondescript house. They were in a residential area of Haven, where many of the houses looked the same. She wondered what significance the house had to Daisuke and why he had led her here after their escape.

The change in Daisuke was fascinating as he entered the house. He took off his sandals and placed them neatly against the wall, where Asa saw a number of other sandals. She frowned.

Daisuke stepped farther inside, and Asa could feel the other lives in the house. One source of energy, a child, ran toward them. Asa's first reaction was to reach for her sword, but she realized the tension of the evening had her thinking foolishly. Daisuke wasn't afraid or on edge at all.

A girl came around the corner and ran full-speed into Daisuke. "Dad!"

Asa's jaw dropped for what felt like the hundredth time that night. She scanned the child with her sense, but she couldn't feel anything unique about her. She wasn't sense-gifted, or if she was, she hadn't displayed any powers yet.

Daisuke knelt down and gave the girl, who was apparently his daughter, a big hug. He picked her up and swung her around. The little girl squealed with joy.

Asa tried to blink away what she was seeing. After everything she had seen from Daisuke—his strong fighting skill, his calm competence under the most stressful combat situations—she hadn't pictured him as a man with a family. Daisuke turned to Asa, his daughter in his arms. "Asa, I'd like you to meet my daughter, Mika. Mika, I'd like you to meet a friend of mine, Asa."

The little girl seemed to be paying a lot of attention to Asa. She turned to her dad. "Is she a nightblade like you?"

Daisuke laughed, a sound that still seemed completely foreign coming from the warrior Asa knew. "She is. How did you know?"

"She looks serious."

Daisuke laughed again and looked at Asa. "Apparently you're going to need to work on your facial expressions if we're going to get you out of the city. Even my daughter can pick you out!"

Asa was still stunned speechless. She wondered if this was some sort of complex joke she didn't understand.

Another person came to the front, drawn by all the commotion. "Daisuke, did you bring over a guest without warning me? I thought we had talked about this."

The woman who came forth was younger than Daisuke by at least ten cycles. She was a short woman with long dark hair that fell below her shoulders, and Asa could tell from the way she stood close to Daisuke, she was very much in love with him. Daisuke was grinning from ear to ear. "Asa, I'd like you to meet my wife, Keiko. Keiko, Asa."

The young lady looked at Asa, and from her expression, it was clear she wasn't pleased to see another woman in the house.

Daisuke put Mika down. "Mika, I need you to go play for a little while. We need to talk about serious adult things. Can you do that?"

Mika nodded, and Asa saw the young girl was curious but obedient. A few moments later, Asa felt the girl playing in the next room, slowly working her way toward the door so she could listen to the adults.

Keiko seemed to know something was wrong. "What's happened?"

Daisuke looked down at her. "Lord Shin is in the middle of a coup."

Keiko's eyes went to the unlocked door, and Daisuke seemed to understand her question. "All things considered, they're doing a superb job. I don't think anyone is going to know until tomorrow morning. But Asa and I just escaped from the palace."

"Kiyoshi?"

"I assume he's been captured or killed. Keiko, the nightblades are taking sides in this fight, and I'm worried about what will happen."

Asa watched Keiko's face as it went through several emotions. Eventually she stood up straighter, and Asa could see the strength of her character.

"What would you have us do?"

"I'd like you and Mika to leave town tonight. There's a small chance that this will resolve peacefully, but I have a hard time believing in such eventualities. I suspect we're going to see war soon, and Haven will be the center of activity. I can't have you here, and I'm worried they will try to close the gates sometime before the sun rises."

Asa expected Keiko to question Daisuke, to beg him to come with her, but she didn't. Asa was impressed.

"What are you going to do?"

Daisuke glanced over at Asa. "First, I need to find out if Kiyoshi is still alive. If he is, we'll need to rescue him. If the king is still alive, we must get him out, too. Hopefully, Kiyoshi has more of a plan than I do. I just need to give him the opportunity to make it happen."

Keiko looked as though she wanted to argue. "We'll get ready. Did you want us to go to my sister's?"

"It is as good a place as any—yes."

Keiko didn't ask any more questions. She turned and went through the house trying to find her daughter. "Mika! It's time for a surprise visit to your aunt!"

—

Asa and Daisuke sat in his dining room. She was still looking around, having a hard time accepting that Daisuke had a family. He watched her eyes wandering the room, smiling at her amazement.

"How did all this happen?"

Daisuke shrugged. "Where would you like me to start?"

"When did you meet Keiko?"

"A long time ago, more than twenty cycles. I was a boy, and she was an even younger girl. I rescued her from a bad situation. Kiyoshi helped me. It is one of many reasons why I owe him everything.

"I helped her escape, and because she was so young, she had a tendency to view me as some sort of hero. Nothing could be farther from the truth, but there was no telling her otherwise. She followed me for quite some time, and finally I gave up trying to convince her to leave. To make a very long story short, in time, she grew up and saw me as I really am. We found love and have been together for five cycles now. Mika is four."

Asa was intensely curious. "I don't know if I've ever heard of a nightblade leading a life like this. What does the council have to say about it?"

Daisuke barked a short laugh. "I suppose Kiyoshi never had a chance to tell you. I was never a part of the census. The council doesn't know that I exist. I serve Kiyoshi, not Starfall."

Asa studied Daisuke carefully. He was perhaps the most interesting nightblade she had ever met. "How is it that Kiyoshi has earned such loyalty from you?"

At that moment, Keiko stepped into the room, and from her expression, she had clearly heard the question. Her eyes saddened, and Asa realized that all she saw was connected. Keiko, Daisuke, and Kiyoshi were all intertwined, and she had just asked the question at the heart of the story.

Daisuke spoke softly. "There was a time, a very long time ago, when Kiyoshi and I would have been enemies. I was just discovering my ability to hide from the sense, and I was being groomed to kill blades. Again, it's a long story, but Kiyoshi and I came face-to-face, and although I'm ashamed to admit it, he overcame me. He had the opportunity to kill me, and he should have. But he showed me mercy. Not only that, but he protected me and trained me for several cycles. Everything I am is because of him."

Keiko interjected. "If not for him, our family and our lives wouldn't exist. I owe him everything."

Asa thought about the man she had met only a few times. "He is something unique, isn't he? I don't know if I've ever met a man quite like him before."

Daisuke nodded. "He isn't perfect. He'll be the first to tell you he's made horrible mistakes. But he tries every day to do the best he can, and I've never regretted a day in his service." He paused. "And he seems to get me into the most interesting situations."

Keiko seemed to read her husband's thoughts. "We're ready to go. Mika is tired and will probably fall asleep as we travel."

With the family ready, they all sprang into motion. Asa noticed a slight edge to Daisuke's actions. The sun was just peeking over the horizon, and she could tell he was worried they had waited too long for his wife and daughter to leave. Nevertheless, they prepared their horse for travel. Keiko climbed on top with practiced ease, and Daisuke lifted a sleeping Mika up to her arms. With that, all four of them left.

Asa scanned the area, but it was still too early in the morning for most people to be awake. Even so, she noticed a great deal of activity in the direction of the wall. Asa also worried they would be too late. She felt for Daisuke. It had been so long since she had been part of a family, but she knew Daisuke would lose focus if his loved ones were in the city, in danger.

When they got to the gate, Asa saw there was a commotion. The atmosphere was quiet but tense. The king's guards were stationed at the gate, but a contingent of about sixteen of Shin's men had come to relieve them. They were carrying orders, and there seemed to be a heated discussion between the two groups. Asa, Daisuke, and his family stopped a little way away from the gate. She was relieved that she couldn't sense any blades nearby.

Daisuke's mind seemed to be racing. He looked at Asa. "We can try to deceive them, but I doubt it will buy us more than a few moments. Will you help?"

Asa didn't even have to think about her answer. She nodded.

Daisuke looked up at his wife. "Keiko, we'll buy you a short window, but you might need to make a sprint for it. I will come for you as soon as I can. But be alert. I'm afraid that if the fires of war start, they will spread far faster than anyone thinks."

Keiko met her husband's gaze. "I love you."

"I love you, too. Travel safe."

With that, their small group stepped forward. Daisuke's voice was commanding, very much unlike his presence. Asa was surprised yet again by her companion. "What's happening here?"

The guards all stopped and turned to see the two nightblades at the gate. One of the commanders turned and bowed. "I'm sorry, sir, but this group of men has come, claiming they are to take control of the gates. But I've gotten no such orders."

Daisuke seemed to study the situation for a moment. If it came to a fight, Shin's men looked as though they would win due to sheer numbers and preparation for combat. The guards at the gate had become far too used to peacetime, and they weren't wearing the armor or weapons that would give them a chance.

Asa stepped forward, deciding to help Daisuke, and addressed the commander of Shin's men. "Minori asked us to come here and take charge of the gate. A small problem has developed to the west of the palace, and your help has been demanded."

The commander looked doubtful. "Why send you here? Wouldn't it be more reasonable if you went directly there?"

She frowned, her mind racing. "It was deemed unwise to send a nightblade into this particular situation. They need guards, not blades."

The commander still looked doubtful, and Asa noticed he kept glancing down at her arm and the red band.

"Very well." The commander turned to his men. "Men, new orders!"

Shin's men soon turned around and marched the other way. Daisuke led Keiko through the gate, and they shared a few private moments on the outside of the wall.

Asa turned to the commander of the gate. "They'll be back, and they'll be angry. Shin is leading a coup."

The commander looked as surprised as could be expected. His immediate reaction was to put on the mask of a brave soldier. "We'll guard this gate with our lives!"

Asa shook her head. "There's no point. At best you can hold out, what, maybe half a day? Shin has far more troops here than you would believe. Better to abandon your posts and live to fight another day. There's nothing to be gained by sacrificing yourselves."

Asa could see the doubt on the man's face. Abandoning his post went against every precept of honor he held to, but frankly, she didn't care.

She looked one last time at the gate. Asa knew that if she had any hint of self-preservation in her, she'd leave Haven now. But Minori was here, and she wouldn't flee without killing him. The chaos of the coup would provide the perfect cover. She would bide her time until opportunity presented itself.

Daisuke came back and stopped next to Asa. "Now we need to find out if Kiyoshi is still alive, and if he is, where he is. Then we break him out." He paused and smiled at her. "Ready?"

"It's my first jailbreak. Hope you don't mind showing me how a professional operates."

Daisuke barked his short laugh.

Asa watched as the sun came up over the horizon.

Chapter 20

Minori believed that too many people put too much stock in the wrong values. Everybody was so concerned about their honor, they were blind to more devious means of seizing power. But if deception meant more people could live, wasn't that worth something? Life was much more precious than honor.

They had sent out the news this morning. The old king was dead, and Lord Shin had been named the new king just prior to Masaki's death. Simply say it and it would become true.

There were complications, of course. For one, the king wasn't dead. In fact, he was in Kiyoshi's windowless room, probably being healed right now. Minori smiled. Kiyoshi would never stop fighting, but he had lost. Minori had achieved a victory over his strongest opponent yet.

The other lords were also a problem. Neither was particularly pleased about being taken hostage and becoming embroiled in lies.

Minori wondered which would chafe more: being confined to their palaces or their people believing they had supported Shin. He supposed it was the latter. And Isamu had been particularly disappointed when he discovered his buildup of guards had been escorted from his castle with the help of a large group of blades.

The Kingdom was far from unified, but if the next few days were peaceful, Minori thought his and Shin's plan would work. Both Juro and Isamu were part of large, powerful families, and if the clans decided they didn't like what was happening, they could always resort to force. But there would be an element of confusion. Forged letters had been sent to both families, claiming the lords had supported Shin's ascension. Even if the letters weren't believed by the clans, they would sow doubt, and by the time the families decided on a course of action, Shin would have solidified his base of power and moved his armies into strategically vital locations. At least, that was the hope. That, and the fact that the heads of their families were being held as hostages.

In all other ways, the takeover had been smooth, almost too smooth. Minori hoped for more violence. He needed more violence. The pieces were in motion, and Minori was playing a very long game. He wanted Shin to have to resort to authoritarian measures so that the blades would soon have a reason to depose him.

There was still hope. Asa and some other nightblade had escaped the palace. It seemed as though Asa and her friend had made some trouble at a gate, too—a strange situation. The commander reported being deceived by two blades, but when he returned to the gate, the posts had been completely abandoned.

Minori wondered if the two had escaped the city or were still here. He couldn't decide. On the one hand, he could see Asa trying to get back to Starfall. She would go to the Council of the Blades, only to find no help there. Minori had their support, even if they might disapprove of his methods. On the other hand, Koji had said Asa was working for Kiyoshi now. She and her blade ally might remain in the city and try to rescue him.

A rescue would be obnoxious, but Minori wasn't worried. Kiyoshi and the king were near the center of the palace, with nightblades roaming the grounds and four guarding the door. Asa wasn't nearly good enough to break Kiyoshi out from such defenses.

At the end of the day, he didn't have enough information to make a decision, so he put the matter out of his mind. There was no point worrying about what he couldn't control—a hard lesson for him to learn, but one he had taken to heart and that had changed his life.

Anyway, he thought as he smiled to himself, there was an upcoming conversation he was very excited to have.

Minori walked through the halls of the palace, preparing for his next meeting. He hadn't spoken with Kiyoshi in any real way since the first conversation they'd held back when Minori had first come to Haven just over a moon ago. That initial meeting seemed lifetimes away.

He was pleased to see the four nightblades on duty were alert. Blades had a difficult time with guard duty. Since they could sense anyone coming, it was far too easy to slip into a state of complacency. Fortunately, the habit didn't seem to be affecting these four. He nodded at the sentries and walked into Kiyoshi's room without pause.

Minori was surprised. He had expected to see both Kiyoshi and the king, but the room radiated a peace he hadn't expected. Incense was burning in the corner, and the light was dim, the entire space lit by a single candle. The combination of smell and muted luminance had the immediate effect of calming Minori. He wondered at the change.

Kiyoshi looked up at Minori. He obviously wasn't surprised at the visit. He would have felt Minori coming from quite a distance. Something had changed in him, though: the older man was looking healthier than he had in some time.

Minori had come in feeling victorious, but something about the atmosphere of the room made him pause. Here in Kiyoshi's sanctum, he was nothing but a healer, and one of the best in the Kingdom. Politics seemed undeniably petty.

The nightblade glanced down at Masaki. The king had once been a great man, but those times were long past. Minori hoped the same fate would never befall him. He would rather die with a sword through his chest than suffer the indignities of an age that took away your abilities. Perhaps he'd still have the chance.

"How is he?"

Kiyoshi frowned, and Minori understood the question must have sounded strange coming from him. He had admitted he'd just as soon kill Masaki, so inquiring after the king's health must have seemed odd. But after a pause, Kiyoshi seemed to understand. Politics and power were one thing. Personal feelings were another.

"Not much has changed. To be honest, there are times when I wonder if I should keep trying. Once, I thought maybe his life would hold off the chaos, but that was overly optimistic of me. Now I wonder if I should just let him pass on his way. Perhaps it would be better for him."

In a flash of insight, Minori understood. Kiyoshi was giving less and less of his energy to Masaki, hence explaining why he was looking so much better. Seized by a sudden feeling of compassion, he reached out and grabbed Kiyoshi's shoulder. Too late, he forgot what Kiyoshi could do through touch, but he wasn't so cowardly as to remove his hand.

Minori needn't have worried. The healer glanced up at him, but then kept staring at the king.

"We don't agree, Kiyoshi, but it's a good thing you do."

A little tension seemed to evaporate from Kiyoshi's frame. Minori let go and stepped back to a safer distance.

Kiyoshi spoke thoughtfully. "I wonder sometimes. Dayblades and nightblades. Two sides of the same coin. Some have the power to take lives; others have the power to save lives. It seems as though one is better than the other, but at other times, I wonder if maybe this power is unnatural. Maybe none of us should have these abilities."

Bespeaking his calm, Minori didn't respond in anger. "There's no point in questioning whether we should have our gifts. We do. All that is left is to decide how best to use them."

Kiyoshi sighed. "But do you think there is a best way? What if by prolonging Masaki's life, I've brought about more suffering? Maybe none of us are wise enough to know what truly is best. Perhaps we should just let the Great Cycle turn."

Minori thought he understood. "I don't know what you've seen, Kiyoshi, but we can't give up. We're not perfect, but we have choices. We can make this world a better place."

Kiyoshi got up from his place near the king and moved to his bed. "I want you to be right, but my heart doesn't believe it."

Kiyoshi looked as though he was debating whether or not to say something. His words eventually came out. "Aligning with Shin is a mistake. He seeks to eliminate the blades from the Kingdom."

Minori scoffed. "Even if that was true, he wouldn't have a chance. We are far too strong to be removed from the board by force."

Kiyoshi looked like there was more he would say, but the older man just shook his head and remained silent.

The two looked at each other, the silence growing. Minori found it deeply saddening that day and night couldn't agree. If they could, their friendship would be the subject of stories for generations. He smiled and saw Kiyoshi notice.

"I'm sorry, I was just thinking of something Koji said. He told me you and I were more alike than either of us wanted to admit."

"He's probably right."

The next silence was broken by Kiyoshi. "Why are you here, Minori? I know you didn't come to gloat. You're a better man than that."

"I wanted to ask you about Asa."

That surprised Kiyoshi. "Has something happened to her?"

Minori was tempted to lie. "No. I don't know where she is, although we are searching for her. I wanted to learn more about her."

"Why?"

"Because although in many ways she seems perfectly unremarkable, my instincts tell me much hinges on her. If I'm going to succeed, I need to understand her. I need to know why she wants to kill me."

Kiyoshi smiled at that. "She wants to kill you because she thinks you're Osamu."

Minori returned the smile, his guess confirmed. "I wondered if that was the case. I told her I was at Two Falls. But she never would have seen any mention of my name."

Kiyoshi nodded, and Minori frowned. "But you know my history. You know why my name never shows up."

"Yes, I know you were the shadow who provided the information to Osamu. I've known about your background for a long time. When you were younger, you were sent as a shadow on some of the most dangerous missions in blade history. You risked more than most of us ever have."

Minori chuckled. "And yet you somehow forgot all this when Asa told you of her suspicions?"

Kiyoshi's grin was devious. "It might have slipped my mind for a moment."

Minori was surprised, but he didn't find himself angry. Perhaps it was the calming scents, or the refreshing honesty between the two men.

"You know, if we agreed on the future of the blades, you and I would be almost unstoppable."

"Perhaps. I don't believe the blades are as infallible as you think. Someone, somewhere would outsmart us."

Minori changed the subject, unwilling to rehash old arguments. "I don't suppose you have any idea where Asa went, do you? I'd rather capture her peacefully."

Kiyoshi raised an eyebrow. "From a man who just tried to have her killed, I find that hard to believe."

"She can't affect the game anymore, and whether you believe me or not, I'd rather not shed unnecessary blood. At least, not from a blade."

"If I did know her whereabouts, I wouldn't tell you."

Minori's anger finally started to break through the surface. He swore. "Kiyoshi, I'm trying to do what's best. But if you don't stop getting in my way . . ."

Kiyoshi stood in one smooth motion, and before Minori realized what had happened, the dayblade was inside his guard, less than a pace away. Minori's mouth stood open. He hadn't sensed incoming movement. Just who was Kiyoshi, and what was he capable of?

"Minori, the time for games has come to an end. You've forced the blades into a place where they need to make a decision. Are they going to take a side, or are they going to stand for the Kingdom? I may respect the honesty you've had with me, but never consider, even for a moment, that I will help you. You will tear this Kingdom apart unless I stop you, and if not for those four blades outside who would come running the moment I killed you, you would already be dead. Fortunately for you, I need to stay alive to finish my work."

Minori stepped back in fear and surprise. Twice now he had been caught off guard by Kiyoshi. It would never happen again.

Every possible retort he had felt empty and meaningless in his mind, so he snapped around and left the room without another word. He had a Kingdom to run.

Chapter 21

Although he didn't show it, Kiyoshi was consumed by uncertainty, a sensation he hadn't experienced in as long as he could remember. He was a man who thought through his actions carefully, but once he made a decision, he committed to it. These traits had always served him well, but ever since Masaki's stroke, Kiyoshi had been beset by doubt.

Perhaps because the stakes had never been higher, Kiyoshi felt as though every decision he made changed the future of the Kingdom.

For the first time, Kiyoshi also doubted his decisions. Was he keeping Masaki alive for the Kingdom, or for his own selfish desires? He had convinced himself it was for the Kingdom, but was he deceiving himself?

Kiyoshi's mind swirled, lost in conflict. In his windowless room, with no exposure to the outside world, it was too easy to lose track of time. His body and mind were tired and needed sleep. Masaki was resting comfortably.

The old dayblade lay his head down on the bed, thinking he would just close his eyes for a while. His world went black, and when he finally came to, he understood he had been asleep for a long time. But his mind was clear.

Out of habit, Kiyoshi knelt down next to Masaki. He was just about to lay his hands on the king when he stopped, sudden clarity striking him.

He was stuck, making the same decision over and over, even though the situation had transformed into something new. His plan, once reasonable, now seemed silly. He had been a fool for not realizing this before, blinded by hope and optimism. But he saw the truth now. Even if he could bring Masaki back to consciousness for a while, his work would never be enough. The king's guard had already been scattered by Shin's forces, and even if Kiyoshi could summon the troops, they were far outmatched by the combination of Shin's guards and the nightblades assisting them.

All he would accomplish by waking Masaki would be to bring his old friend more sorrow. The king had already given everything in service to the Kingdom and deserved a peaceful rest.

Yet Kiyoshi refused to leave him. He didn't think Minori would do anything to harm the former king's body, but he didn't trust the nightblade to give Masaki a proper funeral.

He almost didn't realize he had made a decision. Kiyoshi knew he had to escape the palace. He assumed Daisuke would arrive sooner rather than later. His old friend wouldn't leave him here, and he suspected Daisuke would have Asa with him. If that was true, Kiyoshi needed to be ready to move at a moment's notice. And Masaki needed to be ready as well.

Decision made, Kiyoshi began making arrangements. His first step was to prepare Masaki. He couldn't give the former king all the energy he had been providing. Kiyoshi was going to need more of it for himself in an escape. But he still had some to give, and in the calm environment of his old room, perhaps he could do delicate work.

Kiyoshi rehearsed his escape in his mind. He didn't know what Daisuke would hatch, but he figured that at the very least, he should be prepared to kill the four nightblades guarding his door. Four nightblades would be quite an achievement, one that would live in infamy if the stories ever got out.

He might be a dayblade, but he had plenty of surprises up his sleeve. He was ready.

—

When the moment came, Kiyoshi was prepared. For most blades, it would have been impossible to sense Daisuke. His skill made him one of the most useful nightblades Kiyoshi had ever met, and he was grateful the two of them had become friends. And he had learned, after cycles of trial and error, ways in which to track his old friend.

Between healings, Kiyoshi would extend his sense throughout the surrounding corridors. Fortunately for him, Shin's coup had largely emptied the palace. Kiyoshi didn't know for sure, but he assumed Shin was still running his coup from the safety and security of his own home. The palace was large and expansive, with rumors of tunnels that ran underneath. Kiyoshi knew the rumors were true, and a part of him regretted that Shin had the wisdom to stay away.

Daisuke would be hard to find, especially if he were trying to hide, but Kiyoshi had made himself familiar with Asa's presence. If she entered the palace again, he would notice her.

After several days, his patience paid off. He felt her, moving into the grounds. He sensed they were using one of the two escape tunnels that had been built into the bedrock. Kiyoshi was grateful. He hadn't remembered if Daisuke knew about the tunnels. The passageways would be guarded by Shin's men, who wouldn't have a chance against the two of them. The only nightblades in the vicinity were the four guarding Kiyoshi.

Kiyoshi knew he had some time before his two allies got to him. Daisuke was a cautious man, and he'd try to spare any lives he could. Kiyoshi put the time to good use. He had conceived of a stretcher using parts of furniture from his room, and now he took the time to put it together. The stretcher wasn't well built, and Kiyoshi was sure his handiwork wouldn't last long, but it would help them get Masaki out of the palace. Then he armed himself and stretched out his limbs. A long time had passed since he had fought, but he was confident he would hold his own.

Kiyoshi tracked Asa through the halls of the palace. As he expected, they were moving carefully, but they seemed to be close in no time at all. Kiyoshi took a deep breath, wondering what tricks Daisuke had planned.

He felt Asa pause at the corner of the hall, just out of sight of the guards. The action was silly. She was close enough that each of the four blades outside must know another of the gifted was close. Kiyoshi could feel them all on edge, ready to spring into action. Pausing only gave them more time to sense her.

Suddenly Kiyoshi realized that was the point. Two of the blades left Kiyoshi's door and walked toward her. After they had taken a few paces, she turned the corner, and the pair of blades approached the intruder.

Kiyoshi wished he knew where Daisuke was. But there wouldn't be a better opportunity than now. He drew his short sword and a knife and took a deep breath. He could feel the blades outside tensing. They could feel his actions, and they knew he was getting ready to leave his room.

Kiyoshi went deep inside himself. The sense, as useful as it was, had limitations. No one was sure exactly how the gift worked, but they knew that it recognized intent. The trick, then, to fool the sense was to try to move without intent. The tactic was as difficult as it sounded, but Kiyoshi and Daisuke had practiced together for cycles. That was how Kiyoshi had surprised Minori earlier, and it was how he would surprise the nightblades outside the door.

At the last moment, Kiyoshi changed his mind. He dropped his weapons, and as they clattered to the floor, he slid open the door to his room. In a single moment, Kiyoshi took in the entire situation. Asa was down the hall, only a moment away from engaging the two nightblades who had come to her. From the other side, Daisuke was approaching, clearly intending to attack the two blades who remained by the door. Neither of them had any idea Daisuke was near.

When they saw Daisuke, the two remaining guards at the door almost jumped out of their robes, and a moment too late, they sprang into motion.

The blades started to draw their swords. Kiyoshi reached out to both warriors. One of them was completely off guard, and Kiyoshi got his hand on the nightblade's face. In a moment he was inside the blade, just as if he were going to heal him. He could sense the energy flowing through the young man's mind, and in less than a moment, he followed the related pathway down the nightblade's spine. He felt the confluence of all the energy converging throughout the body, and when he had it, Kiyoshi twisted.

The feeling was hard to describe, but he knew what it did. For a few moments, the mind lost its connection with the body and believed its body was paralyzed. The nightblade collapsed, mind and body unable to communicate. As the blade fell, Kiyoshi held on for an extra moment, untwisting the flow of energy. He didn't want to cause any permanent damage to the blade, but it would take quite some time for the warrior's mind to recover and align itself with his body again, more than enough time to get away.

The second blade had stepped back, giving himself the space to dodge Kiyoshi's grasp. The extra moment of time gave him the ability to draw his sword. It flashed out of its sheath, cutting at Kiyoshi with one smooth motion.

Kiyoshi sensed the attack and leaned backward, allowing the horizontal slice to pass in front of him. The nightblade, still off guard from Kiyoshi's initial movement, had drawn with too much force, and his cut crossed Kiyoshi's entire body. Kiyoshi saw the warrior had realized his mistake. He either could try to stop his blade, or he could try to spin within the tight confines of the hallway and keep his momentum.

The nightblade stopped his cut, but his sword was off Kiyoshi's line, and the old man stepped forward. The blade stepped back, trying to keep distance between them, but his back ran against the wall behind him. Kiyoshi moved inside the blade's guard, his hand outstretched.

Reacting, the nightblade tried to slash at Kiyoshi, even knowing Kiyoshi was too close to cut. Kiyoshi reached out and grabbed the nightblade's arm, throwing the guard over his hip. The surprised blade somersaulted over Kiyoshi and landed on his back.

Throughout the throw, Kiyoshi held on to the nightblade's wrist and moved his body with a speed he hadn't used in many cycles, twisting his opponent into a joint lock. The nightblade, effectively immobilized, didn't know what to do. Kiyoshi didn't give him a chance. He went inside the blade and repeated the process he had used on the other guard. When he was finished, Kiyoshi dropped the arm, dismayed at the suffering he caused to effect his escape.

As his awareness expanded again, he saw, far more than he sensed, Daisuke dash past him. His old friend had apparently decided he didn't need any help, but Asa did. She was fast, but she didn't have an innate sense of combat. Asa didn't know how to use all of that speed to her advantage. He should ask Daisuke to train her.

Asa was fast enough to defend against the two nightblades attacking her, but it was a close battle. If not for her short blade and the confines of the hallway, Kiyoshi was certain she'd be dead.

The whole situation changed the moment Daisuke reached the fight. The two nightblades, so focused on Asa, didn't have the slightest chance of noticing the threat behind them. Daisuke didn't even draw his sword. He came up behind them and slammed the head of one into a wall, knocking him immediately unconscious. The second one, caught by surprise, suffered a shallow cut from Asa, who sensed an opportunity. Daisuke didn't let her kill the last blade though. He understood what Kiyoshi wanted. He punched the nightblade in the stomach, and as the warrior doubled over, brought his knee up into the blade's face. The final guard collapsed.

The fight had taken only a few moments, and Kiyoshi paused to throw out his sense. It didn't seem as though they had alerted any guards. Even so, the palace was regularly patrolled, and he and his allies had only a little time. When the four nightblades came to, they would be plenty upset and out for blood.

The three met in the hallway. Asa eyed Kiyoshi with suspicion, but he didn't have time to worry about her, not now. He embraced Daisuke. His old friend wore a smile.

"I'm glad to see you alive. I worried Minori was going to kill you."

"If he'd had his way, he might have."

They separated, and Daisuke looked Kiyoshi over. "That being said, captivity seems to suit you. You're looking better than you have in a long time."

Kiyoshi nodded. Soon he'd have to let Daisuke know what he had decided. "We need to get the king out of here. I've built a stretcher."

Daisuke tilted his head forward in acknowledgment. "Asa and I can carry him."

Kiyoshi shook his head, his eyes trying to say what his voice couldn't. Daisuke knew Kiyoshi was just as dangerous a fighter as any nightblade, but he couldn't let Asa know that. "No. We need you to protect us. I'll help Asa."

Daisuke understood. "Move then, old man."

Kiyoshi led Asa to his room. He picked up his weapons, which brought another strange look from Asa. Together, they picked up Masaki's stretcher. Kiyoshi noted how light the king had become.

Daisuke led them out of the palace the same way he and Asa had come. They didn't seek out combat, pausing and waiting in shadows and around corners as various guard units patrolled the grounds. The tunnel they used began in the king's chambers, and Daisuke led them there without a word.

Just as they entered the chambers, they heard shouts off in the distance. Kiyoshi wasn't sure if the blades had come to, or if the scene of the combat had been discovered, but it didn't matter. They locked the king's door behind them. Thanks to their ancestors' foresight, the door was thick enough that it would take some time to break down. Kiyoshi led them to the passage. They went through, and Daisuke closed the portal.

Kiyoshi drew a deep breath of relief. They had plenty of time. It would take the guards quite a while to discover the king's room was locked, and more time to break the door down, only to find an empty space. By the time the guards discovered the passage, if they even could, they would be long gone.

The passage was dark and damp, but Daisuke led them through the blackness without problem, putting them out in a house several hundred paces away from the palace walls. Kiyoshi had been disturbed by the presence of life in the house, but when they opened the door, he saw that Daisuke had recruited several of the king's guard.

Together, they put the king on a cart, covering him well. They left the house not long after, moving deeper into Haven, searching for a place to hide from the inevitable hunt.

Chapter 22

Asa was beginning to doubt her recent decisions. A moon ago the only thought she had held in her mind was finding Osamu and killing him. Now she was sitting in a cemetery with Masaki, who by all accounts was still the legitimate king of the Kingdom. Next to her was Kiyoshi, the man who at one time was considered the most influential blade in the Kingdom, and his right-hand man, the ever-competent Daisuke. If she spent any more time with this group, she'd lose sight of her true goal completely.

Despite her misgivings, she remained. She wasn't exactly sure why and she couldn't rationalize her behavior, but for the moment, this seemed the right course of action. She would have her chance to kill Minori, and there was no harm in waiting. At least that was what she told herself.

The cemetery had been Daisuke's idea. Asa had to admit his plan was deviously brilliant. Cemeteries were sacred grounds, considered suitable only for funerals and family visitation. The three blades and escaped king were hiding in a shrine in the largest cemetery in Haven, far enough away that another blade would likely be unable to sense them. If nothing else, a few days would pass before blades and Shin's soldiers even thought about the cemetery, and that gave the group enough time to act.

Kiyoshi was just finishing another round of healing of Masaki. When he came back to himself, Asa couldn't help but notice how much different he seemed. At one point Kiyoshi looked as though he was killing himself to save the king. Now he looked as though he was giving just enough to keep the king alive.

Daisuke gave Kiyoshi a few moments to gather himself, but then pressed the question: "What comes next?"

Kiyoshi didn't answer right away, and Asa was tempted to repeat the question. But Daisuke simply sat, waiting for his old friend to reply. Asa tried to follow his example.

When Kiyoshi spoke, Asa was surprised by the lack of certainty in his voice. When they had broken him out of the palace, Asa had imagined he would come out with all the answers. But he was a man no different than any other, and this was no easy situation they found themselves in.

"I think our best hope is with the other two lords."

Daisuke's face showed his hesitation, and Kiyoshi expanded his idea. "Shin lied about their support. Right now they are both imprisoned within their respective castles. I worry that if Shin's plan is allowed to run its course, we will see war. The other families will never believe the forgeries sent to them. We'll have Isamu's and Juro's forces at the gates within days. We need to free the lords to stop their families from fighting, but to do that, we need to get them out of the city."

Asa raised her hand, an action that felt incredibly childish. "I'm sorry, but no one seems to be asking the most obvious question. There's three of us by my count, and only two of us are nightblades. How exactly are we supposed to break out the two most heavily guarded men in the city? Daisuke is excellent, but you know Minori's going to have blades in addition to Shin's guards. Even the two of us working together would have a hard time, if it's even possible at all."

A look passed between Daisuke and Kiyoshi. Asa wished she had some clue as to what had happened between those two to form such a strong relationship. Daisuke answered her question.

"It's worse than that. If we're going to break them out, we're going to have to do it at the same time."

Asa's mouth must have been hanging open, because Kiyoshi chuckled at her reaction. He took over Daisuke's explanation.

"The moment we break one of the lords out, Minori will understand what happened. In fact, he's probably already expecting an attempt, because it's the only reasonable action I can take and Minori understands as much. But if we give him time to react, he'll throw even more forces in our way. If we're going to free the lords, their escape needs to occur at the same time."

Asa stared in disbelief. "So each of us has to rescue a lord all on our own?"

"Yes."

Asa was glad she was already sitting. If she hadn't been, she would have fallen over. She had always thought Kiyoshi had an edge of craziness to him, but she had never been so certain he had lost his mind.

"There's no way we can pull that off."

"Oh, I wouldn't be so sure."

Daisuke looked over at Asa. "If Kiyoshi wants to do something, he usually has a plan. We may not like it, but his strategy will be our best option. The best part of working for him is listening to his plans."

Asa looked back and forth at the two men, having a hard time believing they were seriously contemplating this. "Do you know about other secret passages?"

Kiyoshi shook his head. "I wouldn't be surprised if they exist, but if they do, I don't know where they are. Also, I'm sure Shin's men are on the lookout. I expect Minori has blades all over, trying to flush out any sense-gifted individuals they can."

Asa gave up. "Fine. Just tell me what the plan is."

It was the middle of the day, and Asa couldn't believe she was going through with this. She had always considered herself a rational person. Even when she discovered she was sense-gifted, she had looked at the legends of the blades with a healthy dose of skepticism. They made for great stories, sure, but every time she listened to them, she couldn't help but think they were concocted. Those stories could never happen in real life.

However, if Kiyoshi's plan worked, she might have to revise her thoughts. On the one hand, the plan was easy to grasp. The best ones always were. Complexity led to failure, in her own opinion, and this one was almost so simple as to be silly. But if it worked and the story got out, it would become a legend in its own time, although Asa wasn't sure she wanted to have her name mentioned.

She took a short glance up into the sky. There wasn't much point in delaying. Asa took a deep breath to prepare herself and immediately regretted it.

Sitting in front of her was a cart halfway filled with night soil, the waste from humans across town. In the Kingdom, nothing could go to waste, and that included waste. The soil was a valuable and potent fertilizer, and more to the point, few people paid any attention to the farmers who traveled around town collecting it for their fields.

To make her even more unrecognizable, she had smeared some of the goods over her face and the clothing she had found for the purpose of her disguise. So long as she breathed through her mouth, the stench wasn't much of a problem, but if she ever made the mistake of breathing through her nose, she paid the price. That stench was exactly what Kiyoshi was counting on. Her only relief was that somewhere in the city, Daisuke was enduring the same indignities.

She grabbed the handles on the cart and continued toward Lord Juro's castle. It had been decided that of the two lords, Juro would be the more lightly guarded. Isamu was lord of the lands Haven sat on, and he had far more troops in the area than his counterpart. Asa had wanted to debate the point, but Daisuke was a far superior blade and clearly should take the more difficult rescue.

Asa approached the servants' gate at Juro's castle. It was a much smaller gate and guarded by only two people. One of them, of course, was a nightblade. Asa recognized the robes immediately. She forced herself to move at a casual pace. Their escape plan was all misdirection and a bit of violence. As Asa walked toward the gate, she struggled against her impulse to use the sense. As a nightblade, she was used to using the gift, particularly in situations that felt stressful. But if she used the sense at all, any other blade would notice it, and no disguise in the world could hide her.

So, she felt blind as she approached the gate, but there was no other way. The gate itself was nothing special, just an extremely thick block of wood that would effectively seal the entrance in case of emergency. Asa was relieved to see that the gate was open and hosted a small amount of traffic. A castle was hard to run, even if you were running it as a prison.

One of Kiyoshi's assumptions had been that Shin would try to allow the castles to run as normally as possible. While the lords would be well guarded, Shin's guards would do everything they could to pretend life was normal. Ultimately, Shin getting the lords on his side would be far preferable to war.

Asa didn't know how Kiyoshi planned to get the lords out of the city, but there was only one task to worry about at a time. She slowed and came to a stop as she got to the gate. Taking a cue from having seen Daisuke in action, Asa looked around, trying to gather all the information she could. There wasn't too much to see. The gate was guarded by one of Shin's men and one blade. There were guards on the walls, making circuits, keeping a wary eye on the surroundings outside.

That was one piece of good news. For Kiyoshi's plan to work, there couldn't be too many people paying too much attention to what was going on inside the castle walls. So far, everything seemed good for her to go.

Asa looked from the guard to the nightblade, trying to figure out which one was in charge.

The guard was trying his best to be professional, but the stench of Asa's cart was intensely foul. He didn't ask any questions. There was only one reason Asa would be there, and although he made a cursory inspection of the cart, he didn't bother getting too close. He also didn't look too closely at Asa. Kiyoshi had been entirely correct. Smear a little waste on yourself, and you become invisible. The nightblade didn't even bother with an inspection. He simply took a few steps away. When the guard looked at his fellow sentry, the blade nodded. He didn't want anything to do with Asa or her goods.

Asa felt offended. She was only pretending to play the role, but to see the nightblade so dismissive of a citizen going about her work was painful to see. Did they consider themselves to be that much better than others?

Asa's mind wandered only for a moment. She needed to stay focused. The guard waved her through, and without a word, she was inside the castle.

Next on her list of actions was to find the outhouse for Juro's grounds. According to Kiyoshi and his information, Juro's castle held two different outhouses. One was for servants, and the other was for the residents and guests of the castle. Fortunately, they were next to each other.

The next part of the plan was outside of her control and put her at the most risk. Asa needed to wait for Juro to use the restroom, and it needed to happen after the guards changed. The latter part of the problem wasn't too difficult. Asa had timed her entry to come just before the guards rotated their position. The other part was much harder. Kiyoshi had tried to send a message to the lords, but there was no way to know if the dispatch had been passed on. They couldn't afford to wait.

Asa decided she would start with the outhouse of the servants. She kept the door open so she could see people going to and from the other outhouse, but with nothing else to do and a disguise to maintain, she pulled a shovel out of her cart and got to work.

If she thought the smell had been bad before, she really didn't have any idea how wretched the odor could get. She thought for a moment her nose would start burning. She worked at a slow but steady pace, fast enough that she wouldn't arouse suspicion, but slow enough to give her as much time as possible by the outhouses.

Unfortunately it was a warm fall day, and as the sun began its lazy descent, the outhouses warmed up and began to smell even worse. Asa finished the servant outhouse, sweat trickling down the waste on her face. She considered leaving then and there, but the idea of being shown up by Daisuke was almost too much to bear.

Asa almost took a deep breath before going into the residents' outhouse, but she remembered her mistake and instead took a shallow breath through her mouth.

She was almost halfway done with the second privy when her moment arrived. She heard them before she saw them, but two guards were escorting a man to the outhouse. Asa had never seen Lord Juro, but the figure matched Kiyoshi's description, and Asa couldn't imagine anyone else would have two guards on a trip to the outhouse. It had to be him.

Both guards wore the uniform of Lord Shin, so Asa assumed neither were nightblades. That made the next part a lot easier. One of them saw Asa and gestured to his partner. They shook their heads in unison, but the second guard, who must have been the junior, had to step into the privy.

"Get out."

Asa thought quickly. In the outhouse, they were hidden from view, but somehow she needed to get both of them inside. She glanced at Lord Juro and saw a strange expression in his eyes. There was an air of expectation there. So, Kiyoshi's message must have gotten through. Asa bowed to the guard.

"Right away, sir."

She turned around, and as she did, she allowed herself to slip and fall against the cart, rocking it dangerously. The cart stayed on its wheels, but for a moment she feared she would be covered in waste. She grimaced in pain, only part of it faked.

"I think I might have broken something. Can you help me up?"

The guard inside the outhouse gave her a disgusted look. "Crawl out. I'm not going to touch you."

Asa thought fast. "Will you at least get my cart, then? I can't pull myself and it."

The guards looked skeptical, but Juro assisted her. He spoke to the first guard. "Oh, get in there and help her. One of you grab her, and one of you grab the cart. I need to go."

The first guard looked like he was ready to retort, but he clearly had orders to make Juro as comfortable as possible. He swallowed his pride and bowed. "Yes, lord."

The first guard stepped in with the second, and Asa didn't waste a moment. She swept her leg, catching the second guard in the shin. As she rotated, she reached up and grabbed the first guard, who had stepped close and was bending down to pick her up. She pulled on his arm, and all three were on the ground in an instant.

Fortunately, Asa was the only one expecting to be there. She got up to her hands and knees and drove an elbow into the face of the second guard. His head snapped back against the solid dirt floor of the outhouse, knocking him out instantly. Without pause, Asa jumped onto the back of the first guard, wrapping her arm around his neck in a solid choke hold. Her other hand came up and covered his mouth, ensuring he couldn't scream for help.

The guard thrashed for what felt like forever, but eventually fell motionless. Asa kept her hold for a few more moments, ensuring he wasn't faking stillness. When she was certain, she relaxed just a little, keeping her hand over his mouth. Finally, she was convinced and stood up.

She looked straight at Juro. "Thanks. Are you ready to get out of here?"

Juro nodded, and Asa went digging into her cart. "I don't think you're going to like this." She pulled out a set of clothes, completely caked in waste.

Juro shook his head. "Leave it to Kiyoshi to come up with such a ridiculous plan."

Asa didn't have any patience or experience dealing with lords. She wasn't used to their pride. She whispered at him fiercely, "You have a choice to make right now. Either you put on these clothes and we get out of here, or I leave you behind. They'll notice the guards soon and know something happened. This is your only chance, so make your decision."

Juro looked as though he wanted to protest, but when he saw the expression on Asa's face, he realized any argument he made would fall on deaf ears. He gave in and held out his hand for the clothes. He took only a few moments to change, but even Asa was surprised by the difference the clothes and smell made. It would take a very aware or very suspicious person to realize the person in front of her was Lord Juro.

"The plan is simple. The guards have shifted since I came in, so hopefully no one will remember that there was just one of me. We walk out through the servants' gate. Keep your head down and don't say anything unless you have to. I don't want to risk having someone recognize you by your voice."

Juro nodded his agreement.

"If things go poorly, I may fight. If that happens, I need you to run into the city as fast as you can. If I can, I'll catch up with you. Don't wait for me."

The look in Juro's eyes told her that he wouldn't have even considered waiting. Asa ignored it.

Together, they each grabbed a handle of the cart and pulled it toward the servants' gate. There they were stopped by the two guards, who, thankfully, were new, just as Asa had planned. The nightblade who was half of the guard pair ran a quick eye over the cart and Asa, but he didn't find anything of interest. He looked as though he found it painful even having to be part of guard duty.

The other sentry was more dutiful, more so than the guard they had encountered on the way in. He walked around and inspected the cart, and at one point even took the shovel and turned over the waste once or twice to ensure there wasn't anything inside. Asa tried to act naturally, or as naturally as she expected a farmer would. She kept her eyes down and refused to pay too much attention to the soldier. When he was done inspecting the cart, he took a long look at both Asa and Juro. Asa fought the impulse to hold her breath. Everything about Kiyoshi's plan had worked so far. The gate was open, and the city of Haven looked wide and inviting. All they needed was to make it past this last step.

Asa hesitated. The guard was continuing to look at them, and she desperately wanted to look up and study his face. Was he suspicious of something? They had been stopped at the gate far longer than she had been coming in. She considered striking out but crushed the thought as soon as it came to mind. The moment she formed an intent to attack, the nightblade would be all over her. No, she needed to stay focused and keep her eyes on the ground.

It felt like the sun was ready to set when the guard finally waved them through without a question. Asa and Juro pulled on the cart, and within a few steps were clear of the walls. Rather than break out into a run and abandon the cart, they stuck to the plan. The duo rolled into Haven and stopped at a bar, where the farmer who owned the cart was waiting. Asa had offered her services for the day free of charge, and had sweetened the deal with an offer to buy a few drinks. All in all, a small price to pay for breaking a lord out of his prison.

The cart disposed of, Juro wanted to change immediately, but Asa told him he had to wait. Following a map drawn by Daisuke, she eventually found the shadow's house. They went inside, and Asa noticed how different and empty the space felt without his family's presence.

Asa, allowed to use her sense once again, felt that they weren't alone. She couldn't sense Daisuke, but that was bothering her less and less. There was another person in the house, and a few minutes later, Lord Isamu stepped into view, with Daisuke behind him.

Isamu looked and smelled just as bad as Juro, but he seemed to be taking his condition much worse. He frowned with disdain as he looked at his fellow lord. "So, I see they got you out using the same methods." Asa could hear the desire for murder in the lord's voice.

Juro was in no mood for small talk. "We need to kill Shin. Now."

Daisuke held up his hand. "I apologize, Lord Juro. I've already had the opportunity to speak with Lord Isamu, but the situation, as you can imagine, is quite complicated. While you are here, you can change clothes and bathe, but we must be on the move again soon. My friends and I were already being hunted by Minori before this breakout, but after it, he will redouble his efforts. Time is of the essence, and we need to get moving. We will meet all together and decide our next steps.

"The bath is that way. You'll have to tend it yourselves so Asa and I can guard the house. There are fresh clothes there as well. They aren't as fine as you are used to, but you'll need to travel incognito for a while yet. Please hurry. We must leave as soon as the sun dips below the horizon."

The two lords complied, even though it looked like they'd rather do anything else. Asa had thought Juro was irritating, but she saw he was far more compliant than Isamu.

Asa and Daisuke exchanged a look, and he spoke, the disbelief evident in his voice. "Lords."

Despite all the indignities visited upon them in the course of their rescue, the two lords were prepared when the sun fell. Daisuke led the party out, with Asa bringing up the rear. They hadn't encountered anyone searching for the two lords yet, but they imagined it would only be a matter of time. The streets, as they had been the past several nights, were eerily quiet.

Asa would have preferred to have more outdoor crowds within which to blend; as it was, four people walking together on empty streets was asking for trouble. If not for Daisuke's experience in avoiding detection, it would have been a difficult journey. As it was, Daisuke often stopped them before turning corners, somehow successfully playing the most complicated game of hide-and-seek Asa had ever played. Juro and Isamu couldn't sense the patrols moving through the city, so they couldn't appreciate just how difficult the task was.

The moon was high in the sky by the time they reached the cemetery where Kiyoshi was hiding with Masaki. Asa watched the faces of the lords as they entered the cemetery. She wasn't impressed. In her mind, a leader was someone who was willing to make any sacrifice to protect his people, and she didn't see that from these two. They had been born into power and didn't understand how to wield it well. She saw this on their faces as they entered the cemetery. Their look of revulsion told her enough. Isamu and Juro were more concerned about manners than about doing what needed to be done.

Regardless, she followed them. Kiyoshi believed they were important, and that was enough for her. They entered the shrine, and Asa almost laughed at the look of shock on their faces as the two lords saw their king.

Kiyoshi stood and bowed, and Asa was struck by how much stronger he seemed. In her free moments, she had been thinking a lot about the dayblade. There was far more to him than he was letting on. She kept replaying their escape from the palace in her mind. Kiyoshi had taken out two nightblades with an ease Asa found incredible. She wasn't certain she could defeat two strong nightblades at all, and certainly not with his ease.

She had only seen glances of his battle, being somewhat concerned at the time with the two blades coming after her, but the way he moved had defied all expectation. The only way Asa could describe it was that he moved like a nightblade.

That was where all of her reasoning broke down. Kiyoshi was known across the Kingdom as one of the land's greatest dayblades. It was why he had been taken into the king's service, and there was no doubt his healing powers were incredible. Asa herself had been one of his patients, and her healing had been as perfect as anyone could expect. There was no way to be both a nightblade and a dayblade. At least, that was what Asa understood. Even though they were two separate aspects of the same sense, the training in their use was far different. Asa had been trying to remember all her lessons from when she was younger, and she was sure such a feat was impossible.

When she saw Kiyoshi rise with the smooth grace of a much younger man to greet the lords, all her questions were brought back to the front of her mind.

There were greetings all around, and Kiyoshi invited the lords to sit. They looked uncomfortable with the idea of sitting on the dirt floor, but eventually joined the blades.

Kiyoshi began. "I'm glad to see you are both safe. It seemed vital we get you out of your homes as soon as possible."

Juro, ever the problem, replied, "Thank you for the rescue. It was unorthodox, but I suppose I can't question its effectiveness. Now I have an order. Kill Lord Shin."

Kiyoshi laughed, and Asa enjoyed watching the rage build on Juro's face.

"Lord Juro, your status means little to me, especially now. We rescued you because you are a person loved by your family and a symbol who wields a great deal of power. But you cannot order me or any of the other blades here. If you believe Lord Shin must die, we can speak about that later, but right now we are here to discuss what our next steps are."

Isamu spoke up. "I respect your words, Kiyoshi, even if they are hard to swallow. But what Shin has done is far outside the laws of the Kingdom. He has committed treason, and the punishment is death. Our duty seems clear."

Kiyoshi nodded. "I appreciate your reasoning, and your line of thought is sound. But these are difficult times, and we owe it to ourselves to ask difficult questions. I am not taking a stand here, but I will challenge your opinion. There is no doubt Shin has broken the law, but I believe we need to ask if perhaps it isn't for the best."

Isamu and Juro both turned their heads at that. Juro shot back, "Of all the people here, you are closest to Masaki, and you're willing to see his throne taken from him while he still breathes? Is your friendship worth so little?"

Asa saw the attack had bothered Kiyoshi, but the frustration passed from his face so quickly she was certain only Daisuke and she had noticed. "He is my friend. One of the closest I have. But this isn't about my personal feelings. It has always been about what is best for the Kingdom. One of the three of you would have been the next king. Why not Shin?"

Juro's retort was sharp. "Because he broke the law."

"And none of you have?"

Kiyoshi let the silence hang for a moment before he continued. "I know he broke the law, and personally, I'm furious. But my concern has always been the same: What is best for the Kingdom? We all know Shin is driven and clever, and his lands have prospered under his rule. Is there a reason to rebel against his coup?"

Asa watched the two lords carefully. Kiyoshi raised a good argument, but she could see the lords weren't swayed. Asa cursed to herself. They were far more interested in their own power and problems and couldn't see the larger picture.

Kiyoshi leaned back and sighed. "Even though I won't kill Lord Shin for you, I will help protect you. I fear your lives are in danger so long as you're here, and the last thing I want to see is war. We will get you out of the city and to your families so that you may decide what is best. I hope you listen to my warnings."

Daisuke, seeing his master needed a break, stepped in. "Getting you out of the city is going to be challenging. By now, Lord Shin and Minori will know about your escape. It would have been nearly impossible to get you out right after escaping. Now I'm not sure it's possible at all. Shin will want to close the gates."

Juro shook his head. "If he shuts the gates, it would expose his lie. He'll need to leave them open."

Kiyoshi responded, "No. He'll come up with some sort of excuse to close the gates. I expect we'll need to fight our way through. Do either of you have loyal troops in the area?"

Juro answered, "If there are any still around, I know where they'll be."

Isamu nodded, indicating the same was true of him.

"Good. We're going to need their help. The plan won't be complicated, but we're going to need bodies. Tonight, rest here. Tomorrow we'll send each of you out with one of the nightblades, and you can recruit as many people as possible. Tomorrow night we'll try to break out of the city for good. We'll take the king with us." Kiyoshi looked down at Masaki, worry in his eyes.

The lords made themselves as comfortable as they could for the night, upset but out of options. Kiyoshi, Daisuke, and Asa sat together for a while longer, planning out their next steps. Asa looked at Kiyoshi. "Are these lords even worth saving?"

Kiyoshi held his grin in check. "Probably not. But they are symbols, and like anyone else, they are important to their families. The difference is, these families will go to war if we don't get their cherished ones safely out of the city."

Chapter 23

Minori looked at his map of the Kingdom. It was an excellent map, one of the highest quality that existed in the land, but over the past few days, Minori had made it his own. His markings and notations covered the map, and as he looked at his writing, he realized it would be completely incomprehensible to anyone but him.

He had been trying to piece together the big picture. Ever since Shin came to power, Minori had been flooded with more information than he thought possible, and the map seemed to be the best way of understanding the dimensions of his new world. There were units, supply chains, towns, and much more all laid out in front of him. As he received new information, he updated the map, and when he was done, he took a step back and tried to imagine it all as a chessboard.

What was the Kingdom but the largest, most complicated game he had ever played? In the back of his mind, he had an itch, a belief that there were underlying principles to everything that was happening. He just couldn't see them. Like any game, there was a pattern unfolding, but it seemed to be just outside his mental grasp. The problem was frustrating, and he kept looking at the map from different angles, trying new ideas to see if they made the information fit into a pattern.

If nothing else, Minori was stubborn. He wouldn't let go of a problem until solved, and this problem, complicated as it was, was no different.

He and Shin had two main challenges within the next moon.

The first and most immediate was the escape of the two lords. He had needed only a few moments to figure out what had happened, but by then it was already far too late. The plan had to have been the work of Kiyoshi.

Minori wasn't certain how much damage the two lords could do. The city was still relatively sealed. The gates were open and people were welcome to pass to and fro, but Minori had tripled the number of guards at each gate, and every single traveler coming in and out received a level of scrutiny that made even the most innocent shudder in fear. Minori was fairly certain the lords hadn't left the city yet, but they could send messages. The only way he could have prevented that would have been to seal the gates, thus ending the public pretense. If Shin had come to power under peaceful means, there wouldn't be any reason to seal the doors to the city.

Minori turned several ideas over in his mind. What he needed was to find a reason to shut the gates. If the gates were closed, there wouldn't be any way for the lords to get a message out. Night had fallen, and if Minori knew Kiyoshi, the old man would be moving fast.

His first challenge was compounded by his second challenge. He had just received word that Juro's army had made an extremely hazardous river crossing and was moving toward Haven. There wasn't any word yet of any of Isamu's armies making the same move, but if Juro's armies had crossed, it would only be a matter of time before everyone had a force outside the gates. Shin had ordered one of his armies across, but he had done so with the king's seal, and the message had taken a few days to make it to the border. They wouldn't be here in time to prevent a siege if that was what it came to.

Minori cursed the other lords and their families. Shin was the best choice to lead them after Masaki's death, but no one else seemed to see that. War, if that was what was coming, was unnecessary. All the lords needed to do was accept the smooth transfer of power.

Minori's anger was beginning to get the best of him when he sensed a presence nearing his door. He stepped over and opened the door, giving the messenger a little start. The man regained his composure and bowed deeply. "King Shin can see you now."

Minori took a deep breath. He understood that Shin had many other tasks he needed to see to, but the challenges Minori was trying to solve had to be first. He had already waited far too long. The messenger retreated, and Minori followed him to Shin's chambers.

To Shin's credit, he didn't seem to be unduly affected by the title of king. He had elected to stay in his house, and for the most part, nothing seemed to have changed for him. When Minori entered, he looked up, and Minori could see the exhaustion in his face.

The king dismissed everyone else in the room, and Minori went up to him. He updated Shin on what he knew of the escapes and of the troop movements he had just received. Shin took all the news in silence, and even after Minori finished, the silence seemed to stretch on. Minori waited patiently for as long as he was able, but he felt the pressure of time pressing against him, an enemy always at his back. Forgetting politeness, he threw out the beginning of his idea.

"My king, if I may, I think we need to create some event that will allow us to shut the gates. It gives us the time we need to make better decisions. If necessary, we can also pin the blame on the lords."

The idea seemed to spark something in Shin, and for a few moments he came alive. He studied Minori closely. Finally, he spoke. "I think I have just the idea, but I wonder how you'll feel."

Minori waited for Shin to continue.

"I think it's time to burn the palace to the ground."

Minori's first reaction was shock, but over the course of his life, he had learned to evaluate ideas based on more than emotion. He thought about Shin's idea further.

Shin waited and watched Minori's reaction as he turned the idea over in his mind. "It's a brilliant idea. It's a powerful symbol, one that the people are very attached to. But at the same time, it doesn't directly belong to any of the great houses, so they won't care. We explain that we're closing the gate to search for the arsonists. A stroke of genius, my king."

"Excellent." Shin's gaze held a question that took Minori a little time to decipher. When he did, his heart sank, but he had already promised himself he would do everything necessary to bring about the freedom of the blades. Once Shin was firmly in power, Minori could make his play.

"I will see to it tonight. I will personally make sure it happens."

Shin nodded his approval. "I can't trust anyone else. Thank you." Shin bowed deeply to Minori, more deeply than was necessary or even appropriate.

With that, the meeting adjourned, and Minori turned and left without another word.

The night was dark and cool, but Minori didn't notice. The evening had been a busy one. After he left Shin's hall, he had blades loyal to him obtain several carts of hay and went to find Koji. He wanted help tonight, and although he wasn't as sure of Koji as he once had been, Koji was still the only really trustworthy help Minori had.

Together the two approached the palace. They remained at the gate, waiting for the carts Minori had ordered. When the blades started lining up the carts of hay purchased from around the city, Koji looked at Minori with a question on his face.

Minori met his gaze. "We need to burn the palace."

To Koji's credit, his face remained impassive. So impassive, in fact, that Minori was having trouble reading him. Minori felt a sudden need to justify himself. "No one is inside. Shin ordered the palace evacuated after Kiyoshi's escape. It's only wood and stone."

"Perhaps, but to many people, it's much more. You'll unleash an anger that will be difficult to control."

"And it will all be pointed at the two other lords. Koji, by doing this, we can help Shin solidify his power. Once he is king and there is no doubt of it, the blades will have the freedom we once had. The steps we take are sometimes unpleasant, but if burning a building will bring about that day for the blades, it's an action I'll take gladly."

Koji shook his head, but he didn't walk away. Together, they brought the carts into the castle and laid the hay in several of the rooms. The work was quiet, but Minori found he enjoyed the physical labor. Minori looked at Koji and decided the next step was one he had to take on his own.

"Don't worry. I'll light the fires. I won't ask you to take this step with me."

Minori walked back into the palace and grabbed the nearest torch. He started at the back of the royal home, touching the torch to the piles of hay, making sure each was well lit before moving on. His pace was quick but deliberate, and there was only one place where he paused: Kiyoshi's old room. Minori had piled far more hay in the room than was necessary. With a fit of rage, he tossed the entire torch in and began to leave. Already the smoke was gathering across the ceiling, and Minori knew the palace only had a bit of life left in it. He walked out and rejoined Koji.

Together, they stared at his handiwork for a few moments. Minori was surprised by how much of the palace had already caught fire. The entire structure would soon be cinders.

He turned to Koji. "Come. It's time for us to leave."

They left just as the city of Haven was starting to come alive. After so many evenings of hiding in their houses, the flames brought people out, many of them huddling with their families in the street, looking toward the center of the city at the fire that consumed the old king's residence.

Koji looked as though he were about to part ways with Minori, but the elder blade laid a restraining arm on his shoulder. "There is another task I'd ask of you."

Koji stared at him silently, and Minori wished he understood what was going through the young man's mind. "I need you to kill the escaped lords. I know they are still in the city, and if they escape, they will cause war to break out in the Kingdom. I can't bear to see that. Begin with Lord Isamu. Of the two, he is more dangerous."

Koji considered the request, finally nodding. Minori breathed a deep sigh of relief and watched as the young nightblade vanished into the darkness.

Chapter 24

Kiyoshi woke from his light sleep. Something was wrong in the world. As soon as he became conscious, he lost the sensation, but he had the feeling that it had been very distinct. His first instinct was to look around and scan the area with his sense, but he discovered nothing out of the ordinary. Everyone was sleeping peacefully in their little corner of the shrine, and Kiyoshi could still hear the labored breathing of Masaki.

Only after a few moments did he realize that the sky was far too light for this time of the night. All vestiges of sleep fled from his mind as he sat up. Light that bright could only come from a fire. A big one.

Kiyoshi got to his feet, which was enough to alert Daisuke. The shadow opened his eyes, but with a gesture, Kiyoshi indicated he should stay where he was. If the situation got out of hand, Daisuke would be able to figure out what was happening and keep everyone as safe as possible. Kiyoshi needed to know what was going on. After his imprisonment and subsequent escape, Kiyoshi was cut off from his extensive network of shadows. He felt like a blind man finding a path through the woods.

He took off toward the light, with a growing certainty that it was the palace that was ablaze. It would have been intentional, and Kiyoshi mentally gave Shin, or Minori, credit. The act wouldn't anger the houses but would provide the perfect excuse to seal the gates. Ultimately, it was no matter. He had expected they'd have to break through a sealed gate.

Kiyoshi moved easily and quickly found himself flowing forward with a growing number of citizens of Haven. The feeling was unusual. After so many days with the streets empty in the evening, seeing so many out and about was like being slapped with a cold fish.

Kiyoshi wasn't surprised when he turned the final corner and saw Masaki's home devoured by flame. What he was surprised by was the totality of the destruction. The arsonists had been thorough. Nothing would be left but ash. Hundreds of volunteers gathered around the palace with water, but for now they were keeping their distance. The fire burned bright and hot, and there was no chance of putting it out.

Kiyoshi found himself reflecting on his memories of the palace, his residence for almost twenty cycles, the closest place he had to a home. And now it was gone. His first reaction was one of anger, but he was too old to remain angry for long. He had too much perspective. What he felt was a deep sorrow, a hole in his heart. The palace wasn't just his home. It had been the heart of the Kingdom. The palace had burned down before, but knowing that the fire was an act to narrow down his options seemed so petty. Despite their differences, Kiyoshi believed some things were sacred, set apart from his machinations. Apparently Minori had no such beliefs.

Torn by the fire, Kiyoshi turned his attention to the crowd. The emotions on their faces matched the feelings in his heart. They were angry and sad, and in addition, they were afraid. Tension had been building in the capital for more than a moon now, and Kiyoshi sensed this was the breaking point. They wouldn't take much more.

He opened his ears and slid through the crowd listening to the citizenry. Several talked about the fire itself, but as he wandered, he picked up on other threads. A number of people, particularly those who were wealthier, were talking about getting out of the city tonight. They could read the signs, and they knew that soon the city would be sealed, if it wasn't already. Kiyoshi saw a few men, who he identified as merchants, ushering their families back toward their houses to pack and leave.

The seed of an idea was forming in Kiyoshi's head, but he was wise enough to continue wandering. The best ideas came of their own accord, the product of an open mind. He kept his ears and his mind open, and was surprised when he heard the whispers that were beginning to run through the crowd.

Someone, somewhere, had seen two nightblades leaving the palace just as it caught on fire. Their robes had given them away, and one of them had been wearing the red ribbon that had been seen around town with increasing frequency. Kiyoshi stopped and tracked the whispers, listening as they spread as fast as the fire in the palace.

An overwhelming sorrow seized Kiyoshi. He sank to his knees, the hole in his heart threatening to swallow him whole. For all of their back and forth, he had never thought it would come to this. Minori had been so intelligent, always thinking steps ahead of his opponents. Had he really been so blinded by his purpose that he missed what was happening?

Kiyoshi, a veteran of the political movements of the court, saw everything unfold before him. Each set of events, falling into place one after the other. From his perspective, he wasn't sure how he could fix the damage that Minori had caused. Everything he had worked for, the past twenty cycles of his life, his redemption, it was all over.

A profound feeling of hopelessness settled on his shoulders, pressing them closer to the ground with its weight. He had never felt as old as he did at that moment, his very frame threatening to collapse under the pressure. He had a short blade hidden on his body, and he wondered what it would feel like to release his energy to the Great Cycle. Who knew how many people he had sent there himself? He imagined the cold steel being drawn across his neck, and he felt no fear. His hand wandered down to the hilt, but some small part of him prevented him from taking that final action.

He had never given up before. Even in his darkest moments, he had followed whatever small light would guide him, and this moment wouldn't be any different. Somewhere, somehow, he would find a way.

Kiyoshi didn't know how long he knelt in the dirt, but eventually he stood back up, slowly and painfully. He was heartbroken, but he wouldn't give up. He could feel that his end was near, but he would fight until that day came. Piece by piece, his mind regained its focus, and he started to think through the next challenges. If there was going to be an exodus from the city tonight, he and his companions had to be part of it, leading to far less loss of life than if they fought their way through a gate on their own.

With a concrete action in front of him, Kiyoshi strode back to the cemetery, his crisis of purpose a thing of memory.

The sun was rising by the time Kiyoshi returned to the cemetery and had prepared everyone for their departure. It had taken time to wake the lords, and Kiyoshi spent time giving Masaki another healing. The healer didn't have a plan. What he saw was an opportunity, and he was wise enough to take it. They left for the smallest city gate just as the sun was beginning to warm the land.

The group moved silently. Kiyoshi had outlined his ideas to Asa and Daisuke, but they would have to improvise based on whatever they found when they reached the gate. All Kiyoshi knew was that time was of the essence.

When they arrived, Kiyoshi allowed himself a small grin. There was a large crowd of citizens at the gate, and the gate was still open. At Kiyoshi's request, Asa found a higher vantage point and reported that several units of Shin's guards were managing the gate. They were letting people through, but slowly. Asa reported that the inspections were intense and thorough. There wouldn't be any sneaking through.

Kiyoshi listened to the sound of the crowd. Off in the distance, smoke was still rising from the burning palace, and the rising sun was darkened by the plume. It seemed to make the crowd more anxious. To Kiyoshi's ears, they were close to rioting. Right now, the drawn swords of Shin's guards were enough to hold them at bay. All Kiyoshi needed was an inciting incident, and the crowd would become a stampede.

He asked Daisuke to get a better idea of who was guarding the gate. The blade nodded and disappeared. While they waited for him, Kiyoshi asked Asa to go through the crowd, asking those who looked most angry what was taking so long.

Daisuke soon returned. Only one nightblade was at the gate, and there were fewer guards than Kiyoshi had assumed. Daisuke's best guess was that only two units were stationed at the gates, a total of twelve guards, not much more than would be on the gate on any other day.

Kiyoshi figured Shin had to spread his units thinner than he wanted. Most of the blades would be searching the city for him and the lords. It was much harder to hide from a blade than from a regular guard. Shin's units—limited in number even taking into account the troops he'd smuggled in—would be pulling all sorts of duty. They had to be managing the crowd at the palace and ensuring the fire didn't spread beyond its walls. They would have normal patrols to keep the city calm, as well as try to manage the gates.

All of this made Kiyoshi's life easier. He waited for Asa to return, and by the time she did, Kiyoshi knew exactly what they would do. He gave out instructions to their small party, and they began. Asa and Daisuke melted into the crowd, leaving Kiyoshi with the two lords and the sick king. Masaki was on the stretcher Kiyoshi had made, carried by Isamu and Juro. The lords hadn't liked being forced to work for their escape, but Kiyoshi didn't care in the least.

Kiyoshi heard Asa's voice from somewhere in the crowd. The crowd, angry as they were, were still being largely respectful. That needed to change. Asa shouted, "Come on! I will not wait any longer!"

From the other side of the crowd, Daisuke shouted, "Yeah, I'm not a criminal! I'm free to come and go as I please."

Kiyoshi hoped one of the guards would rise to the bait, and they did. In a way, he sympathized with them. They were just following orders. One guard, who Kiyoshi noted was higher-ranked than the others, stood on top of a cart. "Every person must be inspected!"

Daisuke responded, still well hidden by the crowd. "I'm not an arsonist. I'm a citizen! I just want my family to be safe."

Kiyoshi could almost feel the crowd respond. These were families and merchants. None had done anything wrong. They were simply seeking safety.

A rock flew from somewhere in the crowd, and Kiyoshi assumed it came from Daisuke. The stone struck the guard in his chest, and he drew his sword and leapt down into the crowd. Asa, right on cue, shouted, "Let me out!"

Kiyoshi couldn't see what happened next, but he could picture it. The guards had formed two ranks in front of the gate, and Asa and Daisuke were supposed to charge. Kiyoshi assumed that the guards would want to do their jobs and carry out their orders, but that they would also hesitate to strike at unarmed civilians. If the two blades could poke a hole in the wall of swords, he expected the units to collapse.

Kiyoshi led the two lords right into the thick of the crowd, pushing and shoving his way to the front. He could hear the commotion and the screams and assumed that his two nightblades were in the thick of it. He had asked them both not to draw their swords. Between their skills and the element of surprise, there shouldn't be any need. The crowd just needed leaders.

Kiyoshi couldn't see whether they were successful and he didn't dare use his sense in such a confined, crowded space, but he could feel the crowd surge forward and he knew their plan was working. A hole must have opened, and everyone was trying to get through it at once. Kiyoshi allowed himself to be pushed around, following the natural currents of humanity as they swarmed the gate.

Without warning, Asa was next to him. He glanced at her and saw she had suffered a small cut on her left arm, but otherwise she looked unharmed. There was no time to speak. Together, they went where the crowd flowed.

A group of three soldiers appeared as if by magic in front of their small band of escapees. Asa took care of the obstacle in her typical straightforward manner. She walked right into one before he realized what was happening, her knee driving up into his groin. The second guard saw what happened to the first, and scared, swiped at her. Kiyoshi meant to shout at her, but she must have sensed the strike. She shifted her weight and let the blade pass harmlessly to her side. She tried to step in toward the guard, but was pushed sideways by a sudden shift in the mass of people.

The final guard saw Kiyoshi and put his hand out to stop him. Kiyoshi's instincts kicked into action, and he grabbed the man's wrist. The dayblade tried to send a wave of energy through the guard, but was distracted by the crowd pushing against him. The guard, regaining his wits, jerked his hand away. Kiyoshi saw a look of recognition flash through the guard's face.

To his side, Asa reappeared, driving the second guard down to the ground. Her knee landed on his chest, crushing the breath out of him. Kiyoshi didn't have time to congratulate her as the final guard drew his sword. Kiyoshi opened up his sense and felt the strike coming, his body effortlessly avoiding the stab. He drove his fist into the guard's neck, dropping him as well.

Kiyoshi avoided Asa's stare and kept leading the two lords. It took a few moments, but they passed underneath the gate. As soon as they did, the crowd dispersed, everyone trying to get away from the walls of the city as quickly as possible. Kiyoshi waved at Asa and the lords, and together they struck out from Haven.

They hadn't been traveling long when they were joined by Daisuke. Kiyoshi had asked his old friend to stay behind and observe what happened after the escape. His report wasn't promising.

"The confusion didn't last for long. The nightblade who was there had the presence of mind to order the gate closed. I was one of the last to make it through. Unfortunately, I did see some civilians on the ground. It looked like, in their fear, some of the guards overreacted."

Kiyoshi felt a pang of sorrow, but he pushed the emotion aside. If they didn't succeed, there were going to be far more than just a few dead. He set his face in a grim mask and led his comrades forward, trying desperately to stop a war that was looking more and more inevitable.

Chapter 25

Asa was impressed by the quiet opulence of the inn they had found. She had enough experience with Kiyoshi by now to know that nothing he did was by chance. This had been his destination all along. From the outside, the inn was an unmarked building in a small village just outside of Haven. There was absolutely nothing remarkable about the structure. Even if one were to step inside, they would only find a common room not unlike any other in the Kingdom.

But there was more to this inn than could be easily observed. There had been two men loitering by the door, and while a casual glance would have passed over them, Asa could tell from their balance and the way their eyes moved constantly that they were warriors. Even more surprising, one of them, according to Asa's sense, was a nightblade.

Kiyoshi had caught her suspicious glance, but his response did little to answer her questions. "The owner here is a friend of mine. He assists in many types of trade throughout the Kingdom."

Asa assumed the trade was both legal and illegal. There weren't many other guests, but the ones who were present were far more vigilant than common citizens. At first, Asa had wondered if this was a place for blades to gather, but she didn't sense anyone else besides the man outside.

Kiyoshi's knowledge of the establishment further complicated Asa's idea of the dayblade. It was easy to fall into the trap of thinking he was an innocent old man, a do-gooder with his head in the clouds. But there was too much evidence against that idea. From this place, it was clear Kiyoshi was involved at least in some way with underground markets, and Asa had replayed their escape through the gate in her mind time and time again.

She had watched the way Kiyoshi dealt with the guard. She had been fighting her own battle and there was a real possibility her mind was playing tricks on her, but she would swear she thought she saw Kiyoshi moving to dodge an attack before it happened. Either the man was an incredibly gifted warrior, or he could use the sense in combat, making him a nightblade.

It came down to the same two possibilities. Either she was paranoid, seeing events that weren't there, or Kiyoshi was somehow both nightblade and dayblade. She couldn't decide which option seemed more implausible.

Asa sighed. She hadn't seen any money change hands, but the room she had been given was the nicest she had ever been in. The accommodations resonated peace, the tatami mats spotless. Even though the chaos of Haven was only a short ride behind, she felt as though she was a full moon away from any problems. Asa closed her eyes and was quickly asleep.

—

When Asa awoke, there was someone outside her door. She reached for her blades, only to sense Kiyoshi's energy. He spoke softly, his voice barely carrying through Asa's door.

"I'm sorry to wake you. I was hoping you would join us to discuss our next actions."

Asa sat up, surprised she had fallen asleep so easily. She glanced outside and saw the sun hadn't traveled far. She was grateful she hadn't slept too long.

"I'll be there in a few moments."

She sensed Kiyoshi's bow, and he walked away from her room, back toward the common area.

Asa was the last to arrive. When she entered the common room, she saw Daisuke, Kiyoshi, and the two lords sitting around a table. Each had a drink, and before Asa joined them, she picked one up at the bar. She assumed Kiyoshi had arranged payment.

She sat down at the last space at the table. Kiyoshi gave her a short nod and began giving his news.

"Now that we are out of the city, I've learned much, and it's concerning."

Asa didn't really wonder about Kiyoshi's information network. She had known for a while that he was well connected, and she assumed one of the reasons he had chosen this particular location was because it was where information would have been left for him.

Kiyoshi continued. "First, there are several big events happening at the same time. Word has been sent out to every corner of the Kingdom: Masaki is dead, and Shin is the new king. The proclamation hasn't been accepted by the other two houses. Lord Juro, one of your armies, stationed at the border, crossed almost as soon as they heard the news. They are heading straight to Haven, and best estimates put them about three days away.

"Lord Isamu, it seems as though your armies have become completely disorganized. Each seems to be operating under a different set of orders. Most important, though, is that you also have an army coming up from the Three Sisters toward Haven. They are expected within five days.

"Unfortunately, Shin is also moving in reinforcements toward Haven. They will be here in four days."

Asa stifled the urge to laugh. If there was one place a person didn't want to be six days from now, it would be in Haven. They had three days of relative peace, but then everything was going to happen very fast.

The lords both looked like they had a number of questions, but Kiyoshi held up his hand to stop them before they began. "I know you'll have several questions about troops and family members, and I will answer as many of those questions as I can in a while. So far, there haven't been any major conflicts between armies. Lord Isamu, your army let Shin's pass because of orders issued from the palace. Lord Juro, your army apparently has developed a bridge crossing system we didn't know about, so they managed to avoid Lord Isamu's patrols without a problem. So far, we haven't fallen to war. My only concern is to make sure we never do. We have little time. In five days there are going to be more than ten thousand troops surrounding the same city. We need to have a solution by then."

Juro looked around the table and settled his stare on Kiyoshi. "What do you expect of us? You've gotten us this far, and knowing you, you've got a plan, don't you?"

Kiyoshi didn't retreat from the lord's stare. "You're asking if my goals contradict yours?"

Juro nodded.

"Perhaps. My concern is the Kingdom. I don't care about petty power struggles. Frankly, I don't much care which of you becomes king as long as the Kingdom remains at peace."

Juro scoffed. "Do you really believe that after everything that has happened, there is any hope of that?"

Kiyoshi didn't hesitate at all. "There is always a way to find peace. It only takes men with enough courage to pursue it."

Juro said, "Shin needs to pay for his treason. No man should ascend to the throne in the manner he did. If the king can't abide by the laws, the very idea our Kingdom is founded on is worthless."

Kiyoshi sighed. "That might be true. But what I am concerned about is the next few days. I want to avoid all-out war."

Isamu interrupted the two men. “Kiyoshi, I agree with Lord Juro. But like you, I wish to avoid bloodshed. If you can get me to my army, I can ensure that engagement is the last action they take.”

Asa studied the large lord. His voice was convincing, but his manners were not. She didn’t care for either of the lords, but Isamu the least. It was hard to believe anything he said, although Kiyoshi seemed to accept his statements without question.

“Thank you. That was my intention. I didn’t think I would be able to convince anyone to come to my point of view today, but I expect to get your respective promises that you won’t immediately resort to force. There are still thousands of innocent people in Haven, and they don’t have any part in your struggles. We will get you back to your families.”

Lord Juro looked skeptical. “And then what?”

Kiyoshi looked uncertain. “After that, there are many options. Lord Juro, if your men can get here even earlier, we might earn a slight advantage. The timing of your troops’ arrival and Shin’s might make all the difference. Perhaps I can lead an excursion into the city to bring Lord Shin out. We can sit you all down at a table and keep you there until you come to an agreement.”

“You think you can do that, even with the nightblade support Shin has?”

Daisuke stepped into the conversation. “Despite anything you may have heard, Lord Shin does not have the support of the blades. Minori may have convinced a handful within the city to support Shin, but they won’t be a problem.”

Isamu’s look conveyed a healthy dose of skepticism. “Forgive me, but even one or two nightblades pose a substantial problem.”

Daisuke spoke, his voice flat. “Hunting nightblades is my specialty.”

The lords looked to Kiyoshi for confirmation, and he agreed. “Daisuke is the most dangerous opponent any nightblade could face. Although I would wish for any other option, if that is what it comes to, Daisuke will be more than sufficient.”

It was a measure of the trust and respect that the lords had for Kiyoshi that they didn't make any comment.

Kiyoshi took one last look around the table. "Asa, you will escort Lord Juro in all haste. Daisuke will do the same for Lord Isamu. Once you deliver them safely to their armies, I'd ask that you return here as quickly as you are able."

Asa nodded and went to grab her things. She had almost reached her room when she realized she hadn't thought about Osamu in almost two whole days. She paused on the stairs, letting that idea sink in.

She turned around on the stairs, considering going back down to tell Kiyoshi she had more important matters to pursue. But she didn't. For the first time, she believed in something beyond revenge. Asa turned back up the steps and continued to her room to pack her bags. She would come back for Minori, but she would take care of Juro first.

It didn't take long for Asa to prepare herself. Lord Juro was a very different story. Lord Isamu and Daisuke had already been gone for half the day, but Juro insisted on sitting with Kiyoshi and picking his brain for every bit of information he could get. Asa used the time to sharpen her blades back in her room.

The sun was setting when she felt Kiyoshi outside her door. "Come in," she said.

Kiyoshi let himself in, studying her with the same gaze he always seemed to have. "Lord Juro will be ready shortly. There was much he wished to learn. Thank you for your patience, and thank you for escorting him."

Asa nodded. "I don't much care about the lords, but if their safety means other families don't have to go through what mine did, I'm more than willing to lend whatever strength I have. Just get me back into the city so I can kill Minori."

Kiyoshi gave her a glance she didn't understand, but he nodded. "I don't think you'll run into any problems, but there is never any telling. Were I in Shin's place, I would consider Isamu to be the greater threat. We are in his family's land, and the surrounding area has more allegiance to him than to any of the others. But his armies are farther away. Juro is certainly also a problem for Shin, however, so I will be curious to see what actions he takes. Be alert at all times."

Asa bowed to Kiyoshi and was surprised when he matched her bow with one of equal depth.

—

Outside, Kiyoshi watched as she and Juro mounted fresh horses. His last words to her were a simple, "Be safe."

After that, they were off, and Asa didn't look back.

Her first surprise of the trip was that Juro became pleasant company once it was just the two of them. There were still times when he acted too much like a lord for her tastes, but as she soon learned, Juro had been a soldier in his armies before he had come of age to lead his family. He rode well, much better than Asa, actually, and the hardships of the road didn't seem to bother him. It was almost as if the more time he spent away from the palace, the more he returned to his personality as a soldier, and the more Asa began to like him.

As they rode, Juro asked her many questions. He was curious about her life as a blade and specifically asked about her training and how she ended up in her current situation. Asa wasn't naïve enough to believe the questioning was all honest interest. She could tell he was trying to understand exactly how the Council of the Blades operated. Regardless, Asa didn't see any reason to lie, and she welcomed the conversation.

Asa returned his interest by asking about the life of a lord, not a subject she had ever considered. But Juro, despite her suspicion, made her curious. As he spoke about his day-to-day life, Asa realized she would much rather be a nightblade than a lord. Politics and paperwork were two tasks she was happy leaving to others.

The moon was high in the sky, but the two riders didn't stop. Both Asa and Juro wanted to reach his army in as little time as possible. A steady pace was best. With any luck, they would come across his troops by the end of the next day.

When Asa saw the silhouette off in the distance, her heart immediately sank. A lone individual appeared, not a scouting party from an army. Although such a coincidence seemed unlikely, Asa felt like there was only one person it could be. Juro spotted the rider as well, and their conversation evaporated.

Juro glanced at her. "Nightblade?"

"I can't sense him from here, but I'm almost certain."

The two paused their mounts, each trying to decide what to do. Their horses weren't exhausted, but they weren't fresh, either. If it came to a chase, they would probably be overtaken.

Asa looked at Juro. "I can try to intercept him. You can make a run for it."

"Can you beat him?"

"As nightblades go, my skills are just above average. If that is who I believe it is, my odds of winning are slim."

Juro looked thoughtful for a moment. "If you can't buy me enough time to escape his pursuit, there's no point in me running. I'll stay and fight with you."

Asa glanced over. The surprise must have been evident on her face.

"You may not respect lords, but perhaps I can change your mind. We aren't as useless as you believe. I am a decent sword."

Asa bowed.

"Whatever happens, Lord Juro, you've made me think there's more to lords than I ever gave them credit for."

"That, at least, is something."

They kicked their horses forward, and Asa extended her sense as far as she was able, to make sure there weren't any lurking traps. The closer they got to the lone rider, the more certain she was that her gut was correct. Before they were close enough for her to see the rider's face clearly, she could sense him, and her heart finished its plummet to the bottom of her stomach.

"It is him."

Juro simply nodded. There wasn't much else to say.

They stopped about twenty paces away from the lone rider, and Asa looked into Koji's eyes. The fierceness she had seen in them the last time they met was still present, but now they were tinged with something else: a rage she couldn't understand.

Asa didn't want to fight Koji. Not just because he was stronger, but because he was the first person she'd had a good conversation with in many cycles. They barely knew each other, but Asa felt a kinship with the younger man. Even if she drew her sword against him, she worried her heart wouldn't be in the fight.

Asa spoke first. "Knowing everything, you still follow Minori's orders?"

Koji turned to her, his expression softening for just a moment before hardening again. "Not quite. My orders were to start with Isamu. This, this is for me."

"What do you mean?"

"Juro is the lord of the lands that betrayed me and sentenced me to death. I saved the lives of his people, and how does the lord repay me? By ordering my death. He is a man without honor, and I want him to die knowing it was his own mistake that cost his life."

Juro was confused. "What have I done?" He turned to Asa. "Who is this?"

Koji didn't give her a chance to answer. "My name is Koji."

The look of recognition on Juro's face was immediate. "You? How?"

Koji didn't bother giving the lord an answer. He kept his gaze on Asa. "I have no quarrel with you. But if you stand between me and him, I will cut you down. I'd rather not do that."

Asa dismounted. She didn't want to, but she had given Kiyoshi her word, and she wouldn't break his service, not when she had just accepted it. "I understand your desire for revenge, Koji, but I can't let you kill this man. His life can save the lives of many others."

Koji's face twisted, and Asa felt a fear she never had before. The forces controlling him were primal. "And if the same was true of Osamu? If his life could save others, what would you do?"

Asa felt his words as deep as any sword. She wanted to claim she would do the right thing and save the most lives, but she wasn't sure. Osamu deserved to die.

"That's what I thought." Koji also dismounted, and Juro, looking one last time at the horizon, got off his horse, too.

Juro drew his sword, and Koji did the same. Looking between the two men, Asa wished there was another way, but she, too, drew her short blade.

Of all of them, she wasn't expecting Juro to be the one to attack, but he was. Courageousness or foolishness, she wasn't sure, but the lord charged Koji head-on. Asa sprinted forward, knowing she wouldn't have much of a chance. Koji easily dodged Juro's attack, and for a moment, Asa thought the battle was over almost before it began. But Koji didn't take the killing stroke that was right in front of him. Asa couldn't believe it. Koji was playing with Juro, prolonging the moment.

His anger gave Asa the time she needed to get to the scene of the fight. She darted in between Koji and Juro, her blade coming up in a defensive posture. But Koji didn't attack, for he had no interest in her. Asa knew he would try to ignore her if he could, but if Juro was going to have any chance of survival, she needed to engage Koji.

Asa sensed Juro regaining his balance, and Koji tried to dart to Asa's side. She sensed the move coming and was just as fast. She shifted and kept herself in between him and his prey. Rage consumed his face, and he didn't restrain himself any longer. He swung at her, but his attack was easy to sense. She moved out of the way and darted in, scoring a shallow cut across his chest.

The cut wasn't dangerous to Koji, but it seemed to drive some sensibility back into him. A look of control came over his face, and Asa knew she had only succeeded in making her job that much harder. Koji took one of his stances, his sword point held low. Asa stepped back and brought her sword to a defensive position. Now the fight would be serious.

Koji stepped forward, his cut clean and controlled. Asa deflected it, her short sword moving quickly. But Koji had clearly expected the block, moving into his next cut without hesitation. Cut after cut drove Asa back, and she was forced into doing nothing but reacting time and time again. She was moving as fast as she knew how, but Koji was always just a little ahead of her. Behind them, Juro tried to angle his way into the battle, but the two blades moved too quickly for him.

Asa deflected one cut off to the side and realized she was inside his guard. She hesitated for just a moment, uncertain of what to do. Koji, his eyes as cold as steel, didn't share her hesitation. His knee came up and drove into her stomach. Asa doubled over as she tried to get air into her lungs.

At just that moment, Juro came in. His cuts were well timed, but against someone sense-gifted like Koji, they were obvious and easy to dodge or block. Koji dodged each thrust, not even trying to deflect Juro's attempts.

Wheezing, Asa caught her breath and moved forward as quickly as she could. Her stomach was still sore where she had been kneed. She joined Juro's offensive, and Koji was forced to dodge both of them.

It was Juro who made the first mistake. Thinking he had an opening, he made a cut with too much force, allowing himself to lose balance. Koji dodged the cut and moved in toward him. He brought his leg up and kicked Juro in between his legs. Juro's eyes rolled up, and he collapsed, struggling to get back to his feet.

Asa, knowing she didn't have many more chances, launched an all-out attack on Koji. She struck as quickly as could, each cut a fatal possibility. But even with all her efforts, Koji was unharmed. Asa had known Koji was a better fighter, but she had never suspected he was this much better. She surged forward again, sacrificing form for speed, and Koji capitalized on the opportunity. He knocked the blade out of her hand and punched her in the stomach, right where he'd hit her earlier.

Asa collapsed, her world going dark. She saw Koji step back toward Juro and forced herself back to awareness. She grabbed her blade and lunged at him, but he must have sensed her coming. He sidestepped her attack easily, pivoting and delivering another blow to her stomach. Asa vomited and collapsed, blackness pressing in on her vision.

Asa grabbed the grass, seeking anything that might provide some purchase, anything her slipping consciousness could hold on to.

In what remained of her vision, she saw Koji kick Juro several times. The lord tried to fight back, but he couldn't succeed, not against a nightblade gripped by rage.

Asa wanted to fight. She wanted to defend Juro. But there was nothing left. She tried getting up, but she collapsed to the ground, unable to move. The last thing she saw before her world went black was Koji punching Juro, his knuckles bloody and raw.

Chapter 26

The sun dawned on a new day, and Minori awoke uncertain. When he had conceived his plan, it had seemed right, the best path forward. However, the world seemed determined to frustrate him at every turn. If he was playing a chess game, he felt like he wasn't looking far enough ahead.

Minori looked out the window of his house, which faced in the direction of the palace. Memories of fire engulfed his mind. The action had seemed necessary, but as he looked at the wisps of smoke in the distance, he felt as though he had sacrificed a part of himself.

Two nights had passed since he and Koji had burned the palace to the ground, and still the ruins smoldered. Shin had sent soldiers in with water to try to quench the remaining flames, but no matter what they tried, the ruins continued to give off wisps of smoke, as though ghosts of the palace were trying to escape. Minori wasn't a superstitious man, but every time he looked at the smoke in the sky, he wondered if it was a sign of his mistakes.

What made the guilt worse was that burning the palace hadn't mattered. They didn't have any concrete evidence, but Minori was certain Kiyoshi and the lords had already escaped the city. Koji had disappeared, and if he was completing his mission, then he was out of the city as well. Minori was surprised by how alone he felt. A strange part of him even missed Kiyoshi.

Thoughts of the healer immediately angered him. If not for the old man, Minori was certain events would never have gone this far. But even though he kept a few steps ahead of the dayblade, Kiyoshi always seemed to manage to find a way to destroy his plans. Minori remembered the fear on the face of the messenger who came to report the incident at the gate early yesterday morning. There was no way of knowing who all had left the city, but the nightblade guarding the gate had been knocked unconscious, and the only person in the city capable of doing that worked for Kiyoshi.

Minori tried sitting to meditate, but his thoughts were a turbulent storm. The world was nothing more than a chessboard, but Minori couldn't focus on all the pieces. All he could see was Kiyoshi on the board.

There was so much more to consider. There were the approaching armies, the other lords, and even the Council of the Blades. All had roles to play, and at one time, Minori had known exactly how to manipulate each of these forces, but they all felt like pawns compared to Kiyoshi.

Minori swore out loud, upset that there wasn't anyone in the room to feel his anger. He grabbed his blade and walked out into the small courtyard of his house, working his way through practice kata. Normally it was something he only practiced a bit each day, but today he needed more. He kept running through the katas taught to him as a child, which he had practiced almost every day since then. His blade sliced through the air, and even though Minori could hear that his cuts were poor, he kept moving through the motions, his mind elsewhere.

Sweat beaded down his body, and as he continued to run through his katas, his mind began to calm. The world of the sword was easier to understand. Minori imagined cutting down Kiyoshi and Asa and Shin, and he immediately felt better.

Exhausted, Minori sat down at a bench in his courtyard. For the first time that day, he was able to think clearly. He avoided contemplating Kiyoshi, afraid that doing so would wreck the small amount of focus he had. Instead, he thought about Lord Shin. In many ways, Shin was his benefactor, but Minori didn't trust him. The lord was far too clever, and Minori needed to figure out a way to control his actions before the usurper cemented his power. Shin needed to appear too authoritarian for the citizens of the Kingdom. They needed to want him gone.

Minori realized he needed to leave his house. The news from the gate had thrown him off-balance yesterday, and he had spent the entire day scouring documents and letters, trying to find the big picture he was missing. If he was going to manipulate Shin, he needed more information. He needed to know what was happening in the city. He was just about to go change when he sensed a person at the gate to his home. Given the circumstances, the visitor could only be a messenger. Minori hoped, for the messenger's sake, that he was carrying good news.

Minori walked to the door and opened it moments before the messenger arrived. "Yes?"

The messenger looked shaken, and Minori delighted in the slight use of his powers.

The messenger quickly recovered. "I come to you from the king. He is making a speech this morning to all the residents of Haven. He requests your presence."

Minori frowned. "Did he say why?"

The messenger gulped, and Minori thought he must have really intimidated the man. The question wasn't that hard.

"The king said he wants you there to reassure the public that the monarchy and the blades are working together to find and punish the traitors who burned down the palace."

Minori contained the laughter he felt. It was a typical move for Shin. Shin would be laughing for days about his speech, promising to pursue the traitors while the person who burned the palace was standing right next to him. But Minori applauded the move. The support of the blades would make a huge difference in the public's mind, and if Minori made an appearance and could even say a few words, he could establish more trust with the people. The show of support could provide future opportunities to increase the visibility of the blades and their work in the Kingdom.

"I will be there."

The messenger bowed. "I will take your response to the king. There will be criers going throughout the city soon. The speech will take place in the streets outside the old front gates of the palace."

Minori nodded. He saw Shin's influence in everything. It was the perfect spot for a gathering. The smoking ruins of the palace would provide a powerful backdrop for Shin, and he was a talented enough orator that he would make great use of the scene. Minori smiled. Shin wasn't the only one who could manipulate people. He would speak at the gathering, and he would begin the long process of ushering in a new era for the gifted.

Minori walked toward the palace, his mind occupied. Although the streets were crowded with people wandering toward the gathering, he might as well have been walking on a street alone. His thoughts consumed him as he tried out different arguments in his mind, examining which ones would seize the public's imagination most.

When he got to the gathering, he worked his way toward the front, where a makeshift platform stood elevated above the crowd. Shin saw him approach and waved the blade up. Minori threaded his way through the crowd without a problem, for as soon as people saw his robes, they moved out of his way. He stood on the platform, and he couldn't help but feel a small swell of pride as he looked out on the masses.

Minori turned to Shin. "Thank you for inviting me. I'm happy to show the blades' support for your reign. Would you like me to say a few words?"

"I hadn't even thought of that, but now that you mention it, yes, it does seem like a good idea. I'll give my message, and once I'm done, you're welcome to say whatever you like. I'm sure the crowd will be interested in what you have to say."

Together they waited for the crowd to finish assembling. The street, while wider than others in Haven for purposes of defense, was still not more than fifty paces wide, and it was packed in each direction with people. Even if Minori shouted, it would be the responsibility of the crowd to carry his message to the farthest corners of the assembly.

Finally Shin stepped forward, and the din of the crowd faded to an eerie silence. Minori had never seen so many people in one place. He couldn't estimate how many citizens were packed in to the street, but thousands had to be there. To be in the presence of so many and to have such silence was an experience unlike any other. For a moment, Minori wondered if he had suddenly gone deaf.

But then Shin spoke, and the illusion was destroyed. His voice was clear and deep and carried across the crowd. Minori immediately paid attention and found himself impressed by Shin's speaking power.

"Friends, I did not come here today to mince words or give flowery speeches. Everyone here knows that the time is dire. The Kingdom, for the first time in many lifetimes, is truly at risk. Rumors abound, and I apologize if the actions I've had to take have caused further confusion."

Minori watched the crowd, every face rapt with attention.

"Here are the facts. Our faithful and strong leader, King Masaki, is dead. Everything was done to save his life, but in the end, the Great Cycle claims us all, and Masaki now leads us on the journey we must all take someday. Although his body was lost in the tragic fire that consumed the palace, one day soon he will be honored with a celebration to mark his passing. But first, we must act to protect the Kingdom he loved so much. Before he died, Masaki wrote a letter willing that I become his successor."

Minori kept his face straight, but it was difficult. The move was bold, but reasonable. Masaki had been a popular king, and his blessing would provide Shin much of the support he needed. The letter would be easy enough to forge, as well. Masaki hadn't written personally in many cycles, and Minori was certain Shin had seized the royal seal in his coup. The only two who knew differently were the other two lords, which meant Shin had another plan for them.

"King Masaki believed I would be the best leader for the Kingdom, but power and politics must play their ugly role. As we speak, armies march toward Haven, and shutting the gates was necessary to prevent spies from leaving the city."

A murmur ran through the crowd, and Minori wondered if Shin had misjudged his audience.

"But have no fear, friends. I have no plans to fight. No good can come from war. Masaki chose me, and I hope that I am worthy, but I will sit down with the other two lords. We will decide the future of the Kingdom not with swords, but with words. That is my promise to you."

Minori, despite himself, was impressed. Even knowing Shin as he did, he couldn't detect a trace of false humility in his voice. Every word rang true, and from his view of the crowd, Minori could tell the king's words had the desired effect. Minori shook his head just the smallest amount. The move was brilliant. If Shin could get the public on his side, and he would if he continued to give such powerful speeches, the other lords would be backed into a corner. Shin controlled Haven, the public believed he was chosen by Masaki, and if this crowd was any indication, the people trusted him. If the other lords cared at all about the Kingdom, they would have little choice but to follow Shin.

The crowd quieted again as Shin raised his hands. The man held their attention like a puppeteer, pulling the strings just right, making them dance to the song only he could hear.

"Friends, although there will not be war, I do come to you with a terrible burden." He paused, and Minori, just like every other member of the crowd, hung on his next words. "Behind me, you can see the embers of the palace that was the symbol of our Kingdom. It was burned out of hate and spite for our land, and I will not stand for it. My shadows and soldiers have identified the group responsible for burning the palace, and I was very disturbed when I found out who it was."

Minori wondered what game Shin was playing. Was he going to accuse Kiyoshi of starting the fire? It would be a strong move, but one that could backfire. As Minori had discovered himself, Kiyoshi was well loved by many blades, and they wouldn't take the accusation lying down.

In the back of his mind, Minori felt that something was wrong, as though there was an insistent buzzing. But he mentally slapped it away, trying to focus on what Shin was going to say next.

"The group that burned down the palace, and who killed several of my guards in the process, were the blades, acting on orders of their council."

The crowd was as silent as Minori, the weight of Shin's words settling on them.

Minori froze in place, his mind racing. What he was hearing—it couldn't be true. He was trying to process all the implications, but his mind felt trapped in a small cage, denial running through his head.

"The man standing next to me, whom I've trusted these past moons, has secretly been the leader of the plot against me. I have learned that the blades seek to overthrow the government of the Kingdom and rule this land. They are tired of serving and wish to rule instead."

Shin glared at Minori and drew his sword in a clumsy motion, his eyes as cold as ice. "Guards, take this man prisoner."

Shin's command snapped Minori to attention. He couldn't process the betrayal and its implications, but he knew imprisonment meant death, and he wasn't ready for that. As his mind caught up to the events of the past few moments, he paid attention to his environment with fresh eyes. The platform was surrounded by guards with spears, and Minori realized there were eight in number, the same as in Shin's nightblade-hunting units.

The guards had been waiting for Shin's signal; they turned and faced the platform. Minori glanced around and saw another pack of eight spears marching toward the platform. Shin wasn't taking any chances.

At that moment, Minori was thankful he had been so frustrated earlier that day. His body was warmed up and ready to move, a much different sensation than most mornings, where morning movement came hand in hand with stiffness. His own anger could be the difference between him escaping or dying.

With the extra group behind him, Minori only had one logical path. He took one last look at Shin and sprinted forward, leaping as high as he could off the front of the platform. There were four guards who had been stationed there, and Minori passed within spear range of two of them. They stabbed out, and Minori felt at least one of the spears tear through his robes.

Minori landed hard and rolled clumsily. He cursed himself for not having kept his body in better condition. In his time in Haven, there had been so much to pay attention to, he hadn't moved as often as he should. Fortunately, although his side and back hurt from the hard landing, he was certain he hadn't rolled his ankles. He had a chance.

Again the crowd parted before him, the well-established fear of nightblades still holding, but in the already-packed space of the road, there wasn't always a place for people to go. Citizens tripped over one another, and when some tried to get away, they only succeeded in being pushed back against Minori. Fast movement simply wasn't going to happen. Still, the guards behind him were bogged down as well.

Minori risked one glance. Shin stood on the platform, back straight, a bemused expression on his face. No doubt he believed his guards would have little problem rounding up Minori. In a moment of doubt, the blade considered just giving up. In combat, he had a chance, but against sixteen of Shin's specially trained men, that chance was exceedingly slim. If it came down to a footrace, Minori knew he was doomed. Perhaps if he didn't resist, there would be an opportunity later.

His mind screamed at him, and he realized he was being foolish. If he were captured, Shin would ensure he was the best-guarded prisoner in the history of the Kingdom. His chances of escape now might be slim, but he had to try.

When Minori reached the edge of the street, he saw that he had been headed off by two of Shin's guards. They were only carrying swords, and Minori assumed they were regular soldiers, present to oversee the gathering.

They both drew their swords and slashed, but Minori was able to sense both strikes coming. He easily slid between the guards and kept moving. Regular soldiers weren't his worry. The group of eight behind him was, as well as the others behind them.

His only real hope was to try to lose the soldiers in the folds of Haven. To do so, he needed narrow alleys and lots of corners and hiding spaces. A market nearby just might serve him well. Minori turned toward it, the sound of footsteps running hard behind him.

Minori didn't feel fear. He had been in impossible situations before. When he was younger, they had been considered his specialty, which was why he had been sent into Two Falls in the first place. When times got tough, when their lives were threatened, most people had a tendency to panic. Not Minori. His breath settled, and he sensed everything around him. He could feel the empty streets and knew just how far away Shin's guards were. An implacable calm settled on him as he knew what he had to do to survive.

He could sense Shin's guards splitting up and going down side alleys. They knew they were faster and would seek to box him in. If he was going to live, he needed to make sure that box never closed. He found the side street he was looking for and sprinted, asking more of his legs and lungs than he had in many moons.

He sensed the soldiers before he saw them, and skidded to a stop. One pair of guards was coming up the cross street in front of him. Minori threw himself behind a cart—a poor hiding place, but he was betting his pursuers wouldn't stop to look carefully. He breathed slowly as his guess was confirmed and they ran in front of him, just glancing to see if their quarry was in the alley. Then the soldiers continued on their way.

The pair that had been trailing him turned the corner, saw him crouched behind the cart, and immediately realized what had happened. They let out a shout, and Minori was back on his feet, sprinting through the intersection perpendicular to the path of the first pair. At the next intersection, he doubled back toward the palace. He had broken through the box once. Now he had to continue to do so.

What he needed more than anything else was a place to hide, a place where no one would suspect him. His mind raced through different options as his body raced through the streets of Haven. The guards had gotten between him and the market, and he could sense all sixteen prowling the area. His options were quickly disappearing.

The pair behind him had eased their pursuit. But he could tell why. His sense told him he was surrounded by guards, and rushing would only put the guards in greater danger. Despite his efforts, he was indeed boxed in, even though the box was large.

Minori turned a corner, thoughts of his earlier life as a shadow returning to him. He had been pursued regularly then, but how did he always evade his pursuers? Then he remembered that there were two directions people rarely looked—down and up. Minori didn't think he'd be able to hide anywhere underfoot, but they wouldn't expect an old man to climb up. He just had to find a place to scale without being seen.

Minori slowed down to a jog, scanning his surroundings. A cold wind picked up, and the blade felt a sudden chill. There was the spot he was looking for. Minori climbed on top of a barrel, and from there onto the top of a wooden wall. He balanced precariously for a few moments before finding his center. He walked along the wall for about six paces. Across the alley, only two paces away, was a rooftop he could hide on. Now all he had to do was make the jump. He hesitated. If he missed his target and fell, everything would be over. He sensed two pairs of guards getting closer. There wasn't any time to doubt.

Minori leapt, trying to get his center of weight over the roof, but he failed. Slowly, he slid backward, his hands scrabbling for purchase on the slanted roof. He caught himself just before he fell, and for a brief moment hung in space. Summoning all his energy and youthful memories, Minori pulled himself up to the top of the roof, grunting through the final effort.

He got his feet up and over the wall just before the guards came in view of the alley. Not seeing him, they continued on their way. Minori knew they would be back, continuing to search the area. But for now, he was safe, and that was enough.

The blade collapsed onto his back, his entire body aching from the effort of escape. He felt a wetness on his face, and it drew his eyes toward the sky. The gathering clouds had thickened, and the first snow was falling.

It was going to be cold, but he wouldn't freeze. He had one thing left to do in this world, and he wouldn't fail. All his plans may have been for nothing, but a new mission had taken their place.

He was going to kill Shin.

Chapter 27

Kiyoshi sat in his room, the rightful king in front of him, breathing peacefully and calmly. If he took a step back, he had to acknowledge how unusual the situation was. Monarch and adviser were on the run, even though Masaki should be in his palace, surrounded by aides. Instead, he was here alone, with only Kiyoshi to look after him. His palace had burned, and all his aides believed he was dead. If they knew the truth, they would never speak of it.

Masaki didn't deserve this fate. There were a handful of people in the Kingdom who knew the sacrifices he had made for peace, but in the end, they would all come to nothing if Kiyoshi couldn't salvage the disaster that currently surrounded them. Masaki had paid the price for peace in blood, and no one knew.

As he looked at his king, Kiyoshi thought about when he had first entered Masaki's service. They had known each other for some time, but Kiyoshi had recently failed in the most spectacular way. He had disappeared for some time, and after a long period of wandering, he returned to the palace. He had laid his blade before Masaki and told him that if he so wished, he would gladly take his own life. In his youth, Kiyoshi had despised the practice, but he had come to understand it. Sometimes death was the only peace one could find.

Masaki hadn't allowed him his death. He asked Kiyoshi into his service, and the blade had remained there for more than twenty cycles now. They hadn't always experienced easy times, but Kiyoshi always looked up to Masaki. He was the only truly selfless leader Kiyoshi had ever met, a worthy man to follow.

Kiyoshi was close to giving up on the Kingdom. Maintaining order in the land was like trying to hold together a piece of pottery that had already shattered.

Asa was in her room, recovering from her injuries. Koji had been a force Kiyoshi hadn't reckoned on. The young boy's power and strength were remarkable. Minori had found a tool more powerful than even he realized.

With Juro dead, there were only two real contenders for the throne. Until this morning, Kiyoshi had thought perhaps it was best to allow Shin to continue his way forward. He was the smartest and the boldest, and if it was a choice between him and Isamu, Kiyoshi would gladly have chosen Shin. But not after the information he had just received.

Here in the inn, his shadows were able to get plenty of information to him, and the most recent news from Haven had been the last cut Kiyoshi could take. Minori, displayed in public as the arsonist who destroyed the palace. Shin, demanding representation from the council, but until then, ordering all blades to turn in their swords. If they didn't, they were guilty of treason and would be hunted. Kiyoshi's note said that groups of citizens were going from house to house, making sure no blades dwelled in Haven. Several blades had already died, unable to escape the sealed city.

The petty part of Kiyoshi wanted to laugh at Minori's misfortune. His game had been a foolish one, and although Kiyoshi believed Minori had meant well, he had come into the game not knowing where all the pieces were. He hadn't known about Shin's desire to rid the Kingdom of the blades. A crucial mistake.

Mostly, though, Kiyoshi felt sorry for Minori. They might disagree, but they both wanted what was best for the blades, via their own opinions. Minori had made mistakes, but going down in history as the most despised man in the Kingdom was a fate he didn't deserve.

Kiyoshi had thought about the problem all morning but couldn't come up with any solutions. They needed some way of keeping the Kingdom from remaining in Shin's hands, but the usurper's plans had been very well thought out. With the blades as a common enemy, he might even manage to keep the families united. Juro, of course, had also been killed by a blade, another step that Shin seemed to have anticipated.

Kiyoshi turned the problem over and over in his mind, like constantly tilling up new earth in a garden. But no matter how hard he searched, no answers came to him.

He was so busy thinking about the problems facing the Kingdom that it took him some time to see that Masaki's eyes were open.

The king was awake.

Kiyoshi was so excited that he jumped to his feet, ready to shout for anyone who would listen. But his sudden movement startled Masaki, and as the king's eyes tracked over to Kiyoshi, the old dayblade saw something that terrified him. Masaki's eyes, usually sharp and attentive, were blank and glassy. Kiyoshi realized Masaki, or whatever was left of his friend, was gone. All that remained was a scared child.

Kiyoshi's heart almost collapsed in grief. After all of this, to have the king come to only to have lost his mind was almost too much to take.

Kiyoshi's healing nature reasserted itself, and he walked slowly toward Masaki, his voice soft and soothing. "Hello, Masaki. Do you know where you are?"

Masaki didn't reply to Kiyoshi, but his lips moved. As Kiyoshi got closer, he could hear some of the words Masaki uttered, largely gibberish, but a few remarks Kiyoshi recognized. Names, places, random sentences that didn't fit into any context Kiyoshi could imagine.

Moving slowly, so as not to frighten Masaki, Kiyoshi moved his hands, placing one on the king's head and one on his chest. Kiyoshi closed his eyes, and the outside world faded away. He took a deep, calming breath as he realized just how sick Masaki had become. The growth inside of him had grown much larger, and it was amazing he could even draw breath. But Masaki's mind was what Kiyoshi was most worried about.

Kiyoshi could feel the energy of Masaki's mind, torn into shreds as though a child were ripping up paper. It wasn't wise, but Kiyoshi dove into Masaki's head, into the heart of the disturbance of the energy. It was time for desperate action. The worst he could do was kill Masaki, and he wasn't sure that was a bad thing anymore. The king had earned his rest.

Kiyoshi focused his own strength and dove into the knot that had defined Masaki's recent existence. Gently, but firmly, he tried to force the energy into patterns he recognized. He didn't concern himself with causing permanent damage. He was driven, partly by desperation, partly by curiosity. What was he capable of? Could he bring the king back after all he had been through?

Sweat beaded down his face, a minor irritation. He worked his way to the center of the disruption in Masaki's mind. The energy there circled and swirled, an angry hive of bees. Kiyoshi couldn't imagine beginning to untangle it or rearrange it, so he tried to cut at it with his own inner force.

Kiyoshi felt something snap in Masaki's mind, and he was abruptly thrown out of his meditation. His eyes took in the room they were in, but he needed a few moments to remember where he was and what he was doing. Dayblades were always cautioned about jumping out of patients. It wasn't good for the mind, and in the schools they told stories of dayblades who had lost their sanity trying to heal. Kiyoshi could understand. His soul felt as though it was trying to stitch itself back together.

He looked down, and what he saw brought joy to his heart, the first real joy he had felt in a very long time. Masaki was looking at him, warmth in his eyes.

"Hello, old friend," said the king.

—

The rest of the day was both depressing and refreshing. It was heartbreaking because Kiyoshi needed to give the king at least a small idea of what had happened while he had been unconscious. The blade tried to be quick, because it soon became apparent that while Masaki was awake and alert, he wouldn't be for long. Kiyoshi caught him drifting time and time again, and his moments of lucidity were getting shorter.

Whatever Kiyoshi had managed to do to the king wasn't a permanent healing. Kiyoshi also noticed that the king's breathing was becoming more labored.

The two sat next to each other, talking in quiet tones. Masaki looked tired, more tired than Kiyoshi had ever remembered him. A part of Kiyoshi regretted his actions. Masaki looked as though he would have preferred to pass into the Great Cycle.

The king looked at his friend. "What would you have me do?"

"You need to declare Isamu the next king."

"He's too weak."

"I agree. But Shin will pursue his vendetta against the blades, destroying the Kingdom. We have no choice anymore."

Masaki was silent, and for a few moments, Kiyoshi worried he had slipped back into his lost mental state. But the king was just thinking. "I hate it, but I agree. The Kingdom needs the blades, even if the people don't realize it."

Masaki asked for paper. It was painful for Kiyoshi to watch the king struggle to write, but for the healer's own conscience, he needed the king to perform the act himself. After all of Shin's forgeries, this document needed to be as authentic as possible. They didn't have the king's seal, which was a problem, but the note would have to do.

The orders signed, Masaki gazed at his friend. "I assume you will take it upon yourself to deliver these?"

Kiyoshi nodded.

Masaki looked out into the distance, out through the window. When he spoke, his voice seemed to come from far away. "I think that if you return, I will not be here anymore."

Kiyoshi's first instinct was to argue, but as he looked at his old friend, he knew the king spoke the truth. He would not survive several days of travel overland to meet at Isamu's camp. Kiyoshi wasn't sure Masaki would survive even a few days in the inn. If Kiyoshi was successful, it would be some time before he could return.

Masaki continued. "When will you leave?"

"As soon as possible. Time is among our enemies right now."

"Would you sit with me for a while? It is a rare gift to be among friends."

Together they spoke of old times, of events and people that had passed into the realm of history, some stories of which they were the only two alive who knew of them. Eventually, talk turned to Yoshi, the king's son, the once prince of the Kingdom.

"Do you think he would have made a good king?" Masaki asked.

Kiyoshi smiled, a sad smile. "Yes. You guided him well, and even though he had a tendency to get distracted by women and weapons, he would have outgrown that. His heart was always in the right place, and like you, he put the Kingdom first. The people would have been lucky to have him as ruler."

"You know, when you were the one that came back, I was so angry at you. He loved you like the brother I was never able to give him, but when I saw you, kneeling there in front of me, you'll never know how close I came to taking your head myself."

"I would have let you."

"I know. It's a horrible thought to hold, but every time I saw you, I thought to myself, it should have been you. But you returned, and he didn't."

Kiyoshi, overwhelmed, felt himself losing control, but the king continued.

"Day after day I watched you. I knew how useful you were, but I wanted an excuse to kill you. I wanted you to be the traitor, but day after day, you gave everything to the Kingdom. And then, as the days went on and we all got older, you became the only link I had left to my son. And here we are, both old men who have outlived our usefulness."

Kiyoshi couldn't handle the king's kindness. The tears streamed from his face, and he made no effort to hide them.

A look of compassion flooded Masaki's face. "Kiyoshi, I've seen you bring yourself to the brink of self-destruction so many times since those days. I've seen your heart, and I know the grief and anger that have driven you for cycle after cycle. At times, I think I understand you better than you understand yourself."

Their eyes met, and Masaki held Kiyoshi's gaze.

"There's something I need you to know. Not just listen to, but know. Kiyoshi, I forgive you. You have absolutely no debt to me, my family, or the Kingdom. I forgive you."

Masaki broke his gaze with Kiyoshi as a fit of coughing overtook him. A trickle of blood came out the corner of his mouth, and Kiyoshi wiped it away with a rag. Kiyoshi couldn't bring himself to say anything. His heart was too full.

"Kiyoshi, do you believe it? You have done everything you could and more. Let the weight of Yoshi's death fall from your shoulders. We are both joining the Great Cycle soon, and I won't have you joining me with that debt weighing you down."

At that, Kiyoshi collapsed completely, falling to his knees in front of Masaki. His body was racked with sobs, emotion tearing through him. They were only words, but Kiyoshi didn't realize how long he had waited to hear them.

He lost track of time on his knees, but when he came back to his senses, the room was beginning to darken. Night came sooner and sooner as winter approached. As Kiyoshi stood, he felt lighter somehow. He looked at Masaki, but the king's eyes were glassy again, and he was muttering gibberish. Kiyoshi wanted to thank him, to let him know just how he had helped in the last days of his life, but he didn't say anything. Somehow he was certain Masaki knew his heart.

Kiyoshi turned around and walked toward the door. But just before he was about to open it, he heard a phrase that froze him in place. "Osamu, it should have been you." Kiyoshi spun and looked at Masaki, but now he was asking about wine. Kiyoshi considered sending the king on his way to the Great Cycle, but he couldn't. Not only was it wrong; he wasn't certain he could physically bring himself to kill his friend. He shook his head and left the room on one last mission for his king.

—

When Kiyoshi left the room, he sensed that Daisuke had returned. He went to the nightblade's room, where the door was open. Kiyoshi looked him over. Although the man looked tired, he looked none the worse for wear. A few days riding was all he had suffered. "You delivered him safely?"

Daisuke nodded. "There was no trouble."

"Juro was killed. The young nightblade Minori befriended, Koji, killed him."

"Asa?"

"Beaten up, but fine. I healed any injuries that were serious."

A look of relief passed over Daisuke's face, and Kiyoshi saw his friend had developed an affection for the younger blade. "What comes next?"

Kiyoshi filled in Daisuke on the most recent happenings, from Shin's recent decisions to how the king had regained consciousness and declared Isamu the rightful king. It was their only chance at preventing war or the downfall of the blades.

Daisuke frowned. "I imagine you mean to leave right away?"

"Yes. Why not?"

"If everything you've learned is true, what good will it do to keep trying? I hate to say this, but maybe it's time for us to find a nice quiet corner of the Kingdom and live in peace. There's no way Shin will give up power, and without the seal, Isamu will have an uphill battle trying to convince the Kingdom he has legitimacy."

"You know I have to try. If Shin has his way and the blades become persecuted throughout the Kingdom, I fear for the future."

"At least let me go instead. Your place is here, next to Masaki."

Kiyoshi hesitated. The idea was a tempting one, but wouldn't work. "As much as I want to, that's not what needs to happen. As you stated, without the seal, Isamu would face an uphill battle convincing people of legitimacy. I can attest to the truthfulness of the letter, adding to its authenticity. Perhaps it won't mean as much to the people, but it could lead the Council of the Blades to declare their support for Isamu. With Shin's recent declarations, Hajimi and the council have to be terrified. This gives them a way out. With the support of the blades, Isamu might have a chance."

"It's still a slim chance."

"But it's the best one we have, and the council won't listen to you, since they don't even know you exist."

Daisuke conceded the point with a nod of his head.

"What would you have of me?"

"Tend to the king if he wakes back up. I don't think it will be much longer now. He's delirious and going in and out of consciousness. Keep him comfortable, and if possible, try to keep Asa away from him. I expect she'll sleep for some time, though."

Daisuke looked confused at first, but understanding dawned quickly on him. He straightened up and nodded. Kiyoshi felt sorry for him. He had just ridden several days with little sleep, and to ask this of him was a lot. Daisuke had to be exhausted.

"What if she finds out?"

Kiyoshi had been wondering about that question himself for some time.

"Let her make her own decision. I hope she can see the consequences of her actions now, but her desire for revenge runs deeper than either of us can imagine. Either way, let her choose."

"Are you sure that's wise? She's not that strong, but she's fast, and you're not as young as you once were. She might beat you if it comes to that."

"Perhaps, but if that is my fate, so it is. Daisuke, I'm tired of trying to control the world. It's like trying to grasp sand. The harder you squeeze, the more it escapes from you. If it comes to that, she and I will finish our story. She deserves that."

Daisuke didn't look like he agreed, but he bowed.

"After the king dies?"

Kiyoshi smiled. "I release you from my service, Daisuke. I ask you to guard the king as a friend and fellow blade. Not as your master, not any longer. I'm not sure where my path goes anymore. If I reach Isamu, you may search for me there. I'm always grateful for your company. Otherwise, return to your family. Find a quiet corner of the Kingdom and take up farming. You have a gift in your wife and daughter more valuable than any I can offer. Don't sacrifice them for anything."

Kiyoshi saw Daisuke's eyes watering and almost chuckled. It was a day for farewells.

"I would ask one other favor of you, if I may."

Daisuke bowed deeply. "Anything you ask."

"If you can, and if you're willing, watch over Asa. The only thing I can give her is your wisdom. She'll never be the strongest fighter, but you can teach her the skills you've learned. Perhaps you can also teach her the true meaning of friendship and family. I fear her beliefs have been twisted by revenge, and she deserves better."

"I will train her."

"Thank you." Kiyoshi stepped toward Daisuke and embraced him, surprising the nightblade. "I know you feel indebted, but know this: you have been one of my closest friends over the past twenty cycles, and any debt you had to me has been paid many times over. I am grateful for your service and ask that you now live for yourself."

Kiyoshi stepped back and knelt down, bowing toward Daisuke. He didn't hold the bow long, as he knew it would upset his friend, but it was the only way he knew to express how he was feeling.

When Kiyoshi stood up, Daisuke's face was as filled with tears as Kiyoshi's was. They might meet again, but Kiyoshi felt as though he were on his last mission, and he wanted Daisuke to know how he felt.

Daisuke couldn't bring himself to speak, but Kiyoshi knew the man's heart. He nodded and turned away, walking down the stairs toward the stable.

Chapter 28

Asa had been in and out of consciousness for some time now. Kiyoshi had healed her body, but he couldn't repair the tears in her heart. She was angry at Koji, sad about Juro, and furious at herself. She had taken her nightblade training seriously, but she had never been the best fighter, not even in her class. Now she wished there would be some way to reverse time, to go back and find the secret of training, to get better than anyone else.

When she brought herself to think about it, she realized that what she wanted more than anything else was to not feel powerless. Despite her strength, she felt as though she was always in situations where she was fighting events and people more powerful than she. She hadn't been able to save her family, and now she felt farther away from Osamu than at any time in the past season. She couldn't defend a lord, and the only reason she was alive was because Koji liked her and didn't want to kill her. Though she had passed the nightblade trials, she felt like a small child, a victim of forces beyond her ability.

So even though physically she felt fine, she couldn't bring herself to get out of bed. She heard, more than felt, Daisuke return. She scowled. Of course he would have been successful. His abilities, both natural and trained, were some of the most impressive she had ever encountered. In her current mood, she wasn't even happy he had returned. She also felt Kiyoshi leave, riding toward the south. She wondered what errand he had put himself to now.

Asa fell back asleep, but when she opened her eyes, it was dark. Her internal sense of time told her that night had not yet fallen, and she walked to the window. Outside, the clouds were thick, portending an early winter storm. Even though her room was warm, Asa could hear the wind outside. She didn't pretend to understand the weather, but she knew she didn't want to be trapped outside anytime soon. Hopefully Kiyoshi would be fine.

Asa extended her sense. The inn was quiet, with only a handful of patrons inside. She was beginning to understand that was typical of this place. She wanted to talk to Daisuke, but couldn't hear him moving about. She assumed he was asleep. Like Kiyoshi, he seemed even older than his years, and perhaps he would have advice for her as she thought about her next steps.

She was surprised to feel the king awake and agitated. That was new. She left her room and went to Masaki's room, letting herself in.

The king was there, but he wasn't. Asa saw the blank look on his face and knew that whatever he had suffered had affected him deeply.

"Hello," said the king.

"Hello," replied Asa, looking around the room and wondering what she should do. Originally she had thought of trying to comfort Masaki, but his agitation wasn't physical, and there wasn't anything Asa could do to help him as he was. Lacking any better ideas, she sat down.

"Who are you?" he asked.

"My name is Asa. I'm here to help you if I can."

The king seemed to hear her, but he didn't reply. On the one hand, he seemed lucid, but from the glassiness of his eyes and the way his body didn't seem to be entirely in his control, Asa could tell he wasn't right. She was torn. A part of her felt sympathy, but she had also never known the king personally, and after the pain she had seen her family suffer, she had difficulty experiencing empathy. It would be a mercy to open his throat and put him out of his misery.

In the next room over, Asa could hear Daisuke stirring from his slumber. She was grateful. Perhaps he would have a better idea of how to help the king. Why had Kiyoshi left? Clearly the king needed something, and of all of them, Kiyoshi was best suited to help. Whatever had taken him away must have been important.

The king's next words froze Asa in her place.

"Are you a friend of Osamu's?"

Asa's world twisted, and everything seemed to happen at once. She could hear Daisuke scrambling from his room over to the king's. Everything that had happened in the past few moons was now thrown into a new light. Pieces fell into place one after the other. There had been suspicions, of course, but never any evidence, never anything real to hold on to.

"What did you say?"

At just that moment, Daisuke burst into the room, trying to keep a look of calm on his face. Asa glared at him, and his face was all the confirmation she needed. But she got more from the king anyway.

"I asked, are you a friend of Kiyoshi's?"

Rage burst inside of Asa, fueled by anger at herself and the deep-seated pain she had carried for so many cycles. Everybody she had grown to trust in the past moon had known. They had known and never told her! There wasn't anything she could say to make her anger clear enough to Daisuke, so she just glared at him. Neither carried any steel, but if he stood in her way, she swore she would rip his throat from his body.

Daisuke seemed to know it was unwise to argue with Asa, so he also said nothing. He stood inside the door, impassive. Asa had to get out of the room. She stomped toward Daisuke and shoved him aside. Her first instinct was to go to her room, but that notion was quickly overridden. Instead, she went down the stairs and out the door of the inn, her whole heart trying to decide what to do next.

She was staring off into the distance when she sensed Daisuke. A light snow had begun to fall, and in time she expected the precipitation would become much heavier. The wind buffeted her thick robes, but inside she felt nothing but rage. Wind and snow couldn't touch her.

She could sense Daisuke, and that meant he wanted her to be able to sense him. That alone should have been comforting. Yet the only thought in her mind was that Daisuke served Osamu, and the men she had once been foolish enough to respect and look up to had proven to be her most dangerous enemies. She was a young girl again, uncertain about the way the world worked.

Kiyoshi had reminded her, in a way few teachers could, just how the world worked. She had traveled alone for so long for a reason. Others couldn't be trusted. Others were nothing more than complications.

Daisuke stepped just a bit in front of her, off to the side. She knew it was a purposeful decision. She could see everything he did. The move was meant to put her at ease, but in her current mood, it had the opposite effect. She wanted nothing more than to lash out, but something inside of her held her back. She spoke instead.

"So, what comes next?"

Daisuke turned around slowly to face her, and she also realized he had positioned himself to block some of the wind. The small kindness infuriated her. He could roll up into a ball and die for all she cared.

"That choice is yours."

"But if I go after him, I have to get through you first, correct?" Asa knew if it came to a fight between her and Daisuke, he would win easily.

Daisuke shook his head. "That would be my preference, yes. But he gave me instructions that if you ever found out, you were to make your own choice. He forbade me from stopping you, although it might be the first order of his I wouldn't listen to."

Asa knew her anger was rising, but she couldn't stop herself. "You think he deserves to live?"

For the first time that Asa had ever seen, Daisuke lost his composure. She hadn't thought he ever felt emotions strongly enough to do so. "I think the Kingdom needs good men like him far more than it needs revenge-obsessed nightblades like you!"

Asa stepped back. As long as she had known Daisuke, which she supposed hadn't been that long, he had always been a placid man, able to take everything that came his way. She considered it one of his greatest strengths. Apparently she had touched a nerve. He did care about Kiyoshi. Despite her anger, curiosity got the better of her.

"Why?"

"Why what?"

"Why do you serve him so passionately when you know what he's done?"

"I've told you what he did for me. Does it matter that it happened when I was a child of Two Falls?"

"But you know he was the one responsible for everything. You rank his one act of kindness above the massacre he committed?"

Daisuke seemed to regain his composure, becoming the man Asa had thought she knew so well. "There is no doubt that a man is defined by his actions. And Kiyoshi, or Osamu, has taken some actions that are reprehensible. But Two Falls was a breaking point for him. Yes, he was responsible, and it was a horrible thing he chose to do. It's why he's worked every day since then to keep the Kingdom together."

He took a deep breath and continued. "You seek to define him by one action, as would many. But I've now served him for more than twenty cycles, and I've seen thousands and thousands of actions, and if he hasn't redeemed himself, there is no hope for any of us who have erred in our choices. I'm not exaggerating when I say every action he's taken since that day has been the best one possible."

Asa could feel herself hardening against Daisuke. At one time, maybe, the words would have had an effect on her, but now all she could think about were scenes from her childhood. Her mother and brother, wasting away against the forces of famine. The two of them encouraging her to eat and to get strong. Her brother coming in from the field, his hands bloody from a full day of working. No forgiveness, not for what happened to them.

"Where did he go?"

Daisuke's body seemed to collapse. He remained on his feet, but his back rounded, and he held his face in his hands. "I may not stop you, but I sure won't help you."

Asa turned on a heel and walked back to the inn. It would only take her a few moments to gather up her supplies. She could be off shortly.

A small pang forced her to turn back to Daisuke. She wanted to say something, but nothing came to her mind. A part of her knew she would miss him, but she had the man she had searched so long for, and that was everything to her now. She couldn't risk losing him. Without a word to her fellow blade, she continued to her room and gathered her belongings.

The snow was falling quickly by the time Asa managed to get on the road. The only place Kiyoshi would have rushed off to was toward Isamu and his camp, so she had taken an extra horse from the inn. She figured Daisuke would have to figure out how to pay for the mount. She galloped the horses, following the trails to the south.

Asa didn't have much worry about finding Kiyoshi. She knew where he was going, and he would be making the fastest line there. All she had to do was ride faster, and she had two advantages over him. First, she had taken two horses to his one, so she could ride faster and longer than he could. Second, she was younger, and now that her mission was so close, she was driven by a will he couldn't match. Once she sensed him again, his time here would be short.

Asa rode through the night. She drove the horses as far as she dared and then switched, making the other one trail. She wouldn't stop, not until she had confronted Kiyoshi. As she rode, she fingered the hilts of her blades, mentally preparing herself for the upcoming fight. She couldn't underestimate him. He might be much older than she, but Osamu was a dangerous man.

The snow fell through the night, and at times Asa worried she would freeze. But she kept going, heedless of the damage she might be doing to her own body.

The sun rose on a clear and crisp day. The clouds had dissipated over the course of the night, but Asa hadn't noticed. It was only the piercing light of the sun coming from her left that made her realize it was dawn. The day was gorgeous, and in the light of the sun, she saw a set of tracks not far from her own, heading toward the south. She joined with them, grateful for the small increase in speed. She didn't assume they were Kiyoshi's, but if they were, so much the better.

It was midmorning when she saw him off in the distance. Together they rode for a while, Kiyoshi well in the lead, Asa trailing far behind him. If they had been in different terrain, he might have been able to evade her, but in the flat plains of the south, there was nowhere for him to hide. Eventually he must have realized he had no chance, because he stopped his horse and waited for her to approach.

Asa didn't hesitate. Kiyoshi wasn't the sort of man who would set a trap. She rode right up to him, charging her horse to only paces away, but he didn't flinch. There was a look on his face Asa had never seen before, and she wondered if, for the first time, she was seeing a hint of the man who had once been Osamu.

Asa leapt off her horse and landed softly in the snow. It was deeper than she realized; she understood that in a battle, she wouldn't have sure footing. She advanced carefully, but with every step she took, she thought of her mother and brother. She thought of her father and her last memories of him. Where once she had seen Kiyoshi, now all she saw was the man who had killed her family.

But Kiyoshi didn't budge, and Asa stopped a few paces away. She had seen his moves several times now, attacks that were far more understandable now that she knew the truth.

"How could you?"

Kiyoshi shook his head. "You already know the answers to all the questions. Whether or not you acknowledge it, you know what I'm trying to do, and now you know why I do it."

Asa knew Kiyoshi was telling the truth, but his answer angered her all the more. She wanted contrition, sorrow, and begging for mercy, not calm rationality. Her family deserved more.

"You deserve to die for what you did to my family!"

Kiyoshi bowed slightly to her. "Perhaps. At one time, I wanted nothing more, but Masaki wouldn't let me."

Asa didn't know what else to say, but Kiyoshi continued. "If nothing else, I owe you and your family a great apology. I didn't know your father personally, but I know how he tried to help on that day. In my rage I killed him; he was a man who stood by his morals when few of us did. I am sorry for what happened, and that regret has driven me for more than twenty cycles. But you must get out of the way. I have one final mission to complete."

Asa didn't budge, and a hint of anger exploded in Kiyoshi's face.

"Grow up, girl! This is far more important than your petty revenge."

Asa's will solidified, and she settled into a fighting stance. "I only have one question."

Kiyoshi didn't respond and didn't move.

"How did you become a dayblade?"

"The reason so few of us become dayblades is because the skills are more challenging, requiring a more intimate relationship with the sense. Most aren't willing to put in the work. But our skills, those of both dayblades and nightblades, all come from the same source. I studied and practiced for cycles. I had vowed not to take another life, and becoming a dayblade was the only way I could serve."

"It was also the greatest disguise you could have come up with. No one would suspect a dayblade of being an old nightblade."

"True. But enough. I don't want to fight you, but I will if that is what it takes. I had hoped to show you a different path. You know everything, and you know what drives me. If you're still set on revenge, there's nothing more I can do for you. Move or fight!"

There was no question which Asa would choose. She drew both her short blades, settling even further into her stance.

Kiyoshi sighed and turned to his horse. Inside the pack, well hidden, was a sword. He grabbed the hilt and pulled it smoothly from the sheath. Asa was impressed by the grace he brought to such a simple motion.

"I had vowed never to do this again, but you leave me no choice."

Kiyoshi settled into a stance Asa had never seen before, and for a moment, everything was still.

Asa wasn't going to wait for the perfect moment. Her time was now. She sprinted forward, covering the distance between them in three steps. She stabbed out with her left sword, a strike that Kiyoshi easily deflected. Asa kept moving forward, allowing her momentum to carry her past Kiyoshi. With a smooth flick of the wrists, Kiyoshi changed the direction of his sword and snapped at Asa's back.

She sensed the strike coming and blocked it with her second sword. Her two-sword technique was her pride, the skill she had worked the hardest to learn. She could attack with one and defend with the other. She felt invincible with the form.

Asa slid to a stop and came in low at Kiyoshi, slashing at his shins and knees. Kiyoshi kept his blade between her strikes and his legs, and nothing connected. She backed off, debating which attack to try next. Kiyoshi stood, silently studying her. It was time to show him something new.

Over the cycles of study, Asa had perfected several striking patterns with the two blades. She had practiced them over and over until they were ingrained in her body. Her strikes were fast, and she had never seen anyone able to deflect them all. Even when she was younger, she had always known she wasn't the strongest. She needed something else, something others didn't practice. Otherwise, how would she defeat Osamu?

Asa slid into the first attack pattern, her blades a whirling wall of steel. Kiyoshi had only a moment to study it, but his reaction was almost instantaneous. He thrust his blade into the pattern, finding a hole no one had ever seen before. Asa sensed it coming but was so confident in her attack, she almost let it through undefended. At the last moment, she realized what had happened and fell to the side, awkwardly dodging the thrust.

If Kiyoshi had wanted to, he could have taken her life in that moment. Instead, he took a step back, keeping a few paces of distance between them. He didn't say anything, but his look said enough. This was a different man that stood in front of her. She had unveiled Osamu, a man who looked at everyone else as a pest to be dealt with.

Asa's anger doubled, and she got back to her feet and brushed the snow off her robes. It infuriated her that she was alive only because of his mercy. She would still take his life.

She stepped forward, coming dangerously close to Kiyoshi's range before launching into another pattern. This time Kiyoshi didn't have any time to study the attack at all. Despite that, his sword seemed to be everywhere at once, deflecting each of her strikes. But there was no way for Kiyoshi's one long sword to keep pace with her two short ones for very long. He stood his ground, and eventually Asa broke his defense, one of her blades lashing out at his chest. Kiyoshi stepped back, but not before she drew first blood.

Asa considered pressing her advantage, but Kiyoshi didn't give her a chance. His retreat lasted for only a moment before he came forward, his sword point leading the way. Suddenly, Asa felt as though she was sensing a double image. Kiyoshi's blade was a snake, seeming to dart inside her defense at will. She became overly reactive, and in only a moment, Kiyoshi's sword found her shoulder, stabbing into tissue.

A new look came over Kiyoshi's face, and he pulled back, getting a couple of paces between them once again. Asa tried to figure his reaction out. Some combination of horror and sorrow. What was going through his mind?

Asa took the time to flex her arm and move her shoulder. It flared with pain, but she still had full range of motion.

Worry was beginning to tinge her thoughts. Twice she had attacked Kiyoshi, and both times she had come out the loser. Yes, she had gotten a strike on him, but that had only been when he was defensive. The moment he had attacked her, even with her two blades she couldn't counter his moves. Somehow he was interfering with her ability to sense what he was about to do, and she didn't know how she would beat him.

They met again, and this time Kiyoshi scored a deeper cut through her side. She looked down and saw the blood spreading. She didn't care. This was the last fight she had to be in. Afterward the Great Cycle could do with her as it pleased.

Asa settled back into her stance, and Kiyoshi gave her a curious look. "You have to know you can't beat me. You're going to die if you don't get help."

Asa didn't respond, coming at him with everything she had left. She took three big cuts, ones easy to avoid. Her body screamed at her, but she ignored the pain. She was counting on him not attacking her. Her bet paid off, and he continued to toy with her, easily moving to the side of her cuts. But she was close and he was moving, and she switched into the final attack pattern she had practiced. Her swords flashed one after the other, and Kiyoshi was again forced to move his blade to deflect her attacks.

Faster and faster their blades cut through the air. Asa was moving as fast as she could, relying entirely on her cycles of practice. If she took even a moment to think about her attacks, she would have faltered. In the work of less than a heartbeat, her blade caught his underneath his guard, snapping the sword out of his hands.

Asa felt a momentary wave of triumph, and she struck out at Kiyoshi, who was falling to the ground. She missed, her blade going just above his head. She shifted and struck downward, but Kiyoshi was falling toward her and she didn't want to lose her balance. Kiyoshi fell into the snow, sending up a light cloud of powder.

Asa tried to shift her weight to strike at Kiyoshi, but her right leg wouldn't move. She lifted it, only to see her leg come out of the snow with Kiyoshi's hand gripped tight around her ankle. She frowned as she tried to puzzle out what was about to happen. The realization came too late.

Suddenly every nerve in her body was on fire. She screamed in agony as she dropped her blades and collapsed, her world going black.

When Asa came to, Kiyoshi was bending down to pick up his blade. Every nerve stung deeply, but as she watched Kiyoshi move away from her, she was seized by a new level of rage, a white-hot fire that burned her heart. She wouldn't be denied, and she wouldn't continue to live knowing she had been spared by a murderer's mercy.

Trying to move only made the pain worse. Moving even a hair's breadth sent waves of agony up and down her body. But as Kiyoshi approached his horse, she didn't care about the pain. Physical pain was something that would only last for a time. The anguish she would feel if he got away would last forever. She stifled a cry as she reached into her robes.

It was difficult to feel where things were, and she wasn't sure she would have been able to if she hadn't practiced this exact motion hundreds of times over her life. Everything was pain, but she trusted her body and trusted her training.

Kiyoshi must have sensed what she was about to do, because he turned around, his blade coming around to defend himself. Asa didn't even see how many throwing blades she had in her hand, but she threw with all her strength.

Luck was on her side. Kiyoshi managed to get his sword up and block two of the blades with his own sword, but the third embedded itself in his right shoulder. It wasn't a fatal attack, but she saw his arm go limp and drop his sword, and she saw her opportunity.

Even though the pain was still incredible, the more she moved, the faster it seemed to dissipate. Screaming rage, she shoved herself to her feet, almost falling back to the ground as her world swirled. She braced herself and kept her feet. Kiyoshi had closed his eyes, like he had gone inside himself, trying to heal the injury he had sustained. She knew she only had a moment. She pulled a knife from its sheath and stepped toward him.

He opened his eyes, and she stopped. The moment was hers.

His eyes were defiant, an unquenchable fire. He met her gaze and spoke with a clear voice. "I forgive you, Asa."

The words didn't register at all. She stepped forward again, and finally the pain was too much for her to bear. Asa fell forward, stabbing out at him as she fell. She felt the blade dig into his body, but then for the second time, her world went black.

When Asa regained consciousness, she felt the warmth of another person's hands. She opened her eyes and was confused when she saw Kiyoshi kneeling over her. Hadn't they just been fighting? She looked down and saw her knife embedded in his abdomen.

Asa looked up again and saw that Kiyoshi's eyes were glazing over. She rolled away from him, then realized something was wrong. It took a few moments for her memory to return, but there wasn't any pain as she moved. She scanned her body and poked at her shoulder and realized she had been healed. She frowned and looked at Kiyoshi. Based on the marks and blood around them, he had struggled forward to kneel over her.

The truth came crashing down around her. She had attacked him, and he had spent the last part of his life trying to heal her. With a knife embedded in his belly. She didn't know the way of the dayblades very well, but what he had done was astounding.

Suddenly feeling foolish, Asa crawled forward to him, tears running down her face. She couldn't decipher the mix of emotions she was feeling. Was she overjoyed or sad? The two emotions seemed to blend into each other, creating something Asa couldn't identify. She got to her knees next to him, and he collapsed into her.

Instinctively, Asa reached up and stroked Kiyoshi's long hair, the way her own mother had soothed her when she had been young. Kiyoshi looked up at her, and Asa thought she had never seen such sadness and emptiness in anyone's eyes, like staring into a void. "I only ever tried to do my best."

Asa wondered what Kiyoshi was talking about. Was he trying to explain away Two Falls? She didn't know, and it didn't seem important.

She couldn't think of anything to say, so she just sat there holding on, feeling the energy drain from him.

Eventually he started to shudder, and a sudden urge came over her. She held on to him tightly and shook him back to awareness.

"Kiyoshi, I forgive you."

He smiled and slipped away from her again. She could feel his breathing slow, and soon she felt the last of his energy leave his body. She traced it as far as she could, unwilling to let him go, but it dissipated, joining in the flow of energy that moved through all living things. Kiyoshi had joined the Great Cycle.

Chapter 29

Minori was trying to remember the last time he hadn't been cold. He had memories of sitting in front of fires and basking in the heat of a southern sun, but he couldn't seem to hold on to them. They were fragments that meant nothing.

What bothered him was that it wasn't even that cold. Some snow had fallen, but he could remember having sat through much worse in his younger days. Minori hated being reminded how his body was decaying on him, especially as he'd found little to eat in the past few days. He had snuck a little food here and there, but it was hard to hide in a city where everyone was looking for you. Posters of the once influential blade were everywhere, and Minori had to admit, the artist had done a good job of capturing his likeness. If he was seen, he'd be turned in.

Minori had watched the events of the past few days with a detached interest. It was hard to worry much when you stood above everyone else, and he had almost been able to smile as he watched the mobs of people searching the city for blades.

Minori had essentially lived on the rooftops of Haven since fleeing from the guards. He had worked his way closer to Shin's household, the new palace of the city, studying it and learning the patterns of the guards. For one of the busiest places in the city, Shin's guards were on top of their duties. Both entry and egress were closely managed, and

Shin's guards had learned lessons from the escapes of the other lords. The servants' entrances were sealed shut, and everyone went through inspection at the main gate.

He knew his decision wasn't logical, but Minori had been driven beyond reason. The betrayal he still felt was no less acute than the moment it had occurred, and Minori still felt anger rise in his heart. He was going to kill Shin. At one time, Minori had been one of the greatest shadows the nightblades had, and it was time to remind people of that fact. He wasn't one to be betrayed so easily.

It had been days now, and Minori couldn't find any weakness in the defenses of Shin's grounds. The walls were high, and while Minori might be able to climb them, there was no chance he could do so without being discovered. The gate was well guarded, and Minori had seen a fair number of visitors turned away. Those who were allowed to enter were examined closely. No one got by without a thorough inspection. Even baskets of rice were searched to ensure no one and nothing was hidden inside.

Minori didn't give up searching, though. He found a rooftop where he could see and sense everything. From long experience he knew patience was a virtue that was almost always rewarded. This would be no different. He assumed he would have to kill some of Shin's guards, but that wasn't a problem.

He had no solid evidence, but Minori was certain Shin was up to something big. The constant stream of traffic into the palace only seemed to increase.

Minori watched and waited, his patience consistent. The time would come. If nothing else, eventually Shin would have to leave his palace, and when he did, Minori would be there. He wanted to live, but sometimes he thought perhaps he would be willing to die, just so long as he took the false king with him.

He had lost track of time when the incident he was waiting for suddenly happened. He felt the swell of life inside the palace, but didn't understand what it meant until dozens of guards swarmed out. They spread throughout the city, and their calls could be heard everywhere.

"Pack your things! An attack on the city is imminent! Hurry; there isn't much time!"

Minori fought his curiosity and remained on top of the rooftops. From his vantage point, he couldn't see beyond the walls of Haven, but he would have been surprised if another army had already reached it. It seemed too soon. In his gut, this felt like another trick of Shin's.

Minori realized with a start he hadn't seen Shin leave the castle with his soldiers, and for the first time in days, the gates were only lightly guarded. Whatever Shin was up to, he had committed most of his men to the plan. Minori could feel the city coming to life as people scrambled to obey the orders of the guards.

Only four guards were at the gate. Minori decided it was time. He stood up and stretched, prepared to assassinate the false king.

—

Minori dropped into the alley from his rooftop perch. He used his sense to make sure no one else was nearby and sprinted toward the gate. He had no reason to build up to an element of surprise. He would get to Shin as quickly as possible.

The guards spotted him and immediately came to attention. They drew their blades as he drew his, but they didn't have a chance. It had been a long time since he had drawn his blade with the intent to kill, but his skill hadn't dulled due to his daily practice.

He slid among them, his sword slicing through the guards as though they weren't even solid. There was no need to stop and admire his work.

The castle grounds were empty, and off to the side, Minori could see the gardens he had once prized so highly. A man of such little loyalty didn't deserve beautiful oases. Minori entered Shin's residence, and only then did he slow down. With corners and hallways, there were plenty of places for traps and ambushes, and he needed to be wary. The situation didn't feel like a trap, but Minori had seen enough to be cautious.

His sense told him that although the castle was alive with activity, few people were left inside, and none seemed to be guards. It was hard to tell with the sense, but he didn't notice any pairs walking the hallways slowly, which would have been a giveaway. Minori hurried, using his sense to try to locate Shin. In all the time they had cooperated with one another, he had never been allowed inside the usurper's inner sanctum. Minori hadn't questioned it at the time, but he realized that was a smart decision, especially if Shin had foreseen and planned these events.

Minori could sense life, but he couldn't sense walls, and he didn't know the castle well. Even if he could find the false king, it would take him time to get to wherever he was. In an emergency, that time could prove to be incredibly useful to Shin.

Minori pushed the thoughts away and focused on the present. He had only one goal here. He didn't need to make it out alive as long as Shin didn't survive. Unsure of what direction to go, Minori kept moving farther inside, waiting until he felt Shin's familiar presence with his sense.

His instinct paid off. Shin was in the center of the castle with others, but they didn't seem to be guards. They were too close for that.

It took Minori a little time to navigate the hallways, but eventually he found himself outside of Shin's receiving hall. The others were still in there with him, and Minori paused before charging in. Their voices floated out of the space.

Minori recognized the first voice as Shin's. "It's all prepared then?"

He couldn't hear their response, but they must have affirmed Shin's question. "Good. The robes are ready. Take the men you've selected and get started. My caravan is waiting nearby, and as soon as I take care of one or two more items, I will leave as well. You can begin as planned."

Minori could sense the other men bow and start to leave the room. He glanced around and found a corner that would hide him well. The other men left and walked right next to him, and as they passed him, Minori could tell from their uniforms that Shin had been speaking with some of his local commanders.

He waited until they were around a corner and then stepped out. His sense told him that Shin had stood and was on the move. Minori followed him, taking his time. With his sense, he felt Shin step into a fairly large room, settling down near the far-side wall. Minori drew his sword and took a calming breath. He searched the castle with his sense but found nothing unusual. He stepped into the room.

In front of him, Shin was sitting at a small table, furiously writing something. Shin's back was to Minori, and the blade took a few more cautious steps into the room. He could almost taste Shin's blood.

Minori took another step, and the wood underneath his foot sang. Minori cursed. He had forgotten Shin had a nightingale floor in this room. Shin turned around, but it didn't matter. The two were alone in the room, and even if Shin sounded an alarm, he wouldn't have enough time to stop his death. Minori launched himself forward.

At the same time, Shin seemed to trigger something, and there was a blur. Minori couldn't see what was happening and he couldn't sense anything, but suddenly, sharp pain erupted all over his body. His vision became skewed, and more by instinct than any thought, he pulled himself backward as he felt chunks of his flesh being torn from his body.

A gong sounded in the wall off to Minori's side. His sense, still functioning on a fundamental level, told him that the remaining people in the castle had started to converge on the room Minori was in. His heart sank as he realized there were eight men, something that hadn't even occurred to him on his way in.

Shin stood, his face calm and impassive. "Minori. I was starting to wonder if I had made the security around here too tight. I expected you earlier. You almost missed your chance entirely."

Minori made to charge again, but Shin shook his head. "I wouldn't try that if I were you." He raised his finger, drawing Minori's focus to a point in between them.

Minori's mind, the prize of all his abilities, couldn't keep up with what was happening. Shin wasn't acting the way a man facing a nightblade one-on-one should. He was calm and confident, and Minori couldn't figure out why.

Then some of his blood fell to the floor, and an understanding dawned on him. Somehow Shin had triggered a latticework of razor-sharp wire. Minori had run into it with his left leg, shoulder, and part of his face. Minori screamed. No wire would stand between him and his prey. He cut at it with his blade, severing one strand but catching his sword on the second. Where had Shin gotten wire like this?

His mind cracking, Minori realized he wouldn't have time to cut through the wire before Shin's nightblade-hunting unit arrived.

Minori's yell was deep and tore at his throat. It couldn't end this way!

But he didn't see any way out but one as the hunting party assembled behind him. Minori turned to face them. He knew he didn't have a chance. He had already been deeply cut by the wires, and his left arm was almost useless. He thought he had maybe lost an eye to the wire as well. But he wouldn't die without a fight. He would die on his feet.

The hunting party showed no hesitation. They advanced, their spears at the ready. Minori swore to himself.

For a moment, everything seemed unfair. He had only tried to do what was best for the blades, but it would cost him his life. Minori didn't know what had happened to Kiyoshi, but he was sure the old dayblade would laugh at him and his foolishness.

Minori did his best to dart forward, but his left leg didn't want to take too much weight. He stumbled, which probably saved him. A spear stabbed overhead, and he felt a second one coming at his chest. He deflected it and tried to move inside the range of the guards, but two more shafts appeared in his way. Minori slapped them away as best he could with his blade, but everything in front of him was a wall of darting spears.

He felt the attack coming from the side and leapt backward, remembering too late he didn't have any space to dodge. He felt the razor wire slice into his back, and he shifted his weight forward, feeling the razors tear more flesh from his body.

He felt sharp pain everywhere. His mind lost all focus, and he couldn't sense any strikes coming. He was disappointed in himself. At the very least, he should have been able to take a few of Shin's warriors with him.

The first spear took him in the side of his stomach. As he doubled over around the pain, a second stabbed into his shoulder, forcing him upright against the wire again.

Minori felt his body collapse, the razor wire tearing more of his flesh as he fell. Blackness crept into the corners of his vision, and Minori was ready to join the Great Cycle.

"Stop!"

The command was instantly obeyed, but Minori didn't care. He had reached a state where his concerns were unimportant. There was only life, and despite everything, it was a beautiful thing.

Minori's peace was shattered as he was rolled over onto his back. He didn't seem to notice the pain anymore. All he could see was Shin in his vision, lips moving, words taking too long to get to Minori's ears.

"Find him a doctor and heal him enough so he stays alive. We'll need him for a few more days at least."

Minori must have had a question on his face because Shin smiled at him.

"You can't die just yet. You will die, but when you do, it will be as the most hated man the Kingdom has ever known. And I captured you."

What was left of Minori was furious, and he tried to move, but his body wasn't responding to his commands anymore. All he could do was glare. He saw Shin pull back his boot, and Minori's world went dark.

Chapter 30

Asa rode back to the inn slowly. After she had been healed, she had been lost, unsure of what to do. The purpose that had driven her for her entire life had vanished as quickly as a flame snuffed out by lack of air. She had stumbled around the site of her battle for most of the afternoon, unable to decide on a path forward. She wanted to leave everything behind and wander, but she felt she owed a debt to Kiyoshi, a debt she didn't want to pay. Every time she tried to mount her horse and leave, her conscience stopped her.

As hard as she tried, she couldn't summon the hatred and rage that had driven her for so long. When she looked at the body, she didn't see the demon Osamu that had haunted her for so long. All she saw was the healer Kiyoshi. She couldn't leave his body to rot out on the plains or be eaten by scavengers. Despite his crimes, he deserved better than that.

Finally, tired of indecision, Asa wrapped Kiyoshi's body in clothes from his saddlebags and draped him over the horse he had been riding on, surprised by how light his body was. He really had driven himself to the edge of life, another reminder of everything he had given.

There wasn't any hurry anymore, no hurry about anything. She wanted Daisuke to be at the inn so she could give Kiyoshi's body to him. He might want to kill her, but she found she didn't care. She had found her revenge, and her family could now rest in peace.

After a day of riding, she found herself within sight of Haven. She was surprised to see a tremendous plume of smoke stretching up into the sky. As she got closer, she noticed that the layer of snow she was riding on had a thin black topping of ash. Although she didn't believe it, there was only one reason for that much smoke: the entire capital was on fire. And the only way that happened was if someone had set it.

Asa was glad she wasn't going to the city. She had thought as she left that if she never saw Haven again, she would be happy, but had never guessed the thought might come true. Even the inn seemed too close for comfort, but she didn't know where else to take Kiyoshi's body.

By the time she got to the inn, the road was full of people without a home. Asa rode through them, handing her horses to a boy who worked for the inn. The tension in the air was palpable and almost too much to handle. All Asa wanted was to be left alone, to rest in quiet. She didn't want anybody else's problems. She was grateful when she slipped into the unmarked inn and found it to be as quiet as ever.

Daisuke was in the common room, and from the look of his table, he was deep into his cups. The image bothered her more than anything she had encountered in the past few days. Daisuke was a rock, always stable, no matter what happened. To see him tossed about like a leaf in the wind was uncomfortable. He looked at her as she came in and downed another cup in one swallow.

Although she didn't think he would do anything, he practically radiated his desire to kill her, and it took all her courage to sit down next to him. She found herself at a loss for how to proceed. She blurted out the first thing that came to her mind. "I brought back his body."

Daisuke filled and emptied the cup again. "Thank you."

The silence stretched between them. Asa fought the urge to apologize. She wasn't sorry, and saying she was would be disrespectful to the man who had saved her life. What was there to say to the man whose master and best friend she killed?

Daisuke had no apparent desire to speak with her, but she couldn't leave, not yet. Every moment, Asa was certain Daisuke would lash out at her and she wouldn't do anything about it. She couldn't. But she couldn't leave as his enemy. She just couldn't.

At a loss for what to say, she led with an obvious question. "What's happening out there?"

"Even someone as blind as you can see Haven is burning. There are reports that men in black robes were running around the city, lighting buildings on fire."

Asa couldn't believe his words. "People believe the nightblades lit Haven on fire? That's ridiculous."

Daisuke fixed her with a cold stare. "Oh yes, people believe it. Our new king, King Shin, has made certain of that."

A sudden thought occurred. "What about the real king, Masaki? Is there anything he can do?"

"He died this morning. Peacefully, in his sleep. Not the way of a warrior, but a good way for a king to pass."

Asa turned the news over in her mind. She wondered what Shin would do next, and she found that as she pondered this question, she didn't really care. All she wanted was to disappear. All she had to do was finish her final task.

"What would you like to do with Kiyoshi's body?"

Daisuke gazed off into the distance, his drink visible in the glassiness of his eyes. "The two of them should be honored together. I think they would like that."

Asa was torn. She didn't have any regrets about killing Kiyoshi. He had earned his just reward. But still, she felt as though she needed to honor the old man. She didn't understand it, but she accepted it. "May I help?"

Daisuke's stare grew longer, and he looked as though he were wrestling with the words he really wanted to say. "He would have liked that."

Asa could feel the tension and knew it was best if she could leave soon. "I will find wood."

Daisuke gave her a short nod and turned back to his cups. Asa hesitated in place, just for a moment, before turning around and leaving him to his grief.

—

The next two days were full of activity but largely devoid of meaning for Asa. Finding wood was proving to be harder than she expected. Most places had been cleaned out by the flood of homeless people from Haven.

The fire that consumed Haven was slowly burning itself out, but from what Asa heard as she wandered the countryside looking for wood, no one planned on returning. People were uncertain and scared. She heard dozens of reports of crime, but so far, no one seemed to be taking any action on it. King Shin had ordered the building of a tent city two days' walk to the east of Haven, and people were flocking to it as a means of temporary shelter.

Everywhere she went, Asa discovered just how deep the hatred of the blades now ran. Fear had morphed into something else entirely—rage. First the palace, and now the capital? Roving bands of citizens armed with everything from kitchen knives to homemade spears combed the land and, if rumors could be trusted, had already killed a few blades.

Asa wouldn't dare to wear her black robes in public, not anymore. Her swords had to be concealed at all times, too. Women weren't in the army, and a woman carrying swords in public was a dead giveaway of one's nightblade status.

The most surprising news came on the first day after Asa had returned to the inn, a whisper that spread like wildfire. The families of both Lord Isamu and Lord Juro had publicly declared their support for King Shin. That day Daisuke took a piece of paper from Kiyoshi's clothes and threw it into the fire, never telling Asa what it had been.

Asa didn't know how Lord Shin had gotten their support as quickly as he had, but the lords were united against a common foe, the blades.

Starfall was silent. Asa had heard no news from the city of blades, and she didn't expect to. Anyone could see that no news from the blades could cool the rage of the Kingdom. She imagined the council would call the blades home soon, if they hadn't already.

Asa had gotten a glance at Minori as a group of guards paraded him around the camps. He was declared as the mastermind behind the burning of the palace and of the city, a nightblade who had plotted to have Shin killed right after he became king. The older nightblade was cut and bloody, and Asa was surprised he had lived through whatever fight he had been in. He was tied with rope to a wooden beam and displayed for all to see. Angry citizens threw rocks at him, and the guards did nothing but protect themselves.

No love was lost for Minori in Asa's heart, but even she had a hard time accepting the fate he endured. He would be vilified for all time as a traitorous nightblade. Flyers spread about his execution a few days away. Asa decided she wanted to be far, far away when that happened.

After everything that had happened, Asa had thought she would feel different, as though she had accomplished something. But all she found in her heart was emptiness.

Daisuke's mood improved after he drank his sorrows away. He still spoke little to her, but Asa was far less afraid of being killed by him now. That moment had passed. He wore his sorrow like a cloak, and he told her he planned on returning to Keiko. Together they would find land, and Daisuke would give up his swords for good.

Asa had already decided what she was going to do, although it could possibly best be described as "nothing." She was going to pack everything up again and wander. She had never considered what life would be like after killing Osamu, and part of her realized that she had always thought she would die completing her task. Kiyoshi could have killed her, but he had taken the easy path away from her. She would have to walk another path, and she was in no hurry. She would walk the roads, and if she could, would help others as she was able. This was, perhaps, a small homage to Kiyoshi and his values. Daisuke approved.

After two days of hunting, she finally found enough wood for a proper pyre.

—

While Asa worked to find the wood, Daisuke had taken responsibility for preparing the bodies, but the way of the blades was a simple one. He cleaned the remains of both Kiyoshi and Masaki and dressed them in the nicest clothes they had, which, given their circumstances, wasn't much. When they were done and evening had fallen, Asa helped him carry the bodies out of the village to the pyre she had built.

At night, the fire that consumed the last parts of Haven lit up the cloudy night sky. Although she had had nothing to do with the fire, she felt a wave of guilt wash over her. She turned her eyes away to face the fire Daisuke was about to light.

He glanced at her. "Do you have any final words?"

Dozens ran through her mind, from anger to compassion, but none of them encapsulated how she felt. They were all dirty reflections. She shook her head.

Daisuke lit the pyre and stepped back.

"Masaki, you were a king who stood for the people, and for that, you will always have my respect. You deserved better, but I hope you find this acceptable."

He paused, and Asa could see a tear forming on his otherwise stony face.

"Kiyoshi, you were the best man I ever knew. Thank you, not just for sparing my life, but for teaching me how to live. I know you said otherwise, but I owe you a debt I can never repay. From this day on, I will try to live in such a way that I am worthy of the honor you showed me."

Despite the icy shield over her heart, Daisuke's warm words stabbed into her, and Asa was torn into shreds. The tears started to fall, and she sank to her knees in the fresh snow. Words weren't enough anymore. Daisuke watched but didn't offer any comfort. The pyre burned as the moon crawled across the sky, and even though its heat scorched at her skin, Asa was frozen in place.

When the sun rose, the last remnants of the pyre were burning themselves out. Kiyoshi and Masaki, two of the most influential men in the Kingdom a few moons ago, were gone for good, their spirits joining the Great Cycle together.

Daisuke turned to leave, and suddenly, Asa felt alone. More alone than she had ever felt in all her cycles of hunting for Osamu. "Daisuke!"

He turned to her call, and Asa realized she didn't know what she wanted to say. Their eyes met, and Asa wanted to apologize, to say she was sorry for taking away his best friend and mentor. But she couldn't. A part of her was sorry, but the greater part of her knew the truth: She had accomplished exactly what she set out to do. To apologize to Daisuke was to lie to him, and that she wouldn't do. She wanted to comfort him but didn't know how.

In the end, she couldn't get any words out. She just looked at him, pleading with him silently. A wind gusted across the plains, throwing up snow between them. For a moment, she worried when the snow cleared that he would be gone, but her fears were unrealized. Instead, he remained where he was, giving her a small bow. When he straightened up, a slight smile was on his face, a smile he couldn't hold on to for very long.

Asa bowed in return, pressing her forehead to the ground. She understood, and she felt his forgiveness. When she sat back up, Daisuke was gone.

Asa knelt there in the snow for a while, the last embers of the pyre keeping her warm. The sun rose completely above the horizon, and although Asa couldn't explain why, she felt an ease, a weight falling off her shoulders. It wasn't happiness, but perhaps contentment.

Asa stood up, feeling the stretch throughout her body. She checked to make sure her swords were still attached and looked off into the distance. She needed to walk, perhaps farther than she ever had before. But she was ready.

ACKNOWLEDGMENTS

It is often said and always true that a book is always the work of many people. I would be remiss if I didn't give credit where it was due.

First thanks always need to go to my family, who tolerate and even encourage this obsession of mine. They gave up nights and weekends and made tremendous sacrifices for me, and I appreciate it.

Thanks to Bryce, my partner in crime over at Waterstone Media. Without his help, there is no way I would have finished this novel.

A special acknowledgment to Adrienne, who patiently waited for drafts and brought this story into the light. I'm always grateful for her hard work.

Thanks also to Clarence, who spent many late hours helping me turn a draft into a story.

And finally, to the entire team at 47North, who all worked diligently to make this story come alive. Thank you.

ABOUT THE AUTHOR

Ryan Kirk is the author of the Nightblade series of fantasy novels and the founder of Waterstone Media. He was an English teacher and non-profit consultant before diving into writing full-time in 2015. For more information about Ryan, visit his website at www.waterstonemedia.net.